The WEDDING VOW

She couldn't pretend he wasn't smokin' hot. . .

Taking her hand, he held her eyes in his bluer-than-the-sea gaze, murmured in that deep, exotic voice, "Thank you, Madeline."

And he kissed her.

On the knuckles. But . . . wow.

In a faraway corner of her mind, the voice of reason piped. *This is how he does it. This is how he gets those supermodels onto his yacht.*

But apparently she was as susceptible as the bimbos, because instead of hitting the fire alarm, she froze like a deer in the headlights, letting his thumb skim her knuckles, rubbing his kiss into her skin, a fiery tattoo.

It was the limo all over again, only more so. Now his lips were involved, warm and seductive. His hair fell forward around his too-dangerous face, thick and glossy and dark as the devil's.

By Cara Connelly

THE WEDDING VOW
THE WEDDING FAVOR

Available from Avon Impulse
THE WEDDING DATE

Coming Soon
THE WEDDING BAND
THE WEDDING GIFT

CARA CONNELLY

The WEDDING VOW

A SAVE THE DATE NOVEL:
THE BILLIONAIRE'S
DEMAND

AVON

An Imprint of HarperCollinsPublishers

This is a work of fiction. Names, characters, places, and incidents are products of the author's imagination or are used fictitiously and are not to be construed as real. Any resemblance to actual events, locales, organizations, or persons, living or dead, is entirely coincidental.

AVON BOOKS
An Imprint of HarperCollins*Publishers*
195 Broadway
New York, New York 10007

First Avon Books mass market printing: October 2014

Avon Trademark Reg. U.S. Pat. Off. and in Other Countries, Marca Registrada, Hecho en U.S.A.
HarperCollins® is a registered trademark of HarperCollins Publishers.

Printed in the U.S.A.

10 9 8 7 6 5 4 3 2 1

For my parents

CHAPTER ONE

SIX THOUSAND, EIGHT hundred dollars, and ninety-eight cents.

Maddie let the bill flutter to her desk, where it settled like a leaf between her elbows. She dropped her head into her hands.

Lucille, her lovable, irresponsible, artistic sister, wanted to do a semester in Italy, studying the great masters.

Well, hell, who wouldn't? The problem was, Lucy's private college tuition was already stretching Maddie to the max. The extra expense of a semester abroad meant dipping into—no, wiping out—her meager emergency fund.

Still, considering all they'd been through, Lucy's carefree spirit was nothing short of a miracle. If keeping that miracle alive meant slaving more hours at her desk, Maddie would make it work somehow.

Knuckles rapped sharply on her office door, Adrianna Marchand's signature staccato. Maddie slid a file on top of the bill as Adrianna strode in.

"Madeline. South conference room. Now." Adrianna

scraped an eye over Maddie's hair and makeup, her sleeveless blouse. "Full armor."

Maddie shook her head. "Take Randall. I'm due in court in two hours and I'm still not up to speed on this case." Insurance defense might be the most boring legal work in the world, but it was also complex, and she was buried. She waved an arm at the boxes stacked on her cherry coffee table, the hundred case files that marched the length of her leather sofa. "Remember how you dumped all of Vicky's cases on me after you *fired her for no reason*?"

Adrianna iced over. "*No one's* job is guaranteed at this firm."

Maddie glared, unwilling to show fear. But she was outclassed and she knew it. Adrianna's stare could freeze the fires of hell, and as one of Marchand, Riley, and White's founding partners, she could, and would, fire Maddie's ass if Maddie pushed back too hard.

"Fine, whatever." Kicking off her fuzzy slippers and shoving her feet into the red Jimmy Choos she kept under her desk, Maddie whipped the jacket of her black silk Armani suit off the back of her chair and punched her fists through the sleeves. Then she spread her arms. "Full armor. Satisfied?"

"Touch up your makeup."

Rolling her eyes, Maddie dug a compact out of her purse, brushed some color onto her pale cheeks, hit her lips with some gloss. Then she poked her fingers into her caramel hair to give it some lift. She wore it spiked, like her heels, to make herself look taller, but at a petite five feet she was still a shrimp.

Adrianna nodded once, then charged out the door, setting a brisk pace down the carpeted hallway. "Step on it. We've kept your new client waiting too long."

Maddie had to trot to keep up. "*My* new client? Because I don't have enough work?"

"He requested you specifically. He says you're acquainted."

"Well, who is he?"

"He wants to surprise you." Adrianna's dry tone made it clear she wasn't kidding.

Before Maddie could respond to that ridiculous statement, Adrianna tapped politely on the conference room door, then gently pushed it open.

Meant for large meetings with important clients, the room was designed to impress, with Oriental carpets covering the hardwoods, and original landscapes by notable artists gracing the walls. But it was the long cherry table that really set the tone. Polished to a gleam and surrounded by posh leather chairs, it spelled confidence, professionalism, and prosperity.

Bring us your problem, that table said, *and we will solve it without breaking a sweat.*

And if the room and the table weren't enough to convince a prospective client that Marchand, Riley, and White were all that, then the million-dollar view of the Manhattan skyline through the forty-foot-wide glass wall would drive the point home. Who could argue with that kind of success?

Maddie's new client stood gazing out at that view, his back to the door, one hand in the pocket of his expensively cut trousers, the other holding a sleek cell phone to his ear.

Through that phone, Maddie heard a woman's tinkling laughter. He responded in rapid Italian. Not that Maddie understood a word of it. Her Italian began and ended with ordering risotto in Little Italy. But she'd had a short fling with a gorgeous Italian waiter, and she recognized the rhythm of the language. It was the sound of sweaty sex.

Clearing her throat to announce their presence earned her a wintry glance from Adrianna. But the man ignored them utterly. Maddie crossed her arms and looked him up and down with an affronted eye.

He was tall, over six feet, and she put his weight at a lean one-ninety. Broad through the shoulders, narrow at the hips, he bore himself like an athlete, graceful and relaxed—as if he wasn't standing six scant inches from thin air, sixty stories above Fifth Avenue.

Though he claimed to know her, she couldn't place him by the sliver of his face reflected in the glass, or by the sleek black hair curling over his collar, too long for Wall Street, not long enough for the Italian soccer team.

Everything about him—his clothes, his bearing, his flagrant arrogance—screamed rich, confident, and entitled.

He must be mistaken about her, she decided, because she honestly didn't know anyone like him. And given his casual assumption that his time was more important than theirs, she didn't want to.

She held it together for as long as she could, tapping her foot, biting her tongue, but as the grandfather clock in the corner ticked into the fifth long minute of silent subservience, her patience ran out. She uncrossed her arms and reached for the doorknob. "I don't have time for this shit."

Adrianna's hand shot out and clamped her arm. "Suck it up, Madeline," she gritted through her teeth.

"Why should I? Why should *you*?" Under normal circumstances, Adrianna had zero tolerance for disrespect, so why was she putting up with this guy's bullshit?

Flinging a resentful look at the mystery man, Maddie didn't bother to lower her voice. "This guy doesn't know me. Because seriously, if he did, he'd know I won't stand here burning daylight while he talks dirty to his girlfriend."

"Oh yes you will," Adrianna hissed. She released Maddie's arm, but caught her eyes. "You'll stand on your head if he says so. He could mean *millions* for this firm."

The man in question chose that moment to end his call. Casually, unhurriedly, he slipped the phone in his pocket. Then he turned to face them.

Maddie's heart stopped. Her lips went icy.

Adrianna started to speak but he cut her off, his vaguely European accent smoothing the edge from his words. "Thank you, Adrianna. Now give us the room."

Without a word, Adrianna nodded once and left them alone, closing the door softly behind her.

His complete attention came to rest on Maddie, a laser beam disguised as cool condescension. Her blood, which had gone cold, now boiled up in response, pounding her temples, hammering out a beat called Unresolved Fury, Frustrated Objectives, Justice Denied.

"You son of a bitch," she snarled. "How dare you claim an acquaintance with me?"

He smiled, a deceptively charming curve of the lips meant to distract the unwary from eyes so intensely blue and so penetratingly sharp that they might otherwise reveal him as the diabolical felon he was.

"Ms. St. Clair." Her name sounded faintly exotic on his tongue. "Surely you don't deny that we know each other."

"Oh, I know you, Adam LeCroix. I know you should be doing ten to fifteen in Leavenworth."

His lips curved another half inch, past charming, to amused. "And I know you. I know that if you'd taken me to trial, you'd have done an excellent job of it. But"—he shrugged slightly—"both of us know that no jury would have convicted me."

"Still so cocky," she simmered. "And so fucking guilty."

ADAM HELD BACK a laugh. Madeline St. Clair might be tiny enough to fit in his pocket, but she had the grit of a two-hundred-pound cage fighter.

When he'd last seen her five years ago, she was a bloodthirsty young prosecutor, spitting nails as her then-boss, the U.S. Attorney for the Eastern District of New York—who had his eyes on higher office— shook Adam's hand and apologized for letting the case against him go as far as it had.

Playing magnanimous, Adam had nodded gravely, said all the right things about public servants simply doing their jobs, and with a wave for the news cameras, disappeared into his limousine.

Where he'd cracked a six-thousand-dollar bottle of Dom Perignon and made a solitary toast to a narrow escape from the law.

It had been his own damn fault that he'd come so close to being caught, because he *had* gotten cocky. He'd made a rare mistake, a minute one, but Madeline had used it like a crowbar to pry into his life until she'd damn near nailed him for stealing the *Lady in Red*.

The newly discovered Renoir masterpiece had been sold at Sotheby's to a Russian arms dealer, a glorified mobster who cynically expected a splashy show of good taste to purge the bloodstains from his billions. Adam couldn't stomach it, so he'd lifted the painting. Not for gain; he had his own billions. But because great art was sacred, and using it as a dishrag to wipe blood off the hands of a man who sold death was sacrilege.

Adam had simply saved the masterpiece from its unholy purpose.

It wasn't the first time, or the last, that he'd liberated great art from unclean hands. He told himself that it was his calling, but he couldn't deny that it was also a hell of a lot of fun. Outsmarting the best security systems money could buy taxed his brain in ways that managing his companies simply couldn't. Training for the physical demands kept him in Navy SEAL condition. And the adrenaline rush, well, that couldn't be duplicated. Not even by sex. No woman had ever thrilled him that intensely or challenged him so completely on every level.

But now the shoe was on the other foot. One of his own paintings—his favorite Monet—had been heisted clean off the wall of his Portofino villa.

Just the thought made his teeth grind.

Oh, he'd find it eventually; he had no doubt of that. He had the resources, both money and manpower. He was patient. He was relentless. And when he got his hands on the bastard who'd infiltrated his home—his sanctuary—he'd make him pay for his hubris.

But in the meantime, he had a more immediate concern. The insurance company, Hawthorne Mutual, was dragging its feet, balking at paying him the forty-four million the Monet was insured for.

Forty-four million was a lot of money, even to a man like him. But it was the company's excuse for holding it up that really pissed him off. They needed to investigate the theft, they claimed, because Adam had once been a "person of interest" in the theft of the Renoir.

In short, Hawthorne's foot dragging could be laid at Madeline's door. She'd damaged Adam's reputation, impugned his integrity. Cast a shadow of doubt over one of the richest men in the world.

Never mind that she'd been right about him.

Because she was visibly chomping at the bit, he moved as if he had all day, strolling to the far end of the room, where a leather sofa and club chairs clustered around a coordinating coffee table. This would be where clients chummied-up with the partners after meetings, rubbing elbows over Scotch and cigars while the lowly associates—like Madeline—scuttled back to their offices to do the actual work.

He poured himself an inch of Scotch from the Waterford decanter on the table and then relaxed into the sofa, stretching one arm along the back, letting the other drape carelessly over the side, whiskey glass dangling from his fingers.

Her steel gray eyes narrowed to slits. "What do you want, LeCroix? Why are you here?"

Lazily, he sipped his Scotch, enjoying the angry flush that burned her cheeks. In the prosecutor's office, they'd called her the Pitbull. He was glad to see she'd lost none of her fire.

Watching her simmer, he remembered how her intensity had appealed to him. How much *she'd* appealed to him. Which was surprising, really. As a rule, he liked a solid armful of woman, and Madeline was barely there.

At the time, he'd told himself it was because she'd damn near taken him down. Naturally, he had to admire that.

But now he felt it again, that tug of attraction. Something about those suspicious eyes, that spring-loaded body, went straight to his groin. An image of her astride him, nails gouging his chest, eyes blazing with passion, flashed through his mind. Was she as hot-blooded in bed as she was in the courtroom?

Regrettably, he'd never find out. Because he was about to piss her off for life.

He crossed his legs with studied nonchalance while all five-foot-nothing of her bristled with temper.

"Hawthorne Mutual is holding up payment on the Monet," he said. He didn't bother to describe the painting; she'd remember it. Five years ago she'd subpoenaed an inventory of his art collection. He'd complied—at least as to his *legal* collection.

"Someone stole the Monet?" For the first time, she smiled, a wicked grin.

He flicked imaginary lint from his knee. "Apparently, even *my* security isn't unbreachable." And wasn't that a sore spot?

She barked out a laugh. "What goes around, comes around, LeCroix. With your history, Hawthorne will never pay—what was the insured value? Forty-four million?" She sneered, clearly enjoying the irony. "They'll keep you in court for years."

He let her savor her last taste of victory. Then he hit her where it hurt.

"Not me," he said, succinctly. "Us. They'll keep *us* in court. Because you're representing me. For as long as it takes, whatever it takes."

Her chin actually jerked as she took the blow. Then he finished her off with a short jab to the kisser.

"From now on, Madeline, you work for me."

CHAPTER TWO

MADDIE SLAMMED HER door so hard her diploma jumped off the wall, glass splintering as it hit the floor.

She didn't spare it a glance, just threw herself into her desk chair and glared at the door, waiting.

Five seconds later, Adrianna barged in, loaded for bear. Planting her fists on the desk, she fired both barrels. "Get your ass back in that conference room and unmake whatever mess you just made. Adam LeCroix is The Most Important Client who's ever walked into this office."

"He's a criminal," Maddie lashed back. "He should be in an eight-foot cell, not strutting around Manhattan thinking he can buy anybody he wants. Thinking he can buy me!" She jabbed a finger in his general direction. "He can go fuck himself. I'd rather starve than work for him."

"Then you'll starve," Adrianna shot back. She drew herself up, breathed in, breathed out. "You're fired."

"Good!" Maddie snapped open her briefcase and dumped out the legal pads. In went her personal things. A photo of Lucy in her cap and gown, smile brightening the cloudy day. Another of Lucy on her first day at college, waving from her dorm window. Lucy again, at her small gallery showing, face alight with wonder and promise.

Maddie stilled. Her eyes dropped to the bill poking out from under *Johnson v. Jones*. No job meant no semester in Italy for Lucy. Hell, it meant no semester of any kind for Lucy, unless the poor kid took on the same crippling school loans that still hamstrung Maddie. That kind of debt took away your choices, killed your dreams. Left you at the mercy of people like Adrianna Marchand . . . and Adam LeCroix.

She had no choice but to give in. Cornered like a rabbit, she lifted her eyes to Adrianna. Who smiled her evil she-wolf smile.

"I knew you'd see reason." Reaching across Maddie's desk, Adrianna hit the intercom button. "Randall, get in here."

"Yes, ma'am!" He snapped out a verbal salute, sped into the office in record time. Cursed with red hair and freckles, he blushed like a virgin when Adrianna turned her carnivorous gaze on him.

"Take this." She scraped *Johnson v. Jones* into a pile and thrust it into his arms. "Judge Bernam's expecting you in his chambers in two hours for a settlement conference. Don't disappoint me."

Randall went pale. "But—"

Adrianna stared him silent.

"Don't worry," Maddie cut in, mercifully, "it's pro forma. The plaintiff's not ready to settle."

Randall's momentary relief died as Adrianna pointed at the boxes on the coffee table, the files on the couch. "Those are yours too. Get them out of here."

As a brand new hire, Randall had the lightest caseload of any associate. Naïvely, he still believed that evenings and weekends were his own. His dawning horror would have evoked Maddie's pity if she wasn't busy reckoning with her own horror: Adam LeCroix, billionaire businessman, international playboy. Art thief extraordinaire.

She swallowed hard, tasting her bitterest defeat.

Five years ago she'd almost nailed him. A circumstantial case, but if only she'd been allowed to take it to trial, she could've made it stick. She could've convinced the jury that LeCroix was not only the mastermind who outwitted Sotheby's state-of-the-art computerized security, but also the Spider-Man who scaled walls, ghosted past armed guards, and, in under four minutes, poofed with the *Lady in Red* rolled up in a three-foot tube.

But her boss was too chicken to take LeCroix on. With his eyes on a senatorial bid, he wasn't willing to risk having a high-profile defeat splashed across the front page of the *New York Times*. So Maddie had watched LeCroix waltz out of her office, wave to the media whores who worshipped him like a celebrity, and cruise away in his black stretch limo.

That had been bad. But this . . . this was a nightmare. She was at the man's mercy. There was no way she could walk away from her job at Marchand, Riley, and White and into another that paid as well. Not in this economy.

She suppressed a shiver. Not since she'd left her domineering father's house had she felt so vulnerable. She'd sworn never to let a man control her again, but now LeCroix had her by the proverbial balls. And he was diabolical. If he learned about her childhood, he'd use her personal demons to turn the screws tighter still.

She couldn't—and wouldn't—hide her revulsion at

working for him, but she could never let him know what it cost her.

ADAM ENDED ANOTHER phone call, checked his watch. Six minutes. By now, Madeline would have capitulated and she'd be processing her defeat. Girding her loins—that image made him smile—for the short walk to this conference room and the crow-eating apology the Marchand vixen would expect her to deliver.

His smile grew to a grin. That would be the day. He might have Madeline's back to the wall, but he knew better than to expect an apology out of her. And he didn't want one.

What he wanted was his forty-four million, and to see Hawthorne's high-and-mighty CEO—Jonathan Edward Kennedy Hawthorne IV—blanch when Adam showed up with his former prosecutor in his corner.

Hawthorne mistakenly believed that because his great-whatever-grandfather came over on the *Mayflower* and started what was now the oldest, most hidebound, hoity-toity insurance company in America, he could jam Adam up. That Adam would quail at veiled threats to dredge up old rumors about the *Lady in Red*.

Not likely. If Hawthorne's smarmy lawyers had done their homework, they'd know Adam didn't give a damn about bad publicity. He didn't give a damn about the press or the public or the next story about him on Page Six of the *Post*.

What he cared about was not getting screwed over by *anybody*. Most assuredly not by some blueblood who thought his money was better than Adam's simply because it had more age on it.

Well, Hawthorne had a big surprise coming. Never in a million years would he expect Madeline to join forces with Adam, when the whole world knew she'd done everything in her power to convict him. Why, the press had made hay with it across the globe, sensationalizing the story of the upstart prosecutor's tenacious pursuit of the self-made billionaire, dubbing it the Pitbull versus the Piranha.

For that reason alone, her mere presence on his payroll would neutralize any once-a-thief, always-a-thief argument Hawthorne could make about the Monet. And if Hawthorne cooked up some other reason to deny Adam his money, then Adam would turn her loose on him. Hawthorne wouldn't have a chance against the Pitbull.

His grin widened. The icing on the cake was that Madeline would hate every minute of it. He couldn't have dreamed up a sweeter revenge if he'd tried.

When the idea had first come to him a week ago, he'd wondered how he could rope her in. The woman had more integrity than anyone he'd ever met. But a quick and dirty investigation into her finances turned up her Achilles' heel—her sister, Lucille. Sixty percent of Madeline's income went to cover the girl's expenses. Room, board, clothes, travel, and the killer—tuition at the Rhode Island School of Design. The kid got some meager financial aid, but she took no loans at all. Madeline covered every penny of it.

She literally couldn't afford to lose her job.

After that, all it took were some vague promises of future business to her shrew of a boss, hinging, of course, on Madeline's cooperation, and he had her right where he wanted her.

The door to the conference room opened and the Pitbull herself strode in. She snarled over her shoulder at whoever remained in the hallway, then slapped the door shut and stalked the length of the room, a short stick of dynamite, ready to explode.

He couldn't suppress another smile. He'd always loved to blow things up.

She pulled up in front of him, close enough that even from her unimpressive height she was looking down at him. She snapped out one word.

"Why?"

He let his brows rise a centimeter. Gave her not one inch of ground.

"Why what?"

"Why me? It's stupid to expect me to help you with the Monet. One thing you're not is stupid." She crossed her arms. "That means you're dragging me into this for revenge. Since it's been five years, and the only price you ever paid for stealing the *Lady in Red* was to get more attention from your fans in the press, why risk a forty-four-million-dollar recovery by putting me in the middle of it? Why not find someone who might *actually believe* you didn't steal your own Monet, and leave me the fuck alone?"

Adam swirled his Scotch. When he'd envisioned this inevitable moment, he'd imagined responding to her attack with a swift accounting of her precarious financial condition, followed by a hard boot in the ass to bring her into line. Now that the time had come, he didn't want to do either of those things. He liked her this way, with fire in her eyes.

The truth was—and this surprised him—he wasn't quite comfortable using her sister as a sword to force her to her knees. Maybe he had a soft spot for sibling affection—he wouldn't have guessed it, having none of his own. But more likely it was his business sense kicking in. After all, her feistiness would be an asset in his battle with Hawthorne. It wouldn't behoove him to break her spirit.

But he did have to show her who was boss.

"Do sit down," he said in an even tone that neither challenged nor gave ground. Then he dropped his gaze to the chair, a clear signal that if she wanted to meet his eyes, she'd have to park herself in it.

After five deliberate seconds plainly meant to show that she was sitting because she *wanted* to, not because he commanded it, she let one cheek touch leather. It hardly made a dent; she couldn't weigh more than ninety pounds soaking wet.

She'd left her jacket in her office, and her sleeveless top stretched over breasts that fit her proportions exactly. Not that he was looking; he kept his eyes on her face, but his peripheral vision caught the action as they swelled up and out with each annoyed breath.

"Listen, LeCroix—"

"Adam," he cut in. "My top advisors go by given names. I find they speak more freely that way." He smiled slightly. "Although you don't seem to have a problem speaking your mind to the boss."

"You're not my boss. I work for Marchand, Riley, and White. You're my client. I'm"—here she choked on her words—"your attorney. You don't pay me. The firm does. I don't report to you. I represent you. That's all."

He tilted his head, did a sympathetic smile this time. "Perhaps Adrianna wasn't clear. It's true that you aren't *directly* on my payroll. But make no mistake. You work *for me*. You report *to me*. I am your *only* client, and my whim is your command."

She shot out of her chair and he almost laughed. He *had* gone a bit far with that last part. But really, she was asking for it.

"You can take your *whim*—" she snarled, but he cut her off again.

"I'm sure you have many fascinating and original ideas about what I can do with my whim," he said, "but that's not what I'm paying for. I'm paying for your time, your efforts, and your undivided attention. And by undivided I mean 24/7."

Her eyes bugged. "I have a *life*, you know."

"Do you?" Insulting.

Her cheeks went up in flames.

He could have told her what he knew right then and there, that not only were her finances in the crapper, her love life was circling the bowl along with them. But why let her know that his private investigators had turned her life inside out? He'd save that bombshell for another day.

Still, her lack of romantic involvements—past and present—surprised him. His investigators had checked as far back as her undergraduate days at Boston College and found no relationships lasting longer than a three-day weekend. Granted, it would take a brave man to bare his junk to her—he'd find himself short a nut if he looked at her crosswise—but even so, there'd been no shortage of interest through the years. It was Madeline who refused to get serious.

Her flushed face told Adam there was a story there. In time, he'd find out what it was. For the moment, though, he had all the leverage he needed.

"Get your things," he said. "I'll take you home."

She bristled. "I can get home on my own, when I'm good and ready to go."

Ignoring her, he set his glass on the table, pulled out his phone. "Fredo, bring the car around. We'll be down in five."

"I'm not riding with you!"

He dropped the phone in his pocket. Rose to his full

six-foot-two, and watched her head tip back to hold him in her furious glare.

He curved his lips, part smile, all menace. "Five minutes, Madeline. With your things, or without them. That much is up to you."

And he walked past her and out the door.

CHAPTER THREE

THE LIMO HUGGED the curb, the open door gaping like a hell mouth.

A good-looking guy with olive skin and a dark suit stepped forward to take her briefcase. "Hello, Ms. St. Clair. I'm Fredo."

"Hi, Fredo. You can call me Maddie." She let her gaze linger just long enough to signal interest, then mentally slapped herself. The last person she should get naked with was LeCroix's driver/bodyguard/confidant.

Well, he was the next-to-last person. LeCroix was the last. Women threw themselves at him; his body count must number in the hundreds, or higher. But she wouldn't be one of them.

Oh, she understood the attraction on a physical level. The man was a god.

But he was also the devil. And anyway, he hadn't shown one iota of interest. Not five years ago, and not now. Ensconced in the forward-facing seat, a laptop propped open on his right, papers fanned out on his left, he didn't even glance at her as she ducked inside.

She took the seat facing him, checked out the accommodations. Top of the line, of course. Buttery leather seats, recessed lighting, stocked bar with a fridge. But surprisingly restrained. Since LeCroix was nothing if not a showoff, she took a moment to recalibrate.

As they pulled into traffic, he said matter-of-factly, "If that's the best you've got, I won't be needing your services after all."

Startled, Maddie did a quick check of her suit, flicked a glance at her briefcase. She looked like exactly what she was, a high-priced lawyer.

Affronted, she scowled at him.

But he was staring out the window. "No, I won't change my mind," he said, and tapped the Bluetooth in his ear.

She felt her cheeks heat up. He hadn't been talking to her. She wasn't even that important.

As if to emphasize the point, he tapped some keys on the laptop. Continued to ignore her while she plotted and stewed.

The problem—the immediate problem, anyway—was that she didn't want him to see where she lived.

Before taking responsibility for Lucy, she'd managed to swing a sweet apartment in Park Slope, a trendy Brooklyn neighborhood where she'd come to know the shopkeepers and students and artists who shared it. Now she still lived in Brooklyn, but not in Park Slope, or Williamsburg, or any other upscale address.

Instead, she was squished into a tiny apartment in a dicey neighborhood that didn't even have a name, its most attractive feature being proximity to the subway.

"Listen," she said, trying to keep the anxiety from her voice. "I need to stop for a few things. Tell Fredo to drop me at Macy's."

LeCroix didn't even look up. "There's no time for shopping. We're wheels up in ninety minutes."

She nearly lifted out of her seat. "Wheels up? On a *plane*?"

"I don't yet own a rocket. Though I'm working on it." He glanced up. "Afraid of flying?"

She was. Deathly, back-sweatingly afraid. "*No,* I'm not afraid of flying. But Hawthorne's headquarters are here."

"And mine are in Italy."

Hours by air. Across the Atlantic.

Sweat trickled down her sides. Heights terrified her. Flying took that terror and poured gas on it, then ignited it with a nuclear bomb.

The limo closed in around her, a rolling jail cell. Flirting with panic, she stared out the window, realized they were crossing into Brooklyn. Obviously, LeCroix already knew where she lived, which explained why he'd been so disgustingly sure of her.

Anger flared in her breast, a welcome reprieve. Scowling at his chiseled profile as he calmly skimmed spreadsheets and scrolled through e-mails, she stoked her fury until it burned away fear, burned away shame.

"Your Monet wasn't stolen, was it?" she said, breaking the silence. "This is just another scam. Another swindle to prove you're smarter than everyone else."

He lifted his head, locked onto her eyes. "If I said it was, that would be a privileged communication between attorney and client, wouldn't it, Madeline?" His lips curved slightly. "Even if I told you I stole the *Lady in Red*, there wouldn't be a damn thing you could do about it, now that you represent me."

She swallowed bile. "Are you admitting you did?"

His eyes, that startling blue, crinkled as he smiled. "Ever the prosecutor, aren't you, darling?"

Her blood pressure spiked. "Don't *darling* me, you son of a bitch."

His smile grew. "Forgive me, Counselor. I forget how sensitive you American women are."

"Cut the shit. You're American too."

"By birth, but I consider myself a citizen of the world."

His background was old news to her. Born to two renowned painters who'd skipped and hopped around Europe, squatting for months at a time in the posh guesthouses of wealthy patrons, Adam LeCroix had spent precious little of his childhood in America.

An only child, fluent in seven languages and blessed with a staggering IQ, at twenty-two he'd sold off the truckload of paintings his parents left behind when they died in a plane crash off Corsica, and parlayed that small fortune into a gigantic one. Five years ago, Maddie had known the net worth of each of his international companies, and the figure was staggering. Since then, his conglomerate had doubled in value.

Now he was one of the richest men in the world. The asshole.

The limo came to a smooth stop. Outside the window, her concrete building loomed grimly.

Fredo came around to open the door. She started to get out, then froze, stooped over, when LeCroix closed his laptop and slid his butt toward the door.

"Wait a minute. I didn't invite you in."

He met her snarl with innocent eyes. "This vehicle has many accouterments, but a bathroom isn't one of them. I hoped to use yours."

What could she say to that? Nothing, that's what.

She stepped out onto the pavement with a crick in her back and a scowl on her face. Fredo flashed a grin that seemed sympathetic. She couldn't help liking him.

Sidestepping between a rusty Honda and a gleaming SUV, she heard Adam say to Fredo, "We'll be out in ten minutes."

Ten minutes to pack for Italy?

Swinging around to tell him what she thought of that, she saw movement under the Honda and leaped onto the sidewalk, expecting a rat to dart out. But nothing appeared.

Then she heard a faint whine and squatted for a look.

"Oh no!" A dog—more dead than alive—blinked at her once and then closed his brown eyes.

Dropping to her knees, she stuck her shoulders under the bumper.

"What the hell—" Adam knelt beside her. Then, "Oh Christ." He caught her arm as she reached for the dog. "He's hurt. He could bite."

She shook off his hand, but he was right. She worked with rescue dogs, had seen even the gentlest soul lash out when wounded. And this fella was in bad shape. He'd crawled under the Honda to die.

Wriggling out, she sat back on her haunches and turned her outrage at the situation squarely on Adam, who was getting to his feet. "We're not leaving him!"

"Of course not," he said curtly. Stripping off his suit coat, he dropped it on the Honda, popped out his cuff links, and rolled up his sleeves. To Fredo, "Get the jack." To Maddie, "Where's the nearest vet?"

"Around the corner." Her friend Parker's place, where she helped out at the shelter he operated next door to his office.

In no time, Fredo jacked up the Honda. When she looked under, Maddie's heart convulsed at the cruelty.

A short-haired yellow dog that should've been sixty pounds but was probably forty lay on his side in an oily puddle, ribs jutting, fur patchy, and a raw, open wound circling his neck where his collar used to be.

Adam crouched beside her. "Hello, boy," he said in a tone that soothed even Maddie's raw nerves. "You look like you've missed a few meals. Let's see what we can do about that."

The ropy tail twitched once, the brown eyes opened. Then closed again.

Adam reached for his suit jacket, shimmied under the car, and wrapped it around the bony body, then shimmied out again with the dog, his head lolling over Adam's arm.

"Take a right at the corner," Maddie told Fredo as he dropped the Honda. "It's halfway down the block." Then she swept the laptop aside and Adam followed her into the limo, the dog as limp as a noodle on his lap.

She speed-dialed Parker. "I've got an emergency. A dog. No, I don't think he's been hit. But he's dying." Her voice caught. The dog's eyes hadn't opened. His neck wound was infected. He lay as if he hadn't a bone in his body.

Parker met them at the door. They cut through the waiting room, past a kid with a squirming puppy, and an old man with a Chihuahua in the crook of each arm, to an examining room at the end of a hallway. Adam laid the dog, still wrapped in his jacket, on the stainless steel table.

"I'll take it from here," Parker said, and shooed them out.

The receptionist waited with a clipboard. "Whose dog is it?"

Maddie opened her mouth to claim him, then bit her lip. Dogs weren't allowed in her building.

"Bill it to me," Adam said.

"What's his name?"

"He's a stray."

The woman clicked her pen, wrote *John Doe Dog* on the form, and offered the clipboard to Adam. "You can put your billing information here, Mr. LeCroix."

Adam didn't bat an eye at his name. Of course not. He was freaking famous. Not only was his face on CNBC every night, but unlike other gazillionaires like George Soros and Warren Buffett, Adam LeCroix was hot, so *People* and TMZ were all over him too, scrutinizing his love life the way Wall Street tracked his takeovers.

It was utterly disgusting. The man was a *felon*. Maddie *always* turned the channel when the reporters started fawning, and she'd once thrown *People* across the salon when she came on a bare-chested photo of him on his yacht, supermodel sunning beside him.

For the moment, though, she refrained from sneering, because Adam handed over a business card and said, "Send the bill here. Whatever he needs."

John Doe Dog would need hundreds in care, and Maddie didn't have it to spare.

Out in the waiting room, they parked in the hard-backed chairs. The puppy squirted out of the boy's arms and raced circles around their feet. Across the narrow room, the Chihuahuas vibrated like cell phones against the old guy's chest, bug-eyes glued to the action.

Adam pulled out his phone, hit speed dial. "We'll be here for a while," he said to Fredo. "Park the car, and tell Jacques to cancel the flight plan and stand by."

"You can go," Maddie said as he pocketed his phone. "I've got this."

"I think not," he said, dryly.

"Well. It was worth a try."

He snorted a laugh, stretched his arm along the back of her chair. She scooted forward, giving him the hairy eyeball.

And for the first time, she noticed the oil staining his white shirt and streaking his tanned (and sinewy) forearms. His dark trousers were grimy from knee to (nicely packaged) groin. And his coal black, longer-than-it-decently-should-be hair was tousled . . . and ridiculously sexy.

She looked away, loathing herself for having non-negative thoughts about him. But wow, she'd never seen him without a jacket, not in person. He was built, and probably hung.

"You're filthy," he said, a smile in his voice.

Her head whipped around. Had he read her mind?

Then his eyes skimmed her suit. *Phew.* He meant her favorite Armani, not her oversexed brain.

She shrugged. "That's okay, I'll expense it. The shoes too." She pointed her toe, displaying the scratch. "I warn you, they cost more than the suit."

His lips turned up at the corners. "I'll have a pair sent over in every color."

"Size six." *Heh heh.* Ten pairs of Jimmy Choos would run him ten grand, plus tax.

"This Parker," he said, "he's a good vet?"

"Of course he is."

"You're not biased?"

"Why would I be?"

"You seem chummy."

"That's because we *are* chummy. I volunteer at the shelter he runs next door. And I'm telling you he's the best vet I know."

"Hmm." Adam's assessing gaze swept the room, and suddenly she saw it through his eyes. The water-stained ceiling, curling linoleum, fly-specked walls.

Her back went up. "In case you didn't notice, this isn't Beverly Hills. People here don't do cosmetic surgery on their pets, but they still love them. And the low rent lets Parker put his money into the shelter. He funds most of it out of his own pocket."

He brought his gaze back to hers. "I admire that," he said, taking the wind from her sails.

"Yeah, well, you should," was all she could muster.

She looked away from his bluer-than-the-sea eyes. It was impossible to meet them without losing her edge, and she needed her damn edge; it was all she really had.

Yet try as she might, she couldn't ignore his presence any more than she could have ignored a panther lounging beside her, sleek and rangy and strong enough to snap her with one swat.

She knew his heritage, knew his parents' best qualities had synthesized in their son. His killer eyes and quarterback's build came from his Celtic father, his glossy black hair and movie-star cheekbones from his fiery Italian mother.

But knowing the genesis of The Sexiest Man Alive didn't make his hotness any easier to handle.

Pissed at herself, she picked at the grit stuck to her knees until Parker poked his head through the door.

"Hey Mads, come on back."

Adam followed behind her. She couldn't stop him, since he was paying. But she refused to like it.

They found John Doe on the table where they'd left him, stretched out on a blanket. Adam's ruined jacket lay on a chair.

Parker glanced up when they came in, eyes only for Maddie.

"He's not as bad as he looks. Right now, his biggest problem is dehydration, that's what almost killed him.

We're setting up an IV in the back to take care of that. He's undernourished, obviously, and without knowing for sure how long that's been going on, I can't tell if there's organ damage."

He ran a gentle hand down the dog's bony spine, then brought it back up to his neck, close to the wound. John Doe opened his eyes, chocolaty brown and filled with misery. "It's okay, boy," Parker murmured. "Nobody's gonna hurt you anymore."

Maddie's eyes smarted, and one tear got away from her. She swiped it off her cheek.

Adam's hand touched the small of her back, oddly comforting. "Will that heal?" he asked Parker in a taut voice.

"Oh, sure. I've seen worse than this. What happens is, the owner doesn't loosen the collar as the dog grows, until eventually it's embedded in the skin. In this case, the fucker must've ripped it off the poor fella before he dropped him on the street."

"Jesus," Adam muttered, anger, disgust, and compassion all rolled into one word.

"I gave him something for the pain. It'll put him out, then I'll apply an antibiotic salve." Parker glanced at Maddie. "Want to help me bring him into the back room?"

"I can carry him," said Adam.

"Thanks, but Maddie knows what to do." Parker stepped around the table, dislodging Adam from her side. "You can get the door, though."

He took one end of the blanket, Maddie took the other, and they shuffled past Adam.

As he started to follow, Parker kicked the door closed behind him.

Chapter Four

Adam caught the door with his hand before it bounced off his chin.

What the fuck?

Not since his boyhood had he been so rudely shuffled aside, and he'd hated it enough to spend the last twenty years ensuring that he was always the most important man in the room.

Apparently Parker hadn't gotten the memo.

Fighting the urge to barge through the door, Adam paced the examining room instead, pausing to glare out the tiny window. It was grimy on the outside, making the narrow alley it faced look grimmer.

He spotted the shelter's entrance, a freshly painted blue door on an otherwise derelict building. A skinny teen in ripped jeans emerged with a chipper husky mix on a leash. The dog's nose immediately went to the ground, sniffing energetically, reading the pavement like a newspaper. The boy ran a hand down its back and it wagged happily, living in the moment.

Adam's chest tightened. The foolish dog didn't know it was a stray. That no one wanted it. It simply took what kindness it could eke out of a cold, cruel world and made the best of the shitty hand it was dealt.

He'd done the same himself, but he'd gone that sorry dog one better. He'd quit looking for kindness at a young age. Stopped craving affection and attachment when none was forthcoming.

He'd even stamped out his old childhood longing for a dog, that one steady companion to take with him when his vagabond parents picked up stakes, tearing him away from what few friends he'd made in whichever strange city they'd roosted in.

Living on others' largesse, as they'd frequently explained, meant traveling light. Bad enough they were saddled with a child. How could they expect their hosts to tolerate a pet as well?

How, indeed. Well, he'd made the best of it, hadn't he? Learned to adapt, to mix with any crowd, from the moneyed offspring of their benefactors to the motley children of the hired help. He'd learned their languages too, and the language of class as well, the intonations and dialects of the posh and the poor, the parlors and the street corners.

He'd taken that experience, along with the brains God gave him and the sixty paintings his parents left behind when they died, all the way to the bank. And the knowledge that the daily landside of cash flowing into his pocket had its roots in the art they'd created at his expense always prompted a smile, not of joy, but of grim satisfaction.

Behind him, the door opened and Parker came through. "I'll keep him comfortable," he was saying over his shoulder, his large frame completely blocking tiny Madeline. "Why don't you come back after hours? You can check in on him."

Adam smirked at the obvious ploy. Parker was good-looking, capable, and obviously intelligent. But apparently there was a second memo he hadn't gotten, the one about Madeline's drive-by "relationships."

Predictably, she brushed him off. "I'll try," she said, heading for the door. "Text me if there's a change, okay? And don't spare any expense." She jerked a thumb at Adam. "It's on him."

Parker swiveled in Adam's direction. Under the circumstances, Adam wasn't surprised to see suspicion and dislike in the other man's eyes. What did surprise him were his own similar feelings. They prompted him to give Parker, a man he'd otherwise admire for his compassion, a haughty stare.

And if that wasn't odd enough, he heard himself say, "Your assistant has my card. Have her notify me as soon as my dog's ready to travel."

Taking Maddie's elbow, he kept her moving out the door. But when they reached the sidewalk, she shook him off.

"What do you mean, *your* dog? *I* found him. You would've walked right past him."

He looked down at her, showing only the mildest interest. "Pets aren't allowed in your building."

She glared up at him, patently furious that he knew so much about her, and undoubtedly wondering how much more he knew. He hid a smile behind a bored facade. She'd burst a blood vessel if she knew how thoroughly his people had turned her life inside out.

The car slid up to the curb. She ran a withering eye down its length, then set off for her place on foot.

Let her walk then. As they glided past her, he saw her middle finger shoot up. Behind the tinted windows, he laughed out loud.

His unexpected appearance in her life, not to mention the reversal of power in his favor, had thrown her back on her heels. But soon enough she'd pull herself together. And as much as he'd like to believe he had her by the short hairs, once she was on her game she was just smart enough to wriggle out of his grasp.

Of course, it was her brains that appealed to him. She was a spitfire, and in his battle with Hawthorne both her intelligence and her cussedness would come in handy.

At the moment, though, the latter quality was directed exclusively at him.

Fredo pulled up to the curb as Maddie steamed past. Adam caught up to her as she jabbed her key into the lock.

"There was a bathroom at the clinic," she snapped over her shoulder.

"So there was." He reached out a long arm to push the door open for her. She let out a low growl, then stomped up the stairs to her second-floor apartment and assaulted another lock.

He pushed that door open too, and together they stepped into a living room not much larger than the limo. Leaving him to fend for himself, she marched down a short, dark hallway and disappeared into the bedroom.

Halfway down that hallway, Adam found the bathroom, so tiny it would fit in the tub at his villa.

Squeezing between the shower stall and the bowl to take a leak, he cased the room. White tile, chrome fittings. Bathmat kicked into the corner, Colgate uncapped on the sink.

Messy, but clean where it counted.

On the wall above the toilet, four framed pencil sketches were arranged in a square. Farm scenes. Horses, a barn, an old hound dog. To his experienced eye, the drawings were the youthful efforts of a talented artist. Unsigned, but he knew who'd done them.

While he washed dirt and oil off his hands, he looked over the contents of her medicine cabinet. Birth control pills, as expected. Otherwise it was mostly over-the-counter stuff, with one surprise. A prescription sleep aid. He checked the label. Just a few days old, which explained why his investigators had missed it. He sprinkled the pills into his palm—all thirty still accounted for.

He poured them back into the bottle, set it on the shelf where he'd found it. Were Madeline's financial troubles keeping her up at night? Good. The more worried she was, the tighter his grip on her.

The bedroom door was still closed when he emerged. He wandered to the living room. It bulged like an overstuffed suitcase, jammed with a few nice pieces she'd likely carried over from more prosperous days. A floor lamp with an extravagantly beaded shade stood between a comfortable-looking love seat and matching chair, upholstered in velvety ruby red. An ornate Japanese chest doubled as a coffee table. And facing the love seat, a flat-screen TV scaled for a much larger room filled the wall, dominating the cramped space like a movie screen.

There was clutter here too. A white fleece blanket balled up on the sofa. The Sunday *Times* askew on the coffee table, the magazine section flopped open to the half-done crossword. A cereal bowl with an inch of milk congealing in the bottom.

Feeling a sudden urge to take the bowl into the micro-kitchen and wash it, Adam shoved his hands in his pockets. When had he last done something so mundane, so normal, as wash a dish? He couldn't recall. But something about this messy little space struck a chord, made him wonder how normal would feel. Made him want, badly, to prop his sock feet on the coffee table and take a stab at the crossword with the chewed-on pencil that was caught between the pages.

It made no sense. In his own world he demanded neatness and order. He owned a dozen houses, each grander than the next, and not an atom out of place. When he set something down, his servants picked it up. All signs of life were quickly erased, making it easy for him to leave, to bounce from house to house. He felt no attachment to any of them, except perhaps his villa.

But this sad excuse for an apartment, dinky and cluttered and the farthest thing from grand, felt . . . homey. Lived-in. He could see himself on that love seat, could almost feel John Doe's heavy head on his thigh.

His gaze lifted to the walls, crammed with paintings. He'd scarcely noticed them, so tangled up was he in his inexplicable longing.

Now he focused his attention on the art.

He knew art—how could he not, growing up as he had? And he collected more than just the old masters. He searched out new talent, even played patron to several promising young artists.

These paintings were Lucy's. He was familiar with her work, had already purchased—anonymously—two of her paintings from a Providence gallery where she'd had a small showing. She was a staggering talent, raw yet, but maturing nicely, and largely unrecognized, so her work went for pennies.

Under other circumstances, he'd be inclined to sponsor her. But becoming her patron would lift the financial burden from Maddie's shoulders, and he had no interest in doing that. She'd made his life hell for six long months, put fear into him for the first time since he'd claimed manhood.

Now he had her under his thumb, and he meant to keep her there.

"You're still here," she said, startling him.

Covering his flinch with a shrug, he continued gazing at the paintings. "Finished packing, have you?"

"No."

He turned, faking mild surprise. She'd changed into faded blue jeans and a sage green T-shirt, both likely purchased in the children's department. "Hurry along then," he said, checking his watch to make the point. "We'll stay at my penthouse tonight, fly out first thing in the morning."

The expression on her pixie face remained calm and cool. "Fine. I'll meet you there later."

Ah. She'd regrouped. She was pretending to cooperate, hoping that if she seemed compliant he'd let her call some of the shots.

Not bloody likely.

Taking out his phone, he buzzed Fredo. "We'll be down in ten," he said, then slipped it back into his pocket and casually resumed studying the art.

He never heard her silent retreat—he'd have to remember she moved on cat feet—but when the itch between his shoulder blades abated, he knew she'd left the room.

He rolled his shoulders, cast a troubled eye around her cramped and cozy space. Forced himself to resist the love seat's siren call, the crossword begging to be finished.

It was utterly unlike him. Yet in the two hours since Madeline had reentered his life, he'd experienced a gamut of unsettling emotions, not least of which was this bizarre yearning for home and hearth. He'd even taken on John Doe, an impetuous move for a man who lived life like a chess game, plotting six moves ahead.

But once again, she'd bumped the board, jarring the pieces off their designated squares, upsetting plans large and small.

Now, staring at her damn cereal bowl, he wondered if getting involved with Madeline St. Clair was such a brilliant idea after all.

LEANING BACK AGAINST her bedroom door, Maddie squeezed her eyes shut.

LeCroix was the devil in a dark blue suit. Forget the heroics with John Doe. The casual bill-it-to-me crap. Forget the oil-stained shirt, the filthy trousers, and ruined shoes. It all amounted to pocket change to him.

Okay, so maybe he seemed to genuinely care about John. He'd just farm him out to one of his many estates. He didn't understand that a dog, especially one like John, needed love.

But what did Adam LeCroix know about love? Nothing, that's what.

He was all about money and stuff and taking what he wanted, even if he had to steal it. *Especially* if he had to steal it. Stealing was fun for him, a game, a hobby, and she'd been *so close* to nailing him.

Now he was out there sneering at her apartment. So what if it was small, and modest, and, okay, kind of messy at the moment? Downsizing had forced her to pare down her possessions, to bring only what truly mattered. Like the love seat that cuddled her after a long day at the office. Her oversized TV, perfect for escaping into movies with popcorn and Cabernet.

And Lucy's work, of course. Bold and colorful and full of life, just like her sister. Inspiring Maddie to be better, work harder. To do whatever it took to care for the young woman she'd abandoned as a girl.

Now LeCroix's cooties were on all of it.

Grinding her teeth, she rifled her drawers. Underwear, bras, and socks hit the bed. Yoga pants and T-shirts and a cotton nightie followed. Pawing through her closet, she yanked out two Gucci suits, periwinkle and gunmetal gray, and the blouses and accessories to match.

Then she dragged her garment bag out from under her bed and layered the whole kit and caboodle into it, stuffed her toiletry bag, still stocked from her last business trip, into the outside pocket, and was done packing with four minutes to spare.

Not that it was a competition.

Slinging the bag over her shoulder, she cast a long last look at her sleigh bed with its comfortable-as-a-cloud mattress and reminded herself to stop in the bathroom for her sleeping pills. She'd done without them until now, but things were going downhill like a pig on ice.

Adam was waiting by the door when she emerged. She dropped her bag and brushed past him, then pulled up short. "Where is it?"

"Where's what?" He looked bored.

"My cereal bowl."

"I washed it."

"You *washed* it? Why?"

He hefted her bag. "To move things along. Leonardo times his carbonara to the minute."

She snatched her purse from the counter as he opened the door. Damn it, she hated to be rushed. But carbonara was an art form, and it happened to be her favorite dish.

"I take it Leonardo's one of your lackeys," she said snottily.

"It's unlikely he'd characterize himself as a lackey." Adam stepped back so she could precede him down the stairs. His manners were flawless, double damn him.

"How about flunky?" she lobbed over her shoulder. "Grunt, stooge, minion?"

He laughed, and she realized she'd never heard him sound genuinely amused.

She redoubled her efforts to be abrasive.

"It must suck knowing that everyone around you is there because you pay them. No friends, just hired hands."

"Whereas you," he said lightly, holding the outer door, "are awash in friends and lovers."

"I have friends," she snapped, managing to step on his toe as she passed him. Fredo opened the car door and she plunked herself on the forward-facing seat.

LeCroix eyed her through the open door.

"I get carsick if I ride backwards," she announced. "You want me puking all over the place?"

"Certainly not. Slide over. We'll share the seat."

She had no intention of sitting that close to him. Their knees might touch.

She crossed her arms, a truculent two-year-old.

"Madeline." With a definite edge. "Shove over, or I'll shove you over."

She stared straight ahead. Let him try it.

Then—whoosh—the bastard scooped her up like a feather and deposited her two feet to the left! He dropped onto the seat beside her, Fredo closed the door, and five seconds later they were under way.

"I guess you've been working out," she snipped, masking wounded pride. "Planning another heist?"

He broke into a smile, amusement again, and she felt an unwelcome tingle. Some perverse part of her liked being the center of his attention.

His eyes, midnight blue in the waning light, flicked over her once. "What do you weigh? Ninety pounds?"

She narrowed her eyes. "It's rude to ask someone's weight."

"Rudeness is hardly the worst you've accused me of."

"True, but it's your latest offense. Along with touching my person. That's battery."

He grinned now, and damn it, her insides fluttered. She pinched it off. Reminded herself *why* she was sitting here with a goddamn felon. Because he was *blackmailing* her.

"Keep your mitts to yourself, LeCroix. You might've hijacked my services as a lawyer, but don't even *think* about getting into my pants, because sex isn't part of this deal."

He dropped the grin. "I don't deal for sex, Madeline. It never crossed my mind. But since it appears to be at the forefront of yours, let me be clear. I've never bought sex, never coerced it in any manner. I don't use sex as a tool, a weapon, or a means to an end. For me, sex is about desire. *Mutual* desire. We'd both have to want it.

"And frankly, darling"—he smiled apologetically—"diminutive women don't do it for me."

WATCHING THE FLUSH rush up Madeline's neck, Adam wished he'd stopped short of making it personal. It was beneath him to poke at another's physical attributes. He'd been bloody lucky in that department, through no doing of his own, and always found it boorish when others mocked those less fortunate.

Now he'd gone and done it himself. Not that there was anything wrong with being petite. Some men undoubtedly preferred their women pocket-sized. He'd begun to see the attraction himself. But she was obviously self-conscious about it, so it wasn't fair to taunt her.

He wanted, desperately, to blame his transgression on her. The woman deliberately got under his skin, pricked his ego. But it was no excuse for his own bad behavior.

There was no making up for it now, not without drawing more attention to both her size and his indiscretion. Best to ignore the whole thing and hope she forgot about it.

Like that would happen.

He gave it a try anyway, opening his laptop to the latest quarterly report on his most recent acquisition. He had decisions to make. A change in management was overdue, and he'd be plugging his own people into key positions before the week was out.

He jotted some notes, sent a brief e-mail. But he couldn't concentrate. Madeline was thinking too loudly. He could almost hear her plotting.

Foolishly, he hadn't fully thought through his plans for her. Again, he'd acted impulsively, even recklessly, his usual clear-sightedness blurred by the tantalizing thought of having her at his mercy. He hadn't considered that keeping Madeline close was like cuddling a live grenade.

It was bound to go *boom*.

He could, he supposed, strand her on one of his more remote estates. Leave her to chew through the woodwork while he went about his business, summoning her only when the Hawthorne matter required it.

But now that he had her, he was oddly reluctant to let her go. Not only did the old adage fit—keep your friends close and your enemies closer—but he was man enough to admit she'd captured his interest. She was a puzzle begging to be solved.

And despite his crass comment about diminutive women, she was damn desirable.

In any case, it behooved him to keep her too busy to plot. And after his digression into name calling, he needed to reestablish their professional footing.

Him, boss; her, minion.

So, taking a file from the stack on the seat, he held it out to her without looking away from the screen.

"What?" she asked without touching it.

"I'm installing a new CFO at a software company I've just acquired."

"So?"

"So this is her employment contract. Look it over. And pay special attention to the noncompete clause." It would give her something to do besides plan his castration.

She sniffed. "I'm here to squeeze Hawthorne, not help your crusade for world domination. Give it to one of your lackeys."

He looked over at her then, and was startled to see that instead of steely gray, the eyes glaring back at him were a pale and luminous sea green.

He blinked.

It was her sage-colored shirt that brought out the hue. But a hint of it must have been layered beneath the steel, which explained why he'd always found her eyes so arresting. Green eyes hit him below the belt.

He recovered quickly. "I *am* giving it to one of my lackeys. You."

Those arresting eyes narrowed.

He feigned surprise. "Did you expect to loaf? Draft a few motions and then lounge by the pool? At five hundred dollars an hour?"

"You make a good point," she said in a tone that meant anything but. "Why hire me full-time when I can draft those motions in a couple of hours? They'll still have my name on them, so you'll get my"—air quotes—"stamp of approval. And you'll save yourself a fortune."

Allowing a faint smile, he launched a decoy to draw her away from the sound point she'd made. "Yes, but it's my fortune, isn't it? And I wouldn't keep it for long if I frittered it away on lazy lawyers."

Her lips flattened out. "This lazy lawyer came within an inch of taking you down."

"Ah, but a decisive inch it was." He dropped the folder on her lap and went back to his laptop like he'd lost interest in the conversation.

With a great many muttered fucks and damns, she pulled out the contract. Two minutes later she slapped it down on the seat. "You're kidding, right? This is the language you always use?"

He gave her his full attention. "Why do you ask?"

"Because it sucks." She pulled a pen from her bag and circled a phrase, jabbed it with the point.

He picked it up, read it, gave her a questioning look.

She rolled her eyes. "This is basic. I can't believe it hasn't bitten you in the ass."

He lowered the contract. "This happens to be the first contract drafted by a firm I've recently retained. But my own attorneys reviewed it and found it ironclad."

"That's because the problem's so obvious that they overlooked it. Happens all the time. You expect to see something, so you see it. Even when it's not there." She snatched the contract, wrote three words—"directly or indirectly"—and dropped it again.

"How's that for lazy, LeCroix? You were *an inch* from getting fucked."

And didn't that conjure up some interesting images?

Five years ago, he'd entertained a few fantasies about her. Lifting her skirt, bending her over the desk. The usual thing.

But now he threw her down on the seat, cuffed her wrists. Tore her blouse, popped her tits out of her bra. She pretended to fight him, thrashing her head, cursing his name. But when he mounted her, drove into her, she bucked up to meet him, shuddering as she came.

Yes, this time around it was hardcore porn fast-forwarding in his brain, hardening his dick while he looked steadily into her eyes.

"Thank you, Madeline," he said, managing a civilized tone, while his inner barbarian stripped her naked.

She must have sensed the atmosphere change; the heat rising from his skin, the primal scent of lust. "Whatever," she muttered, but she didn't look away. She wanted to, he could tell. But their eyes had locked.

Color rose in her cheeks as the moment lengthened. Her lips went dry; she touched them with her tongue.

He broke his gaze to stare at it, hungrily. Only willpower kept him from biting it, sucking it . . .

Then the door opened. He hadn't even realized they'd stopped.

Maddie leaped over him and out of the car.

CHAPTER FIVE

RATTLED DOWN TO her genes by the pheromone explosion in the limo, Maddie's resistance took another hit when Adam's private elevator opened onto a magnificent foyer twice as large as her apartment.

Determined not to show weakness, she hid shock and awe behind an insouciant facade, barely glancing at the chandelier—as big as a Volkswagen. Or the Persian rug—as wide as a hockey rink. And she refused to acknowledge the art dripping from the walls, or the life-size bronze nude she knew to be a Rodin.

A gaunt man in a black suit was harder to ignore. He dropped a tight bow and spoke with a high-toned British accent. "Mr. LeCroix, a pleasure to have you back with us so soon."

"Thank you, Henry. This is Ms. St. Clair. She'll have the emerald suite."

Henry nodded at a hovering maid, who disappeared to do the master's bidding.

"Please tell Leonardo we'll dine early. Say, half an hour."

Henry nodded again, then turned to Maddie. "If you'll follow me?"

Half a mile of art-lined hallway later, he opened the

door to a suite more luxurious than the most opulent hotel. Ankle-deep cream carpet, fireplace fronted with jade marble, sofa and chairs upholstered in ultra-soft sage, all designed with elegant comfort in mind.

The art here was museum quality too. Every surface boasted artifacts from around the world. And the paintings. Good God. On one wall a Remington, on another a Turner. And above the fireplace, a Cezanne rounded out the eclectic collection.

It was tasteful and stylish and snug all at once, and if the fourth wall hadn't been glass—albeit draperied in emerald chenille—Maddie would have been forced to call it perfect.

"The bedroom is through there." Henry spread an arm toward double doors. "Bridget is unpacking your things. She'll attend you while you're in residence, and assist you with your bath if you wish. In any case, you may summon her—or any of the staff—simply by picking up any telephone."

"Great." Maddie gave him a friendly smile, hoping she didn't seem completely out of her element.

He reciprocated with an infinitesimal curve of the lips. "Dinner will be served in thirty minutes. Bridget will escort you to the dining room."

Not a chance. She wasn't going near LeCroix tonight, not after they'd almost jumped each other in the limo.

"Thanks, but you can send me a plate."

Henry's sunken eyes widened. "But Mr. LeCroix will expect you."

"He'll get over it." She put a hand on the doorknob, a clear signal to scram. "We're leaving tomorrow, so if I don't see you again, thanks for everything."

He backed into the hallway, surprise written large on his dour face. She did a bye-now finger wave, then went hunting for the maid.

She found her—the slender woman from the foyer—folding her panties into tiny triangles.

"Hey, Bridget, I'm Maddie." She stuck out her hand.

The stunned woman stared at it, eventually reaching out to touch it—barely—before pulling hers back and dropping a quick curtsy.

"Shall I draw your bath, then, ma'am?" she asked in a soft Irish brogue.

It was *Downton Abbey* come to life. Butlers, and parlors, and curtsying maids.

"Thanks, but I've got it from here." Hustling the girl into the hallway, Maddie looked both ways and dropped her voice. "Listen, Bridget, why don't you take the night off? Hit the movies, or a club. I promise not to tell."

And giving the gaping girl a parting grin and a wink, Maddie closed the door in her face.

"SHE SAID *WHAT*?" Adam stared at Henry.

Henry crossed his arms, his amusement apparent. Gone was the prim and proper butler. His demeanor now was less servant than friend, and his accent less Queen's English than cockney.

"She's blowin' you off, mate."

Adam pushed his fingers through his hair. He'd hoped to follow up on their interlude in the car. *Mutual desire* had definitely hung in the air.

He should have known she'd fight it. Any other woman would have thrown herself at him, but she'd thrown herself *over* him to get away.

Not only that, but she was patently unimpressed by the resources at his command. He had to respect her for that, but damn it, he wanted her to acknowledge his place in the world.

And he wanted her to dine with him.

He pushed back his chair. "All right, then. Serve dinner in the emerald suite. For two." And taking two flutes in one hand and the icy Prosecco in the other, he strode from the room to take on the Pitbull.

She wasn't happy to see him.

"What?" She kept her hand on the knob like she'd slam the door in his face if she didn't like his answer.

Ignoring her question, he strode into the suite like he owned it, which he damn well did. Setting the glasses on the cherry dining table that stood before the window, he twisted the top off the Prosecco. It popped loudly, then fizzed invitingly, foaming as he poured it.

He lifted a flute and held it out to her.

Her pixie nose wrinkled. "I'm not drinking with you."

"Your loss." He took a sip from the glass. "You'll find it's just the thing with Leonardo's carbonara."

"I'm not eating with you either."

He smiled. She was such a contrary imp. Totally unlike the other women who came in and out of his life, so anxious to please, to tease, to bewitch him with their talents. Not that he discouraged them. But Madeline didn't even *pretend* to like him.

Why did he find that so alluring?

Behind her, Henry's "Excuse me, madame," made her jump. Pushing past her, he wheeled the dinner cart to the table and commenced setting two places with Wedgwood and silver.

"Hold on." Maddie fisted her hips, stretching her T-shirt taut across her breasts. "I asked for a plate, not service for two. Get that stuff out of here."

Ignoring her, Henry set a covered platter between the plates, along with a bowl of Bibb lettuce tossed with vinaigrette, and the coup de grâce, Italian bread, a whole loaf, so hot from the oven that the knee-buckling aroma filled the room like smoke.

Maddie stopped bitching, her eyes nailed to the bread.

Then Adam lifted the lid from the platter, heaped with carbonara. "Rustic," he said, "but Leonardo elevates peasant food to high art."

She licked her lips. Took one step closer.

Then she stopped. Her eyes went to the window, then back to the table. Then the window once more. And she turned away.

Puzzled, Adam studied the twilit view. Nothing objectionable there. New York looked its best from this lofty height, silhouetted against the pastel sky.

He looked to Madeline again. She'd flopped on the sofa, stacked bare heels on the coffee table.

Well. Let her sulk. She wouldn't hold out for long. He happened to know carbonara was her favorite meal, and she was defenseless against Italian bread. And while martinis were her cocktail of choice, she preferred a crisp Prosecco with her pasta.

He took a seat, let the serving fork clatter as he scooped pasta onto his plate. Then he sawed the bread noisily. Crunched a mouthful of crust.

She crossed her arms under her breasts, unwittingly propping them up for his viewing pleasure.

He poured another glass of Prosecco, let it fizz loudly. Sucked a sip . . . and her feet hit the floor.

"Enough with the chewing and slurping," she snapped. "I know it's delicious. Even *I've* heard of Leonardo."

"You're free to join me."

"You've got it backwards. Eve gave the apple to Adam, not the other way around."

"So you're casting yourself as Eve in this drama?" He tsked. "Playing against type, don't you think?"

She shot a death ray over her shoulder . . . just as

he lifted his fork. A strand of pasta dangled from it, coated in cream.

Her gaze fixed on it.

He let the fork hover between them before sloooowly taking it into his mouth. His tongue wrapped around it, his lips came together, and—whoa—she looked hungry for more than just pasta.

Lust hit him like a fist in the gut. His balls drew up, his abs tightened reflexively.

And his pasta went down the wrong pipe.

He tried to cough. No air got through. He dropped his fork, lurching to his feet, clutching his throat. His hip hit the table, upending his glass. Spots flickered at the edge of his vision.

Then—oof!—a gob of pasta erupted from his throat, splatting on his plate. He leaned over the table, gasping gratefully.

"You okay?" Maddie's arms encircled him, her small hands fisted over his solar plexus. "Need another one?"

"I'm fine," he croaked, overstating the case. His throat burned. His eyes watered like faucets. "Thank you. I believe you saved my life." *After almost killing me with that eye-fuck.*

"Yeah, well"—she released him—"it hasn't exactly been my lucky day."

Turning his head, he caught her rueful shrug. He let out a laugh. And as if he'd popped a cork on a bottle of bubbly, he kept laughing.

He couldn't seem to stop.

It turned into a fit. Tears streaked his cheeks. A stitch in his side bent him over.

God, he hadn't laughed like this in years, that gut-clenching, gasping hilarity that swung between pleasure and pain, self-perpetuating, irrepressible, one slippery step from hysteria.

Even as his side split, he knew it for a reaction to his near-death experience. But Maddie had triggered it. She went straight to his funny bone.

He managed to look up, saw that she was laughing too. *At* him instead of *with* him, for sure, but he'd never seen her laugh at all, certainly not a belly laugh like this, like a teenager in the grip of high school hilarity. Free, uninhibited.

And God help him, breathtakingly sexy.

MADDIE WIPED A tear from her cheek. LeCroix completely losing his shit was the funniest thing she'd ever seen in her life.

Too bad the tabloids weren't around to catch it. His badass rep would be down the toilet, because the mighty Adam LeCroix laughing his ass off was *not* an intimidating sight.

When he was laughing, he didn't seem dangerous at all. He seemed perfectly normal, and . . . well . . . nice.

Not that she believed he was actually either of those things. But she couldn't pretend he wasn't smokin' hot. God, when he'd wrapped his lips around that carbonara, her panties had melted into a puddle.

Thank God he'd almost choked to death before she'd done something stupid, like let the lust that streaked through her body show up on her face.

Whatever. It was over now and he had himself in hand, looking down at her from his six-foot-two, making her feel like an ant.

She searched her repertoire for a snide remark, but all that laughter had released a crapload of endorphins. She'd lost the snarky mood. Hell, she felt almost charitable toward him.

He must have sensed her weakness, because he took full advantage, doing something she'd never ordinar-

ily have allowed. Taking her hand, he held her eyes in
his bluer-than-the-sea gaze, murmured in that deep,
exotic voice, "Thank you, Madeline."

And he kissed her.

On the knuckles. But . . . wow.

In a faraway corner of her mind, the voice of reason
piped up. *This is how he does it. This is how he gets those
supermodels onto his yacht.*

But apparently she was as susceptible as the bimbos,
because instead of hitting the fire alarm, she froze like
a deer in the headlights, letting his thumb skim her
knuckles, rubbing his kiss into her skin, a fiery tattoo.

It was the limo all over again, only more so. Now
his lips were involved, warm and seductive. His hair
fell forward around his too-dangerous face, thick and
glossy and dark as the devil's. And his thumb was
practically giving her an orgasm.

He lowered her hand, gave it a light squeeze, and let
go. She looked down at her knuckles. They looked the
same as before.

Huh.

He turned away, toward the table, and it was like a
light had gone out. Or the sun had set.

Before she could process that feeling, he turned to
her again, taking her arm and drawing her toward the
sofa. She went along like a trauma victim.

Sitting her down, he put a glass in her hand. "Mine
broke," he said. "We'll have to share."

Whoa. Share a glass with him? She should probably
object.

Before she could, he was back again, this time with
the bottle and the platter of pasta. Sitting down beside
her, he wound some strands around his fork and
brought it to her mouth.

She pressed her lips together instinctively.

Then he smiled, damn him, and now that she'd felt those treacherous lips on her hand she couldn't look away from them. She stared as he spoke.

"Madeline, it's only pasta. What can it hurt?"

That was a very good question, and there was a very good answer hovering just out of sight.

Gently, he rubbed the warm carbonara along her bottom lip. She couldn't stop herself. She opened up and let him in.

The pasta was fresh, made within the hour, the sauce light but substantial, the pancetta tissue-thin. It came together in a magical blend, everything carbonara should be, and more.

Sex on a plate.

It hit her tongue and her eyes rolled back. She hummed a long, blissful note.

Then she snatched the fork and swirled another bite. Adam wrapped his hand around hers and steered it his way.

"Hey! Get your own fork."

"If you insist." He made to stand, taking the platter with him.

"Whoa! Bring that back!"

He raised an eyebrow. She narrowed her eyes. Took a pull on the Prosecco. "Fine, we'll share."

He reached for the glass, finished it off, and poured another while she gobbled down two hasty bites.

"Mine," he said, eyeing the third. She fed it to him, keeping possession of the fork. "The bread's likely still warm," he mentioned.

Hissing impatiently, she hotfooted to the table, brought back the loaf. "I forgot the knife."

"No matter," he said, tearing off a hunk and passing it to her.

She moaned as she bit into it. The crust shattered,

scattering crumbs across her T-shirt. She hunted them down with a wet fingertip, chased them with Prosecco.

He'd found her weaknesses, all of them, and she couldn't be bothered to care.

"Pasta," Adam murmured, and she twirled him a bite. As he took it with those lips, his eyes flicked up and caught her staring, swamping her in a sea of blue.

Dazzled, she held his gaze while he chewed. Time slowed. She balanced the fork in midair. She was drunk, but not on wine.

He took the glass from her other hand, brushing her fingers with his, drawing her eyes. She'd never noticed his hands before.

Now she was riveted.

Their elegance disguised their size, broad, long-fingered like an artist's but, curiously, not soft at all. Lightly callused, in fact, with faint scars crisscrossing the knuckles, visibly white against his tanned skin.

A cut on his palm caught her eye. Without thinking she took the glass from his hand, opened his fingers for a closer look.

"Did you do this today? On that rusty Honda?" Her thumb slid over it. He didn't flinch, though it must have been tender. She angled it to the light. "It's deep. You need a tetanus shot."

"I had one last week." He pushed up the sleeve of his thin cashmere sweater to show her a healing gash on his forearm.

She forgot about the carbonara, captivated by sinewy muscle, more defined than any businessman had a right to. "How did it happen?"

"Rock climbing. Missed my footing, and had a bad moment before I recovered it."

She traced a finger along the scab. "You could've died."

"Disappointed?"

She shrugged. "Hope springs eternal."

He laughed, and she laughed along with him. It felt good. Easy and comfortable.

Her conscience pricked. She should be hating him, not flirting with him. But diabolically, he'd snuck past her defenses. First by playing the hero with John Doe, then by practically choking to death, giving her a turn to play hero. And instead of getting embarrassed and defensive like most guys, he'd gone giggly instead.

She honestly couldn't remember when she'd laughed so hard.

As if that wasn't enough, he'd blown her away with one stupid kiss on the hand, like he was some kind of knight and she was some kind of lady, two things that couldn't be further from the truth.

But damn it, it got to her. Now she'd gone gaga over his stupid lips and eyes and, God help her, his hands. It was all she could do not to kiss his palm and make it better.

Worst of all, they were swapping spit on a fork like they were lovers or something.

And it didn't feel awful. Her skin wasn't crawling.

To be perfectly honest—

Her phone burst out in the "Stray Cat Strut." Parker's ringtone. Leaving the fork on the platter, she headed to the bedroom, dug her phone from her bag.

"Hey, Park. How's John Doe?"

"On his feet, sniffing every nook and cranny."

"No way."

"Way. Once he was hydrated, I couldn't keep him down. Want to come see him?"

She frowned. "I can't."

"Working?"

"Sort of." It was too complicated to explain. "When can he leave?"

"Tomorrow, but he'll still need to take it easy." He paused. "Is that guy really going to take him? Because as far as I'm concerned, you brought John Doe in. If you don't want me to release him, I won't."

She hesitated, but what could she do? "Adam'll see he's taken care of."

"You don't sound enthused."

"I'm not. He's an ass and I doubt he's got an affectionate bone in his body." *His way-too-sexy body.* "But he'll find a good home for John."

"What the hell, Mads? If the guy's an ass, what're you doing with him?"

"Trust me, I'm not doing anything *with* him. It's strictly a work thing." *And I need to keep it that way.*

"Oh." Relieved. "So, brunch on Sunday before we walk the dogs?"

"Sounds good." It was only Wednesday. Surely she'd be home by Sunday.

Going back to the parlor, she found Adam at the window, hands in his pockets, gazing out at the Manhattan night. All remnants of dinner had been removed, and the air of intimacy had gone the way of the dirty dishes.

She refused to be disappointed.

"John Doe's on his feet. He can leave tomorrow."

"I see." Adam's voice had a cynical edge. "So your hero works miracles too."

Her back went up. "Parker's awesome. He's a gifted vet, and he's selfless too. I'm sure that's not a quality you appreciate, but I do."

He turned his head, raked her with those penetrating eyes. "So why haven't you married him?"

"*What?*"

"He's in love with you, and you're fond of him as well."

"Parker's *not* in love with me."

"Parker's unquestionably in love with you."

"You're nuts. And anyway, I'm not marrying him, or anybody else." Catching herself before she got any more personal, she turned it back on him. "Besides, what do *you* know about love? Or marriage, for that matter. You can't even keep a girlfriend."

His brows arched insultingly. "And you know this how? From reading the tabloids?"

Her cheeks heated up, but she fired back. "So you've got a girlfriend stashed on an island? Or maybe a wife?" She didn't want to care about the answer, but she did.

His lips curved in a smile that had drained of all warmth. "Why would an ass without an affectionate bone in his body need a girlfriend, not to mention a wife?"

The last of her endorphins fled the scene. What could she say? He was quoting her own words, and she'd meant them when she said them. Or maybe it was habit that brought them trippingly to her tongue. Either way, they damned her.

She lashed out anyway, defensive, resentful. "Adding eavesdropping to your rap sheet?"

He dropped his gaze, so the light went out of the room again. Quietly, he said, "Who's the ass now, Madeline?"

She stared after him, tongue-tied, as he walked out and left her.

Henry passed him in the doorway, continued into the room, and set a tray on the table.

Cheesecake, her favorite. One slice, two forks. And two steaming cappuccinos.

Damn him.

*   *   *

ADAM NEEDED TO work off his mad before he did something stupid. Something stupid like go back for more. More insults, more frustration. More Maddie.

Striding into his suite, he flicked the door shut behind him, kept moving into his walk-in closet, shedding his trousers, ripping off his sweater, rifling his drawers as he churned over her hurtful words.

Especially hurtful because he feared they were true.

Could he feel affection? Or had his childhood stunted that emotion too?

He thought about it as he yanked a T-shirt over his head, punched his arms through the sleeves. His parents hadn't known what affection was. They fought like alley cats, flinging barbs and crockery, and even fists. Once, after his mother caught his father with the mistress of whatever manor they were squatting on, Adam had to pull them apart, but not before she'd torn off his father's ear.

The old man used to joke that he started painting like Van Gogh after that, and in fact, he'd swung to a darker palette. But even with a missing ear, his dark good looks and brooding mien were irresistible to women of all ages and intellect, and he exploited it, fucking them without scruple until he tired of their adulation.

And yet his continuous cheating never drove Adam's mother away, though it frequently drove her into other men's arms. Which inflamed his jealousy, as she meant it to do, and the cycle began anew.

So yes, his parents had strong emotions, jealousy foremost among them. But love and affection were in short supply, and whatever positive emotions they did possess, they channeled into their work.

Geniuses, both of them. But as role models, they sucked.

Adam hoped to do better in his own relationships.

The precious few he considered true friends, he held close. In fact, most of them worked for him. Henry, Fredo. A handful of others he'd met along the way. Men who'd fought beside him, literally, when he'd landed in a new place and had to make his own way.

Adults were cruel, children crueler, and Adam was always the odd man out. The townies found him too cultured; the upper crust too common. He fit in nowhere, which made him vulnerable. He couldn't count the times he'd been kicked black and blue by the local bullies, his parents too self-absorbed to notice when he came home with a black eye or worse.

Here and there, though, someone had taken his part. And while he'd long since left the enemies of his youth to their inconsequential lives, he'd sought out those who'd stood with him. Like Fredo, who butted into a losing battle in a Florence park at midnight. And Henry, who had Adam's back in a Liverpool alley.

So, yes, he told himself as he threw open the door to his gym, yes, as he racked two hundred pounds on the bench press. He felt affection, even love, for Fredo and Henry. And for the others too. Men and women from back when he was nobody.

Well, he wasn't nobody anymore, and he'd built an empire to prove it. *Just try me now*, his billions sneered with a shake of the fist. *Just fucking try me now.*

Few did, he thought, as he benched his body weight. Those who dared it—like Hawthorne—didn't come at him with a knife or a sap, but crept up through the boardroom, deadlier than any back-alley brawler.

Even so, it paid to stay in shape. Who knew when some competitor's tactics might change?

Or when another masterpiece might need liberating from unclean hands.

Which brought him back around to Madeline. She

was the only person, past or present, to tackle him head-on. No sneaking through dark alleys, no sleight of hand. In his mind she occupied a category all her own.

If he was honest—and he believed he was ruthlessly so—tiny Madeline loomed large in his psyche. A worthy adversary, too cagey to let out of his sight. Why, if ever she uncovered hard evidence on the *Lady in Red*, she'd take him down at any cost.

He had to admit that he admired her for that. That she was . . . important to him. That he cared about her.

But not in an *affectionate* way.

Or so he would have said that morning. He'd also have said he owed her for besmirching him, for causing him some sleepless nights. That he had a healthy interest in making her squirm.

But now he didn't know *how* he felt. Except that he wanted to wring her neck.

Finishing a punishing set, he made for the dumbbells and pumped out a set of flys that would have been impossible if he weren't so pissed.

He worked his shoulders, his back, fuming at her indifference to what he'd made of himself, her utter disregard for his achievements.

Curling sixty pounds with each arm, he let the burn in his biceps fuel his anger.

She was driving him mad. He wanted to shake her. Berate her.

And God help him, he wanted to fuck her.

CHAPTER SIX

"Just how big *is* this place?" Maddie wanted to know.

"I couldn't tell you dimensions," said Bridget, "but it occupies this entire floor, as well as the one above."

Must've cost a mint.

"On this level you'll find the guest suites, the dining room, the gallery. All the rooms where Mr. LeCroix does his entertaining." The girl spoke with pride. "The upper level, that's Mr. LeCroix's private quarters. His suite, the gym, the indoor pool. And then there's the roof, of course."

Of course.

"Quite beautiful, it is," Bridget waxed on, "with gardens galore. A greenhouse, with herbs for the kitchen, and more flowers than we know what to do with." She swept an arm at the burgeoning vases on every surface. "There's a fine terrace for parties—"

"Yeah, yeah, I get the picture. Lifestyles of the rich and famous."

"Oh indeed." The sarcasm sailed over Bridget's head. "We've a regular roster of famous folk. Actors and musicians. Even some of those supermodels."

She dropped her voice disapprovingly. "Eat like birds, they do. Drives Leonardo mad when his lovely food comes back to the kitchen picked over like a sales rack." Then she smiled. "Not like last night, eh? He was quite pleased with how you took to his carbonara."

"Right." In any comparison to supermodels, Maddie could only come up, well, short. "Anyway, thanks for the coffee." She rose abruptly from the sofa to cut off the conversation.

Bridget got the message and pokered up. "You'll find breakfast set out in the dining room. Or if you'd prefer, you can ring the kitchen and I'll bring whatever you'd like." She did the curtsy again and closed the door silently behind her.

Maddie felt like a heel. She'd snubbed the poor girl over a sudden stab of . . . what?

Supermodel jealousy?

Not possible. Last night's attraction to Adam was a fluke brought on by a long day full of unpleasant surprises, culminating in an unusual evening in an unfamiliar place. Like any stranger in a strange land, she'd gravitated toward the only recognizable thing, which just happened to be someone she despised.

That was her story, and she was sticking to it.

And just to corroborate it, she'd have breakfast in the dining room. Not because she wanted to see Adam, but to prove she *didn't*.

When she got there, after a winding path through hallways, galleries, and a ballroom—yes, a ballroom— complete with frescos and a dozen Waterford chandeliers, she found him standing, as was his unsettling habit, at the window wall, phone to his ear and his gaze on Central Park spreading out umpteen stories below.

His posture was as far from relaxed as she'd ever seen it.

"I don't give a fuck," he said with feeling. "I want it back. But more than that, I want the balls off the fucker who stole it. And if it's an inside job, I want to know about it yesterday." He paused to listen. "No, keep the *polizia* out of it. They'll blunder around and scare the bastard off." He checked his watch. "I'll be there in twelve hours and we'll decide how to proceed."

He dropped the phone in the pocket of another five-thousand-dollar suit. Then he turned, slowly, an unpleasant smirk on his much-too-handsome face. "Eavesdropping, Madeline?"

Having had all night to regret jumping to conclusions, she knew she deserved that. And here was her chance to be the bigger person and apologize.

She couldn't stomach it.

Instead, she crossed the room, past a gleaming table long enough to land a Cessna, to the sideboard groaning under the weight of chafing dishes.

Scooping scrambled eggs onto a china plate, she said over her shoulder, "You've obviously got a lot going on in Italy. I'll only get in your way."

"On the contrary. Your presence is indispensible."

He strolled up beside her, all nonchalance once more. She caught a whiff of his soap, clean and crisp. No cologne, damn him. She hated cologne on men. She could have added it to her list of grievances.

He lifted the lid on a different chafing dish. French toast, her favorite breakfast. Her mouth watered. But she'd already heaped eggs on her plate. She couldn't very well scrape them back into the pan.

As she vacillated, Adam took the dish from her hand.

She bristled. "What now? You're cutting me off?"

"I'm sparing your conscience. The starving children and so forth."

"There *are* starving children. Not that you'd care."

He leveled a look.

Her cheeks heated up. She knew very well his charitable foundation fed children by the thousands. But her mouth had shot off ahead of her brain again, and this time her conscience made her give the devil his due.

"Okay, that was uncalled for." She swallowed hard. "Sorry."

His brows rose slightly and he assessed her with those devastating eyes. At this range, she could see every facet, glittering like sunlight off the deep blue sea.

Talk about unsettling.

Then he forked three slices of French toast onto a plate. "The starving children," he said, "won't begrudge you French toast. With warm maple syrup."

Her eyes narrowed. Funny how her favorite foods kept popping up on the menu.

Ignoring her scrutiny, he piled bacon on her eggs and kept them for himself.

"I assume you brought professional attire," he said, taking a seat at the table. "We meet with Jonathan Hawthorne at ten."

She sat down three seats away. "Aren't you jumping the gun? I read through the contract last night, but we haven't discussed the case. I don't even know what you want to accomplish today."

"What I want to accomplish," he said, shaking an unhealthy amount of salt over his eggs, "is to introduce my counsel in this matter. To wave you under Hawthorne's nose, so to speak."

"Hmmph." She forked in a bite of French toast. And *whoa*.

It crunched, then squished. Syrup drenched her tongue.

She made a noise in her throat. Squinted to savor the flavors—subtle vanilla, earthy maple—and the texture. Lord, the texture. Crusty outside, custardy inside.

Adam smiled. "Deep fried."

He filled her cup and she chased the syrupy sweetness with the smoothest, richest roast she'd ever tasted.

A killer combination.

"Okay," she said, feeling much more agreeable. "Hawthorne's a prick. Let's go make him sweat."

SUITED UP IN periwinkle silk and four-inch pewter heels, accessorized with the diamond studs some guy had given her and the Cartier watch she'd gotten on deep discount, Maddie flashed the Pitbull's you're-going-down-asshole sneer in the mirror. She still had it goin' on. If things went her way, Hawthorne would fold on the spot.

But then, things hadn't exactly been going her way.

Her phone jangled—"Cruella de Vil"—her bestie Vicky's ringtone, an ode to Vicky's mother, the evil Adrianna. Somehow, Vicky had taken that malevolent DNA and spun it into gold.

"Hey Mads, how's it going?"

"Great," she lied. No way would she tell Vicky about the assignment from hell. Vicky would call Adrianna in a rage, and for nothing. Adrianna would never back down.

"How's rehearsal?" she asked, shifting the focus to Vicky's new role in an off-off Broadway play, her second since being fired from Marchand, Riley, and White.

"It's coming along." Vicky paused. "Um, listen. We set a date."

"For the opening? Great, I'll be there."

"No. For the wedding."

"Oh. Well. I'll be there for that too, I guess."

"Come on, Mads. Be happy for me."

Maddie plopped on the bed. "I am, sweetie. I'm glad you're in love. It's just"—she rubbed her temple—"why do you have to get *married*?"

"Are you still mad at Ty? Because, trust me, he's made up a thousand times over for being a jackass."

"If you say so." Tyrell had inched higher in Maddie's esteem, but she'd never forget how miserable he'd made Vicky before he got his shit together.

Even so, Ty wasn't the problem. The problem was marriage, an overrated, outdated institution that gave a man altogether too much leverage over a woman. Who needed it? This was the twenty-first century, for Christ's sake. Unmarried people could have sex. They could own property together. Why the compulsion to tie the knot around their necks?

Vicky was too excited to let Maddie bring her down. "It's the second Saturday in July. Save the date."

"Whoa, wait. That's, like, two weeks from now!"

"I know it's short notice, but we're working around Ty's semester and my opening. Otherwise, we'll have to wait until Christmas."

"What's wrong with Christmas? Fresh snow. Twinkle lights. And six more months to make sure you're compatible." Maddie did the voice of reason. "Right now it's all X-rated sexts and nailing each other five times a day—"

"Have you been spying on us?"

"I'm serious, Vic. What happens in six years when you've got a kid or two? Ty can basically hold you hostage."

Vicky sighed, full of sympathy. "Listen, sweetie, neither of us grew up with the Waltons. My mother's a nightmare. And your father was—is—a hundred times worse."

No, actually a thousand times worse. But Vicky knew only part of the story, the part where he came down on Maddie like a hammer for everything she did. If she had her nose in a book she was a loser without any friends; if she played with her friends, she got grounded for blowing off homework. If she ate her food, she was shoveling; if she picked at it, he threw it in the trash and she went hungry. If she moved around normally, she was an inconsiderate brat making a goddamn racket; if she tiptoed, she was a sneaky little thief.

She could, literally, do nothing right. And there was no such thing as flying under his radar. If she breathed, he disparaged. It was constant and relentless. And it was just the tip of the iceberg.

Yes, Vicky knew about the emotional abuse, but there was much more that she didn't know. And still she couldn't understand why Maddie's mother hadn't intervened. "Honestly, Maddie, shame on your mom for not protecting you and Lucy."

"You don't know my father." This was old, painful ground. "He's a big shot in our town. He runs the town council, the school board. My mom had no money, no skills, no family to fall back on. And two kids he held to her throat like knives."

A hundred times he'd threatened to take them away from her. A hundred times she submitted so she wouldn't lose her children.

And in the end, she'd lost them anyway when they left home and never went back.

How, coming from a horrible father and an ineffectual mother, could Maddie ever trust herself to be better?

"Anyway"—she brushed it aside—"*you're* happy about your wedding. That'll have to be good enough for me."

"Good, because I want you to be my maid of honor."

"Oh, jeez." Maddie was touched and dismayed at once. "Are you sure? Because I don't have a clue about showers and gowns and all that sh— stuff."

"Don't worry. Isabelle"—her brother's wife—"has everything covered. All you have to do is show up and hold the hankies. Ty and I are writing our own vows, so tears *will* be happening."

Writing their own vows. Maddie shuddered. The only wedding vow she'd ever make was to never make a wedding vow. If that made any sense.

"I'll text you as I come up with them," said Vicky. "You can tell me what you think."

"I can already tell you what I think. *Cor-ny.*"

"Just keep an open mind, okay? And don't forget the hankies."

"The hankies I can handle. The hankies and the pre-nup."

Vicky laughed. "I love your optimism. But, seriously, I'm not worried about a pre-nup. Ty's got a lot more money than I do—"

"For now. But when you're an A-list actor making twenty mil a movie, you'll thank me." It was the only thing she could do to protect her friend, so she dug in her heels. "That's the deal. You sign, and I'll carry the hankies."

"Okay, okay. I can't fight the Pitbull."

Satisfied, Maddie threw her a bone. "I hope you never need it, Vic. But a pre-nup's like a condom. It's better to have it and not need it, than need it and not have it."

PERIWINKLE. A COLOR Adam had always favored. Now he reconsidered.

True, it cast Maddie's eyes an unusual and interesting

shade of gray. But gray was the color of the steely-eyed prosecutor who'd nearly nailed him. He preferred the aqua-eyed woman he'd shared a fork with, the warm-blooded sensualist who licked cream off her lips and made carbonara an erotic experience.

He'd plotted last night's meal for the precise purpose of taking down her defenses. But he'd outfoxed himself, hadn't he? Because watching her enjoy it had taken down his.

Just as well that things had taken a sharp turn for the worse before he'd made an even bigger fool of himself. Mixing business and pleasure was always a bad idea.

Never worse than with Madeline St. Clair.

Sitting beside her in the limo, he flipped open his laptop and pretended to ignore her. Those silver stilettos were driving him mad. He could almost feel them digging into his back, her legs locked around him—

"Call your Parker," he heard himself command, the better to remind them both that she was, indeed, his minion.

"He's not *my* Parker," she bit out in an unminionlike tone. "And what am I supposed to tell him?"

"That we'll pick up John Doe at eleven."

"Where're you planning to dump him?"

The disdain in her voice as much as the question brought his head around. "I'm not *dumping* him anywhere."

"You know what I mean." Apparently, the benevolent effects of French toast had worn off, because her eyes were flat. "Which one of your properties are you shipping him to?"

He'd been mulling that very question, but now he closed his laptop and angled his body toward hers. "I'm keeping him with me," he said, more to be contrary than because he'd thought it through.

"Then you'll need stuff. There's a PetSmart on Broadway." She gave a thin smile.

She'd boxed him, and slickly. It chafed, but he covered it with an impatient nod.

"About Hawthorne," he said. "You need to know that we have a history. The details aren't relevant. It boils down to this. He's offended by new money. I'm offended by blueblood snobs."

"And I'm offended by both of you." She spread her hands. "Always an advantage to see both sides."

How completely she discounted him. It stung like vinegar in a fresh cut.

"See as many sides as you like," he said curtly, "but remember whose you're on. I pay your fee. And I can cut it off."

"Oh, I remember, LeCroix." Her scorn was caustic enough to peel paint. "Otherwise, I wouldn't go near you with a ten-foot pole."

He set his teeth. Now she'd gone too far. It might be true that she disliked him, maybe even despised him. But sitting in this very spot just yesterday, he'd felt the heat between them flowing *both* ways.

And last night on her sofa, they were less than *an inch* from kissing when her phone killed the mood.

So fuck her ten-foot pole, he thought, perversely, and fuck mixing business with pleasure.

He wanted her. He was going to have her.

And she was going to like it.

CHAPTER SEVEN

Vicky: Tyrell, I promise to always be kind
to you, to never deliberately make you
mad, and when you do get mad,
to meet your anger with kindness.

Maddie: And a hard boot in the ass.

NEITHER MAN WOULD concede home turf to the other,
so the meeting took place in a well-appointed private
room at a trendy midtown restaurant. A silver coffee
service and a plate of mouthwatering pastries sat on
the table, along with four china cups.

Two for the duelers, Maddie thought, and two for
their seconds.

That's how it felt, like Adam and Hawthorne were
thirsting to draw blood.

Oh, it was all civility on the surface. Hands were
shaken, introductions made. But their dislike shimmered like heat waves in the air.

Hawthorne had brought along his own counsel,
Jason Brandt, a broad-shouldered Ivy Leaguer with

an easygoing smile and raptor's eyes. He made a point of shaking Maddie's small hand carefully, as if afraid he'd break it. Then he all but dismissed her as beneath his notice.

Until he saw his silver-haired, big-shot boss go pale. Then Brandt narrowed those predator's eyes at her. His expression said, *I eat little girls like you for lunch.*

She flipped him off with a bored glance. She ate big boys like him for breakfast.

Commandeering the floor while Brandt was still sugaring his coffee, she opened by laying it out for Hawthorne. The contract terms, the company's liability, the ugly lawsuit that would ensue if they refused to pay.

She followed that up with the media play-by-play. The Anderson Cooper interview she'd do beside Adam. The *Wall Street Journal* headline: "Too-Big-to-Fail Hawthorne Reneges on Its Policies." The *60 Minutes* segment featuring the media darling's battle with the insurance behemoth.

Then she outlined the damage: tumbling stock prices, balking policyholders, dwindling profits in advance of the inevitable takeover.

When all that had sunk in, she announced their terms: Pay up in thirty days. Or else.

It took less than ten minutes. Hawthorne and his sidekick hustled out of the room.

Adam favored Maddie with a smile. "I think Brandt wet his pants."

She snapped her briefcase shut. "Fifty bucks says he's never set foot in a courtroom. Hawthorne brought him along to play up the old-money angle. 'Look at us, with our blond hair and white teeth and country club parties.'" She snorted. "Why they'd think that would intimidate you, I can't imagine."

He held the door for her. "That almost sounds like a compliment."

"Sure, if ballbuster's a compliment."

"I concede that title to you. Hawthorne's icing his as we speak."

She shrugged. "We surprised them. Now that he knows I'm involved, he'll quit the shenanigans. He'll trade in the pretty boy for someone who knows his stuff, and then he'll either face facts and roll over, or he'll let that big ego of his call the shots and we'll end up in court."

"Either way, we'll prevail." Adam sounded dead certain.

Despite herself, she puffed up, flattered by his confidence. He'd held back during the meeting, letting her take the ball. She appreciated it as the mark of a pro. He knew enough to bring in an expert and then let that expert call the plays.

A casual observer would have described him as confident, in-charge, and ultimately unconcerned, as if, win or lose, his ego wasn't in the balance. Since she knew that wasn't entirely true, she had to admire his panache. Not to mention his genius in bringing her on board. It might qualify as the worst thing to happen in her adult life, but for Adam's purposes, it was brilliant.

She slid into the limo, tossed her briefcase onto the opposite seat. Out on the sidewalk, Adam said to Fredo, "Stop at the first Starbucks. Bold for me." He poked his head into the limo. "Early in the day for a celebratory drink, but I'll spring for Starbucks."

"Skinny mocha latte with a shake of vanilla."

He repeated it to Fredo, then slid in beside her, gave her a study as the car moved into traffic. "I'm hard to impress."

She let her eyebrows rise a skeptical half inch.

"I admit," he went on, "I expected a halfhearted effort. But you convinced even me that you're in my corner."

"I got an A in drama. Besides—and I know you hate for Hawthorne to beat you at anything—he's an even bigger, even more arrogant asshole than you are."

"Well now. There's no call to hurt my feelings."

She laughed in spite of herself. How could she not? She was flying high after trouncing the preppies. And he was funny. Not to mention that his smile was just ridiculously gorgeous, all white teeth, full lips, and sparkling eyes, aimed right at her.

He angled his lean body toward her too, stretched out his long legs, invading her half of the car. His stupidly glossy jet hair swept the snowy collar of his shirt, and his suit fit his frame like it was tailored to his exact dimensions, which of course it was.

He wore it the way a quarterback wore his uniform, like a second skin.

In fact, his whole world fit him like a second skin. The swanky penthouse, the luxury limo, the obsequious staff. He made it look effortless. Natural.

And all that confidence was oh-so-seductive.

Okay, enough. She buttoned down her smile. Took out her phone and scrolled through her e-mail, deliberately rude. If she ignored him, he'd pull in his legs and his smile, go back to his laptop and stop chipping at her resolve.

It worked, sort of. He took out his own phone, seemed to lose interest in her.

Then *ping*. A text popped up from ALeCroix: I trust you packed your passport.

She typed back: Oops.

Nice try.

You don't need me in Italy.

I'll be the judge of that.

Meanie.

Brat.

Damn it, she was smiling again. She shut off her phone, looked out the window instead. Fredo had double-parked across from Starbucks. Now he was crossing the street toward them with three coffees in a cardboard holder.

Acting like her smile had been for him all along, she lowered her window, took the two he passed through. She gave Adam his tall bold without making eye contact. The man was altogether too dangerous.

Shifting her butt another six inches away from him, she wedged herself in the corner. Then, trying to look relaxed instead of feral, she stretched out her own legs. And accidentally touched his foot with hers.

Whoa! Electricity jolted up her leg.

She yanked it back, jostling her coffee. It spurted out the hole, missed her suit by an inch but dribbled on the seat. "*Shit*," she blurted, scrabbling for the napkin that had landed on the floor.

Calmly, Adam blotted the spill.

"Thanks." She took a breath, got ahold of herself. Christ, half an hour ago she'd had Hawthorne by the throat and his bag carrier Brandt by the balls, and she hadn't broken a sweat. Now she was sweating like a linebacker.

Adam smiled, drawing her eyes to his mouth. His sensual mouth. "You're dripping," he said.

Is it that obvious?

"You might want to lick it."

Yep, I'd love to, but it's a bad idea for sure.

"Madeline."

She tore her gaze from his lips. He was pointing at her cup. "You're dripping."

"Oh. Right." She caught the drip with her tongue, let

her gaze go back to his lips. They were parted, but he wasn't smiling anymore. She raised her eyes to his and got scorched by blue flame.

Oh no. Oh no.

The limo rolled to a stop at PetSmart and she made a break for it, crossing in front of Adam to open the door before Fredo could get it.

Adam followed her onto the sidewalk. Her temper flared. "Stay here. I don't need you."

He gave her one of those assessing looks, like her sanity was in question. Which it was. He was driving her crazy.

Calmly, he took the coffee from her hand and passed it to Fredo. "Keep that warm, would you?" To Maddie, "I've never owned a dog. I'd like you to show me what he needs."

Grrrr. He sounded so freaking reasonable.

"Fine," she bit out, and stalked to the door. He managed to get there first and open it for her. *Grrrr.*

Since he was paying, she went top of the line. A plush bed, fuzzy blankets, expensive food and lots of it. Toys, bones, a fancy harness collar. Into the cart it all went.

Adam followed her down the aisles, asked intelligent questions, offered suggestions on size and color, and was generally agreeable while she snapped and snarled. And when she unloaded the cart onto the counter, he paid the staggering bill without batting an eye.

But hey, the whole pile probably cost less than his necktie, so it was no skin off his nose, was it?

Back in the car, he spoke to Fredo. "Stop at Ms. St. Clair's building before we pick up John Doe."

Maddie gnashed her teeth. "You don't need me in Italy."

"Madeline." Infinite patience. "Is it such a hardship to travel to the most beautiful country in the world? To stay in your own luxurious suite in a palatial villa overlooking the Mediterranean?"

"You're right, it sounds nice. Why don't I go, and you stay here?"

"So the problem with Italy is me?"

"You're the problem with everything." Especially with the limo, which shrank a little more each time they got inside. In here, she couldn't ignore him. Not his presence, not his scent, not his freaking pheromones.

He chuckled, which made her head whip around.

"It's not funny," she ground out.

"Oh, but it is." He stretched out again, invading her space. "Unsettling you is surprisingly enjoyable."

"Fame and fortune must be overrated if this is how you get your jollies."

"And how do you get your jollies, Madeline?"

"None of your business."

He did that assessing look again. "You have no hobbies," he mused.

"I work a lot."

"And earn a healthy salary for your efforts."

"I'm worth it. And if you think snooping into my finances will tell you who I am, you're dead wrong. There's more to me than my bank balance."

"There'd have to be, wouldn't there?"

So he *had* been snooping. No wonder he was so smug. He knew she was tapped out.

"And yet," he went on, "all your friends together wouldn't fill this car."

"I'm picky," she snarled.

"Too picky, perhaps? Is that why you've no husband, nor any prospects in that area?"

That tipped her over the edge. "Listen, Mr. Nosy, I don't want a husband, and I don't want a boyfriend. Men are only good for one thing, and I get plenty of that."

"Sex?"

"Of course, sex. What the hell else can a man give me that I can't get for myself?"

"Love."

She made a rude noise.

"Romance."

"Are you sure you're not a girl?"

"Not last time I looked."

Which made her look too. Just for a second, then she yanked her eyes away.

But her mind's eye was harder to divert. She had a picture in her head, and it was porn.

"Told you," he said.

"Pfft. Anybody can carry a roll of quarters."

He smiled, all masculine confidence. "In any case, love and romance aren't the exclusive province of women."

"What's your point? That men are suckers too?" She snorted. "You're not exactly a poster child, LeCroix. I've never seen two pictures of you with the same woman."

"You will, when she's the right one."

A huge eye roll. "You *are* a romantic. Let me know how that goes."

"I'll do that." His head tilted. Another assessing look, this one with heat. It seared through her clothes, her skin. Sizzled straight to her core.

Oh no. Oh no.

"In the meantime," she snipped, her voice steadier than her pulse, "butt out of my business." *And out of my panties too.* "I'm not here for conversation." *Or sex.*

"We're not friends." *Or lovers.* "If you want to talk about your *feelings*, call someone who cares."

And keep your stupid roll of quarters in your pocket!

WHILE MADDIE MARCHED—under protest—into her apartment for her passport, Adam sat in the limo and stewed.

The illusion that she was merely a tool in his toolbox was becoming harder to sustain.

The trouble was, he'd gone beyond lust. Lust was easy. Uncomplicated. He wanted; he'd take. Her sweet little body was his.

But he craved more. He wanted to penetrate her shell, unravel her twisty brain. She was a puzzle crying out to be solved.

Take her mysterious aversion to romance. It must be rooted in childhood, because his people had found nothing in her post–high school years to account for it.

He dialed his private investigator, Giovanni, who answered on the first ring.

"Mr. LeCroix, sir, I'm sorry but I have nothing new to report since this morning."

"I'm sure you're doing your best." Adam tolerated nothing less. "This is about Madeline St. Clair. I need you to go deeper, back to her childhood."

"Are you looking for something specific?"

"Traumatic events. Possibly sexual assault. A cheating boyfriend. Something that might turn her off men."

"Um, Mr. LeCroix, if you'll recall, she's had a number of liaisons with men. None with women, at least none that turned up."

"It's not her sex life that concerns me." He knew more about that than he wanted to. At first, her liaisons hadn't bothered him. After all, he was in no position to judge. But he felt differently about it now. "She's had no long-term relationships. I want to know why."

"I understand. I'll put someone on it immediately."

She stormed out of her building and, without sparing him a glance, steamed down the sidewalk toward Parker's.

Adam beat her to the door, of course, which galled her. As she flounced past him, he realized again just how tiny she was. Her personality was so much larger than life, he kept forgetting she was just a sprite.

A tenacious, bloodthirsty sprite.

Parker waved to her, then pushed open the door to the back room. Out trotted John Doe. He spotted them and his head came up, his ropy tail wagged.

He made straight for Adam, and for the first time in his life, Adam felt the simple joy of being greeted by his dog.

He bent to scratch the floppy ears, and John leaned into his leg, a sorrowful sight, scrawny and patchy, his neck wound gleaming pinkly through a shiny salve. But his heart shone out of his big brown eyes.

When he turned those eyes on Maddie, she relaxed visibly, temper draining out of her like water. She squatted, and John slotted his bony body between her knees, squinting blissfully as she scratched his belly.

Adam squatted beside her, stroking John's knobby head. "He's a rack of bones," he murmured. "Is dog food the best we can do for him? Perhaps Leonardo—"

John lifted his nose into Adam's palm and licked his hand.

Sweet Jesus. It electrified him. Emotion surged in his chest, an overpowering need to protect this sweet creature from the cold, cruel world. To shelter him. To earn the affection he offered so freely.

Then Parker loomed over them, said in bitter tones, "I guess he'll be okay going with you."

Adam glanced up at his scowl. Maddie must be clue-less not to see the man was gone for her.

Rising smoothly, he put himself between them. "We'll take good care of him," he said, more to work in the "we" than to reassure Parker.

Parker stiffened predictably. "He'll need attention for the next few days. And affection."

"We'll keep him with us constantly."

Maddie got to her feet, wobbling a bit on her high heels. Adam steadied her with a hand on her waist, amazed again at how narrow it was. He could circle it with both hands.

How could such a tiny person absorb so much space in his life?

With her help, Parker fitted John's new harness collar around him, their coordinated movements proving they'd worked together often.

Seeing their casual intimacy, hearing them murmur back and forth, Adam was suddenly, irrationally sure they were lovers. Jealousy flared in his breast. Not thinking, just reacting, he took a step toward Parker.

And Fredo stepped squarely in front of him. "Should I cancel the flight plan?" he asked innocently. "Give John a chance to rest?"

Adam blinked. Refocused. "Yes." A deep breath, and a firm grip on his emotions. "Yes, we'll leave to-morrow instead."

Maddie peeked around Fredo. "I can stay here with John."

Adam ignored her. The villa was the closest thing he had to a home. She was damn well going whether she liked it or not.

Out on the sidewalk, Parker eyed the limo. "You sure about this?" he said to Maddie under his breath.

"It's fine." She gave him a brighter smile than she'd ever given Adam.

Taking John's leash from Parker's reluctant grasp, Adam thanked him curtly. Maddie spread a blanket on the rear-facing seat. John hopped in, circled once, then curled up with his head on his paws.

Parker leaned in to pat his flank. "You're traveling in style, buddy." He patted Maddie too—not on the flank, but even her knee was too much for Adam. "See you Sunday, Mads."

"No you won't," said Adam, nudging Parker aside as he slid in beside Maddie. "We'll be in Italy. But we'll be sure to let you know how John's faring." He nodded to Fredo.

With a polite but firm glance that warned Parker to step back, Fredo closed the door.

Instantly, Maddie's finger drilled Adam's biceps. "What the fuck is wrong with you? Parker's the nicest guy in the world, and you were a total dick to him!"

"And *you*," Adam shot back, "see only what you want to see. The man's besotted with you."

"*Besotted?* Where did you learn *that* word?"

"I can read, can't I?" He should quit now, but he couldn't. "He wants to sleep with you, or has he already?"

"No he hasn't slept with me. And what's it to you, anyway? You don't—"

John whined.

Maddie cut off, stricken. Her voice dropped to a croon. "We're upsetting him." Kneeling on the carpeted floor, she stroked his bumpy spine. "I'm sorry, John."

Adam swung over to sit with him. "He's likely heard plenty of shouting. He'll expect a kick to follow."

"We'll never hurt you, John." Maddie's hand touched Adam's inadvertently and he couldn't help himself, he covered it.

She didn't pull away, but looked up at him with tears sheening her silver eyes.

How had he ever thought them cold? They were luminous.

He tried a smile. "A truce, for John's sake?"

After a moment, she nodded, giving him hope. "Just try not to piss me off, okay?"

FAT CHANCE. THE elevator hadn't closed behind them when Adam said to Fredo, "Put John's bed in my suite."

"Hang the hell on." Maddie faced off with him. Then John butted her knee.

Swallowing her rant like a bitter pill, she said sweetly, "I'd like John to sleep with me."

"He's my dog," Adam said pleasantly. "But you can visit him whenever you wish."

She sulked all the way to her suite. The "truce" was already cramping her style.

Getting back into her jeans helped her mood, but not much. She was slumped on the sofa feeling sorry for herself when Bridget popped in to take her lunch order.

"I'm not hungry," she groused at the girl. "Just give me whatever the big cheese is having."

Bridget's brow furrowed.

Maddie rolled her eyes. "The boss man. The string puller. The great and powerful Oz."

"Ah, yes. Mr. LeCroix requested a light lunch of Caesar salad with two of Leonardo's popovers piping hot from the oven."

Mmm, Caesar salad. And popovers, well, those didn't grow on trees. When was the last time—

Her eyes narrowed. "Is that his usual?"

"I wouldn't know, ma'am. Mr. LeCroix seldom eats lunch in. Will you be dining with him?"

"No." Then, "Wait. On second thought, where's he eating?"

"In his suite, with John." Bridget smiled benignly. "A skinny one, he is, but Mr. LeCroix will fix him up. He's a good hand with strays."

"You mean he's done this before? Taken in a stray dog?"

"Oh dear, no. I meant people. Like Fredo and Henry and me. We were at loose ends, each of us, when Mr. LeCroix came calling. Paying his debts, he said, to the folks who stood by him in his youth."

"You knew him as a child?" This could be interesting.

"Not myself, no. But my husband, Ian, did him a good turn in a Dublin pub. Something to do with a lass and a dirk, though I never did get the details."

She touched the small cross she wore on a fine gold chain. "Ian was a reckless sort, and back in the day Mr. LeCroix was cut from the same bolt of cloth. But he mended his ways, made a name for himself. Came back to give Ian a leg up, not three days after he was shot down in a Finglas alley.

"Mr. LeCroix found me at his graveside, not a penny to my name. And look at me now. A steady job and money in the bank."

She hit her stride. "Now, Henry, his hard luck began as a boy—"

Maddie's phone whistled the Mayberry theme. Lucy's ringtone.

"Sorry, we'll have to finish this later." She herded Bridget toward the door. "I'll have lunch upstairs." With John. She'd be damned if she let LeCroix hog him.

Settling on the sofa again, she stacked her heels on the coffee table, in a better frame of mind. If anything could cheer her up, it was a nice long chat with her sister.

"Hey, Luce."

"Maddiiiiiieeeee! I can only talk for a minute."

"Okay." Disappointing.

"I just wanted to tell you I'm coming for the Fourth!"

Maddie shot out of her seat. "Of *July*?"

Lucy laughed. "Yes, of July. I used your Visa to book the train, I hope that's okay."

"Sure, but—"

"And I'm bringing Crash. My boyfriend."

"*Boyfriend?*"

"That's his band rehearsing across the hall."

Which explained the racket. But nothing else.

"I didn't know—"

The din ratcheted higher. "I can hardly hear you," Lucy bellowed. "Listen, we'll be there tomorrow afternoon."

"*Wait! What—*"

"I'm *dying* for you to meet him!"

"But—"

"Gotta go." The "music" crescendoed, then died. "See you tomorrow! Bye!"

Maddie stared at her phone as if it was to blame.

Things weren't bad enough? Lucy had to pick now to get a boyfriend? She had to bring him to New York the day Maddie was supposed to leave the country?

It changed everything. She couldn't leave them alone in her apartment. Lucy having sex was hard enough to accept. Lucy having sex in her bed with *Crash*—a *musician*? That was just not gonna happen.

Italy was out. LeCroix would have to see reason. Or else.

CHAPTER EIGHT

APPARENTLY THINGS *WEREN'T* bad enough, because Maddie walked into Adam's suite only to find that he'd changed into ass-hugger jeans and a snug black T-shirt that showed off The Best Arms she'd ever seen. Ever.

And she knew arms. Half the reason she haunted the gym was to ogle arms. Now LeCroix's were right in front of her, sun-browned and roped with lean muscle. Just the way she liked them.

Stepping past him, she dragged her gaze from The Arms and scanned his parlor. Twice the size of hers, its neutral palette kept the focus on the art, enough to endow a university. The gas fireplace was black marble, with a leather sofa and club chairs sharing an oversized ottoman in front of it, pushed aside now to make room for John's bed.

A small but elegant dining table stood much too close to the window wall that overlooked Central Park. And Adam's desk, L-shaped and tricked out with three jumbo monitors, had probably once belonged to the president.

Diabolically, after letting her into the suite, the man

himself proceeded to pay her no mind, his tight butt propped against the edge of the desk, ankles crossed, nose in a prospectus, while with the flat of one hand he rubbed his awesome chest, a move that bulged his biceps, stretching his sleeve to the breaking point and whipping her overwrought libido into a full-on frenzy.

Severely disadvantaged, she fell back on surliness. "Where's lunch?"

He looked up, distracted, and nodded at the phone. "Tell the kitchen you're dining here."

"Bridget already knows." She did a toothy smile. "You said I can spend as much time with John as I want to, so I'm basically moving in."

And hoping to aggravate him out of taking her to Italy, she plunked on the sofa, pulled out her phone, and proceeded to check Facebook.

MOVING IN, WAS she? Well, that was fine with him.

Plenty of room for her in his king-sized bed. And if she kept eyeing him the way she'd been doing since she walked in, she'd find herself on her back in the middle of it.

"How convenient," he said mildly. "I've another employment contract for you to review, and a stock option agreement with some thorny language that could use fresh eyes."

He sifted through a short stack of folders, pulled out two, and walked them to Madeline. She took them without a word, dropped them on the seat, and went back to her phone.

He plucked it from her hand.

"Hey!" She grabbed for it. He held it just out of reach. She leaped to her feet. He held it higher. She came around the couch, jabbed him in the chest with her pointy finger. "Give me my phone, you jerk, or I'll knee you in the nuts."

He slid it into his back pocket, intercepted her knee with one hand, and used it to tip her, very gently, over the arm of the sofa.

She landed on her back, outrage all over her face. "That's assault! I'm pressing charges!"

He laughed.

Her eyes glinted.

John Doe whined softly.

They looked at him, then back at each other.

"See what you did?" Snarling lips belied Maddie's dulcet tones.

"My apologies, John." His voice was pure honey. Stepping around the sofa, he lifted Maddie gently by the waist, set her on her feet. "See now? We're all friends here, aren't we?"

"Bosom buddies," she got out. But her voice had gone breathy. His pulse sped up in response.

He let himself look down into storm-tossed eyes. Dangerous waters, but he felt reckless.

Then her tongue touched her lips. An invitation?

He took a half step closer. Her breasts rose and fell just a whisker from his chest. Her hands slid up his forearms. Every hair prickled in response.

God, she was light as a feather. He could lift her up and taste those lips if he wanted to.

He wanted to.

His hands tightened on her waist.

And then Henry, double damn him, rapped twice on the door, and the spell between them shattered like glass.

Up shot Maddie's knee. Adam twisted, taking it on the thigh. Her knee glanced off and she overbalanced.

He had only to release her, and her butt plopped ig-
nominiously on the sofa.

Meeting her scowl with his most condescending
smile, he left her simmering while he explored the
lunch Henry was spreading on the table. Airy popovers, crisp Romaine, fresh-grated Parmesan. He could
get accustomed to eating Maddie's favorite foods.

"Will you dine in tonight?" Henry asked. "Or perhaps, since you're here, you'll reconsider the gala?
You'd mentioned that Mr. Hawthorne would be there."

"Good point, Henry. Let Dyan"—his secretary—
"know that I'll attend after all. And I'll be bringing a
guest."

That got Maddie off the couch. She came at him like
a bullet from a gun.

He flicked a glance at John, which had her dialing
down the volume. Instead, she blasted him with her
eyes and kept her tone conversational.

"I'm not going to any gala with you. Period."

He pretended not to hear. "Send for Raquel," he said
to Henry. "Time's short, so I'll rely on you to give her
the details on the event. As for the gowns, tell her a
size zero should do."

He sized up Maddie's breasts. "She can always take
it in."

SHE COULDN'T TEAR him a new one in front of John
Doe, so Maddie stabbed up both middle fingers instead. "Read my lips, LeCroix. I won't be seen out on
the town with a felon."

Oh, he didn't like that one bit. His eyes glinted, onyx
and sapphire. "Read *my* lips, Madeline. You're going to
the gala, on my arm. As my date."

"Not a chance." She vibrated with the agony of sup-
pressing a scream.

"You'll call me Adam"—his voice was velvet over steel—"and you'll do it with *affection*. No one who sees us tonight will doubt your absolute belief in my innocence."

"I won't do it. I won't go." Her conviction was rock solid.

His jaw flexed. He stepped away, poured a glass of Pellegrino, and took a long swallow, visibly summoning his composure. Then he turned to face her.

"You forget, Madeline, that you have skin in this game. You've held yourself out as my attorney. The business press will break that story before the day's out. If the entertainment news doesn't beat them to it."

Fury rose up like a dragon. "You *leaked* it?"

"I didn't have to. Hawthorne was already spinning it as he left the room, calculating how to turn it to his advantage."

"And how would that be?"

The look he gave her was almost pitying. "He'll say I bought you, of course. That you sold out for money. He'll paint you as a greedy mercenary without principles or integrity."

The truth of it hit her between the eyes. How had she missed it?

She'd been too busy feeling sorry for herself, that's how. Too worried about John Doe, too distracted by Adam's sexual mojo to see that the sterling reputation she'd built as a prosecutor, and that she'd hoped would leverage her back into the U.S. Attorney's Office once Lucy was settled, was tarnished for good.

She swayed, clutching the back of the sofa for support. "You knew. You planned this."

He stepped to the window, looked out. The draperies were partially drawn, but sun streaked through the opening, winking off the bubbles in his glass.

"Of course I knew," he said quietly. "I wasn't actively seeking revenge, so I didn't set out to harm you, if that's what you mean. But as collateral damage, well . . ." He shrugged one shoulder.

She stared at him mutely. Now that the scales had fallen from her eyes, her mind made up for lost time, fast-forwarding through a hundred humiliating scenarios, both social and professional.

He stared down into his drink with an expression that might have passed for regret on a person with a conscience. But when he looked up, his eyes were bland. "Odd as it may seem, attending the gala with me could undo some of the damage."

She huffed out a half laugh, all the breath she could muster. "Right. Let's make like we're dating. That'll help."

"Affairs of the heart are easily forgiven. Better that people believe I've turned your head than lined your pocket."

The fact that it made some kind of sense put the whole disaster into horrifying perspective.

"I need to think." She dropped down on the couch, head in her hands to stave off the further disgrace of fainting at his feet. Low blood pressure was an inconvenient fact of her life. She was, mortifyingly, a fainter.

John Doe stood up and shook himself, long ears flapping like Dumbo's, then came to lean against her leg. Stroking his head absently, she second-guessed her every move. Clearly, she should have said no to LeCroix at the outset, told Adrianna to suck it, and gone looking for another job while she still had her reputation.

Now, forget it. Everyone would think she'd sold out to a felon. And the worst of it, the bitterest pill, was that she *had* sold out. Maybe LeCroix's cash wasn't directly lining her pocket, but money had driven her decision.

"Madeline." Adam sat down on the ottoman. "You needn't fawn over me. We'll simply be seen. We'll drink, we'll dance, and we'll leave. Together."

She looked up. "What's in it for you?"

"I'm not above tweaking Hawthorne, letting him believe you have a personal stake in my affairs."

She scratched John's ear, reminded herself that she'd gotten into this for Lucy. And her job wasn't finished. "If I do it," she said, "I want something in return."

"We've just established that you're getting something. The chance to appear lovelorn rather than mercenary."

"That's not enough." She rose, paced the floor, giving the window a wide berth. "I need to stay in New York."

"Why?"

She held her temper by a thread. "I don't have to explain myself to you."

"That's not entirely true. You work for me." He held up a finger to cut off her retort. "Let's not play semantics. You work for me, so if you have a good reason not to accompany me to Italy, I'll hear it now."

Grrr. The things she did for Lucy.

"My sister's coming tomorrow. With her boyfriend. They expect to stay at my place."

"And will be pleasantly surprised to have it to themselves."

"Exactly." Her nails dug into her palms. "I have to be there to . . . you know."

"Chaperone? Madeline, she's a college senior. She's had sex."

"I know. But this is her first *boyfriend*. I haven't met him. I don't know anything about him."

"I'll have my people run him. What's his name?"

It felt like spying, but she didn't care. "She called him Crash, is that enough?"

"Probably. Gio's very good."

When he finished the call, she said, "Even if he comes back clean, I need to be here."

"Why?"

"Because she's my *sister*. She's innocent. She needs protection."

"Leave a box of condoms on the pillow."

"Not that kind of protection. Well, okay, that kind too." She paced some more, getting desperate. "The thing is, Lucy's naïve. She thinks no one's ever going to hurt her. She thinks she's safe now."

"She wasn't safe in the past?"

The sudden focus in his tone brought Maddie's head around. The last thing she wanted was LeCroix prying into her family.

"Nobody's safe," she said. "I can't go gallivanting off to Italy without seeing how he treats her."

"Then we'll bring them with us."

That stunned her silent.

He stood and walked to the table, filled the other glass, and brought it to her.

She glugged Pellegrino while her mind raced. "You've got an answer for everything," she said at last.

"I like to think so."

"Suppose they don't want to go to Italy?"

He gave her a pitying look.

"Okay, what if Crash doesn't have a passport?"

"Call your sister and find out."

"Why are you doing this?"

He spread his hands. "You want to observe Crash with your sister, don't you?"

"What's in it for you?"

He looked annoyed. "That's twice in ten minutes you've questioned my motives."

"Because you always have one. I just can't figure it out this time."

He gave a short laugh. "Sometimes," he said with apparent chagrin, "my motives puzzle even me."

WHAT *WAS* HIS motive, anyway? He didn't know. But his gut told him to bring Madeline to his villa, and Adam never ignored his gut.

Turning away from those thundercloud eyes, he pulled out a chair, beckoned her to take it. "Let's eat, shall we? Raquel will be here shortly."

But Maddie shook her head, the stubborn wench. Nothing was simple with her. Nothing was easy or obvious.

Take her sister. There was another mystery. Why had Maddie taken charge of her when Lucy was sixteen, given up a career she prized to become a high-priced law-bot, then spent every cent sending Lucy first to an insanely expensive prep school, and now to one of the costliest colleges in the country?

She'd taken nothing from her parents, not for Lucy. And not for herself. She'd paid her own way through Boston College with loans and part-time jobs, then earned a partial ride through Harvard Law with stunning grades and near-perfect scores on the LSAT.

After that, she'd focused like a laser on her career. The U.S. Attorney's Office had snapped her up, and realizing they had pure dynamite on their hands, dropped her into their Manhattan office, exactly where every bloodthirsty young prosecutor longed to be.

In the five years that followed she'd made a name for herself with a string of convictions that seasoned prosecutors envied. Adam himself was her singular failure, and only because politics had, as usual, trumped justice. Then Lucy appeared on her doorstep, and the very next day Maddie threw it all away. She went to work for that soulless Marchand vixen, and since then nearly bankrupted herself giving Lucy every advantage money could buy.

Now she was sweating over Lucy's boyfriend, to the point of pleading with Adam to leave her in New York. He'd wager that hurt more than the tens of thousands bleeding from her bank account yearly.

What drove her to sacrifice everything, to worry herself sick over her sister? Nothing he'd seen explained it, and he doubted she'd offer it up.

But Lucy might.

With both sisters in Italy, he could unravel the mystery. Satisfy his curiosity about the maddening Maddie.

Meanwhile, Caesar salad was her favorite lunch. She'd eat it or he'd know the reason why.

IN THE END, though, Maddie didn't eat it, and Adam didn't know why.

She'd refused—without explanation—to sit at the table and share a civilized meal. If not for John Doe, he would have resorted to raising his voice, the woman was that frustrating.

Now Raquel was threatening to walk out.

"She's a bitch, Adam. And so *short*." Coming from Raquel at five-foot-ten, the latter was the greater insult.

"She's difficult, I know. And not as tall—"

"Or as built." Raquel cupped her own double Ds. "You usually go for the tits. This chick's got nothing." She wrinkled her nose as much as Botox allowed. "I don't get it."

And he certainly couldn't explain it. "You showed her the gowns?"

"Sure I did. The little squirt turned her nose up at everything. She's shrimpy, but she's got a shitload of attitude."

She tossed a mile of blond waves over one shapely shoulder. "You better talk to her, Adam. If she gets shitty with me again, I'm outta here. She's not exactly a poster child for my designs anyway."

That was going too far. Maddie could be a pain in the ass, but she was beautiful, and no one, even Raquel, a friend who went back to the old days, would say differently.

She kept up her rant. "I hope this isn't some phase you're going through. Razor-tongued pipsqueaks—"

"Raquel." His chilly tone brought her up short. "Madeline is dear to me."

That put surprise on her face. She blinked a few times. "I didn't mean anything."

"I'll speak to her." He could smile now that she'd gotten the message. "Why don't you ring for Henry? He'll bring you something while you wait."

Riding down in the elevator, Adam rolled his shoulders like a boxer waiting for the bell. He'd lead with diplomacy, but if it came to a fight, he was ready.

Maddie answered his knock, locked and loaded.

"Keep her away from me. She's a psycho."

He lifted a brow. "Bridget?"

"Har har." She stepped back and he followed her inside, amused when she plunked down on the arm of the sofa, arms crossed, jaw set.

"Raquel's a talented designer. She dresses all of my dates."

"Yeah, I heard about them. Brandi and Sylvie and Wendi and Allie and this-y and that-y." She rolled her eyes. "Don't any of them have *real* names?"

"Like Maddie?"

She bounced to her feet. "Shut up. Just shut up and get out." She pointed to the door. "Take Raquel to the gala, she's got all the right *assets*. Nobody'll make fun of her."

Startled, he bit off the ultimatum simmering on his tongue.

This was more than sensitivity about her height. She was insecure about her figure too.

Well, he could ease her mind about that.

He curved his lips, went for sensual, not mocking. "Madeline, darling. Your assets"—he walked his eyes down her perfectly proportioned body—"are delightful. You needn't worry about them."

She reddened fiercely. "I'm not *worried*, dickhead. But I don't want Lucy getting upset that her sister's an international joke."

That stymied him. "A joke? Why in God's name would you be a joke?"

"Oh please. Can't you see the headlines? 'From Pitbull to Lapdog.'" She did air quotes. "'LeCroix Keeps Pitbull on a Short Leash.' With hooks like that, FOX News can flog the story for weeks. I can't wait to see the graphic they come up with. My face on a dog's body? Studded collar with a leather leash?"

She paced the floor. "Whatever. I can live with the professional bullshit. It's the personal stuff, the way they'll gloat about you *lowering* your standards. Developing a taste for *shrimp*." She jabbed a finger in his direction. "Give me ten bucks for every 'Tinker Bell' and I'll be as rich as you are."

He bit down on a smile. He loved her humor, even her gallows humor. But now wasn't the time to tell her.

And sadly, she wasn't wrong. The press dissected every woman connected to him. Madeline wouldn't be spared. Add their history, and the vultures would pick her apart like carrion.

Once again, he regretted not thinking things through beforehand. But even if he had, he wouldn't have focused on her stature. Who knew she was so touchy about it, particularly when he found it increasingly appealing himself. She wasn't his usual type, that much was true. But tossing her lithe body around his bed had quickly become an obsession.

In any case, it was too late for second thoughts. CNN had already broken the story. The best thing he could do for Maddie now was take her to the damn gala and show everyone in the room that he found her the most alluring woman there.

Ditching flattery since it didn't impress her, he tweaked her pride instead. "I had no idea you're so sensitive."

That stiffened her spine. "I'm not *sensitive*. I just happen to care about my sister's feelings. *She's* sensitive. In a good way. She'll hate seeing me ridiculed."

"Won't she hate it all the more if she thinks you're miserable to boot?"

"I *am* miserable!"

Maybe *he* was too sensitive, because that stung like a slap. He dropped the act, gave in to frustration.

"Why, Madeline? Why are you miserable?" He spread his arms wide. "This is hardly a prison. You have the run of it all—the gym, the pools. Ask for anything and you'll have it. Food or drink? Only name it."

He dragged a hand through his hair. "Is it such a trial to come with me tonight? We might even enjoy it. We can dance. I like dancing. I thought you liked it too."

He ran out of steam, feeling like an ass. Maddie's

eyes were round, questioning his sanity. Well, fuck it all, he *was* losing his mind.

Furious with himself, he made for the door with his last remnants of pride.

"You're going," he shot over his shoulder. "You can suck it up and cooperate with Raquel, or I'll bloody well dress you myself."

How THE HELL did LeCroix know she liked to dance?

Pacing the suite from hearth to Jacuzzi, Maddie weighed the evidence. It added up to a lot more than a standard background check. He'd identified her friends, her favorite foods, her interests. He probably knew more about her finances than she did.

And he knew enough about Lucy to push Maddie's buttons.

But he didn't know her family's ugly secrets. She'd be able to tell if he did, by the disgust on his face.

A bird streaked past the window, catching her eye, making her shiver. Why did people insist on living up so high, with all that *space* out there, empty and ominous, and utterly useless? It wasn't like you could step out and walk around on the clouds.

She averted her eyes but didn't draw the drapes. That would raise too many questions. The last thing she needed was LeCroix gloating about her fear of heights.

Especially since she'd soon be up in his plane, floating in space above the deep blue sea.

Talk about empty, ominous air.

A rap on her door brought her back to earth. Raquel poked her head in. "Um, Ms. St. Clair, are you ready to try on the gowns?"

Ms. St. Clair? What happened to "gremlin" and "munchkin" and her parting shot, "hobbit"?

Maddie narrowed her eyes. "Whatever."

Raquel slunk through the parlor and into the bedroom. Maddie followed in her own sweet time.

She had to admit, she was curious about the dresses. She loved beautiful clothes—Fashion Week, anyone?—but she'd been too busy trading insults to spare a glance for the gowns.

They hung from a bar in the walk-in closet, three glittering jewels—sapphire, onyx, and emerald—as far beyond Maddie's budget as their faceted namesakes.

"I can alter any of these to fit your slim build," said Raquel, politely. "The sapphire"—her fingers stroked lovingly over the beaded bodice—"would make the most of your figure, and also complement Adam's eyes."

"Why would I give a rat's skinny ass about Adam's eyes?"

The reformed queen of snark let it pass as rhetorical. "The onyx, of course, suits any occasion." She touched the chiffon skirt; it drifted like smoke. "But Adam prefers the emerald." Her eyes flickered to Maddie's. "He mentioned . . . yes, it brings out the green."

Startled, Maddie blanked on a snotty reply. Most people didn't notice her changeable eyes, at least not right away. She glanced back into the bedroom. The emerald suite.

Huh.

"I agree with Adam. The emerald suits you."

"Hold on." Maddie found her voice. "I can choose my own dress."

Feeling like a midget next to Raquel, she approached the gowns, toyed with the fabrics. The black chiffon was so light the slightest breeze made it flutter. The sapphire was regal; classic movie-star wear.

But the emerald. Oh my. She ran a hand over the bodice. The fabric was textured, with a faint metallic sheen.

"Dupioni silk," Raquel said helpfully. "The silk-worms are reared by hand, and the fabric is handspun and woven in the traditional methods. The gown is one of a kind, of course."

"Of course," Maddie murmured. She couldn't fathom the cost.

She wanted, desperately, to reject it on principle.

But even more desperately, she wanted to wear it. To feel, for one night, as beautiful as any woman. Beautiful enough to be on Adam LeCroix's arm.

It was foolish, for sure. He was a criminal and she shouldn't care if he thought she was a hobbit.

But she did, Lord she did. And though it stung to admit it, she wanted him to see her in that dress, and be awed.

CHAPTER NINE

Vicky: I promise to stand with you against
adversity of all kinds, be it enemies
or illness or poverty or loss.
I will be at your side.

Maddie: Unless it's zombies.
Then I'm outta there.

HENRY WAS WAITING for Maddie in the foyer. "If you'll come with me, madame, Mr. LeCroix will meet you downstairs."

So much for making her grand entrance. Adam hadn't even bothered to wait for her. Disappointment drizzled on her parade.

Well, it was his loss. She lifted her chin, gave Henry a phony confident smile, and stepped into the waiting elevator.

Henry followed, pressing the button for the lobby. "May I say, Ms. St. Clair, you look absolutely stunning."

"Yes, you may." Her grin was genuine now. "But only if you call me Maddie."

He returned her smile. "You'll shine as brightly as any star at the gala."

Her smile vanished. "Star? Like movie stars?"

"Dozens. They all band together for this cause."

Great. A herd of long-legged gazelles trying not to trip over the Chihuahua in their midst.

"Um, what cause would that be?" She should've asked before now.

"Raising funds for disabled actors. It draws all the big names."

She clutched her beaded bag with all ten fingers, made herself focus on the farce, spending zillions on a fancy party so a few pennies could trickle down to the poor slobs at the bottom of the Actors' Guild pecking order.

It was a joke. A photo op. How did she let herself get sucked into it?

The elevator pinged, the door slid open. "Madame." Henry stepped out, ushered with his arm.

Maddie didn't move, just stared out into the lobby, so grand and elegant and far from home, feeling exactly how Cinderella must have felt when the carriage turned into a pumpkin and she realized she was still just a servant girl after all.

As always, Maddie reacted to helplessness with a sharp burst of anger. *To hell with LeCroix. He can pound sand. And then he can pound some starlet all night. It's not my problem. I'm out of here.*

She punched the button for the penthouse. The door started to close. Henry put out a hand to stop it.

And Adam walked through the front door and into the lobby.

She blinked like the sun had come out from behind a cloud.

The tuxedo, it seemed, was designed with Adam in mind. Six-foot-two was the ideal height, one-ninety the perfect weight. And confidence the ultimate accessory.

And his face, God, his face. The old masters would have wept to paint it on Apollo, with that sweep of glossy hair and those lips, wide and full.

His spontaneous grin when he saw her tilted her world on its axis.

Before she knew what she was doing, she was standing before him, the elevator closing behind her. He took her hands, held them wide. His gaze swept up from her four-inch heels to lock on her eyes.

"You're dazzling," he said.

Heart beating like a crow's wing, she mustered a shrug. "You clean up pretty good yourself."

He laughed, a lighthearted sound. Keeping hold of one hand, he led her across the grand lobby and out onto the sidewalk. "Thank you, Peter," he said, handing the doorman a bill as they passed.

"No problem, Mr. LeCroix," he called after them. "That's some sweet ride."

Maddie swiveled her head, expecting the limo to stream up to the curb. But Adam kept her moving toward an altogether different vehicle. A metallic blue—

"Ohmygod!" Maddie clutched her chest. "A Bugatti Veyron!" She gaped at the car. Gaped at Adam. "Is it . . . are we . . . ?"

He was grinning. "It is, and we are."

She crept up on the two-million-dollar sports car like it might spook and take flight. She stroked the gleaming metal with a tentative hand.

He came up behind her, touched her back lightly. "I thought you might like it."

So he knew she subscribed to *Car and Driver*. So what?

He opened the passenger door and she slid into the seat, admiring the recessed gauges, the compact controls. "It's a cockpit," she said as he took the wheel. "It feels like an airplane."

"And it flies."

He hit the gas and the Bugatti jumped away from the curb. He shifted smoothly, zipping around traffic, and the city rushed past in a smear of colored lights.

"I'd open it up"—he flashed her a smile as hot as the car—"but I wouldn't want to get arrested."

She laughed, and the wind caught the sound, swirling it around them. The top was open to the twilit air. Tipping her head back against the seat, she gazed up at the skyscrapers, their lights climbing all the way to the stars.

In the face of such unearthly beauty, her troubles shrank to pinpricks.

Sweet heaven, she was in a Bugatti Veyron with the hottest, most thrilling man on the planet.

She really was Cinderella.

It made Adam feel like a king, the rapture on her face, knowing he'd put it there.

Her hand stroked over the seat, the power of twelve hundred horses pulsing through supple Italian leather.

"You've got some nice toys, Adam, I'll say that for you."

Oh, but she'd said so much more, hadn't she, just by using his given name at last?

"We'll fly it out to Texas sometime," he said offhandedly. "They don't take speed limits so seriously out there."

She laughed again, a surprisingly addictive sound. "Even Texans might get pissy at two hundred and fifty miles an hour."

"They'd have to catch us first, wouldn't they?"

He braked at a stoplight, Times Square's multicolored neon refracting like a firestorm off the gleaming hood. Maddie peered around as if she'd lost her bearings, seemed surprised to find herself on Forty-second Street.

"Where are we going, anyway?"

"Cipriani's."

She sighed. "Wouldn't you rather just drive around all night?"

She looked bedazzled, cheeks glowing, hair tousled, like a woman who'd just had great sex and wanted more. When her eyes met his, they glittered so green and gorgeous that he gripped the wheel to keep from reaching for her.

He made himself look away. "Later. First we knock them dead. Then I'll take you anywhere you want to go."

He only hoped that would be to bed.

Outside Cipriani's, the sidewalk was abuzz with arrivals, limos disgorging beautiful people by twos and threes.

Adam tossed his keys to a goggle-eyed valet. Maddie grasped his arm. "Are you nuts?" she hissed up at him. "You're letting him drive the Bugatti? What if he steals it? Or dings it?" She glared at the teenager sliding in behind the wheel.

Adam smiled down at her. "Darling, it's just a car."

"A two-million-dollar car! The fastest street-legal car in the world, for Christ's sake. What if he takes it for a joyride? Hits one-fifty on the JFK?"

"Then he'll spend an uncomfortable night as a guest of the NYPD. And he'll have a whopping story to tell his grandchildren."

"How can you be so casual about it?"

Her jaw thrust out indignantly. He couldn't resist cupping it in his palm. She was so fierce. So desirable. And as fine as bone china.

His thumb stroked her cheek. His other hand drifted up her arm, sliding over silk until it reached the silkier skin of her throat. He held her like that.

And then he kissed her.

OH, HOW HE kissed her. Gently, no tongue, just warm lips closing over hers. His strong hands cupped her face, a delicate touch, as if she were a flower that could be carelessly crushed.

Some way-back part of Maddie's brain howled, *Push him away!* She flattened her palms on his chest to do just that.

But then he angled his head. His tongue, hot and wet, licked the seam of her lips. Like Eve, she opened to taste him, delicious, forbidden. The best thing she'd ever had in her mouth. And instead of pushing him away, she fisted his lapels and yanked him in.

In a finger snap, their pent-up desire went nuclear. His spectacular arms seized her, dragging her up on her toes. She mashed herself to his chest, fused her hips to his hard-on as if they had no history and she could fuck him with impunity. Only their clothes kept her off his cock, or they'd have been doing it right there on the sidewalk.

It lasted only an instant, that quick flare of insanity, before a deep-throated chuckle behind her cut through the horny haze.

She pulled back from the kiss, dazed and confused.

"You two oughta get a room," drawled the chuckler in a broad Western twang.

Adam's gaze flicked over her shoulder, an irritable glance. But his lips curved into a reluctant half smile. Turning her around by the shoulders, he said, "Maddie, meet Dakota."

She froze like a statue. *Dakota Rain.* Probably the

hugest movie star in the world. Certainly the only person who could have distracted her from Adam.

"Dakota, this is Maddie St. Clair."

"The lady prosecutor." Dakota grinned his trademark I've-got-the-world-by-the-balls grin. "Nice to meet you, Miz St. Clair."

She gulped. "The same, Mr. Rain."

She shook his offered hand, going giddy when he slickly hooked her fingers through his elbow. "How 'bout Maddie and Dakota?" he drawled. "I got a feeling we'll be friends." He took a step toward the door.

Adam's hand fell on his shoulder. "Find your own woman," he said, unhooking Maddie's hand and tucking it under his own arm. Then he tipped his head toward the street. "Isn't that Ashley getting out of her car?"

"Aw, hell." Dakota all but ducked. "That girl can really hold a grudge." He dropped a quick wink at Maddie. "See you later, gorgeous." And he disappeared inside.

"You needn't look so disappointed," said Adam, dryly.

"Disappointed?" Maddie gave him an are-you-nuts stare. "*Dakota Rain* just called me *gorgeous*."

"Yes, and you were spellbound." He sounded disgusted.

"Well, duh. I've seen *every one* of his movies."

The doorman waved them into the jam-packed lobby. Adam nudged her out of the fray. His voice was stern, and seriously annoyed. "Don't trust Dakota. He's not the romantic hero he plays on screen. He'd have you out of that dress in a New York minute, then never return your calls."

She rolled her eyes. Like she expected to ride off into the sunset with Dakota Rain.

Still, it was a timely reminder and she took it to heart, if not exactly how he meant it. "Thanks for the tip, but I know very well there's no such thing as romance."

Then she nipped off the conversation by tugging his hand toward the ballroom. "Come on, let's find the food. I'm starving."

"I told you to eat lunch," he muttered, with his nose out of joint. But he laced his fingers through hers and they stepped into the stream.

It was a crush, celebrities rubbing elbows with politicians and socialites, everyone glittering in sequins and jewels. Maddie took it in stride, managed to do blasé while she soaked up the swank. Until she hit the ballroom.

Decked out for maximum glitz, it was totally, riotously over the top. Soaring columns, brilliant tapestries, gigantic feathers spearing from oversized vases. And trees—actual full-sized trees—sheathed in twinkling lights.

It was a fairy tale, brought lavishly to life by the star-studded crowd circulating through it.

Their entrance drew stares, as expected, but it still made her cringe. She shunned the limelight under the best of circumstances, which these definitely weren't.

Still, the gawkers weren't as annoying as those who pretended she wasn't there at all.

"Oooh, Adam." The delighted purr came from a long-stemmed beauty with a waterfall of blond. She coiled around his arm, gazing up at him from eyes so vividly violet that they must have been enhanced.

Like her rack was enhanced, Maddie thought snidely. She could pitch lawn chairs on that balcony and serve cocktails for four.

"I haven't seen you in *ages*." One crimson nail traced Adam's collar. "You don't call, you don't write."

He smiled with what looked to be genuine warmth. "Andrea. You look lovely." He nudged Maddie into her sightline. "Maddie, darling, this is Andrea Lyon."

The violet eyes dropped ten inches to meet Maddie's, and widened slightly. A smile quirked Andrea's lips, like she was expecting Adam to pat his little sister's head and send her off to play.

Instead, his hand on Maddie's waist tugged her closer, so her shoulder bumped his chest. "Andrea, meet my date, Maddie St. Clair."

It was a cheap thrill watching the A-list beauty fall speechless. But the woman had talent to go with her looks and she drew on it now.

Morphing from pouting lover to pure femme fatale, she slid Adam a sultry wink. "I'll be in New York all weekend," she stage-whispered, "if you get tired of Tinker Bell." Then she melted into the crowd.

Maddie held out her hand. "Ten bucks."

Adam grinned. "Why don't I buy you a drink instead?"

"Fine. Because if you've screwed as many of these women as I think you have, I'm gonna need it."

They inched across the room, waylaid by former—and wannabe—lovers cooing over Adam, by politicians back-slapping him, millionaires rubbing elbows, and A-list actors buddying up. Everyone wanted a piece of him. And all were patently surprised when he glued most of his attention to Maddie.

"I thought the plan was for everyone to think *I've* lost my head over *you*," she said when they reached the bar. It was their first moment of privacy since entering the ballroom. "So what's with the caveman act?"

His brows rose half an inch.

"You know. The Clint Eastwood squint, the possessive arm around my waist." She jabbed the offending limb with one pointy finger.

He tightened his grip, brought her hips up against his. "Who said it's an act?"

She licked lips that had gone suddenly dry. "Yeah, right. Anyway, you've got everyone thinking *you're* into *me*. It's all over the Twittersphere by now."

"That doesn't trouble me in the least."

"Well, it's troubling every woman in the room."

"Even you?"

"No. Because I know you've got something up your sleeve."

The bartender appeared and Adam looked away long enough to order two dry Beefeater martinis, up, with extra olives.

She regarded him balefully. "Your private dick tailed me into a bar?"

He shrugged. "Could be coincidence. Beefeater martinis happen to be my drink of choice."

"No way."

He grinned. "Way."

Her lips twitched as she fought a smile. "You're a jerk."

"Ah, a step up from asshole."

"They're not mutually exclusive."

Two frosted glasses appeared on the bar, tiny shards of ice shimmering in the gin, three gargantuan olives speared on oversized toothpicks.

Adam passed one to her without releasing her waist, lifted the other to clink against hers. "To fast cars and faster women."

"To muscle cars and muscular men."

Chuckling together, they sipped, eyes locked over the rims. Their steamy sidewalk clinch shimmered in the air.

Then Adam's gaze flicked past her shoulder. His good humor dimmed. "Hawthorne spotted us. He's coming our way."

"I thought that was the point."

"I suppose it is." Adam released her and she took a small step back.

A reluctant step, she realized, missing the press of his hips. They'd been standing much too close, but damn it, she'd liked it. And who could blame her? Half the women in the room would dump their dates to bump against Adam.

As it was, he didn't let her go far, just enough so she could turn and face what was coming. Then his hand settled lightly on her waist again, surprisingly comforting. As if they were united in more than just this one battle.

Hawthorne ignored Adam and focused on her.

"Ms. St. Clair." Malice slid like grease under his polished delivery. "I must say I didn't expect to see you like this." He looked down his long nose, taking in Adam's hand on her hip. "But since you're whoring yourself out, you may as well go all the way."

Adam stiffened, but she set a hand on his arm. She didn't need backup.

This was Pitbull country.

"Two words, Hawthorne. *Punitive damages.*" Her smile was needle sharp. "Juries love sticking it to greedy insurance companies sitting on their bailout money. So bring your checkbook."

She half turned, then sneered over her shoulder. "While you're at it, bring a real lawyer. I could blow Brandt out of court with one good fart."

And flicking her fingers like the man was a gnat, she turned back to her martini.

For one speechless moment, Hawthorne stared red-faced at Adam, his pulse throbbing visibly above his starched white collar. Then off he strode, blustering clichés about hired guns, while Adam choked back a laugh.

"Priceless," he murmured into her ear, "but next time warn me so I can get it on film."

With her future in ruins and "whore" ringing in her ears, Maddie's high spirits collapsed. Reality set in. "As your attorney," she said stiffly, "I advise against that."

"Tell me you wouldn't love to see it on YouTube."

A network news anchor hovered not four feet away. "I think this case will get plenty of screen time." In her book, that was nothing to celebrate.

Edgy now, she pushed her martini away. "Any idea where the ladies' room is?"

He pointed, and she gauged the time it would take to shimmy through the gazelles. "I might be a while. Where will I find you? Near the door, I hope."

He laughed, and looked damn hot doing it.

Grrr. Weren't things complicated enough? Did she have to lust after LeCroix like one of his idiot starlets?

Scowling, she plunged into the jungle. But she never made it to the ladies' room.

Senator Michael Warren, former U.S. Attorney for the Eastern District of New York and her onetime boss, the very man who'd sold her out on *United States v. LeCroix*, intercepted her.

Taking a firm grip on her elbow, he maneuvered her into an alcove, put her back to the wall, and used his own broad one to close them in.

His square jaw was rigid with anger. "Maddie. What the fuck?"

"No, *you* what the fuck." She drilled a finger into his chest. "Quit dragging me around like a caveman." She was surrounded by them tonight. This one was blond and brown-eyed, but no less of an alpha.

He caught her finger in a chokehold. "Don't turn this around. LeCroix's a goddamn felon."

"I know what he is."

"Then why are you cuddling up to him?"

"I'm not cuddling," she snapped out, but her face went hot. "I'm representing him, you idiot. I'm in private practice now, in case you forgot."

She tried to wriggle her finger free but he turned his hand, laced their fingers together.

His stern expression softened. So did his voice. "I haven't forgotten anything about you, Maddie. Not in five years. Not in fifty."

She rolled her eyes. "Oh please. We had sex once. And then you *screwed me*."

"Don't pretend that's what happened to us. You wouldn't have gotten involved with me anyway. That's not your style. I'd have been lucky to sleep with you a few more times before you kissed me off."

True, but she wouldn't admit it. "Boo hoo. Now let go of my hand."

He tightened his grip. "Does LeCroix know you'll drop him next week? Next month if he's lucky? That you'll crush his heart like a grape and he'll never be able to forget you?"

"Honestly, Michael." *What a drama queen.* "Save it for the voters. And don't waste any sympathy on LeCroix. Even if he had a heart, he wouldn't hand it to me."

"Believe me, sympathy's the last thing I feel for that fucker. Jealousy, maybe, and outrage that he's sucked you into his latest scam."

"It's not a scam," she said, admitting aloud what she'd avoided admitting to herself. "I thought it was, at first. But somebody actually ripped him off and he's pissed as hell. He's got a squad of private dicks on it."

"Don't be naïve, Maddie. He's putting on a show." Michael leaned in to make his point. "With the *Lady in Red*, he didn't care if you thought he was guilty. He just wanted you to believe you couldn't convict him. This time he's got more at stake."

She wanted to dunce-slap him. "Seriously, Michael, you've lost your edge. He has *less* at stake now." Her tone broke it down like he was a dummy. "I'm his lawyer. It doesn't matter what I believe, I'm stuck with him unless he out-and-out tells me he's committing a fraud, and even then all I can do is withdraw."

He shook his head, hissed it out. "You don't see it, do you? *He wants to fuck you.* It's written all over him."

"Pfft. That's jealousy talking." In a fresh surge of annoyance, she yanked her hand free. Her funny bone cracked the wall and pain sang up her arm. "God*damn* it! Get out of my way!"

She gave his chest a shove that didn't budge him. He took her shoulders, gave her a shake. "Listen to me, Maddie. He stole the *Lady in Red*. Who knows what else he's done? Who he's hurt?"

"Stop right there, Michael. He stole the painting. But he didn't hurt anyone doing it."

"If he stole one, he stole others. We don't know the collateral damage."

She dug in her heels. "You're being ridiculous. He's not that bad."

He stiffened away from her. "I can't believe you're defending him."

"I'm sticking to the evidence. All we had on him was the *Lady in Red*, and I won't impute murder and mayhem from that. And anyway, if he's so evil, how do you justify kicking him loose?"

Michael's nostrils flared. "I'll tell you now what I told you then. I can do more good in the Senate than LeCroix can do harm out in the world. Or at least I thought so until tonight. Until I saw you hanging all over him—"

"Senator." Adam's big hand fell on Michael's shoulder, gave it a not-so-friendly squeeze. "I see you've found my date."

Michael held Maddie's eyes, his own hot with resentment. His voice was a jagged blade. "Hands off, LeCroix. You're assaulting a senator."

Adam squeezed harder. "And you're harassing a defenseless woman."

Michael swung around to face him, dislodging Adam's hand. "I'm talking some sense into her. Trying to protect her."

"By backing her into a corner? Looming over her like a goon?" Adam's quiet menace frosted the air. Michael's temper flared white hot in response.

Maddie stepped between them. "That's enough, boys, keep your dicks in your pants." A quick glance at the crowd caught a dozen curious stares. "Now smile, both of you."

Michael caught her elbow. "Maddie—"

"Smile, Michael, or I'll knee you in the nuts and give everyone the scene they're hoping for."

Her level stare must have convinced him, because he pressed his lips shut, forced the corners to curl upward. He could have been gritting out a prostate exam, but it would do.

She turned to Adam. He gave her a level stare of his own, wildly blue, darkly furious. "I'll smile when he unhands you."

She shook Michael's hand off her elbow, kept her gaze fixed on Adam's.

Gradually, his jaw unlocked. One corner of his mouth twisted up. Without another glance at Michael, he took that same elbow.

"We're leaving. Now." And he strode for the door.

CHAPTER TEN

MADDIE WAITED TILL they hit the sidewalk before elbowing Adam's ribs. He released her to clutch his side. "Damn it, what was that for?"

"For manhandling me, that's what. And for going all barbarian in there. *Unhand my woman*. What's that about?" She pointed a finger at him. "You called me *defenseless*."

He looked amazed. "He's got a hundred pounds on you. He *shook* you, for Christ's sake. I should've laid him out for that alone."

"Quit it." She advanced on him. "Just quit with all the hero shit. John Doe, and Bridget, and the starving children. Because I know you're a crook." She nodded once. "You're a crook, not a hero."

That made him smile for real. "They're not mutually exclusive," he echoed at her.

She seized on it. "So you admit it? You admit you stole the *Lady in Red*?"

The look he gave her was bland as toast. "It was simply an observation."

She simmered silently while the same valet wheeled

the Bugatti to the curb. Adam didn't seem to care that he screeched to a stop. He peeled bills off his wad and handed them to the kid, but she blistered the boy with a glare that shrank him like a raisin. Then she hoofed it to the car to open her own door before Adam could beat her to it.

Defenseless. Not hardly.

Still, he managed to catch her elbow before her butt hit leather. She shook him off. "It's an elbow, not a rudder. Quit using it to steer me around."

He held his hands up, palms out. "I thought you might like to drive."

"Oh. Well." That was thoughtful. Too bad she couldn't take him up on it. "Thanks, but I'll ride."

A voice boomed from the doorway. "Leaving already?" Dakota swaggered to the car, eyed Adam shrewdly. "Just when things were shaping up for a fight."

"Maddie made me keep my dick in my pants."

Dakota roared. "You're a rare one, Miss Maddie. Most women are after him to take it out."

She should have had a snappy comeback, but she was pitifully star-struck, blushing up at Dakota like a tween.

Adam stepped between them, said dryly to Dakota, "Going home empty-handed?"

Dakota spread his palms. "I shook off the babes when it looked like you might need a hand with the senator. Now I've got to start all over again." He peeked around Adam at Maddie. "Got a sister? 'Cause if she looks like you, I might hang up my spurs."

Adam strangled a snort, gave Dakota a half-serious shove, and strode around the car. Sliding behind the wheel, he said over his shoulder, "Consider your invitation revoked." Then he gunned it and shot into traffic.

Most of the cars at that time of night were cabs.

Adam wove through them like they were standing still. Maddie held her tongue, but when they skinned past one with nothing to spare, she sucked a breath through her teeth.

"Jesus, Adam. Why do you let Dakota get to you?"

"He doesn't *get* to me," he lied, but he eased off the gas.

"He's a joker," she said. "He doesn't take anything seriously, least of all himself." Which was a disappointment to a fan who preferred his rare dramatic roles to his usual action fluff.

Adam braked at a red light, glanced her way. "Dakota's a good friend. He wouldn't have thought twice about punching a sitting senator if it came to that. But he has an irritating habit of wanting what he can't have."

"He's Dakota freaking Rain, what can he possibly want that he can't have?"

Adam's smile was razor-thin. "At the moment, that would be you."

"You're wrong about that."

"No, I'm not. He wants you."

"I meant you're wrong that he can't have me. Turn the car around and I'll prove it."

The look he shot her was dark and dangerous. When the light turned green, he did zero to sixty in two point five seconds, leaving her stomach back at the intersection.

"Shit, Adam!" She almost swallowed her tongue.

"You could've driven," he said as if that excused him.

She looked out the side window at the Broadway lights, knew she'd have to tell him. "I don't have a license." She mumbled it out.

He throttled back to a reasonable speed. "I beg your pardon?"

She set her teeth, kept her gaze on the street. "I said I don't have a license, okay? I live in New York City. I don't need one."

Silence.

She broke it. "Just say what you're thinking. Spit it out."

"I'm thinking about pizza." He coasted to the curb in front of a hole in the wall. The unremarkable sign said "Luigi's."

"We can't leave the car here," was her first thought.

"We're not getting out." He beckoned to a dark-suited giant who stepped out of the shadows. "Roberto," he said, and let loose a stream of Italian as the big man nodded along. Then Adam passed him a fifty and he disappeared inside.

She eyed the unassuming storefront skeptically. "The pizza's good?"

"The best in New York."

"No way. Anthony's is the best, down the block from my place."

"Twenty bucks says Luigi's."

"You're on."

Roberto emerged with a box. Adam handed it off to Maddie.

"That was fast." She sniffed the box noisily as he jetted into traffic.

"I called it in after you left me." His voice hardened. "Obviously, I should've stayed with you instead. I'm sorry Warren cornered you."

"Forget it." She flipped up the lid. "Oh God, oh God." Thin crust, thick sauce, and cheese . . . lots of cheese.

Adam downshifted for a turn. "I didn't know you'd been lovers."

"Good. Because it's none of your business."

Even though she knew better, she went for a slice, ended up sucking burnt fingers.

"He fell in love with you," Adam persisted.

"Michael falls in love twice a week. He's a smart lawyer and he's probably a good senator, but he's an idiot about his love life."

"So it was one-sided?"

"Remember how I said it's none of your business?"

"Humor me."

"Bite me."

"Don't tempt me." He showed his teeth, and she laughed.

He pulled up outside his building. The doorman hurried over. "I'll garage it for you, Mr. LeCroix," he said, palming the bill Adam slipped him.

As they crossed the lobby, Maddie griped. "You must be down two large in tips tonight. I'd be better off as your doorman than your lawyer."

Adam keyed in the code to call his elevator. "But you'd miss out on the city's best pizza."

"We'll see." When they stepped out into the penthouse, Maddie twirled her finger at the splendor. "Luigi's seems a little lowbrow for a guy who lives like this."

"He's a friend."

"Ah. Like Henry's a friend, and Bridget. And Fredo too, I suppose?"

He looked surprised, but he let it go. "I knew Luigi in Sicily. He dreamed of his own restaurant, and I dreamed of his pizza."

He took the box with one hand, traced the other lightly up her bare arm. His eyes glinted, an impossible blue. "And you, Madeline? What do you dream of?"

She wasn't playing that game. It led straight to his bed. Instead, she tapped the lid. "Three slices with one of your fancy reds, and another piece of that cheesecake."

He walked his gaze down from her eyes to the hollow of her throat. His lips curved up on one side. "That seems a little lowbrow for a woman wearing emeralds."

She'd forgotten about the necklace he'd loaned her, a thumb-sized stone on a braided gold chain. "It belonged to a princess," he said, "in the fifteenth century. A betrothal gift." He touched it, then her skin, with one fiery fingertip. Her heart, already drumming, sped up like a bongo.

She faked flippant to cover her jitters. "Sounds pricey. How'd you end up with it? Five-finger discount?"

"No, Madame Prosecutor, I didn't steal it. I won it in a poker game."

Whoa. "What did *you* put in the pot? A tropical island? The space shuttle?"

"The Bugatti."

She gasped. "Are you nuts? I was kidding!" Then the full force of it hit her—she was wearing a two-million-dollar necklace!

"Shit! Shit! Get it off me!" She went for the clasp, but he brushed her hands away, laughing.

"Darling, it's just a necklace."

"And the Bugatti's just a car. To *you*. Not to me."

"I'm accustomed to the best." He traced a finger along the chain. "You do it justice."

It was exactly the right thing to say. But then, seduction was his second language. He was fluent in it.

Proving it, he hefted the pizza. "Speaking of bets, we have twenty riding on Luigi's." His hand drifted down her arm. He laced his fingers through hers. "I'm willing to go higher if you are."

She tried to look unaffected by his touch, by his tone. "Sorry, no sports cars or priceless jewels here."

"I can think of other things." He raised her hand

to his lips, did that knuckle kiss again. It was a killer move. She had no idea how to counter it.

Magically, Henry appeared to relieve him of the box. "My suite," Adam told him. "And another Brunello."

Then he tugged her back into the elevator, and like a bubble-eyed starlet, she went with him.

AN HOUR LATER, Adam was pacing his suite when Maddie rolled in like thunder. She tossed John's leash on the desk. "You *do* think I'm helpless. You sicced Henry on me."

He refused to apologize. "The park isn't safe at midnight."

"I can take care of myself." She waved her Mace. "I've been doing it for years."

She spoke in a singsong for John's benefit, but steam whistled from her ears.

After pizza, she'd shed the emerald gown that he'd never forget and changed into blue jeans and a sweater the color of ripe plums. Her hair was windblown, and her eyes, pearly gray, were narrowed to slits.

He wanted to eat her up.

But that wasn't going to happen.

Somewhere between the elevator and his suite, his smooth seduction had hit a bump. He wasn't sure how it happened, what he'd said or done, but things had gone downhill with a bullet.

It started when she plopped the third largest emerald in the world on his desk with a short, severe lecture on how two million dollars could be better spent on the starving children. Granted, he hadn't helped matters by mentioning her lack of qualms about the Bugatti, but really, she was asking for it.

Then she'd fussed about the candlelight, claiming she couldn't see her hand in front of her face, much less her pizza. She wouldn't quit until he lit the place up like Wal-Mart. Talk about killing the mood.

Finally, after sourly handing over the twenty bucks she damn well owed him for the bet, she'd announced her intention to walk John. Solo.

As if he'd let her wander nighttime New York with only a rickety dog to protect her. And he shouldn't have to take shit for it, either.

He paced to the window, feeling surly, looking for trouble. "Did you speak to your sister?"

"I did," she bit out.

"Crash has a passport?"

"He does."

He checked her reflection in the glass—arms crossed, brow lowered, staring holes in his back.

"I'm sure they'd like privacy," he went on, throwing gas on the fire. "There are several guest houses on the property—"

"No!" She clutched her head. "No, no, no. Main house, separate bedrooms. In fact, Lucy can bunk with me."

"And when she sneaks out in the middle of the night?"

"She won't. Not if I stay awake."

"For a week? A brilliant plan."

"What, you think I should just deal with it? Pretend some loser called *Crash* isn't debauching my sister two doors down the hall?"

"The debauching is well under way. It's probably going on at this very moment."

"Thanks for putting that picture in my head." She stalked to the sofa, threw herself down. John roused from his bed to rest his head on her knee. She scratched him absently.

Hands in his pockets, Adam wandered a restless circle around the room. His ultimate aim was the sofa, but he'd have to sneak up on her like a cat stalking a mouse. If he startled her, she'd bolt back to her room.

He wasn't in the mood to let that happen.

Pausing at the window, he pretended to ponder the skyline. "Sex needn't be sordid, you know."

"Said the man who's screwed his way across six continents."

Okay, he'd walked into that one. He tried again. "When two people care about each other—"

Her snort cut him short. "Thanks, but my mother gave me 'the talk' when I was twelve. I know all about tender feelings transforming the base biological act into something precious and sacred. Not."

He drove his fists deeper into his pockets. He couldn't find his footing with her. He'd never felt so off balance.

Pressing his lips together and determined to keep them that way until he could think of something bulletproof to say, he moved to the bar, poured the last of the Brunello into two glasses.

"Thanks," she said when he brought it to her. "This whole situation might suck, but at least the food and wine rock."

That stung, but he let it go. He reached down to scratch John's ears. The hopeful dog did a drop and roll, sticking his feet in the air, and Adam, taking his cue, sat on the ottoman to rub the scrawny belly.

"If it helps," he said, "I got the run on Crash."

"He's a serial killer, isn't he?"

"By *serial* do you mean more than two?"

"Funny. Spill it."

Shifting to the sofa, he stretched his arm lazily along the back and tried to remember the last time he'd worked so hard to get close to a woman.

He couldn't, because he hadn't. They dropped into his lap like ripe peaches.

"George Lemon is his name. Twenty-one, from Ogunquit, Maine. Caucasian, three younger sisters, parents still married and gainfully employed. A nice middle-class home."

He thought she'd be relieved, but instead she sneered. "You never know what's happening inside those *nice* middle-class homes."

Her cynical tone said more than her words. Had her years as a prosecutor jaded her? Or was the trouble closer to home?

"What else?" she wanted to know. "Drugs? Baby mamas?"

"No arrests, no rehab, no illegitimate children."

Her eyes narrowed.

Why did he find that so hot?

She bit her lip.

Even hotter.

He shifted slightly and made himself stop staring at her teeth. He was still half hard from playing lovers at the gala. Touching her, kissing her, rubbing against her. A lifetime of experience had programmed his brain and his body to expect sex after an evening like that. With any other woman, things would be well under way.

But Maddie wasn't like other women, and as much as that fascinated him, at the moment it was causing him some serious discomfort.

"You're borrowing trouble," he said, making himself focus. "According to my people, he's fit, good-looking, and intelligent. He also plays guitar in a band. And reaps the rewards that come with it."

He held up a hand when she came to attention. "That

doesn't make him a pervert. It makes him a healthy young man with a normal sex drive."

"And who knows what diseases."

"Your sister risks that with anyone she has sex with."

Maddie went pale.

"In any case," he went on, "he's an A student with a wide range of artistic and musical talent who's thriving at RISD and has no obvious violent tendencies or chemical dependencies. He doesn't appear to be a danger to Lucy. And with a name like George Lemon, it's hard even to hold 'Crash' against him."

That drew a reluctant chuckle out of her. "Okay," she said, "he can live. For now."

She finished off her wine, slid her butt to the edge of the sofa. "Thanks for checking him out. I feel at least ten percent better."

"You're welcome." He reached for her hand. She let him take it, hold it, stroke his thumb over her delicate palm. Protectiveness rose up in him, hand in hand with desire. She was spun glass; he could crush her if he wasn't careful.

He tugged her closer, and she came against him without resistance. Why, he wondered, had he worried so much, struggled so hard? She was supple as clay. He stroked up her side, let his thumb glide over her breast. Jesus, he wanted her. He could hardly breathe with wanting her.

She lifted her eyes to his, her lips a scant inch from his own. Her voice, when she spoke, was a whisper.

"If you think I'll fuck you because you did me a favor, think again."

His hands froze. He backed away slowly.

"Madeline." His lips felt rigid. "That's not it at all."

"You don't want to fuck me? You've been working up to it all night."

"No, I do." He pushed a hand through his hair. "I mean *yes*, I do. Of course I do. But only if you want me to." Her flat gaze made him feel like an amateur.

"I can see that you don't," he added. "I misread your feelings. Please accept my apology."

She wavered, wanting to hate him; he could see the struggle on her face. But she recognized the truth when she heard it. Her shoulders softened. So did her jaw.

Not that she rushed into his arms.

"Whatever." She rubbed her stomach like it ached. Then she kissed John on the head and went out without even a good night.

He watched the door close behind her, then he looked down at his dog. "That went well."

John's brown eyes were all sympathy.

Henry knocked twice and walked in, smirking. "You can direct Fredo's next paycheck to me," he said. "Your perfect record's been broken."

"Since when have you started betting on my sex life?"

"Since it finally got interesting. Tell me, how does it feel to strike out for once in your charmed life?"

It felt like shit, but he wouldn't give Henry the satisfaction.

"If you're done gloating," he said, heading for the bedroom.

"Not nearly." Henry rubbed his hands together. "But I'll pause long enough to tell you I spoke to Gio."

"And?"

"It's definitely an inside job. External security was never breached. Not the perimeter, not the villa. The only system affected was the alarm that should've triggered when the painting was lifted off the wall. It had to be overridden from inside the villa."

"Well, fuck me." Adam dragged his hands through

his hair. He'd tear the thieving bastard apart. "Gio doesn't know who did it?"

"Not yet." Henry paused. "Maybe not ever."

"Unacceptable. There must be electronic finger-prints."

"The only fingerprints of any kind are yours."

Adam swore again. "When Hawthorne hears this, he'll never pay up." But the money was insignificant beside the breach of trust. "I want the fucker, Henry. I want my hands around his ever-fucking throat."

He took a breath, thought it through. "Maribelle?"

"She hasn't the skills, Adam. All she knows how to do is spend your money."

"She hates me enough to pay someone to do it."

Henry shrugged, acknowledging the obvious. "But if you caught her, she knows you'd boot her out. Why kill the goose that lays the golden eggs?"

"People do all kinds of things for hate. More than they do for love."

"You wouldn't say that if you'd ever been in love."

Adam wasn't so sure. But he couldn't argue with the fact that love had eluded him. Of the handful of women who stood out in his memory, his infatuation with each had been short-lived, and in Maribelle's case, disastrous.

"My money's on Maribelle," he said. "You can put up your next paycheck. If I'm wrong, I'll double it."

He dug out his phone, put through a call to Gio and grilled him. When he got nothing new, he issued an icy reminder. "I want the bastard who fucked with me. Turn everyone at the villa inside out. And look hard at Maribelle."

"She's at the top of our list." Gio paused. "Sir, about Ms. St. Clair. We found no reports of sexual assault in her youth. No abusive boyfriends either."

"You've gone back through her teens?"

"All the way to the cradle. Her upbringing appears unremarkable. Her mother was a homemaker. Her father's been mayor for twenty-five years and sells real estate on the side. They were married for thirty-five years and lived together until her mother died. As far as we can tell, sir, she grew up in a nice middle-class home."

"Yes," Adam echoed, thoughtfully, "but you never know what's happening inside those nice middle-class homes."

"Would you like us to keep digging?"

"No." He'd get to the truth himself. "Put everything into finding the thief. And when you do"—he let himself relish the thought—"don't call the *polizia*. Save him for me."

"Amusing," Henry said after Adam hung up, "that you, of all people, are out for blood. Things have come full circle. Did your mother never teach you the Golden Rule? Do unto others . . ."

"My mother *did unto others* every day, which left her precious little time to teach me anything." He tossed his phone on the desk. "What I learned from my parents, I learned from watching them fuck up their lives. At the end of the day, I can only be glad they ignored me, or they'd have fucked me up too.

"As for your Golden Rule," he added, "it doesn't apply. I steal art for art's sake. The *Lady in Red* spent a hundred years under a sheet in a dusty French attic. She deserved better than the wall of Akulov's *dacha*."

He paced. "That thug was behind what happened to Rasheed, to his whole family. You know it as well as I do."

Rasheed was another old friend Adam hadn't been able to save, like Bridget's Ian and a handful of others who'd met a bad end before Adam had the means to change their lives. And none had a met harder end than Rasheed. Except Rasheed's daughter.

"Revenge, perhaps?"

Adam waved that away. "Akulov never believed I stole the *Lady*. He told me to my face that I don't have the guts. In any case, an eye for an eye wouldn't satisfy him. He'd have taken my hands, not my painting."

"Then it's personal."

"It has to be. The thief walked past six paintings as valuable as the Monet, and took only that one. Why?"

"It held pride of place. An obvious favorite."

"Exactly. Instead of waltzing out with a quarter billion in hand, he took only the painting I prized most highly."

"So it wasn't the painting he wanted. It was this." Henry swept a hand at the groove Adam was wearing in the carpet. "He wanted you to wonder, to worry. To think about him. Hunt for him." He shrugged again, eloquently. "He wanted your attention, and he got it."

"Yes, he did. As only someone aware of my *interest* in art would fully understand."

"Which makes you look at Maribelle." Henry shook his head. "She's too lazy. She wouldn't risk her soft life. And if she did, if she hired someone to get inside, it would be for profit. The subtlety of stealing only your favorite would be lost on her."

Henry made sense. Maribelle, his biggest mistake, was interested only in Maribelle. She wasn't likely to derail the gravy train, even to make a point.

But he wanted it to be her, the one person at the villa he didn't trust. The others were like Henry and Fredo, people who'd stood by him when they had nothing to gain. He trusted them, and tainting that trust was something Maribelle would savor.

He tried to shake off his black mood. "Any more on the Matisse? Do we know when they're moving it?"

"A week from tomorrow. I'll know the details forty-eight hours beforehand." Henry hesitated. "Perhaps you should let this one go."

Adam swung around, surprised. "And let Rosales have it? He traffics in children, for God's sake. He cleaned out the Brazilian orphanage." One of several operated by Adam's foundation. "They'll be in Thailand by now, those kids."

"It's bad, Adam. But you take it too personally."

"Like hell. I'm only taking the man's painting, not his balls, which would be far more satisfying."

"Even so, I think you should reconsider. Under the circumstances."

"Which are?"

"Maddie, of course. I don't understand why you're bringing her to the villa, where all your secrets are hidden. The *Lady in Red*. Maribelle. And your—"

"I'll keep Maddie occupied," Adam cut in. "As for Maribelle, tell her to keep to her villa while I'm there. Tell her," he added with an edge, "that if *anyone* wanders *anywhere* that Maddie might go, I'll hold Maribelle responsible. And she won't like the consequences."

CHAPTER ELEVEN

Vicky: I promise to work with you,
to help you achieve whatever
you want to accomplish.

Maddie: Unless it's stupid.

MADDIE WAS UP with the birds, squinting into the mirror at the shadows under her eyes. The tossing and turning was starting to show.

She hefted the bottle of sleeping pills. Through all her troubles, she'd never turned to drugs, legal or otherwise. Even so, she wished she'd taken a pill last night, because sleep might've helped her cope with the day ahead.

First, LeCroix planned to drag her into his New York office, allegedly to work, but more likely to find new and imaginative ways to humiliate her now that she'd spurned him.

Ha. If only he knew how she'd yearned to give in, so desperately that it spooked her into doing just the opposite, throwing a sopping blanket over his steamy seduction. Then, when he played the favor card, she'd had no choice but to throw it back in his face. Her brain she'd trade for money or favors, but her body wasn't for sale.

Turning away from the mirror, she let her shoulders sag.

Sucky as the morning promised to be, the afternoon shaped up just as ugly. Lucy, her favorite person in the world, the sister she lavished her love on, was due after lunch, and instead of scrounging museum passes and lining up show tickets, Maddie was looking down the barrel of an excruciating evening making nice to *Crash* when what she really wanted to do was go Pitbull on him.

And those were just today's dramas.

Tomorrow they'd fly to Italy.

Adam had postponed their departure for another day to accommodate Lucy's arrival, but already dread filmed Maddie's skin like sweat. Flying reduced her to a terrified child. That Adam would see her like that appalled her.

Then, when they landed—*if* they landed—the booby prize was a week at his villa, dancing to his tune every day, lusting for him every night, while Lucy, her sweet, innocent Lucy, threw her tender heart away on George Lemon.

The worst of it, what made it borderline unbearable, was that she'd lost control over her emotions. Bad enough was her anxiety over Lucy and Crash. But at least that was perfectly rational.

With Adam, though, she careened from lust to laughter to fury to frustration so quickly and unpredictably that she lost her footing completely.

She wanted desperately to hate him for what he'd done five years ago, for what he was doing now. But inexplicably, she didn't.

In fact, she kind of *liked* him.

That was another emotion she didn't know what to do with, besides keep it to herself.

Along with her hands. She *really* needed to keep those to herself. No more feeling up his arms. No stroking his chest while his tongue licked over every inch of her mouth.

No more kissing. None.

And absolutely, definitely, no sex. No matter how much she wanted him.

ADAM SUMMONED MADDIE to his office at half past ten.

She arrived with blood in her eye and a stack of papers in her hand. "What? I'm busy."

"Busy irritating everyone in my legal department," he said mildly. "My chief counsel asked to have you removed."

"Your chief counsel's an idiot." She waved the papers. "How the hell have you bought up half the free world with that nincompoop in charge?"

He moved away from the door to stand behind his desk, the power position. This office was his turf. She wasn't going to push him around here.

"You could come to work for me," he said. "Clean house. Build your own team."

"Not for a million bucks."

Now that was an insult. "You'd rather return to the unpleasant Adrianna?"

"At least she's not a felon."

His calm demeanor went out the window. He jabbed a finger at the second, much smaller, desk in the room. "Dyan sits there when I require her presence at a meeting. You'll find it has everything you need."

Her eyes slitted. "I'm not working in here with you."

"Oh yes, you are. You've pissed off everyone in the building. There's nowhere else for you to go."

She crossed her arms, tried to wait him out, completely unaware that her outthrust lip just begged to be bitten, that her hipshot stance tempted a normally civilized man to drag her off to his cave.

For a moment, just a moment, he pitied Michael Warren and every other man she'd seduced and then dropped. Well, damn it, she wouldn't use him the same way.

"Sit," he barked out, making John Doe jump up from his bed.

"Don't tell me what to do," she growled, all but daring him to spank her.

Enough was enough. Circling his desk, he scooped her up, all five-foot-nothing of her, and dumped her in the chair.

The look on her face was priceless. "You . . . you . . ."

"You asked for it," he said, walking back to his desk.

His phone rang. As he answered it, he shot her a no-bullshit glare that said to keep her smart mouth shut. "Yes, Dyan? Put him through." And swinging his chair around to face the fifty-story view, he got back down to business.

HE'D MANHANDLED HER, that's what he'd done. Picked her up like ninety pounds was nothing at all.

Well, no kidding. With arms like that, he could bench me like a barbell.

Yes, but he'd moved her against her will. Taken her from one spot and put her in another.

And wouldn't that be fun in bed. He could toss me around, tie me up.

Whoa. She shoved that picture out of her head. Bondage wasn't something Maddie dabbled in unless she was the one doing the binding.

Which just showed how dangerous Adam was. He pushed all kinds of buttons that were strictly off-limits.

Her eyes strayed to his desk, a mahogany U imposing enough to dominate even this monstrous office, studded with sleek monitors and a sleeker telephone console.

From a desk like that, he could launch the space shuttle, or World War III. And he looked perfectly capable of doing either, his chair tipped back as he rattled off projections and rates of return. It was gobbledygook to her; a second language to him.

What really sucked about the whole thing, what burned her ass, was that he looked so hot doing it. She wasn't normally drawn to the bespoke-suit, master-of-the-universe type. A sweaty fireman was more her style. But Adam, damn him, oozed virility. He was the exception to every rule.

He swung his chair around, catching her red-handed before she could quit ogling him. "You can talk to Willis about that," she heard him say, and then he ended the call.

He kept his gaze on her. Then he said her name. "Madeline."

She swallowed. "What?"

"Is there something you need?"

I need you naked, pinning me down on that big-ass desk.

"No, I'm good. I mean, not *good*, since I'm stuck here listening to you wheel and deal. But there's nothing I need from you. Not a damn thing."

His brows rose a hairsbreadth, as if he was on to her. She tore her gaze away, split the papers into two piles. "Like I was saying, your chief counsel's a nitwit. These insurance contracts"—she slapped a hand on one stack—"have holes in them you could fly your jet through. And these sales contracts"—she slapped the other stack—"aren't exactly my area, but they're funky."

He rose and walked toward her. "Funky? Is that a legal term?"

"It's a smell." She sniffed. "I just have to figure out where it's coming from."

Her desk wasn't half the size of Adam's, but it would have been wide enough to keep him at a safe distance if he hadn't come around to her side.

Leaning over, he spread the insurance contracts with one hand, scratched John's head with the other.

Maddie rolled her chair a foot away, giving herself some breathing room. He didn't wear cologne, but he had his own unique scent. He should bottle it and call it RichPowerfulSexy. He'd make another mint.

"I see what you mean," he said, skimming the high-lighted sections. "What can we do about it?"

"We—I mean *you*—can try to have the contracts amended. And change the language going forward." She slid her notepad under his nose. "It should read like that."

He read it over, then shifted those cobalt lasers to her. "Two million," he said.

"Nope." To get some distance, she rose and crossed the room to the credenza, poured a glass of ice water from the Baccarat pitcher.

"Five."

"Knock it off. You wouldn't pay me five million even if I'd take it."

He ambled toward her, hands in his pockets, but his tone was anything but casual. "I don't make promises

I'm not willing to keep. Five million and all the upper-management perks."

She circled behind the sofa, hating herself for being tempted. But hell, who wouldn't be tempted by five mil a year?

"Thanks," she said, "but I'll muddle along with my two hundred K. Chump change, I know, but it keeps me in chips."

He closed in, and she hit a dead end, trapped between the sofa and the wall, with him blocking her escape.

He stopped a foot from where she'd made her stand. His eyes, impossibly blue, searched her face. "You've backed yourself into a corner. Do I frighten you, Madeline?"

"Pfft. No."

"The pulse beating in your throat says differently." He took one hand from his pocket, laid his fingers against her skin. If her heart hadn't been racing before, it took off like a stallion now.

He moved a step closer, skimmed her jaw with those fingers. "Five million would solve so many problems," he murmured. "No more worries about money."

His whisper was a tropical breeze over her hot skin. His fingertip a feather on her lips.

She should pull away, but it felt so good, so paralyzingly sexy. His touch, his nearness, the heat in his eyes, all of it had silvery threads of desire slipping and sliding under her skin.

Then he lowered that seductive mouth, brushed it lightly against hers. "I can take care of you, Maddie. I can—oof!" He doubled over as she sank her fist in his gut.

"I'm not a hooker, LeCroix. You can't buy me." She shoved him aside, bulled her way past him. "Find some other way to get your rocks off, because it won't be by fucking your prosecutor."

THAT'S WHAT HE got for letting his dick do the talking.

Adam dropped into his desk chair and rubbed his stomach. He'd taken harder shots without flinching, but Maddie had caught him off guard. She always did.

He hit the intercom. "Which way did she go?" No need to specify who he meant. She would have stormed past Dyan like an F5 tornado.

"She tried to take your private elevator. When it wouldn't open without your thumbprint she, ah, employed some choice language, and then took one of the others."

He drummed his fingers on the desk. "Did you happen to notice where she went?"

"I checked the security cameras. She got off at forty-eight."

"Of course she did." The legal department.

"Oh, and sir? I have Mr. Brady on the line for you."

"Put him through." Adam massaged his temple. "What's the problem, Brady?" As if he didn't know. Brady was his chief counsel.

"She's back, that's the problem." Brady's asthma wheezed when he got worked up. "She's pissing everyone off. Alice just threw a stapler at her."

"Did it hit her?"

"No, but only because the little imp's light on her feet." He wheezed. "Seriously, Adam, she's got to go."

Tension drilled a fiery spike between Adam's shoulder blades. "Put her on the phone."

A minute passed while Adam stared out the window. He was looking at the Chrysler Building but seeing Maddie's face, up close as he'd seen it a few moments before.

It pulled him in, that face, the fine bones overlaid with satin skin, the steely eyes underscored with shadows from a sleepless night. She was beautiful and troubled and mad at the world. How could he not want to protect her?

She blasted his eardrum through the phone, making him wince. "What?"

He took a mild tone. "You're causing trouble in my legal department again."

"*I'm* causing trouble? These people are out of control. Alice just threw a stapler at me. A stapler! You're goddamn lucky she missed or you'd have a lawsuit on your hands, and these idiots wouldn't have a clue how to handle it."

The spike drilled deeper. His tone got sharper. "We're leaving now." He'd handle his calls from the penthouse. "Fredo has the limo out front. Go directly downstairs and get in. And for God's sake, don't say another word to anyone."

Hanging up the phone before she could backtalk him, he shoved a handful of folders into his briefcase and cursed her roundly under his breath.

And yet it was his own foolish fault for bringing her along. It was bound to be a disaster. Still, some stubborn part of him wanted her to acknowledge what he'd built, one of the biggest conglomerates in the world.

It would never happen. She couldn't care less. When she looked at him she didn't see the man the rest of the world saw. She saw a criminal, and a lecherous one at that.

And perversely, the fact that she was at least partially right only made him want her more.

He found her waiting in the limo, backed into the corner like he was contagious. John Doe hopped up on the seat and flopped his head on her lap. She gave him the adoring look Adam wanted for himself.

Knowing what he had to do didn't make it any easier. Best to get it done while he had her captive, and while John was there to keep a lid on things.

"Madeline, my offer had nothing to do with sex. I'm sorry if it came across that way. I realize I went too far. Blurred things together, made it sound ambiguous—"

"There was nothing ambiguous about it."

Frustration made him blunt. "Yes, all right, then. I wanted to take you against the wall. But that had nothing to do with the money. The five million was for work, not sex. And the offer stands."

For thirty silent seconds, he could have heard a pin drop. Then, "Thanks, but the answer's still no."

He released the breath he hadn't realized he was holding.

"Seriously, though," she went on, "you've got a weak link in Brady. He wants to get in Alice's pants, so she leads him around by his dick."

Feeling a moment's kinship with his chief counsel, Adam almost smiled. Then he sat back, relaxed for the first time all morning. "So, which one of them has to go?"

BRADY WAS OUT, Alice was in. "My work here is done," Maddie said, satisfied.

Adam smiled, devastatingly. "Only if you're sure you won't take the job yourself."

So tempting in so many ways. And unequivocally out of the question.

Looking away, she focused on John Doe, stretched out on the seat between them, all four feet in the air. "Parker has to see this." She dug out her phone, snapped a shot, and e-mailed it with a brief note about John.

When she looked up, Adam was eyeing her. "You seem close, you and Parker."

"I told you he's a good friend. Not that it's any of your beeswax."

His grin was ridiculously gorgeous. "I haven't heard that phrase before."

"Because you didn't grow up in the woods of New England."

"Far from it. What was it like?"

"A lot more provincial than your upbringing." He'd been everywhere; she'd been nowhere. Her one and only flight had been so disastrous that she'd written off the rest of the world as out of reach.

He shrugged in his uniquely European way. "Small-town life is usually portrayed as idyllic. You didn't find it so?"

"Not a bit." Short and sharp, to cut him off. She'd talk business with him all day, but no personal stuff.

He didn't take the hint. "You don't miss it? Your friends? Your family?"

"My friends are here. And my parents are dead." No way was she talking about her father, who, unfortunately, wasn't *actually* dead, just dead to her.

"We have that in common," he said. "We're orphans, alone in the world."

"I'm not alone. I have Lucy, and other people who matter to me."

His gaze was too steady, too penetrating, so she turned the tables. "You're not alone either, not with a different babe on your arm every weekend."

"Speaking of which." He pulled the *Post* from his briefcase, flopped it open. And there it was in black and white.

The sidewalk lip lock.

For ten humming seconds, she stared at the picture as every drop of blood drained out of her head. "You knew when you kissed me that this would happen."

Why did that hurt so much? Why, given their circumstances, did it feel like a betrayal?

"Actually," he said, tossing the paper on the seat across from them, "at that moment I wasn't thinking about paparazzi."

"Yeah, right." She went for sarcastic but it came out pathetic instead. She turned her face to the window, tried to wrangle her chaotic emotions. She was embarrassed in a dozen different ways, not least of which because she'd believed in that kiss. She'd believed Adam was, for that one moment, as overcome with desire as she was.

"I'm sorry, Maddie."

"Please." She hit the sarcastic note this time. "I'm sure you feel shitty about humiliating me publicly. You've got nothing but my best interests at heart."

She lowered the window so cool air hit her face. Outside, Fifth Avenue slid by. Saks and Lord & Taylor. High-heeled shoppers and ladies who lunch.

She refused to feel sad. Mad was better, easier. Adam had messed up her life. It hadn't been a perfect life, but it was hers. She'd lived it her way, made her own choices, for her own reasons.

"Maddie." He covered her hand where it rested on John's belly.

She shook him off. LeCroix held the purse strings; she was stuck with that. But no way was she letting him know she was into him, that he turned her on just by saying her name.

"We talked about this." His tone was firm. "It's better this way, if people think you've suddenly lost your head over me."

She thunked her skull against the window. He didn't know how true it was.

"It's better if your sister believes it too," he said.

That brought her head around. "I can't let Lucy think I'd fall for you! I'm not much of a role model, but I'm all she's got."

His eyes, that startling blue, went flat. "Surely you don't want her to know the real reason you're in my company."

Well, shit. If Lucy knew Maddie was sacrificing her pride and her future to pay for college, she'd withdraw from RISD on the spot.

"I-I'll have to think about it."

"While you're thinking, you might consider that she'll likely see our picture before she arrives. It's running in most of the usual news outlets."

He was right. "Don't people have anything better to give a shit about than who's banging Adam LeCroix?"

"Given our history, your name is as prominent as mine."

She glanced at the *Post*, still open to the story. Her original guess hadn't been far off. "Piranha Has Pitbull Eating Out of His . . . Hand."

"Why didn't they just say pants? That's what they meant."

"The *Post* would never be so uncouth."

She snorted, then trained her gaze out the window again. "I can't tell Lucy the whole truth, but I'm not pretending that you and I are a *thing*."

"Suit yourself. But we should get our stories straight."

She took a breath, thought it through. "Lucy was still in high school when you stole the *Lady in Red*. Odds are she doesn't remember much about the case. It wouldn't have been discussed at home."

"No? I'd think your parents would've been proud of their eldest daughter making international headlines."

She let that bait float past her. "She'll get the back-story now, of course. They'll dredge it up to go with the picture. But you and me, we'll play it down."

She relaxed as the story unwound. "I'll tell her we were never archenemies, it was just media bullshit to sell newspapers, blah blah. The whole thing ended amicably, which the press never bothered to report because where's the story in that? So when you needed someone to help you with this insurance thing, you naturally thought of me."

"And the kiss?"

"A dare." She liked that idea. "Yeah, your buddy Dakota dared you to kiss the Pitbull, just to see if she'd chew your tongue out." She laughed. "Lucy's smart. Once she meets you, she'll know you'd never turn down a dare."

"I'll take that as a compliment," he said, dryly, "since I'm not likely to get another from you."

"Or another kiss either." She showed her teeth. "Next time you try it, I'll bite."

CHAPTER TWELVE

"Maddiiiieee!" Lucy swallowed her sister in a bear hug.

"Hi, Luce," Maddie mumbled into Lucy's armpit.

Adam grinned. Maddie hadn't mentioned that Lucy had six inches and thirty pounds on her.

Lucy released her, did a twirl around the penthouse foyer, her flouncy skirt billowing around her thighs. "Ohmygod, this place is gorgeous!"

Then she stilled. "Is . . . is that a Rodin?" She took a hesitant step toward the bronze figure mounted on a marble pedestal.

"Yeah," Maddie said like it was no big deal. "Adam's got art coming out of his ass."

"Not quite," he said, stepping forward, "but if you're fond of Rodin, there's a bust in the gallery you might enjoy."

Maddie's mouth twisted into a smile. "Lucy, meet Adam LeCroix. This is his place. One of them, anyway."

"It's lovely to meet you," he said, shaking Lucy's hand, so much larger than Maddie's. They hardly looked like sisters. Lucy's strawberry blond hair was straight as a pin and parted like silk around her shoulders. And her eyes, the incandescent blue-green of the Mediterranean, danced with humor and delight.

"Thanks for having us." She skipped a few steps away to stand beside the lanky young man who'd stepped off the elevator with her. His streaky blond hair touched his shoulders, his jeans were frayed at the knees, and his black leather jacket gapped open over a vintage Metallica T-shirt.

Beaming like the sun, Lucy slipped a slender arm around his waist. "Mads, this is Crash."

She announced it like she'd won the blue ribbon and knew her sister would be so proud.

Adam cut a look at Maddie. She stood perfectly still, steely eyes assessing the guy. Crash took it like a man, didn't flinch or shuffle. Instead, he tipped his lips up on one side, a question as much as a smile, like he knew he was being weighed and measured and was curious, but not nervous, about the verdict.

Realizing the stalemate could go on all night, Adam put a hand on Maddie's back and carried her forward with him. "A pleasure," he said, shaking Crash's hand. Then he pinched Maddie, not hard enough to make her jump, just enough to irritate her into action.

"Hi, *Crash*," she said, just this side of a sneer. She did a quick, hard shake that Crash seemed to take in stride.

"Lucy talks about you all the time," he said in a warm tenor more mature than his lean face. "It's great to finally meet you." And he broke into a heart-melting smile.

Unfortunately for Crash, Maddie was immune to heart-melting smiles, as Adam could attest. The smile she returned was more of a bone crusher.

The resilient Crash let it roll off like rain. To Adam, he said politely, "Thanks for taking us along to Italy. We're real excited about it."

"Yeah, thanks," Lucy said. She smiled conspiratorially. "What drugs are you giving Maddie to get her on the plane?"

Drugs? Adam looked at Maddie; she'd gone cherry red. She wouldn't meet his eyes, seemed to have lost her tongue.

Why hadn't she said she was afraid of flying? It was nothing to be ashamed of. Yet here she was, terrified, and too proud to tell him.

"My Gulfstream hardly feels like an airplane," he said, keeping his tone casual, hoping to allay her fears. "More like an apartment. And my pilots are the best in the business."

Lucy reached out and rubbed Maddie's arm. "I'll be right there, Mads. We'll hold hands all the way."

"Pfft." Maddie managed a sickly smile. "I'll be fine."

Crash gave Lucy a squeeze. "Don't worry, babe. Your sister doesn't look like she scares easy." He tipped his head at Maddie, a friendly half smile on his good-looking face. "In fact, she looks like she'll chew a hole in the plane if it gives her any shit."

That startled a laugh out of Maddie.

Lucy laughed too. "You have no idea. Maddie's not into subtlety. One time at this bar, Blue-something, I can't remember the name, these really obnoxious drunk guys kept hitting on us. They wouldn't quit, so Maddie had this idea, and on three, we pulled out their pants and poured our cosmos down the front. It was *hilarious*!"

Lucy caught Maddie's hand, an unconscious show of affection. "We were laughing our asses off, because, you know, cosmos are really sugary, so their balls would be sticking to their—"

"We get the picture," Crash cut in.

"All too well," Adam said. He was glad to see the sisterly love flow both ways. "Maddie, darling, why don't we show Lucy and Crash to their rooms?"

Maddie pounced on it. "Come on, Luce, you're right next to me." She led the way, saying over her shoulder, "Crash, you're at the other end of the hall."

Lucy sent Crash an I-told-you-so eye roll. He sent back a don't-worry-babe wink.

And envy snuck up and stabbed Adam where it hurt.

He wasn't used to envying anybody, much less a stripling like Crash. But the world had upended in the last forty-eight hours, and unless something set it to rights before bedtime, the new reality was that while the boy spent the night balls deep in a beautiful woman, Adam would be stuck with the palm of his hand.

LUCY PLOPPED ON Maddie's sofa and patted the cushion. "Quit pacing and sit with me. Did you know all the green in here brings out your eyes?"

"Mmm." Maddie sat. "So. What's the deal with Crash?" She was going for girl chat, but even she heard the edge in her voice. She cleared her throat like a frog was to blame, crossed her legs like she was relaxed.

"He's hot," she said, trying again. And it was true. Blond hair, blue eyes, and that wicked cute smile. He had heartbreaker written all over him.

"Isn't he gorgeous?" Lucy sighed. "And so sweet. He's always doing little things, like bringing me Milk Duds. You know how I love them. And he cooks." She let her head fall back. "Red sauce like you Would. Not. Believe."

Maddie could hardly blame her sister for falling for food when she'd practically sold her own soul for carbonara. But still.

"Cooking is good. But"—she couldn't help herself— "he's in a band, right? So there must be girls."

Lucy gave her a look. "He's not fooling around on me. He wouldn't, and anyway, I'd be able to tell."

"All women think they'd be able to tell. Look at Vicky. She didn't know Winston-the-shit-stain was cheating until we walked in on him banging her secretary."

"Totally different situation. Winston was a jerk from the get-go. I don't know what Vicky ever saw in him."

"True. But Crash is *in a band*."

"And Adam LeCroix is *an international playboy*."

"So?"

"So, the guy's a player, Mads. Why would you get involved with him?"

"I'm not involved. I'm working for him. See?" She waved an arm. "I've got my own suite. It's just business."

"Baloney. I saw you kissing him on TV."

"No." Maddie shook her head. "We're just . . . that was a dare. That kissing thing was a dare. His . . . his friend dared him." She sounded like a guilty teenager.

"Right. Adam LeCroix stuck his tongue down your throat on a dare. And now you'll tell me you hated it. That's why you were fighting him off *with your arms around his neck*."

A knock on the door rescued Maddie from that one. Bridget stuck her head in. "Dinner in twenty minutes."

Lucy got to her feet. "Thanks, Bridget. And thanks for unpacking my stuff. But you really didn't have to. We're leaving tomorrow."

"I'm not sure about that, ma'am. I heard Mr. LeCroix tell Henry to cancel the flight."

Maddie shot to her feet. "What the f—" She headed for the door. "I'll see you at dinner, Luce. I need to talk to Adam."

She hammered Adam's door, then barged into his suite. "Listen, LeCroix— Oh jeez." She covered her eyes. "Do you have to walk around like that?"

"Without a shirt? In my own suite? Call me an exhibitionist."

She dropped her hand. At least his junk was in his jeans.

"Listen." She focused on a point somewhere over his left shoulder. His broad, tanned, beautifully defined left shoulder. "Bridget said you canceled the flight."

"That's true. I changed my mind. We'll work from here."

She gritted her teeth. "You did it because of what Lucy said. About me not liking to fly."

He came toward her. She couldn't help dropping her eyes, first to his face, then lower, to his chest, and lower, to his—

She forced them up again. He caught them, held them, closing the distance until she had to tip her head back.

"Madeline."

Why did her name, which she'd never really liked in any of its forms, sound so exotic, so thrilling on his tongue?

"Darling."

Why did that casual term of endearment that had pissed her off two days ago now sound perfectly natural to her ear?

His fingertip traced her brow. "I wish you'd told me."

Why did she stay perfectly still instead of stepping away from his touch?

"I don't want to see you frightened."

Okay, spell broken. "I'm not *frightened*, okay? I get a little nervous, that's all. Only an idiot wouldn't worry about flying over the Atlantic in a tuna can. Maybe you're an idiot, but I'm not. And we're *going* to Italy."

His lips quirked, amused. "You've fought it for days. I finally concede, and now you're insisting we go. Why? Because I'll think less of you?"

"Pfft. I don't care what you think of me." *Liar, liar, pants on fire.* "We're going because you got Lucy excited about it, that's why."

He shrugged that perfect left shoulder. "They can go without us."

"Oh no." She shook her head. "That kid's hot and he knows it, and Lucy's crazy about him. If I'm not there, they'll be banging like bunnies."

"They'll be banging like bunnies anyway. Do you honestly think you can keep them apart? And really, why would you want to?"

"Why?" It was the stupidest question ever. "You've met Lucy. She's . . . she's magical. Untouched." Circling around him, she paced to the fireplace where John Doe snored peacefully, supper bulging his belly.

"If it was just sex, I wouldn't think twice about it," she said. "But she's *involved* with him. *Emotionally* involved."

He sent her a baffled look. "You'd prefer she have meaningless sex with men she doesn't care about?"

"Of course not. Well, maybe." She waved her arms. "You're not getting it. No boy's ever hurt her, and I don't want some doper musician with a perpetual hard-on to steal her heart and break it."

"Why do you think he'll break her heart? Maybe she'll break his."

She pointed a finger at him. "I told you, you don't get it. You've never been in love."

He pointed a finger back at her. "Neither have you."

She opened her mouth to retort, closed it again. Then, "I know people who've been in love. They get hurt." She nodded along with herself. "Or they get married and *then* they get hurt, and then they're stuck because they've got a couple of squalling brats—"

"Is that what happened to your mother? Were you and Lucy the squalling brats?"

It hit her like an openhanded slap. She fell back a step, landed on John's tail. He shot to his feet with a yowl.

"Oh Jesus." She dropped to her knees, put her arms around him, but he was already apologizing for his overreaction, licking her cheek, bumping against her so she landed on her butt.

"I'm sorry, John." Tears geysered up; she couldn't swallow them fast enough. She pressed her face into his fur, tried to hide her disgrace from Adam, but how could she, when he'd dropped to the floor beside her?

He reached out to stroke her hair. She ducked away from his hand. "Stop it," she snapped. "John's the one who's hurt."

"Is he, now?" He ran his other hand over John's back, but kept his gaze on her. "Then why are you the one crying?"

"Because I hurt him, that's why." She lashed it out like a wounded animal. John let out a soft whine. "And stop making me snap at you. It upsets him, for God's sake."

To her everlasting shame, a sob racked her. She fisted her hands till the nails dug into her skin. Damn it to hell, why did she have to start bawling? Why did Lucy have to grow up and fall in love? Why did people have to turn their cruelty on innocent animals like John? Why, oh why, did Adam have to smell so good?

It was too much for her. Too much. Her circuits overloaded, the last shreds of control slipped.

She gave up and let him pull her into his arms.

"RISOTTOOOOO!" LUCY PRACTICALLY bounced in her seat as Bridget set the plate before her. "I love risotto! It's Maddie's fave too."

"Is it?" Adam feigned surprise. He sat at the head of

the mile-long table, Maddie on his right and Lucy on his left, with Crash beside her.

"Totally." Lucy slid a forkful between her lips, rolled her eyes back. "Ohmygod, it's yummy. Mads, can you believe it?"

"Yep, it's delicious," Maddie said, but Adam thought she seemed more interested in her wine. She hadn't met his eyes since taking her seat. Somehow she'd erased the crying jag from her face. Looking at her, no one would know that twenty minutes before, she'd been sobbing in his arms.

For about ten seconds, that is, before she bolted from his suite.

"Good stuff," Crash decreed, digging in with a twenty-one-year-old's appetite. He polished it off and looked around for seconds, obviously disappointed when Bridget cleared his plate.

"Filet mignons for the next course," Adam informed him. "All you can eat." He nodded discreetly to Bridget, who disappeared into the kitchen to tell Leonardo to butcher another cow.

"Excellent." Crash grinned appealingly. He draped his arm across Lucy's chair and stroked her neck with two fingers, the move so casual it implied a much deeper level of intimacy.

Maddie glugged her wine.

Adam was contemplating just how drunk he could in good conscience allow her to get, when Henry stepped through the door. "Mr. Rain," he intoned, and stepped aside so Dakota could stride into the room.

"I know I'm late," he boomed out in his famous twang, "but the first two stores I stopped at didn't stock Brunello."

Adam eyed him unhappily. "I uninvited you, remember?"

Dakota flapped a big, bronzed hand. "Aw, I knew you were jokin'." He dropped a kiss on Maddie's blushing cheek, then reached across the table to shake Lucy's hand. "Dakota Rain," he said, striking her dumb.

"That's Lucy," Maddie said. "My sister."

"You're kidding me." Dakota busted out a laugh. "I called that one, didn't I, darlin'? But you didn't mention she's got a boyfriend."

"Yeah. That's Crash."

Dakota clasped his hand in a friendly shake. Crash nodded politely, but he didn't look thrilled with Hollywood's heartthrob.

Adam knew exactly how he felt.

Dakota settled into the seat next to Maddie, held up his hands to let Bridget slide a place setting in front of him. "Thank you, darlin'," he said with a smile that made her titter. "Do me a favor, will you, and tell Leonardo he doesn't have to catch me up. I'll just take two of whatever's next. And bring me a corkscrew, will you? I gotta get Adam drunk before he tosses me out for flirting with his woman."

"I'm not his woman," Maddie piped up. "I'm his lawyer."

Adam held his tongue. What could he say? It was true.

"Is that so?" Dakota sent Adam a game-on look, scooted his chair an inch closer to hers. "How long you staying in New York?"

"I live here." She'd lost interest in her wine, Adam noted, batting her eyes at Dakota like a starlet.

"Then maybe you can help me out. See, I've got this thing tomorrow night—"

"We're leaving tomorrow," Adam cut in. "For Italy."

"We are?" Lucy tore her big blues away from Dakota. "I thought you canceled the trip."

"Maddie talked me out of it." Adam smiled tightly, feeling guilty, but not guilty enough to let Dakota get his hands on her.

"Well, that's too bad." Dakota uncorked the wine, poured a round into the fresh glasses Bridget provided. He clinked his glass to Maddie's, smiling all over her. "But I'm filming here all summer, darlin'. We'll get together when you come back."

It infuriated Adam, the way Dakota just assumed Maddie would fall into bed with him. The fact that he was right only pissed him off more.

Before he could say something stupid, Crash took his shot. "I'm a big fan of your brother's," he said, earnestly. "He's a hell of an actor."

Dakota sat back in his chair, gave Crash another look, like he was seeing him for the first time. Adam did the same, growing fonder of the kid by the minute.

Then Dakota nodded, every bit as earnest. "He sure is. I hate to say it, seeing as how he's my little brother and all, but he can act circles around me."

"That's *so* not true." Lucy leaned forward so abruptly Crash's hand slipped from her neck. "You were *unbelievable* in *Cry for Me*. We watch that movie *every single time* I come to visit, and we *always* cry when you have your breakdown, don't we, Mads?"

Maddie nodded vigorously. "That part when you're holding the knife . . . It just kills me." She put her hand on her heart.

"And when the police come and take you . . . your expression . . . God . . ." Lucy actually sniffled.

"I still can't believe you didn't win the Oscar," Maddie huffed. "You were robbed."

"Totally," Lucy said with feeling.

Adam caught Crash's eye, his grim expression. The women had circled the wagons around Dakota, who, in another Oscar-worthy performance, was playing the aw-shucks role to a T.

Even his twang hit a humble note. "I sure hate to disagree with a couple of intelligent beauties like yourselves, but Denzel deserved it that year." He shrugged a shoulder wistfully, topped off their glasses. "Maybe I'll get another crack at it someday."

"Oh, you will!" Lucy's wide eyes overflowed with encouragement.

Maddie nodded along. "Another role like that and the Academy will *have* to recognize your talent."

Her hand patting *poor* Dakota's arm pushed Adam over the edge. He gave a snort of disgust that brought both women's heads around.

They glared at him with identical offended expressions, which pissed him off enough that he made the same rookie mistake Crash was still regretting.

"Before you ladies waste anymore sympathy on Dakota, you should know that behind his self-deprecating facade he's imagining a ménage with both of you."

Maddie's lip curled. "That's disgusting. You're just jealous."

Oh, that was the last straw. His blood pressure spiked. "Jealous, you say? Why would I be jealous?"

"Because Dakota's famous and handsome and hot," she shot back.

His temper sizzled like fat on a fire. "Is that why you're throwing yourself at him?"

"I'm not throwing myself at him." She scorched him with burning eyes. "I'm enjoying the company of a nice man who's *not* an egomaniac."

"I'll differ with you there," he scoffed, ignoring their spellbound audience. "But that's beside the point."

"And what *is* the point?"

"The point is—" He stopped. What *was* the point? It had nothing to do with Dakota, that much he knew.

He leaned back in his chair, took a deep, slow breath. The infuriating woman knew just how to get a rise out of him.

But there was a pattern at work, he realized, in the still-sane corner of his brain. And now that he saw it, things finally made sense.

He'd shared a moment with Maddie in his suite, a moment where she let down her guard. That vulnerability scared the hell out of her. So she lashed out.

The same thing had happened the morning after they shared carbonara. And again after the gala. It happened whenever mutual desire flared up between them.

It was her defense mechanism. Each time she softened up and let him get close to her, she reacted by pulling back farther. Hitting back harder. Building her walls higher.

He scared her, he realized, not because he'd threatened her livelihood, but because he threatened her defenses.

It was a startling, and heartening, revelation. The harder she slapped at him, the deeper he'd gotten under her skin.

Viewed through that lens, the day had been a rousing success.

And the night ahead didn't look quite so hopeless after all.

CHAPTER THIRTEEN

Vicky: I promise to try not to hurt you,
and if I do, I promise to say I'm sorry.

Maddie: But not without
talking to my lawyer first.

MADDIE WASN'T THE only St. Clair who moved on
little cat feet. Lucy was halfway to Crash's room before
Maddie realized her sister had snuck past her door.

Legging it down the hallway after her, eyes focused
on her quarry, she nearly leaped out of her slippers
when a door whipped open behind her and a figure
darted out. Before she could yelp, a hand muzzled her
mouth, an arm circled her waist, and she was lifted off
the floor and hauled backward into her own darkened
suite.

Her abductor kicked the door closed and leaned
back against it, setting her feet on the floor but clamp-
ing her tight to his chest. In another time or place, she
would have been terrified. Now her heart drummed
not with fear, but with fury.

"Darling." Adam's voice, amused, tickled her ear. "You really don't want to follow her."

"Yes, I do!" she shouted.

His hand muffled it to "Mmm, m mm!"

She tried biting his fingers but he'd cupped his hand just enough that she couldn't sink her teeth in.

Frustrated, she kicked his shin, but her slipper skidded off denim. She stomped his toes, but the wily bastard had worn shoes.

His voice was a silky caress against her straining throat. "I've got a hundred pounds on you, darling. You're not going anywhere."

Quivering with thwarted violence, she threw every cussword she knew against the palm of his hand. God help him when she got loose. He'd see what ninety pounds of pissed-off Pitbull could do.

For the moment, though, she was helpless.

And the totally fucked up thing was, some perverse part of her *liked* it.

This was why she'd resisted him. Even more than the felon thing, his wicked way of making her like things she shouldn't like, want things she shouldn't want, was too dangerous, too unpredictable.

Like now. The arm at her waist slid down so his strong hand gripped her hip, lifting her, pinning her against his erection, hard and huge. She should be panicking. Instead, flames licked her skin. Heat flooded her core.

She wanted . . . she wanted . . .

No!

Wriggling like a snake, she tried to slither from his grasp. He sucked a breath through his teeth. "Do that again. Please." Jacking her higher, he pressed against her.

And her ass, her traitorous ass, lifted into him.

This was wrong, wrong. She should be fighting him. She slapped at his arm. But then his teeth scraped her earlobe, and the moan she let out was nothing about resistance, and all about *take me*.

It seemed to unleash him, that moan. He turned her head, exposing her throat, pulling her tighter as he sank into the long muscle of her neck, holding it in his teeth, predator and prey, growling as she quivered, waiting to be devoured.

His hand tunneled down into her nightshirt, his rough palm scraping her nipple, his fingers working her breast greedily. It sapped the last of her fight.

Giving in to lust, she reached around behind him, digging her nails into his thigh muscles, pulling him closer, closer. She would have pulled him under her skin if she could have. His name slipped from her lips. She begged him, begged him, to do something, anything. To give her more, more.

"Christ," he rasped, spinning her roughly, turning them both so her back hit the door. He jerked her shirt up, her panties down. Sucked a nipple into his mouth, sank his fingers inside her. "Jesus," as she flooded his palm.

He pulled out, drawing a moan straight from her core. Took her mouth, swallowed it with his lips, then filled her again, more fingers, faster, driving her higher.

His lips dragged across her cheek, he breathed fire in her ear. "Spread your legs. Let me in."

"You're in. God, you're in." She panted it out as tension coiled and built.

"Wrap your legs around me. Take me inside."

"Yes." She moaned it. "Yes. Yes." Nothing mattered now except fucking him. She kicked off the panties that chained her ankles, clawed at his buckle, his zipper. "Condoms," she gasped. "I don't—"

"I do."

Frantic with need, she worked his jeans over his hips as his teeth tore through foil. She reached for him, desperate to feel him, to handle him, but he batted her away.

"Later," he got out through gritted teeth. "I'll come if you touch me."

"No don't, not yet." She wrapped her arms around his neck, tried to climb him like a tree. His breath hissed through his teeth as he rolled on the condom.

Then his hands scooped her ass, lifting her, spreading her, and oh, thank you Jesus, he drove hard and deep, one thrust that filled her, that nailed her to the door.

He was big, so big, but she was soaking wet. Arching, she took him deeper, lifting her hips, riding him, thighs gripping his waist, ankles twist-tied behind him.

The darkness made it dreamlike; he could have been anyone, a stranger, a madman. But he was all Adam, his animal scent, his muscle-roped arms. She raked his biceps with her nails, scraped the length of his forearms, bulging with the strain.

Pumping harder, he found her mouth, bit her lip. "Come with me," he panted, "come all over my cock."

"Yes," she said again, as wild as he was. "So close. Don't stop." She threw her head back, whacked the door and didn't notice, as every cell, every sensation spiraled down, coiled tighter . . .

She heard her own voice cry out as the orgasm shook her, heard Adam's voice too, drawing out her pleasure, telling her he'd fuck her all night, that he wouldn't stop. Again he slammed into her, again, and again, and one last time.

Then his fingers flexed, digging into her cheeks. His

muscles, every one, went hard as iron. He threw back his head, neck arching, tendons rigid.

His knees buckled, and gave. And locked together, they slid down the door to the floor.

OPENING HIS EYES, Adam got his bearings, not unhappy to discover himself cross-legged on the floor with Maddie straddling his lap, still impaled on his cock.

Before he had time to savor the sensation, she started to stir. Cinching his arms around her, he stroked a hand over her head where it rested in the notch of his shoulder.

"Give it a minute," he murmured into her hair, and she surprised him by letting her taut little body relax. He hummed his appreciation, enjoying it while it lasted. Soon enough she'd start squirming again, trying to get away from him, to brush him off like lint.

Well, good luck with that. Whatever was between them, the heat, the connection, demanded to be explored.

She'd want no part of it, of course. She'd laugh in his face, tell him to grow up. She'd claim it was just sex, a one-off with no strings, no emotion. But he'd had plenty of just-sex, and never was it like this. Never had he wanted every part of a woman, her body, her heart, her sharp edges, her venom.

Not even with Maribelle, who he'd once imagined he loved, had he felt this desire to have it all.

Maybe he was a fool, the moth to Maddie's flame. But he hadn't gotten this far in life by playing it safe. He took chances. Now he'd take one on her.

Whether she liked it or not.

And she wouldn't. She was still hung up on the *Lady in Red*. And more than that, she was hung up on relationships.

On that score, he had little room to talk. He hadn't given a woman more than a weekend in ten years. And if he'd been looking for a girlfriend, he wouldn't have looked at Maddie. They couldn't be more different, the prosecutor and the thief.

Perhaps that was the fascination. She was black and white; he was shades of gray. She was all about right and wrong; he zigzagged across the line.

Whatever it was, this thing between them was powerful stuff. He'd tried to say no to it, and couldn't.

Now was the moment to begin convincing her to say yes to it too, to show her how good they could be. She was loose and limber, wrapped around him like spaghetti.

Right where he wanted her.

Her nightshirt had flopped down over her back. He slid his hands up under it, a soft stroke up to her shoulders, then down again over the swells of her ass. She didn't object.

Up again, thumbs grazing her breasts. She didn't balk, didn't quibble. She let him play with her, let him thumb her nipples lightly until they tightened to perfect peaks.

They were just right, her breasts, just a handful, all he wanted. He palmed them, felt the pulse in his cock, the erection that hadn't fully gone away.

He'd have to shift her, withdraw, dig a new condom from his pocket. Not that they needed protection. He'd seen her medical record—Gio was nothing if not thorough—and it was as clean as his own. But he needed her to tell him that in her own time, and to trust him when he told her the same. That was something that couldn't be rushed.

So for now, he'd allow a thin layer of latex between them. But soon even that would have to go.

Rubbing his jaw along her temple, he smiled, smugly.

She was docile as a lamb, enjoying his handling but too proud to let him know it.

Her pride amused him; he loved that about her. And he hated to nudge her along before she was ready. But things were getting dicey. His growing erection had to be dealt with. And when he'd taken it in hand, sheathed it anew, then he'd take her to bed, make her writhe, make her . . .

Snore?

He took her shoulders, sat her up. She blinked at him blearily. Then her focus sharpened, her eyes narrowed to slits. "What?" she said, annoyed as ever.

"You're asleep." Indignation made his voice rise an octave.

"I *was*. You woke me up." She flattened her palms on his chest, pushed back to arm's length. A shaft of light from the bedroom slanted across her knotted brow. "Grab ahold of that thing"—she pointed her chin at the condom—"because I'm getting up."

"For Christ's sake," he muttered, doing as she asked. "Is that the best you can do after getting fucked against a door?"

She scrambled to her feet, leaving him on the floor, hard-on poking up stubbornly from the V of his jeans.

Tugging her nightshirt down over everything he'd handled so confidently, she tossed her head. "What the hell do you think you're doing in here?"

"Do I really have to explain it?" He scraped together the tatters of his pride. "We just made love."

"Pfft. You mean we had *sex*. A quickie. Slam, bam, thank you ma'am. Now scram." She jerked a thumb at the door.

He clambered to his feet, hamstrung by his sagging jeans. Hoisting them, but not zipping them, he shook back his hair. "No."

She goggled at him. "No? No?" She stuck out her chin. "Yes. And make it snappy. I've got things to do." She scooped up her panties, reached for the doorknob.

He caught her arm, yanked her up against him. "You're not pestering your sister. Not under my roof."

Wrong thing to say. Steam whistled out of her ears. *"Don't you dare—"*

He kissed her. He had no choice. Her mouth was right there in front of him, tempting, irresistible. She jerked her head, but he splayed a hand on the back of it, crushing her lips, tasting her fury.

Living dangerously, erotically, he thrust his tongue past her teeth. He didn't care if she bit it as long as he had something inside her.

She moaned in spite of herself, hooked his tongue with hers even as she tried to twist away; ground her hips against his even as she shoved at his chest. She was a mess, a snake pit of contradictions.

He was wild for her.

"Bed," he mumbled against her lips.

"No," she got out, but he swallowed it, scooped an arm under her butt and carried her off anyway.

Her bed was untouched. He tossed her in the middle. She bounced up on her knees and he knocked her back with his body. She hit the pillows. He landed on top of her.

"Get off me, you big ox." She whacked his shoulder with a sharp fist.

He levered up on his elbows, looked down into her snarling face. "Maddie." His voice was gentle but firm. "I'm going to kiss you again."

"Like hell! This is sexual assault and you're going down for it."

Her face was puce, but he knew the difference between fury and arousal. He dropped his chin, held her eyes. They glowed sea green in the bedside light.

"I won't hurt you, Maddie. I'll never hurt you." He let it sink in, then, "Kiss me once. Just once. Then I'll leave if you want me to."

Trembling like a leaf, pupils dilated with desire, she swallowed, convulsively. Nodded her head half an inch.

And with everything hanging on it, everything balanced on the head of a pin, he dipped his head, took her lips.

He held back this time, chained the animal within, and kissed her softly, licking inside, nipping lightly at her swollen lips.

She lay perfectly still, clutching the blanket, rigid with tension. And he sank deeper, still gentle, but his tongue wanted inside. She let it stroke hers, let it learn the shape of her teeth.

His hand came up to cup her cheek. His thumb grazed her jaw, touched the corner of her mouth. Then pushed inside.

A wanting sound hummed in her throat. It vibrated through her chest, quivered her limbs. He felt it run through her; it ran through him too, resonating on a primal plane. He held on to himself by one fraying thread, moving nothing but his lips, his tongue, and that thumb.

She fought him on a cellular level; he felt the battle in the sweaty sheen on her skin. She didn't know it yet, but she'd lost before she'd begun. When she'd stepped into that conference room, she was his.

He stroked his thumb along the silky inside of her cheek; she shook harder, moaned deeper. And then her tongue surrendered, circling his thumb. Her hands came off the bed, fisting his hair, dragging him down, down.

Rolling with her, he pulled her over to straddle him, shoved her shirt up until she sat back on her haunches and yanked it off. He reached for her breasts, those perfect handfuls crying out to be palmed, but she went up on her knees and hooked his jeans with her fingers, backing up, dragging them down until he kicked them away.

Then she crawled up his body, lips parted, eyes dark. "T-shirt. Off."

He obeyed, then caught her arms and pulled her down, tits to chest, skin on skin. He slid one hand through her hair, wrapped the other around her ass, fingers dipping into wet heat. "Fuck," he breathed.

"Definitely," she gasped out, squirming against his hard cock as she groped through his pockets.

His laugh was a panting, desperate sound. "Wait. I want to taste you."

She tore foil with her teeth. "Later."

"Swear it."

"On a stack of bibles." She sat up, rolled it on. Then her eyes rolled back as she mounted him. "Nice. Cock."

"All yours, all night." His eyes feasted on her, so slender, so lithe, glistening with sweat as she rode him. She dropped forward, hands flat on his chest, perfect breasts within reach. "Open your eyes." He needed to see her as he palmed her, needed her to see him.

"Shut up," she panted. "Keep doing that and shut up."

"No." He surged up and rolled her, put her on her back, pinned her with his chest. The shock on her face made him grin savagely. Her eyes were damn well open now.

Stroking, never stopping, he dipped down, bit her

jaw. She turned her head; he turned it back. "Used to calling the shots, aren't you?" He stroked in and out. "Keep the boys begging, that's the way you do it. But not with me, Maddie. Not with me."

"Don't—"

He cut her off, took her mouth. Jammed his tongue in and stroked in rhythm with his cock. Her nails dug into his ass, a painful grip that barely registered. He was lost in her, lost in fucking her, lost in taking her, breaking her.

He never slowed, never changed his rhythm, let her fight her inner battle, let her surrender on her own terms. And when she did, when she caved in and circled him with her legs, pumped her hips up to meet his, then everything, everything in him aligned with everything in her, a cosmic rhythm, the very beat of their hearts.

His hand pushed down between them, found her center, her core, and stroked it exactly as he knew she'd want it. And when she came, screaming, he pumped himself into her, taking her, and losing himself.

CHAPTER FOURTEEN

MADDIE NEVER TWITCHED when Adam slipped from her bed. For a long moment, he stood over her, watching her sleep, the gray dawn deepening the shadows under her eyes.

She looked so small in the big bed. So defenseless.

She'd hand him his head if he said that out loud. Awake, her whole being was focused on convincing everyone—herself included—that she was tough as bark. But it wasn't true.

What she was, was wounded. And like any wounded animal, when someone got too close, she snapped at him.

He'd need to learn what caused her pain and help her heal it. Because after last night, he was hooked. He'd ripped through her defenses, and the woman underneath the thorny facade was every bit as supple and giving as he'd hoped.

He wanted more of that woman. He wanted all of her.

For now, though, he let her sleep.

Stepping into the hallway, he came face-to-face with

Lucy, sneaking back to her room. Her eyes popped out of her head.

"Good morning," he said easily, as if he always bumped into her outside her sister's bedroom with his T-shirt wadded in his hand.

"Um, good morning." She looked confused. "Maddie said you guys weren't sleeping together."

He gave her a wide grin. "We weren't. Now we are."

She cocked her head, appraised him. He waited for her to tell him not to hurt her sister. Instead, she said, "Be careful, Adam. She'll break your heart."

Then she tapped her finger to her lips. "Don't tell her you saw me, okay?"

He nodded, and she slipped into her room.

Back in his own suite, he greeted John Doe with a chin scratch. "Sorry I abandoned you, boy. Tonight you can sleep with both of us."

He smiled to himself. Lucy was wrong. One night wouldn't be enough for Maddie. A week, a year, a decade might not be enough for either of them. He was hard again just thinking of her.

He crossed to the window. He didn't often catch the New York sunrise. It was spectacular. Golden sunbeams lit the tops of the city's tallest buildings, setting them on fire while the streets below remained in deep shadow.

Yes, it promised to be a beautiful day. He could hardly wait to get it started.

He went to the phone, but before he could call for coffee, Henry tapped twice and entered with a pot on a tray.

"You're a mind reader," Adam said.

"I heard the elevator." Eyeing the shirt in Adam's hand, Henry tsked. "Talked the fair Lucy out of her lover's bed, did you? Fast work, my friend, even for you."

"She's practically a child. Get your mind out of the gutter."

"Maddie, then?" Henry's brows rose a full inch. "So Fredo recovers his paycheck, and half of mine to boot."

"Betting on my sex life again?"

"It's usually not worth betting on. But our Maddie's brought some interest to the game."

"Not anymore."

"Finished with her so soon?" Henry looked disappointed. "Too bad. I'm fond of her. We all are, prickly though she can be."

"She's more bark than bite. And we suit very well, so you can hold on to your paycheck. I won't tire of her anytime soon."

Ignoring the stunned silence that met that little speech, Adam nodded at John's leash, dangling from Henry's hand. "I'll walk him this morning." He felt exceptionally energetic considering how little he'd slept.

John did a happy dance as they passed through the door, leaving Henry still speechless behind them.

"Shit." Maddie stared at the ceiling. "Shit shit shit."

What the fuck had she done? Why the fuck had she done it? And how the fuck was she going to *undo* it?

She rolled off the bed. *Ouch ouch ouch.* Her girl parts had gone from rusty to overworked in one marathon night.

Limping into the bathroom, she caught a glimpse in the mirror. *Oh God.* She leaned over the sink, turned her head side to side. Bruised, her lips were bruised. Her whole body felt bruised.

She blasted the shower as hot as she could stand it, all five heads scorching her from every angle. When she got out, she could almost move normally.

Bridget knocked on the outer door, sang out, "Good morning" as she waltzed into the parlor.

Maddie decided she'd never get used to servants barging in, then reconsidered when the girl brought a steaming mug to the bedroom.

"It's a beautiful day," Bridget said brightly. "I'll get you packed up while you're at breakfast and send your things down to the car. What'll you be wearing for your trip?"

"Jeans. And a T-shirt. And that sweater." She pointed at the plum pullover. Then the caffeine hit her bloodstream and she worked up a smile. "And good morning, Bridget. How are you today?"

"Oh, I'm good as gold. Though I'll miss the lot of you while you're gone." Moving to the bed, Bridget picked up the bedspread that had been kicked to the floor. "I'll have your suite all polished up for you when you come back."

"Thanks, but I won't be back. This is good-bye."

The girl cocked her head. "But Mr. LeCroix just now told me you'd be back in a week and I'd be at your service again."

"Well, Mr. LeCroix was wrong." *The nerve.*

Bridget was canny enough to drop a hot potato. "Your lovely sister's already in the dining room with her beau. Such a nice, polite fellow he is."

Oh God. She'd forgotten all about Lucy and Crash. They'd probably done it all night. The kid looked like he knew his way around a woman's body; Maddie could hardly blame Lucy for wanting to sleep with him.

And who was she to talk anyway? If she hadn't gone under from sheer exhaustion, she'd still be at it herself. And Adam would be right there on top of her, doing things she hadn't known she wanted done, ringing bells that had never been rung.

Even her imagination, which was randier than most, hadn't gone where they'd gone last night.

The difference was, unlike her silly sister, Maddie wouldn't fall in love.

In fact, there was no reason that one hot night should change *anything* between her and Adam. This wasn't her first rodeo. She'd worked with Michael for months after their hot weekend together. If Adam got any stupid ideas, she'd give him the same stony stare that made Michael tuck his tail.

Because she wasn't getting involved with *anyone*.

She found Lucy and Crash alone in the dining room.

"Morning," she sang out, taking a page from Bridget's book.

"You're in a good mood." Lucy's smile edged toward a smirk.

Maddie narrowed her eyes and growled, "So?"

"Ah, there's the Morning Maddie I know and love."

Maddie grimaced at her, then managed a sour smile for Crash. He lifted his fork to her with a sunny grin, then went back to shoveling sausage and playing slap and tickle with Lucy.

Stalking to the sideboard, Maddie tried to ignore their giggling. How could she have let Lucy slip past her last night? It was unforgivable.

She drowned a mountain of French toast in maple syrup, took her plate to the table, and plunked herself down across from the lovebirds.

"Crash, could you"—*get your hand out of my sister's lap and*—"pass the coffee?"

"Sure thing." He passed the pot, nothing but obliging. *Grrr.*

"So. How'd you sleep?" Lucy was wearing that half smirk again.

"Like a baby." Maddie tossed it off casually. "You?"

"Same. The beds in this place are like sleeping on a cloud."

Ever the lawyer, Maddie homed in on the details. *"Beds?"*

Lucy shrugged. "Well, you slept late, so you must like yours too." Her blue eyes blinked innocently. "I mean, you *were* sleeping, right?"

Enough talk about beds. The subject was a minefield.

Pointing her fork toward the door, Maddie said, "Did you swing through the gallery, check out the Rodin?"

That did the trick.

"Ohmygod, the gallery!" Lucy was off and running. Rodin blah blah, Degas yakkety yak.

Maddie sat back and sopped up syrup.

She was on her second cup of most excellent coffee when Adam strode in. He wore tailored black slacks and a dark blue pullover that fit him like a department store mannequin and pushed his impossibly blue eyes another notch along the color wheel.

She'd just taken a swallow, and at the sight of him, she caught her breath . . . and sucked coffee straight down her windpipe.

Dropping her cup with a clatter, she blasted a cough that spattered droplets across the white tablecloth and onto Lucy's pink T-shirt.

"Maddie!" Lucy was around the table in an instant, hauling her from the chair, Heimliching the hell out of her.

Maddie flapped her arms. "I'm okay! I'm okay!"

Lucy stepped back, concern on her sweet face. Maddie patted her arm. "It just went down the wrong pipe. I'm fine. Go eat."

Face burning like a campfire, Maddie took her own seat, dabbed at the tablecloth, refusing to meet Adam's gaze. She'd seen enough to know that his hair was still damp from the shower, finger-combed back, glossy and unaffected, and that when she'd choked, he'd streaked across the room, reaching her a split second after Lucy did.

And even without looking, she knew he was watching her as he filled his plate, as he took the seat beside her, as he poured his coffee. Watching her. Waiting for her to meet his eyes.

She carved a hunk of French toast but didn't dare put it in her mouth. Her throat was still tight, and it wasn't from choking.

It was Adam. He was too close, too warm. His scent was too potent. It brought everything back, his touch, his lips, the sweet, scorching words that fell from them.

It seemed that one hot night had changed something after all.

But she didn't have to admit it.

Scooting her chair away, she said crossly, "This table's as big as an aircraft carrier. Quit crowding me, will you?"

So THAT'S HOW it would be. Adam sipped his coffee, disappointed but unsurprised.

Lucy chuckled. "Morning Maddie's a crab, Adam. She needs at least two cups of java before she's civil. Three if she didn't get enough sleep."

"I do not," Maddie crabbed, proving it was true. "What I need is elbow room. Why's everybody climbing all over me?"

Unfazed, Lucy rolled her eyes, said to Adam, "What time do we roll?"

"Nine o'clock."

"Are we limo-ing?"

"Is that a word?" Maddie snipped. "Limo-ing?"

"If it isn't, it should be." Adam smiled at Lucy. "Yes, we're limo-ing. Henry's gone ahead with John and the luggage."

For the first time, Maddie swung around to face him, puffed up with indignation. "You're not sticking John in the baggage compartment."

"Of course not," he said easily, noting tension around her eyes that had nothing to do with John Doe. "He'll be in the cabin with us."

He leaned back, stretched his arm along the back of her chair. She leaned forward until her breasts bumped her plate. Which gave him the interesting idea of dripping maple syrup all over them.

Soon.

For now, she'd have to get used to his proximity, because he planned to spend a great deal of time inside her personal space.

Crash came up for air. "How long's the flight?"

"Seven hours," Adam said. He saw it hit Maddie like a brick. The color drained from her cheeks.

She'd been too distracted, he realized, to brood about the flight. Too busy worrying about her sister. Too busy riding his cock.

If they were flying alone, he'd keep her busy with that all the way across the Atlantic. As it was, he said, "My pilots expect a smooth flight."

Crash blundered in. "That's what they said last time I flew to L.A. Then we hit one of those air pockets where the plane drops, like, a mile in two seconds." He laughed. "Freefall, baby. Like skydiving without a chute."

Lucy pinched him.

"Ow," he said. "What'd I do?"

Maddie had gone whiter still, seemed to sway in her seat. Adam covered her icy hand with his. She didn't shake him off. He was glad, but it broke his heart that she was too distressed to fight him.

"We'll be perfectly safe," he said, looking at Lucy, but speaking for Maddie's benefit. "Safer than on the drive to New Jersey."

"Totally," Lucy said, like it went without saying. "We'll play poker all the way, right, Mads? You can try to win back some of the fifty K I'm up."

Maddie pulled herself together, a perceptible process of straightening her spine, loosening her jaw. She did it for Lucy. The power of her love was awesome.

"Yeah, sure." She slid her hand out from under Adam's without sparing him a glance. "Let's get the party started. I can hardly wait."

ALONE IN HER suite, Maddie let herself shake. How had she forgotten about this morning's flight? It was like forgetting you had a breakfast date with the lions at the Colosseum.

She sank down on the sofa. The nice earthbound sofa. It might be forty stories in the air, but it was attached to solid ground by steel girders and other reliable materials—unlike the plane that would shortly be floating untethered a mile above the bottomless blue sea.

Her stomach cramped. She hunched over to hug it. Why had she wolfed down half a loaf of French toast? She hated, hated, hated to puke. It always went up her nose.

Lucy knocked on the door, poked her head in. "Oh, honey." She came to sit beside Maddie, wrapped an arm around her. "Crash is a blockhead. I chewed him a new one, Maddie-style."

She worked up a ghost of a smile. "If I wasn't such a wimp—"

"Stop right there. You're the bravest, smartest, savviest woman I know. You've got *one* little phobia. So what? Who doesn't?"

"You don't. You're not afraid of anything." She leaned into Lucy, let her sister rub her back. "I want your optimism."

"Well, you can't have it, because it comes from having you as a sister. It's impossible to worry when the Pitbull's got your back."

"I can't help you if the plane goes down." Maddie rubbed circles over her stomach. That usually kept a lid on things.

Lucy glanced toward the bedroom. "Let me get one of your pills. You can sleep through the flight."

"And be out when we make an emergency water landing? No thanks."

"Okay, well, what did you do last night?"

Maddie stiffened. "What do you mean? I slept, that's what."

"Exactly. I figured you'd lie awake all night worrying, but you said you slept great. So, what did you do to relax?"

Maddie sagged against her again. "With all the action, I just forgot about flying."

"You got some action? With Adam?"

Oh jeez. She'd walked into that one. "I meant having dinner with Dakota Rain. Trying not to jump him."

"No kidding. He's even hotter in person. And he's got flirting down to an art." Lucy snickered. "Crash wanted to kill him. And Adam was even worse. Dakota's crush on you was making him nuts."

"Pfft. Dakota's a crush-a-day guy. He'll never settle

on one woman. And it's none of Adam's beeswax anyway."

"So there's nothing going on with you two?"

She evaded. "He's a crook, Luce. You need to keep that in mind. Keep your guard up."

Lucy laughed. "Yeah, he might steal my . . . oh, wait, I don't have anything worth stealing."

"You have your heart and your trust and your good reputation. He chews those things up and spits them out."

"Mads"—suddenly serious—"did he hurt you?"

"No." Well, he'd pissed all over her reputation, but Lucy didn't need to know that. "He can't hurt me, not really, because I know what he's about. He's trouble."

Lucy tilted her head to catch Maddie's eye. "Are you sure about that? Because he seems really kind. I mean, you've seen him with John. He dotes. He's thoughtful too, taking me and Crash to Italy. And he's so sophisticated about art and travel and everything."

It was all too true. But Maddie didn't want to consider it. Adam belonged in an eight-foot cell.

"Not to mention," Lucy added as if more need be said, "that he's so freaking good-looking I could stare at him all day." She punched Maddie's arm lightly. "Don't tell Crash I said that."

"Yeah. About Crash." Maddie changed the subject gladly. "How serious are you guys?"

"We're in love."

She said it simply, matter-of-factly, as if an asteroid hadn't just crashed into the planet and sent it spinning toward the sun.

Maddie rubbed her stomach.

"We met at one of his gigs." Lucy's eyes went dreamy. "You should see him on stage. It transforms him."

"From what to what?" A skinny guy with a stevedore's appetite to a skinny guy with a guitar?

"From the sweet, adorable guy-next-door to a hot sex god. Girls go crazy over him, lifting up their shirts, begging him to sign their tits."

"Tell me you're not one of them."

"Me?" Lucy looked appalled. "Not in this life. I was actually leaving the club, cutting out a side door when Crash ducked out for some air."

"He just happened to follow you out. Uh-huh."

"No, seriously. It was a total coincidence. Anyway, I told him I liked the band, he told me he liked my smile"—she shrugged—"and the rest is history."

"You're too young to have history. And what makes you think it's love? Lust, maybe, and intense *like*, but you just met him, what, two weeks ago?"

"Actually, it was last Saturday."

"*What?*" Maddie sat up, stomachache forgotten. "You've known him for a week and it's love?"

Lucy shrugged, serenely. "Sometimes you just know."

"Baloney. Next you'll tell me it's fate, or karma, or some other happy hooey." She glowered at Lucy. "You can't know if you're in love after a week. You just can't."

"Well, I do. I wish you'd be happy for me."

"Not gonna happen. What *will* happen is Crash—and what the fuck kind of name is *Crash*?—will break your sweet, innocent heart." She shot out a finger like a bullet from a gun. "Tell me you're on birth control. At least two kinds."

Lucy laughed. "Don't worry, neither of us is ready for kids."

"Oh God, you've talked about kids already?" Maddie fisted her hair.

"Sure. We're in love, we talk about everything." Lucy glanced at the mantel clock. "Sweetie, we've got to go. The limo's waiting."

Maddie let go of her hair and clutched her stomach.

It was too much to process. Lucy was in *love* with a rocker. Adam had invaded her body and—face it—her mind. And now she had to get on an airplane.

What next?

Her phone buzzed a text. Another wedding vow from Vicky.

"Argh!" She threw it at the sofa.

ADAM'S GULFSTREAM G650 was state-of-the-art. No executive's preowned castoff for him. This baby had rolled straight off the assembly line into his hangar.

Frozen like a rabbit on the tarmac, Maddie watched Lucy and Crash skip up the stairway and disappear inside.

"Maddie, darling." Adam stroked a hand down her arm. "Wouldn't you rather we called this off?"

Her dry throat convulsed on a swallow. "I'm fine." She took a small step, then her feet seemed to go numb.

Adam took her hand in his warm palm. "You're freezing," he murmured. "It's seventy degrees and your skin is like ice."

A shiver ran through her.

"That's enough." He lifted a hand to the pilot. "I'm not putting you through this."

"No!" She pulled on his arm. "I need to get on that plane."

"Darling, there's no shame in it."

"It's not shame," she said, trying to explain what she scarcely understood herself. "Okay, maybe a little. But it's more than that." She took a deep breath, set her teeth. "It's me against the plane now. I can't let it win."

She half expected him to laugh. Instead, he nodded as if he finally understood. "Ready then?"

"In a minute." Her feet were set in concrete. "I just need . . ." Something. But what?

Then John poked his head out of the plane, gave a gusty woof. And the breath that was trapped in her lungs hissed out through her teeth like air from a balloon.

John clambered down the steps and barreled across the tarmac to fetch them, eager to get the show on the road.

Crouching to meet him, she wrapped her arms around his scabby neck, buried her face in his patchy fur. He was so courageous; his heart was so huge. How could she be less?

On rubber legs, she let him lead her onto the plane.

Lucy and Crash were already living it up, checking out the sound system, sipping mimosas and undressing each other with their eyes.

If they'd had sex in front of her, Maddie couldn't have cared less. Sweat trickled in a thin, steady line down her spine.

Adam's hand on her back kept her moving down the aisle, maneuvering her into a seat, one of a pair that faced another pair, all cream-colored leather. He sat beside her. John flopped on her toes.

"Can I bring you something, Maddie?"

She glanced up at Henry. She must look like a ghost to put such concern in his eyes.

"Not just now," Adam answered for her. "Perhaps once we're cruising. Please tell Jacques to lift off as soon as possible."

Reaching across her, Adam fastened her seat belt. He didn't ask again whether she wanted to cancel the flight. Which was a good thing, because she would have said, *Yes, please, yes.* As it was, she bit down on her cheek to keep from blurting it out anyway.

Then Lucy appeared across from her, strapping into her seat, handing off her glass to Crash so she could clasp Maddie's knees.

"I'm right here, sweetie. Adam's here too." She gave him an approving smile.

Maddie noticed that he'd laced his fingers through hers. She was gripping so hard, her knuckles were white. "I'm fine," she repeated through lips gone numb.

Crash nudged Lucy's arm. "Have some more mimosa, babe." He gave Maddie a once-over. "You could use some too, Mads." He held out his own glass.

"That's thoughtful," said Adam, "but let's get up in the air before we challenge her stomach, shall we?"

Then the engines revved. Terror zinged through Maddie. The plane shuddered slightly as it began rolling forward.

She whimpered, she couldn't help herself. The engines drowned it from everyone but John. He nudged her shin with his nose. Her head was frozen in place, but she dropped her eyes, met his brown ones, full of sympathy and comfort.

She tried not to blame him for luring her onto the plane.

They picked up speed, faster, faster. Then liftoff plastered her head to the seat, glued her eyes shut. Tension tied her muscles into knots, tight enough to cut off blood, choke off air.

Then Adam's fingers caught her jaw, turned her face toward his.

And he kissed her.

His warm lips centered her. His tongue, when he gave it to her, was real, it was now. It tangled with hers, giving and taking. For a moment or three, she let herself lean in. Let herself lean on him.

Then she opened her eyes and met his, brilliant as cut sapphires and filled with promises and questions more dangerous than any trans-Atlantic flight.

Reluctantly, resolutely, she pulled away, released his hand. "Thanks for the distraction."

"Is that what it was?" he murmured. "I thought it was a kiss."

"A distracting kiss. And look at that, it worked." She jerked a thumb at the window, afraid to actually look out, but conscious of the clouds rushing by. "We're practically there."

He smiled, but she had a strong sense he wasn't happy.

Too bad. One night's poor judgment didn't make a relationship. Sure, his body was a wonderland. And he delivered, hands down, The Best Orgasms of her life. So good that she wasn't ruling out a short, sexy fling in sunny Italy.

But Adam LeCroix, former person of interest and present ruiner of her life, would *not* be adding *boyfriend* to his list of offenses.

Henry approached with mimosas. She let Adam pass her a glass. "To distractions," he said.

She couldn't argue the point, since they'd reached cruising altitude and she hadn't crumpled in a faint. But more-than-sex wasn't happening, and he needed to get that from the get-go.

"To distractions," she echoed, then let him sip before adding, "as fleeting as they may be."

CHAPTER FIFTEEN

> Vicky: Even if we don't see eye to
> eye on something, I will try to
> understand and respect your position.
>
> Maddie: And then explain why you're
> wrong.

BARRELING INTO ADAM'S suite, Maddie flung her
hands in the air. "You put them in the other wing!
How am I supposed to keep an eye on them?"

"You're not. They're consenting adults. They can
have sex if they want to. And darling, they want to."

"Exactly." She pointed one finger. "They're doing it
right now, and I can't even find their rooms. This place
is a maze."

"Actually, the layout's quite simple. The west wing
is a mirror image of this one. Lucy's rooms are where
yours are, next to Crash's. As yours are next to mine."

"Yeah, what's with that?" Her fists went to her hips.
"Why am I over here on top of you?"

He smiled, slowly.

A flush slid over her cheeks. "Don't get any ideas," she said, but her voice was hoarse.

"Too late." He covered the distance between them until she had to tilt her head to hold him in her narrow-eyed glare. He ran one fingertip lightly around the shell of her ear, let it trail like a feather along her rigid jaw.

Then he captured her chin between his finger and thumb. Held it still while he lowered his lips.

He half expected her to pull away. Instead, her stormy eyes glazed. Her lips parted under his. And then they were kissing, again, tongues sliding past teeth, finding each other, thrusting and sucking.

She tasted like strawberries. He'd had a bowl of fresh fat ones placed in her rooms, knowing she'd devour them. She was a sensualist, though she tried to deny it.

He'd teach her to accept it. He'd drench her in food and wine and art and all the beauty that was Italy. Make love to her under the stars, in the sea, everywhere.

He'd start in his bedroom, in the moonbeams that streamed through the window.

Drawing his fingers up her arm, over her slender shoulder, he cupped her neck. She was delicate as an orchid, as rare and as lovely. Tonight he'd make love to her, sweet and slow. Take his time, let her feel the connection between them, the tenderness swamping him.

Her fingers touched his waist, and a thrill shivered over his skin, fleeting, intoxicating. He deepened the kiss, giving her his breath, his heart . . .

And she tore at his belt, scraped his zipper down, taking him in her hot little hands. "Got any more of those condoms?" She kicked tenderness to the curb. "Let's get this done."

"Maddie, wait." He didn't want a quickie. He wanted to make love.

He pulled at her hands but she had a good grip. "What's the matter, tough guy, not enough foreplay for you?" She threw it out like a challenge while she stroked him relentlessly.

"I thought—"

"Don't think, just fuck." She snaked a hand up under his shirt, raked five nails across his ribs while her other hand pumped him toward insanity.

He took a last shot. "Let's—"

"Let's not." She sank her teeth in his pec. Every drop of blood drained straight to his cock.

"Ah, fuck it," he breathed, and pushed her down on the sofa.

WARM WATER SLUICED over Maddie's sensitized skin. This Italian shower was even more awesome, with even more showerheads, than the one at the penthouse. A couple of them were removable too. Handy for sex games.

Maybe she shouldn't have blown Adam off when he'd tried to lure her into his. But as she'd made crystal clear, she only showered with a man when they both wanted hot, slippery sex.

Not so they could, like, *bathe*.

He definitely had a head full of wrong ideas about this little affair, but she'd knock them out of there. She'd have to, because she didn't want to give up the sex, not yet. It was extreme, the best she'd had by a mile. It was almost spooky how they knew where to bite, where to squeeze, exactly how to pull the trigger.

It helped that they both went balls out, so to speak. They were adventurous, their bodies interlocking like puzzle pieces no matter how they twisted. They got into it, totally lost in each other.

But physically. Not, like, *emotionally*.

Drying off with a fluffy towel, she checked the floor-to-ceiling mirror, not surprised to see eight purple fingerprints on her ass. Her pale skin bruised like ripe peaches. Hence the bite mark on her left breast, another on her right thigh.

It had been that kind of night. The out-of-their-minds kind, with no judging or worrying or thinking about tomorrow.

Which was now today. And already they'd been at it again. Half an hour later, she still felt his weight pressing her into the cushions. His quick, careless strength, his skin slick under her palms.

She rolled her shoulders. It was like she'd had an itch between them she couldn't reach, and then Adam scratched it and it felt better than anything, a huge relief, total gratification. But as soon as he stopped scratching, right away it started itching again.

Well, she had a week to get scratched. And scratched and scratched. As hard as possible, as often as possible.

But if Adam thought he could scratch his way to her heart, he'd soon find out how wrong he was.

She was immune to romance.

Food, though, was another story. Adam had ordered calamari over fresh pasta for dinner, and she'd worked up quite an appetite. Wearing the only frivolous garment she'd packed, a sleeveless navy dress with beaded fringe at the neckline, she set out for the terrace at a clip, zooming over terrazzo floors and under elegant archways, past statuary and friezes and tapestries woven by women whose great-granddaughters' great-granddaughters were long dead and buried.

Bursting out through the wide double doors, she saw Lucy and Crash standing at the far edge of the candlelit terrace, arms twined like vines. Adam stood with them, the three of them chatting companionably, looking down at the colorful lights of Portofino encircling the bay far below.

Adam was probably bamboozling them with ultra-suave billionaire small talk, which annoyed her enough that she would have rolled in and busted them apart like bowling pins, except that six inches past where they stood, the world ended in an inky abyss.

No light, no shadow, nothing between them and Portofino below.

Detouring to a table instead, where votives cast a soft glow over the mosaic surface, she poured a tall glass of Prosecco and looked everywhere but toward the pit of doom.

Again, she couldn't fault Adam's taste. The terrace was the size of a supermarket, but stone urns holding flowering trees and terra-cotta pots spilling over with blossoms subtly divided it into intimate areas. Lounge chairs and café tables were spread around for socializing or privacy as desired.

At one end, the terrace widened out around a swimming pool glowing with underwater lights, an aqua oasis in the darkness. And the dining area held not one large table, but five smaller ones, each suitable for four people. Theirs was angled so everyone could enjoy the view.

All in all, it was a perfect setting for a romantic girl like Lucy to fall more deeply in love.

Grimly, Maddie forced a few steps in her sister's direction. All three of them turned their heads. Adam held out a hand. "Maddie, darling, come and see the view."

"I can see it fine from here."

Lucy skipped to her side and linked arms. "It's okay,

Mads. It's just a few inches down to the grass, and the slope's really gentle. Nothing to be scared of."

"I'm not *scared*," Maddie muttered, letting Lucy lead her forward. At the edge, she made herself look down. Not a precipice after all. She wouldn't tumble into the darkness tonight.

Adam stroked a hand down her back, let it settle on the curve. She thought about stepping away, but the breeze was chilly and his palm was warm.

"Dude," said Crash, "this place is incredible. If you need another gardener or butler or whatever, I'm your man. I could live here forever."

"Mmm," hummed Lucy, leaning into the circle of his arm, "I can't imagine anyplace more romantic."

Maddie scoffed. "It's just a big house with a nice view." She wasn't getting on the romance train. It wasn't going anywhere good.

Lucy gave her an are-you-tripping stare. "Mads, look around. They could set a movie here. And it would absolutely be a love story."

"Yeah." Crash gave Adam an approving nod. "It's, like, built for seduction."

Maddie jumped on it. "Seduction, yes. Not the same thing as love. Way different." She did the wise older sister. "Sex isn't love, Luce. It's just sex."

"Not always," said Adam.

"You stay out of it." Maddie tried to step away from him, but he curled his hand around her waist and pulled her hip-to-hip.

"You're just being contrary. You know very well that sex can be empty and meaningless—if still enjoyable—or it can be part of something deeper."

She fought back with her best weapon, the sneer. "Is that your advice for the lovelorn, Dr. Phil? Screw as many women as you can, preferably supermodels, until you find one where it feels meaningful?"

He studied her with hooded eyes. "It worked for me."

Annoyed out of all proportion, she brushed his arm off with her elbow. "I guess I'll have to keep trying, because it hasn't worked for me yet."

He smiled, an infuriating curve of delicious lips. "Liar."

"Oh please. If you think a couple of"—she bit back *meaningless sexual romps*—"hot Italian supermodels— and make mine men, please—can show me the light, then send them to my room. I'll report back tomorrow."

He just gave her that smug smile.

Damn him.

Lucy and Crash drifted away, snuggling. She would have pursued, but Adam moved in on her. "Stop treating her like a child."

"She *is* a child." She pushed it through her teeth.

He rubbed her arm lightly. It was more comforting than sexy, so she didn't belt him. "Madeline, look at her." He turned to stand beside her, giving both of them a clear view. "Imagine seeing her on the street, a stranger. Would you think, *Ah, there goes a pretty child*, or would you simply admire a lovely young woman, mature enough to manage her own heart?"

"If she was hanging all over some stud like Crash, I'd think, *There goes another sucker, heading for heartache and despair.*"

"He seems as smitten with her as she is with him. In any case, you interfere at your peril."

He had a point, damn him. Breaking them up—even if she could—wouldn't endear her to Lucy. But maybe if she glared at Crash hard enough, long enough he'd think twice about leaving home without a raincoat.

A broken heart would mend; a kid was forever.

Adam touched her jaw, turned her face to his. His eyes were almost black in the candlelight. "What happened to you, Maddie? Why did you stop believing in love?"

"Who said I ever started?"

He tilted his head. "I thought I was jaded. I'm a wide-eyed optimist next to you."

"I'm not jaded. I'm realistic. I thought that was one thing we had in common."

"We have many things in common."

"Like what?"

"A love for food and wine. An icy Prosecco. Calamari fresh from the sea."

Okay, maybe that. "Pfft. Who doesn't like good food and drink?"

"All right then. The Bugatti. How many people would even recognize it, much less appreciate it?"

"Lots," she said too fast. Then, "Okay, the Bugatti. Speaking of which, what do you drive around here?"

"Usually the Ferrari."

Her pulse b-bumped. "Which model?"

"Four-fifty-eight Spider."

"Red?"

"Is there another color?"

She wet her lips. "Um, do we have to go anywhere? For work, I mean?"

Slowly, he shook his head. "Not for work, darling. For pleasure." He ran those fingertips up her arm again. A tingle she'd rather deny raced from the point of contact straight to her belly, then lower.

"I have a place on Lake Como," he said. "Small, quiet, with a view you'll never forget. We'll spend the night, just the two of us." His voice was exotic as a jungle. As low and deep as a drum. "We'll eat pasta and drink Brunello and make love under the stars."

A thrill shivered up her spine. She shook it off. "You mean we'll fuck under the stars."

"Oh, we'll do that too. But first we'll make love."

"Not happening." She did a slow side-to-side head-shake. "If it's sex, I'm in. If it's romance you're looking for, keep your Ferrari in the barn. You're not gonna need it."

CHAPTER SIXTEEN

HENRY POURED TWO mugs of coffee, passed one to Adam. "Forget about stealing the Matisse. It's a foolish risk."

Adam set the mug on his desk without drinking, paced to the window, and gazed down at the pool. Lucy and Crash romped in the water with John. And Maddie—he swallowed—Maddie lounged on a chaise in a pink thong bikini half the size of a Kleenex.

He made himself look away. "Gio will have the thief by Friday." And then he—or she—would answer for the crime. To him, not the police.

"It's not only that, Adam. You're involved with Maddie now—"

"Maddie's not a factor." He raked a hand through his hair, made the ego-shriveling admission. "She's not *involved* with me. She just wants to fuck me."

"Well, well." Henry snorted a laugh. "I've lived to see it. Ninety pounds and she's taken you down at the knees."

Adam glanced out the window again. What could he say? He'd finally found a woman who touched him, whose mysteries he wanted to unravel, and she treated him like every other man who'd passed through her life, good for a few fast orgasms before kissing him good-bye.

"Cut her off."

Adam turned to stare at his friend. "What do you mean?"

"I mean, don't fuck her anymore. She's got a hard shell, that one. You won't break it with your dick."

Which was exactly what he'd been trying to do.

"You can't be sure I won't wear her down."

"You won't," Henry promised. "So don't give her what she wants until she gives you something in exchange. Stop fucking her."

"Impossible." After a second scorching night plundering her body, feeding on the intimacy she allowed only in the dark, all he could think of this morning was getting inside her again.

Henry gave a hopeless shrug.

"Fine." Desperation made Adam snappish. "If you're such an expert, advise me."

"Do what you were doing. Keep her close. Tempt her with the things she loves. Share yourself with her, make her part of your world. It was working, wasn't it? It got you into her bed."

"Which you're telling me was a mistake. Make up your mind."

"Giving her a taste wasn't your mistake. Handing her your dick like a schoolboy, that's where you went astray. Now she'll lead you around by it."

"Perhaps I'll lead *her* around."

"The dream of men through the ages." Henry shook his head. "Make her work for it, Adam. Make her come out from inside that shell to get it. Or send her home now before you fall any deeper in love."

* * *

"JOHN HAS NO skills." Lucy bounced the ball in her hand as John gazed up at her with clueless devotion. "He can't catch, or fetch. I won't even bother with a Frisbee."

"He can swim." That from Crash, sprawled on a poolside chaise. Shirtless, he looked lean instead of skinny. Lucy ate him up with her eyes.

"You threw him in," Maddie grumped. "What choice did he have?"

"Sink or swim, so he swam." Adam strolled into view. Her gaze skimmed his long length, from the sapphire silk shirt that slipped and slid over his chest, down to his package wrapped in snug faded denim.

He moved closer, and her gaze tracked back up to his face. His smile said he could read her mind. Well, good for him. Maybe he could tell her what she was thinking, because *she* couldn't make sense of her thoughts.

They'd ended up in the sack again last night, burning up the sheets till they collapsed from exhaustion. Which was all well and good, until she'd woken up between bouts spooned against his chest, his arm tucked around her, hand cupping her breast.

Snuggling wasn't her style, but he'd worked so hard and was sleeping so peacefully it would have been heartless to disturb him. So she lay quietly instead, feeling, of all things, peaceful, even happy.

It was all wrong, of course, dangerously deceptive, and eventually it freaked her out enough that she took the bull by the horn, so to speak, and got things moving again.

But now, watching him saunter her way, she realized she was still freaked out.

Hooking a hand under her crossed ankles, he lifted

them without asking and sat himself down on the foot of her chaise, propping her heels on his thigh.

So familiar, so sure of himself, when she was a bundle of doubts and misgivings.

"We'll teach him to play," he said, stroking her sole with his knuckles. His other hand caressed the top of her foot, a slow slide of his palm from her toes to her ankle and back again.

Saliva pooled in her mouth. She couldn't make herself pull her feet away, but she managed a sour puss.

"Life's not all fun and games," she informed him. "You dragged me over here to work."

"You're right," he said. "You should be hunched over a desk under fluorescent bulbs, squinting at small print. Instead you're lazing in the sun, admiring the sea view. I don't know why I allow it."

She glowered. "I'm not here to lounge around your fancy pool. Do I look like a Playboy bunny to you?"

Stupid, stupid question.

His gaze inched up her torso from her way-too-high-cut bikini bottoms to her way-too-low-cut top. The suit had appeared on her bed while she was showering. The price tag was still attached, apparently to prove it hadn't been worn, but it also had the effect of dropping her jaw.

Who in their right mind would pay nine hundred and ninety-five dollars for two scraps of nylon that, sewn together, wouldn't cover a ham sandwich?

She suppressed a flush by main force. "I meant," she added stiffly, "why am I idling around the pool instead of working?"

His lips quirked. "Because it's fun?"

"It's not fun." She pulled her feet away from his seductive hands, swung them around, and planted them on the ground. "Quit handling me."

"I can't." His finger trailed up the back of her arm. "I love how you feel. Velvet over steel."

He traced a lacy pattern on her shoulder.

She should stand up. Stamp across the terrace and storm inside. She could picture herself doing it.

Instead, she closed her eyes. Goose bumps shivered up her spine.

His knuckles brushed her neck, then her cheek, as light as feathers, softer than silk. She swallowed, throat tight, willing them to dip lower, to scorch a fiery trail down to the swell of her breast . . .

And then they were gone.

She leaned in, infinitesimally, seeking what she'd lost. When it wasn't forthcoming, she opened her eyes to find him on his feet looking down at her, his sunglasses hiding his expression.

"We have a lunch meeting in the village," he said.

"Okay. Good." She pulled her shoulders back, shook off his sexual mojo. "When?"

He glanced at his watch. "Forty minutes, under the portico. You'll find what you need in your closet."

She stiffened. "I'm not Barbie. You can't dress me."

"I think you'll approve of my taste." He half smiled. "In any case, it's that or go naked. Your choice, but you can imagine where I come down."

"You did *not* get rid of my clothes." She stated it as fact.

"Every stitch."

She popped up like a cork. "Give them back."

"Too late. They're headed to New York, where they're eminently suitable. You'll find a different climate here."

"Is that so? People don't wear suits on the Riviera?"

"Not to lunch they don't." He held up a hand to belay her next volley. "We're taking the Ferrari."

*   *   *

FROM THE CLOSETFUL of designer clothes Adam had tasked Raquel with providing, Maddie had chosen a halter dress as white as the fair-weather clouds. The silky fabric crossed over her breasts, then wrapped around behind her, leaving her taut belly bare.

It crossed again at a spot just below the small of her back, then came together in a shallow V two inches south of her belly button. From there, layers of filmy scarves fell in a scalloped skirt that fluttered like butterflies around her thighs.

The effect was magical.

She'd tried to hold on to her annoyance, but the Ferrari had taken the edge off her temper. The catcalled compliments as they strolled through the village had silenced her wardrobe rant. And when she realized that lunch would be served aboard his yacht, she threw up her hands and claimed she'd make the best of it.

Now, standing on the deck of the *Signora in Rosso*, the aqua Mediterranean tinting her eyes the same spectacular sea green, she looked like a movie star. And she was smiling.

Around them, Portofino's parti-colored shops and houses clung to the coastline, an Impressionist painting come to life. Forested hills rose steeply in the background, dotted with villas, including his own, windows flashing in the noonday sun.

Ahead of them, the sun splintered off the water, sparking like diamonds strewn across the sea as the seventy-five-foot cruising yacht putt-putted through the harbor, heading toward open water.

Stroking one hand from her neck to her waist, he let it settle in the curve. Her arms, her shoulders, her satiny back, all were bared to the sun. "As much as I hate to cover one inch of your skin, you'll burn to a crisp."

She turned her face up to him, pulled her sunglasses down from her crown to cover her gorgeous eyes. "I dipped myself in number sixty."

"Everywhere?"

"Everywhere that's likely to see the sun." She put a hand on her hip, a move that brought her breasts into play, though he doubted she realized it. "I thought you had a meeting."

"I do." He lifted a hand to summon Gio from the stern. "This is Giovanni. He's investigating the theft." He switched to Italian. Things would be said that he'd rather Maddie didn't hear.

"Gio, this is Ms. St. Clair. I'd prefer that she believe you speak no English."

"I understand." He shook the hand Maddie offered and smiled politely.

Adam skipped over small talk. "You've made progress?"

"The thief used your desktop."

"My personal desktop? In my office?"

"Yes. He—or she—logged on with your password and breached the security system from your desk."

Adam let that thought simmer, then, "What about the fail-safes? The passwords required at key points in the process?"

Gio looked chagrined. "Somehow—and we're still trying to figure out how—the thief infiltrated the programming and rewrote it. The passwords were eliminated."

"That's not possible."

"It's not *im*possible." He rattled off tech speak. Adam let it roll past him. He understood more about computers than most people, but this was several levels beyond him. "Only a handful of people could do it," Gio summed up, "and none of them works for you."

Adam crossed his arms. "Then one of them works for someone who works for me."

"I'm checking out the experts now, verifying their whereabouts on the date in question."

"It's unlikely they did it personally. But they could've talked someone through it." He leaned back against the rail. "Follow the money, Gio. That's how you'll nail them."

"It was the first thing we did, and we got nowhere. We've traced every transaction in and out of your people's accounts for the past six months and confirmed every one."

"Even Maribelle's? The woman goes through millions a year. She could slip something through."

Gio shook his head. "Her expenses fall into three primary categories—clothes, travel, and remodeling her villa. I went over her finances personally, took them back a full year. Everything checks out."

"It has to be her." Maribelle fancied herself a woman scorned. She might be American, but Italian blood ran in her veins. A ten-year vendetta would be nothing to her.

"My opinion," said Gio, "based on all I've learned about Maribelle and on my own interactions with her, is that she's too smart to jeopardize her villa and her stipend just to steal one painting that she'd have trouble fencing."

"Henry says the same, and I agree it doesn't make sense. But you don't know her like I do."

They held swords at each other's throats, Maribelle and he. No telling when she'd try to draw first blood.

"Send her records to me," he said. "I'll review them myself."

They spoke for a few moments more, then Gio motored back to shore in the launch and Adam turned his attention to Maddie. She'd pushed her sunglasses up and was watching him through narrowed eyes.

"I take it the Monet is still missing."

He cocked a brow. "I thought you didn't believe it was stolen."

"It would be an elaborate charade, wouldn't it? Especially since—as you love to point out—I'm your lawyer now."

She'd finally accepted that much. Now he wanted her to be more. How could he make her accept that too?

He began by telling her what Gio had found.

She listened closely, then bottom-lined it. "So you've got a traitor on staff."

"Apparently." He'd left out any reference to Maribelle. Someday soon, if things went as he hoped, he'd have no choice but to explain. But not now.

With his hand on her back, he guided her to the stern. The crew had set up a small table under the awning; white tablecloth, red grapes, and Pinot Grigio chilling in a silver ice bucket.

She took a seat, kept silent while he poured the wine. Then she sipped, and a low humming came from her throat, the sound she made when something tasted delicious.

The same sound she made in bed. It drove him mad.

Her tongue touched her lip. He struggled not to stare.

He made himself look out to sea. They'd left the harbor behind, and the captain had opened the throttle to cruising speed. Vessels of all types dotted the glistening water, from small fishing boats to a yacht several times larger than his.

"I figured you for one of those," Maddie said, tilting her chin at the superyacht.

"Does size matter to you?"

"Anyone who says it doesn't is lying through her teeth." She plucked a grape from the bowl, sucked it into her mouth. "But you don't have anything to compensate for."

Music to his ears. His trousers shrank two sizes in appreciation.

"Still, any old tycoon can have a yacht like this." She waved a hand like she was a yacht expert.

He refocused with an effort. "I had a superyacht and sold it. It raised too many expectations. Every business associate felt entitled to accompany me on a month-long cruise."

"With supermodels and movie stars?"

"At the very least. A smaller craft restricts the guest list."

"And exclusive orgies are so much more intimate."

"You shouldn't believe everything you read about me."

"Pfft. I don't *read* about you."

He eyed her.

"I don't," she insisted. "But you're ubiquitous. Turn on the TV and there you are. Sit down at a bar, you're up on the screen. War and famine can't buy a headline, but Adam LeCroix's every burp and fart is covered from every angle."

He laughed. "Good God, I hope not."

"You know what I mean. And you love it."

He sat back. "Is that what you think?"

"That's what everyone thinks."

"Then I'll have to give my publicist a raise."

"For convincing everyone you're a media whore?"

"For keeping the media's attention where I want it, on my public profile, and off my private life."

She looked unconvinced. "So Cannes and St. Tropez and canoodling with the world's most beautiful women, those are all publicity stunts? The *real* Adam LeCroix likes to sit home with Sudoku?"

"I prefer crosswords. But yes, I feed the press regularly. It keeps them from peering over my fences, looking for a story."

She studied him, considering. For the first time, she looked interested in something above his belt.

He let her look. He wanted her to see past the persona.

"So you're telling me that under all the flash you're really a private person?"

"I've never thought of it in those terms, but I suppose I am. I like, even need, time to myself. When I socialize for my own enjoyment, I prefer to be with a few close friends. And when a woman genuinely interests me, I don't flaunt her in front of the cameras."

He brushed a knuckle down the back of her arm. "You don't see any paparazzi now, do you?"

She didn't take the bait, but she didn't pull her arm away either. "Okay, that explains the puny yacht, but not the sprawling villa or ginormous penthouse. Those cry out for houseguests and parties."

"I enjoy both on occasion, as long as they don't encroach on my personal space. My penthouse suite, as you know, is far removed from the guest suites. And here at the villa, guests stay in the other wing. My wing is off-limits."

"You put me in your wing."

"You're the first. The only."

Most women would eat that up. Maddie sniffed

instead. "You want to keep me away from Lucy and Crash. For some perverted reason, you get off on them screwing under your roof."

For a brilliant woman, she could be annoyingly obtuse. "Oh yes," he said impatiently, "that's it precisely. I hope they're doing it right now, on his bed, her bed, and a float in the pool. Why must you badger them?"

"Because Lucy doesn't know what she's doing, that's why."

"And if she doesn't experiment, how will she learn?"

"She can learn from me." Maddie drummed her fingers on the table. "I thought we were having lunch. Where's the food?"

He ignored her ploy. "What will she learn from you? What relationship wisdom do you have to impart?"

"That's there's no wisdom in having a relationship. Period."

"And you learned this through your own vast experience with relationships?"

She gave him the stink eye. "What do you know about my relationships?"

"I know you've never had one."

Her jaw dropped. "You snooped into my *personal life*?"

He could have bitten off his tongue. But it was too late, so he shrugged one shoulder as if it were only natural. "I don't hire a person into a position of trust until I'm certain nothing in their past will compromise them."

"Really? Then how'd you end up with a traitor in your house?"

"When I find out, I'll tell you."

Lunch arrived before war could break out, delivered

by six-foot-studly Armando. Maddie ogled him. When
he lifted the silver lid, she gasped, "Pizza!" and dazzled him with a smile.

"He didn't cook it," Adam pointed out after dismiss-
ing the poor man. "You've given him an erection he
doesn't deserve."

"Then take me to the chef. I'll be glad to make out
with whoever put this together." She sucked cheese off
her finger.

"Sorry to disappoint you, but the chef is a woman."

"For this pizza, I'd swing both ways."

Jesus, now he had that vision to torment him.

MADDIE'S DRESS WAS an instrument of torture. It
barely covered her best parts under a skim of silk and
left the rest of her satiny skin gleaming in the sun.

Standing at the bow, she squinted against the sunlight refracting off the water, eyes fixed on the ap-
proaching shore. Adam turned his back to it, leaned
his elbows on the rail, and watched her instead.

The wind feathered her hair, fluttered her skirt. Her
feet were bare, her toenails pink.

She'd abandoned her sandals under the table after
her second glass of wine. After her third, she let him
slide his hand under that diaphanous skirt.

Then she tried to drag him down to the stateroom.

He'd resisted, God help him. And God help Henry if
abstinence failed to win her.

She'd shrugged it off, but her frustration was patent,
a mirror of his own. Desire leaped like a living flame
between them. Fighting it took all of his willpower
and a steady eye on the prize. He wanted more from
her than another quick fuck. He wanted to learn what
drove her, what moved her.

So far, she'd deflected every personal question. Now he went for an opening she couldn't resist. "Ferrari or Bugatti, which do you prefer?"

Her lips pursed. "Hard to say. It was stoplight to stoplight in Manhattan. And here, we never broke thirty."

"I have an interest in a racetrack near Milan. We can take the Ferrari there and open it up."

That got a grin out of her. "Okay. But that gives it an unfair advantage."

"When we get back to New York, we'll take the Bugatti to Watkins Glen. You can decide after that."

She didn't say yes, but she didn't say no. He shifted his arm an inch so it lay along hers. Electricity tingled his skin.

He slid a pry bar into the opening he'd made. "Why haven't you learned to drive?"

She hesitated, and he wasn't sure she'd answer. Then she shrugged a shoulder as if it was inconsequential. "I missed my chance. Everyone else learned in high school. I didn't. And once I got to college, I was living in the city. I didn't need a car."

"But you love cars."

"I can love them without driving them. Besides, I can't afford a real sports car, so what's the point?"

"What if I gave you the Bugatti? Would you learn then?"

She laughed, his favorite sound, second only to that sexy humming. "Sure. But nobody gives away a two-million-dollar car."

He wriggled the bar another inch. "Why didn't you learn in high school?"

"Because no one taught me."

"Why not?"

Again she hesitated. He flicked nonexistent lint off

his shirt, glanced up at the sky as if only idly interested in her answer.

"My mother didn't drive," she said after a moment, "and my father . . . we didn't get along."

He'd assumed as much, since she'd claimed the man was dead when he wasn't.

"No aunts or uncles? Family friends?"

"My father didn't allow it. And like I said, by the time I was old enough to learn on my own, it wasn't a priority."

She must have decided she'd gotten too chummy, because she stepped away from the rail, slamming the door on his pry bar.

"I hope you're happy," she said over her shoulder. "You dragged me out here for a five-minute meeting that I couldn't understand anyway, then dawdled the day away while Crash and Lucy went at it like bunnies."

Weren't they the lucky ones.

And she walked away, the scarves dancing the dance of the seven veils around her satiny naked thighs.

PORTOFINO, MADDIE DECIDED, was the prettiest place in the world.

For the best part of an hour, they strolled the waterfront, winding in and out of shops, sipping cappuccino under an awning at a trendy café.

Then Adam drew her down a side street, into a tiny gelato shop where all the colors of the rainbow winked at her from the freezer case.

"Adam!" A middle-aged woman rushed out from the back to kiss him on both cheeks. She gushed a stream of Italian, incomprehensible but overflowing with affection, punctuated by arm patting and cheek pinching.

When he introduced Maddie in the same language, the woman's eyes popped. Clasping Maddie's shoulders, she did the two-cheek thing, greeting her like a long-lost daughter.

"Magdalena's an old friend," said Adam.

"Let me guess. You staked her so she could open this shop."

"Now she has seven, up and down the Riviera."

Bustling behind the counter, Magdalena shooed aside the young women working there. They were busy batting their eyes at Adam, smiling for all they were worth.

"Her daughters," he said, "Angelina and Maria."

"They want to jump you."

"Then you should stake your claim." He smiled down at her, lacing his fingers through hers.

She should have made a face, but who could blame her for staring instead? His jet hair was wind-tossed, his skin freshly bronzed. And his eyes, bluer than the sea, glinted with pleasure at her obvious bedazzlement.

Magdalena packed two cones with rose-colored gelato. "Cherry," Adam said, passing one to Maddie. "Her newest creation."

Maddie licked it and the flavor melted into her tongue, cold and creamy, subtle and sweet.

"Mmm," she hummed.

And Adam kissed her.

His lips were cool and tasted like cherry. So did his tongue, sliding across her teeth. "That sound," he murmured against her mouth. "It goes right through me. Do it again."

Hunger tightened the muscles low in her belly. Hunger for him. She bit him, lightly.

"Magdalena's watching," she murmured. "She'll think there's something going on."

"Darling, there is." He bit her back.

Behind the counter, Magdalena's daughters tittered, but the sound faded out like the ending of a song. Adam's gaze was hot enough to melt her gelato.

She wanted him. She'd wanted him on the yacht, and for hours before that. When he'd slid his hand up her skirt, she'd all but thrown herself at him. But even though both of them were panting like wolves, he'd fended her off, claiming he wanted to talk.

Talk! Most men dreamed of sex without strings, but Adam wanted *conversation.*

Obviously, her resistance to jabbering about herself had piqued his nosiness. She'd thrown him a bone when he grilled her about her license, but it wouldn't be enough. If she wanted another crack at what he was packing in his pants—and she did—she'd have to play along. Dribble out some harmless factoids to let him think she was into sharing.

The downside risk was minimal. In seven days, they'd be back to their separate lives. True, that was five days more than she'd spent with any man, but she wasn't afraid of getting in too deep. She was commitment-proof.

She took a big sloppy slurp of her cone, watched his eyes dilate.

Yep, a little fake intimacy and he'd roll over like a puppy.

CHAPTER SEVENTEEN

Vicky: If something's important to you,
I will make it important to me.

Maddie: But not if it's silly.

LUCY LOUNGED ON Maddie's couch, bare heels stacked on the arm. "Did you know there's another villa on this property?"

Maddie toweled her hair, then poked her fingers through it. "Probably servants' quarters."

"Nope. Henry and the rest of them have rooms upstairs in my wing. And there's a separate fence around the villa, like it's a compound or something."

"Ask Adam if you're curious."

"I did. He said not to worry about it. And not to go over there."

Maddie's ears pricked. Maybe he'd stashed the *Lady in Red* there.

"Anyway," Lucy went on, "you guys were gone a long time. Did you have fun on the yacht?"

"Eh."

Lucy eye-rolled. "Yeah, I bet it sucked cruising

around the Mediterranean with the coolest, hottest guy in the world."

"Hottest, I can't argue with."

"Coolest, too. Crash worships him."

"I noticed." Maddie segued into the question she didn't really want an answer to. "So, what did you guys do all day?"

"You know. Swam and sunbathed. Took a nap."

"Nap" was code for sex. Maddie went for nonchalance. "You should get off the grounds, see the town. Hit the beach."

"We will. But it was so quiet here, and private. We wanted to take advantage of it."

Maddie twisted the towel, couldn't stop herself from saying, "You're getting too serious about Crash. He's a nice guy, but he's still a guy. You don't need a relationship tying you down right now."

"Mads." Lucy sat up, sympathy on her face. "You've got to let it go."

Maddie played dumb. "I'm serious. You don't need a boyfriend."

"I'm talking about Dad. You've got to let it go."

Maddie quit faking. "No, I don't. And you shouldn't either. You grew up in that house!"

"Yes, and it was a sick environment. Dad's a freaking pervert, and Mom was a classic victim of emotional abuse. It was awful, but we're away from it now. So is Mom."

She rose and went to Maddie, took the towel from her clenched fists and tossed it on a chair. "You had it tougher than I did, Mads, because you were older. You defended me when I was little. Made yourself a target to draw him away from me. And then, when the worst happened, you had no one to turn to." She took Maddie's hands. "I had you."

Maddie's heart ached as she looked up at her sister, so strong, so sure. "Do you want to end up like Mom? Can you really take that risk?"

"Sure I can." Lucy made it sound simple. "Because I'm not Mom. I'm not helpless, or alone, and I don't have the bad judgment to hitch myself to a creep like Dad." She squeezed Maddie's fingers. "Honey, you have to trust yourself not to make Mom's mistakes. Trust yourself to be the awesome, independent woman I love and admire."

Maddie shook her head. Lucy was right about one thing; it had been worse for Maddie. When their father came into her room on the night of her sixteenth birthday, she'd fought him. And when she couldn't win, she'd done the only thing left to her. She'd gone out the window, fallen two stories into the inky night.

The arm she'd broken throbbed just thinking of it.

"Adam's a nice guy," Lucy went on. "He takes care of his friends, like Henry and Fredo. He loves John Doe to pieces. And honey, he's crazy about you. He took in Crash and me—who could've been crackheads for all he knew—just so he could spend the week with you."

"You don't know the whole story."

"I know enough. I know he can't keep his eyes off you, or his hands. I know he's got a big heart. I know he's nothing like the press paints him. Sure, he's cocky and confident, but God, he's a self-made zillionaire. Why shouldn't he be cocky?"

Lucy walked to the table, plucked a strawberry from the bowl that had been magically refilled while Maddie was out. "Forget Mom and Dad. You and Adam are nothing like them. Don't let your life go by without taking a chance on love."

She popped the berry in her mouth. When the flavor hit her taste buds, she giggled with pure enjoyment.

Watching her, Maddie wrestled both fear and envy. Fear because Lucy so easily dismissed the lessons of their past and opened herself to the perils of the future.

And envy because by doing those very things, her little sister had accomplished what Maddie had always believed to be impossible. She'd stepped out of the shadow and into the light, and was marching bravely along the bumpy road to happiness.

"ADAM, IS IT okay if Fredo drops us at Madrigal?" Lucy asked.

Maddie looked up from her silky crème caramel. "That sounds like a club."

"Where the royals party with the merely rich and famous." Lucy's eyebrows bobbed. "Henry said showing up in Adam's limo would get us in."

Maddie frowned. When she'd suggested Lucy get off the grounds, she'd meant a tame lunch at a waterfront trattoria, not a night of debauchery with a roving pack of self-indulgent Eurotrash.

Still, she couldn't forbid her to go.

So she'd have to pull herself together and go with her.

It was the last thing she wanted to do. After too much sun, too little sleep, and two glasses of Chianti, she was practically comatose.

Still, she couldn't leave her sister to the dubious protection of Crash. He might hold up in a frat-party brawl, but in an anything-goes nightclub where half the patrons would have bodyguards, Lucy needed the Pitbull.

Setting her napkin aside, she started to rise. Then Adam said to Lucy, "Gerard will take you. He knows his way around that crowd."

"Who's Gerard?" Maddie wanted to know.

"He handles my personal security."

In other words, a bodyguard. And if he was on Adam's payroll, he was the best. Maybe even as good as the Pitbull.

"Thanks," she said after the lovebirds departed. "You hear stories about those places."

"Largely exaggerated," he said, "but we'll both feel better this way." He touched a hand to her back, guided her so smoothly toward the edge of the terrace she didn't think to resist.

Below them, Portofino's colored lights curled like a necklace around the harbor. More lights bobbed on the water; yachts, large and small.

"I'm surprised you didn't want to tag along," she said.

"Clubbing's lost the appeal it once had."

"Right, I forgot. It's crosswords in your rocker now."

He shot her an amused glance. "I'll get my cane and hobble after them if you want to show off that dress."

She rubbed the fabric between her fingers, red silk, cut low in front and even lower in back, and so short it barely covered her butt. She loved it, as she loved every one of the runway dresses that had supplanted her suits.

But his high-handedness still chafed, so she pulled a face. "It's a little extreme for dinner on the terrace, don't you think?"

"I think you were born to wear silk."

"You didn't leave me much choice."

He slid his palm up her back, then down again, slowly. "You prefer suits, then?"

"No." That much she'd admit. "But I'm used to hanging out in jeans, not zillion-dollar dresses."

"Indulge yourself, darling. You're on the Riviera."

"Exactly. I don't belong here." She shrugged. "But

I'm stuck for the week, so if dressing up is part of the job, I'll suck it up."

"Your sacrifice is inspiring. Let's send Adrianna a picture so she knows what a martyr you are."

That made her laugh. "Let's not. She'll dock my pay the price of this number."

His hand continued that mesmerizing stroke. "She does seem difficult. Why did you go to work for her?"

And there it was, the nosy question, disguised as small talk.

"She's my best friend's mother, so I had an in." *Dribble dribble.* "And as small firms go, it's top of the line."

"But defending insurance behemoths is a far cry from locking up criminals. You seemed, shall we say, *passionate* about your work."

He had reason to know that was true, so she dribbled out a little more. "Government work doesn't pay like the private sector. I needed more money. It's that simple."

OH, BUT IT wasn't simple at all. And if Maddie hoped to appease him with dribs and drabs, she was doomed to disappointment.

"So you relaxed your principles enough to take Adrianna's filthy lucre," he said, "but I can't woo you to LeCroix Enterprises with five million."

She actually smiled. "It's one thing to quit prosecuting felons. Another to take their filthy lucre."

"Still obsessed with the *Lady in Red*, are you? Darling, you've seen the gallery here. When I desire a painting, I simply buy it."

"That argument might've worked if you made it to a jury," she said, "but I know it's bullshit. You're in it for the thrill, the adrenaline. You get off on the danger. On the chance of getting caught."

He skimmed her shoulder with his knuckles. "That would make us quite the couple, wouldn't it? Me thumbing my nose at prison, you determined to throw away the key."

"Yeah, it would be pretty twisted. If we were actually a couple."

He let that pass. "The flaw in your case, Counselor, is that I can do my thrill seeking in other, much less complicated, ways."

"Like rock climbing? Skydiving? Sure. You could even afford to race balloons around the world like the Virgin Atlantic guy. But it still wouldn't be enough. Because all of those things just get you one up on *gravity*."

She jabbed his chest with a finger. "You like getting over on *people*. Smart people, the best in their fields."

And didn't that just prove she was the smartest of them all?

"That hardly seems enough motivation to risk my freedom," he said, wondering if she'd divine the rest of it too.

"I agree. And that's the part I don't get. Why risk prison for another painting when you've got more money than God and art coming out of your ass? I mean, with the lawyers you can afford, you'd probably walk even if you went to trial. But there's always a chance—small, but real—that you'd end up doing hard time as some bruiser's girlfriend."

"Well, now you're just hurting my feelings. I'd like to think I could handle myself, even in prison."

"Sure you could, if you wrangled a country club, which you probably would. But in Sing Sing, a pretty boy like you would get passed around like a five-dollar hooker until some lifer decided to make you his bitch."

A chill chased down his spine. "A lovely image. It's heartening to know that you worked your hardest to make that happen. And would again, given the chance."

Silence met that remark. Then she said, quietly, "I can't condone stealing. And I believe people should be punished when they do something wrong. But . . ." She shrugged.

He let that "but" hang in the air. Ambivalence was progress. Not the acceptance he wanted from her, but a step in that direction. Someday soon, he'd make her understand that by keeping art out of criminal hands, he was seeking justice in his own way.

For now, though, he wouldn't push his luck.

He brought the conversation back around in Lucy's direction. "Many people," he said, neutrally, "leave government work for private-sector wages. There's no shame in wanting a higher standard of living."

"Yeah, I'm rolling in dough." Sarcasm dripped. "As if you don't know where my money goes, Mr. Privacy Invader."

Why bother denying it? "Lucy was still a minor when she moved in."

"So?"

"She was your parents' financial responsibility."

"Everything isn't always about money," she said sharply.

"Darling, you're the one who brought money into it. And in my experience, it's often at the core. Did your parents cut her off? Was she was into drugs?"

Maddie hit the roof. "Lucy's never even looked at drugs! Why would you say that? Why would you even think it? She's strong and beautiful and way too smart to screw up her life."

He flattened his palm on her back, a gentling touch, even as he pushed harder, knowing she'd be most likely to open up in defense of her sister.

"Young people make mistakes," he said. "And Lucy left home for a reason. It's logical to assume your parents threw her out."

"Don't give me logical, buster." Her eyes flamed. "Lucy left that house on her own, and she came to me because she knew I'd understand and take her in and she'd never be frightened again. I quit my stupid job so I could take care of her the way she deserves, and I never thought twice about it. So don't you dare think one bad thought about her. She's sweet and innocent and her life will be *perfect*."

She was trembling. She tried to slap away his hand, but he used it to curl her to his chest.

"Maddie, darling, forgive me," he said, undone. Carelessly, arrogantly, he'd ripped a bandage off a wound that hadn't healed in five years. It was deeper than he'd imagined, gouged into her heart.

Her breath hitched hard in her throat, and he wrapped her in both arms, shaken by his thoughtlessness, staggered by his own emotion. "Let me hold you," he murmured. "I need it, even if you don't."

He stroked her quivering skin, whispering endearments. When at last she quit resisting and leaned into him, locking her slender arms around his waist, accepting his affection, his shelter, he felt ten feet tall. The primal desire to protect her roared like a lion in his breast.

And with it, the primal need to mate.

SOAKING ADAM'S WARMTH into her icy skin, Maddie rubbed her cheek against the silk of his shirt, the hard planes underneath. In her ear, his heartbeat drummed, a primal rhythm calling to her DNA.

She should be biting out his heart. He'd all but called Lucy a druggie.

Instead, she let her head fall back, let him press his lips to her throat, hot and needy. He trailed kisses over her jaw, a fiery path to her ear. His voice, low and deep, was almost a growl. "I want you. Here. Now."

Her body lit up like a torch. All day he'd held himself hostage. Now his hands were everywhere, pushing the straps off her shoulders, disappearing down her dress.

His lips dragged across her cheek, taking hers, swallowing her breath. In her throat, a moan rose up, a yearning hum that vibrated through her skin, through her clothes, through the universe.

He took it as she meant it, as if he had a right to her body. Brushing silk aside, he palmed her breast, working her like he'd held back for a lifetime. Like he might never get at her again.

She welcomed it, let him have all the control for a fast, steamy moment. Then out came her nails. She tore at his shirt; buttons pinged off flagstone. Finding his skin, sleek over hard muscle, she raked him, bit him, moaning her need.

Lifting her with one arm, he swept the table with the other. Crockery shattered and she found herself on her back, laid out like dinner, feasted on.

He stepped back to shed the tatters of his shirt. Stepped in again to flip her skirt up to her waist. Then his big hands slid up under her butt, her lacy excuse for panties went *snap*, and—"Oh God!"—his hot lips fastened on her. His talented tongue went to work, so good.

So good, she was losing control. She should tell him to stop. She even lifted her head.

Then his fingers joined his tongue. Her head thwacked back on the table. She arched up onto her shoulder blades, fisting his hair so he couldn't quit if he tried, begging him to stop, to release her, to for-God's-sake end it now.

He ignored her as usual and did what he wanted, going deeper, and faster, pushing past her limit, forcing her to the place where her body ruled and pesky second thoughts were ignored.

In that place all that existed were his mouth and his hands; all that mattered was what he did with them. All she cared about was coming.

Tension tightened like the turn of a screw.

And then, with his tongue and his thumb and two fingers of one hand, he completely erased her mind.

NEVER HAD ADAM gotten off just from making a woman come. But Maddie turned him inside out. Gutted him.

And if she got an eyeful of the stain on his trousers, she'd have his balls too, because she'd know hands down who held the cards in this affair.

For the moment, though, she was limp as a noodle, the rise and fall of her chest the only sign of life. He crawled up on the table, propped himself on an elbow. Her eyes were closed. Her flat belly quivered under his palm.

"Maddie darling," he whispered in her ear.

"Mmm." The barest hum.

"You taste delicious."

Her lips turned up at the corners.

Fuck abstinence. He might as well quit breathing. "I'm going to carry you to bed now. And keep you there."

"Hmm."

It wasn't jubilation, but it wasn't an argument either.

He scooped her up. John Doe scooted out from under the table and padded through the villa behind them.

In his bedroom, Adam threw back the covers and laid her out, her red dress vivid against the stark white sheets.

She was out cold, so he stripped off the dress along with the shreds of her panties, then took the chance to admire her fully naked and unawares; the long, sooty lashes he seldom noticed when her bright eyes were open; the mobile lips, so expressive when she was awake, now still and slightly parted in sleep.

Her shoulders were slender, her arms delicately muscled. And her perfect B-cups begged the question: Why had he wasted years on Cs and Ds?

His eyes wandered down to her belly, where her tan line gave him pause. Thanks to Gio, he knew she'd earned it on a topless beach on St. Maarten during a long weekend with a friend of a friend.

Tom Raskin was his name, and he was her usual type. Single and fit, someone she'd known for a while. Maddie didn't pick up men in bars; she wasn't careless that way. For a sexy weekend, she chose a familiar face. She even managed to stay friendly with some of them afterward.

But not Tom Raskin. Like others before him, he'd wanted more than two nights. So she'd kissed him off, kicked him to the curb.

Just like she planned to do with Adam.

He wouldn't be so easy to shake.

She'd fight him, and she'd put up a hell of a battle. But for tonight, the field was his.

He stripped off his trousers. Then he climbed into bed and curled his large body around her small one, holding her safe, sharing his warmth. Her hair tickled his nose. She smelled of strawberries.

He closed his eyes and slept.

CHAPTER EIGHTEEN

"I REMEMBER BEING able to sleep till noon," Maddie said, grumpily.

Adam shifted into third, glanced her way. With the Ferrari's top off, sunlight picked out the blond in her hair.

"It's a narrow window in life," he pointed out. "Be glad they're able to enjoy it."

"I might, if they weren't cuddled up like puppies. *In Lucy's bed.*"

"Which you wouldn't know if you hadn't poked your head into her room."

She crossed her arms. "I knocked. She didn't answer. I had to make sure she got home okay."

"Gerard would've alerted us if there was a problem."

"Says you."

He laughed. There was no winning an argument with Maddie. She was stubborn and unreasonable, and she was in snit because Lucy and Crash were heading off on the yacht to cruise the Riviera for a few days, unchaperoned.

"They were snoring like chain saws," she groused.

"I don't know how either of them could sleep through that racket." She stared out the windshield as they pulled onto the main road. "He had his hand on her breast. Like he had a right."

"Darling, we slept the very same way. And it didn't hurt a bit, did it?"

She aimed her aviators at him. "Don't get too comfy with my breasts. You had permission, not rights."

He chuckled, more at his own perverse taste for this prickly woman than at her absurd declaration. Of course he had rights. She just hadn't admitted it yet.

Predictably, she was in push-back mode, reacting to an intimate evening and mind-blowing wake-up sex by lobbing grenades and machine-gunning civilians.

"Where're we going, anyway? Another pointless meeting? One day of farting around with the idle rich is okay, but I don't want to make a habit of it."

He pulled off on the shoulder. "Should I turn around, then? You don't want to test this car on the racetrack?"

She rubbed her hand along the leather seat. "You didn't tell me we were going to the racetrack."

"I'm telling you now. Do you want to keep going?"

He watched her struggle with it. She'd boxed herself in with the idle rich nonsense. "I guess we'll have to," she said, feigning reluctance. "You got everybody hopping, right? Changing plans so the big cheese can play around on his speedway."

He swung a U-turn and punched the gas, streaking back toward the villa. He picked up his cell phone, driving one-handed. "Change of plans, Marco. I don't need the track today. *Ciao*."

Maddie huffed. "How's that better? Now you made them change plans twice."

He tossed the phone in her lap. "Call him back if you want to. I can turn around again."

She squeezed the phone in her hand. He bit down on a smile. She wasn't used to anyone calling her bluff. Especially not twice in two minutes.

"Seems like a nice day for it," she said.

"Seventy degrees and sunny. It's a nice day for anything." He wasn't helping her out of this. If she wanted to go to the track now, she'd have to ask.

She fidgeted. "So now what? The track sits there *unused* all day?"

"I suppose so." Adam shrugged as if it made no difference to him.

"Isn't that a waste of money?"

"I can afford to waste some."

"Damn it." She slapped her hand on the seat. "All right, okay. I *want* to go."

"Darling, that's all you had to say." He pulled another U-turn, held out his hand for the phone.

IT WAS, HANDS down, the most fun Maddie ever had in her life.

Adam made her wear a helmet and a fireproof suit, the latter of which was a few sizes too large, but it didn't lessen the thrill of flying around the track at warp nine. She'd had her heart in her throat the whole time.

Now as the cute waiter poured a sparkling Prosecco into her glass, she didn't even think to flirt with him. She was too busy ogling Adam. His hair was sweaty from the helmet—hers probably was too, but who cared?—and dark glasses hid his heart-stopping eyes, but his smile was as wide as hers. He'd had fun too. Cool as a cucumber around the hairpin turns, but she sensed the adrenaline still pumping through his veins.

"Did they open the dining room just for us?" she asked. The trackside view was stupendous.

"If I say yes, will you berate me for ruining every-one's day off?"

"Nope." She grinned. "I'm sure you're giving them a week's pay to compensate."

He was like that, she'd discerned, surprisingly thoughtful, and generous with money.

Generous in bed too. Or on the dinner table, as the case may be.

"We'll take the Bugatti to Watkins Glen next week," he was saying. "I've already arranged it."

Whoa. Next week was another kettle of fish.

"I'll be back at work," she said. "At the firm."

"Hawthorne hasn't conceded. He'll hold out as long as he can."

She shook her head. "One of two things will happen. Either your buddy Gio will find the painting within the next few days, or it'll be gone for good, in which case Hawthorne will pay up. Trust me, he doesn't want a trial."

Adam smiled. "Only because you frightened him."

"Exactly. My work here is done." She lifted her glass, an air toast, and took an icy swallow.

He didn't drink along. "Maddie, I've already notified Adrianna that I'll be using you through the summer."

She stiffened. "Using me? Is that Italian for fucking?"

"Sorry. Poor choice of words. I meant that I need you to see this through. And to reorganize my legal de-partment. And a few other matters that will take us into September."

"You just said summer. Now it's September. I don't like moving targets. And I don't like being *used*. I'm a lawyer, not a hooker."

"For pity's sake, Maddie." He sat back in his seat. "I'm not paying you for sex. You're the finest attorney I know, and as you've pointed out repeatedly, my organization needs help in that area. My attraction to you is beside the point."

"Then why am I here at the racetrack instead of hunched over contracts or helping Brady pack up his office?"

"I thought you enjoyed yourself today." He sounded hurt.

She dialed down, softened up. To be fair, she'd wanted to come. "I did. It was great, the chance of a lifetime. I can cross it off my bucket list. But it's not legal work, Adam. It's fun and games."

"So consider it a vacation. A few days of rest and relaxation before we head back to New York."

"R and R and mutual orgasms?"

"Why not?" He smiled one of his devastating smiles.

She set her glass down, ran her fingertips through her matted hair. Things were getting too serious. He needed to understand that their little fling would end when they got off the plane.

"Listen, Adam. The orgasms are great. So's the car, the yacht. And I never thought I'd hear myself say this, but you're a nice guy. The thing is, I'm still me, you're still a felon, and I don't do long-term anyway."

"You don't even do short-term," he said. "Why not?"

"Because it's easier to keep things light from the start. Getting involved isn't an option for me."

"Why not?"

She shrugged. "I've seen a lot of bad marriages. A lot of kids caught in the middle. I don't want to be part of that."

"Everyone's seen those things," he said, taking off his sunglasses, hitting her with a bolt of blue. "I've seen them myself, close up. My parents were so focused on

their art—and so committed to torturing each other—
that they more or less forgot about me."

She hadn't known. "That sucks," she said, "but
except for the stealing thing, you turned out all right."

"Did I?" He spread his arms. "Do you see a doting
wife? Loving children?"

"Oh please. Every unmarried woman on the planet
and most of the married ones would give ten years off
their lives to be Mrs. Adam LeCroix."

"And yet you begrudge every moment in my company."

She let out a laugh. If he only knew how she'd come
to dread the end of the week, to count the shrinking
days. She'd had to admit it to herself that morning
when she woke up spooned against his chest.

All the more reason to shut him down.

"Everyone's seen bad marriages," he said again,
circling back to his point. "It doesn't stop them from
hoping for something better for themselves."

"I'm one of those rare individuals who actually
learns from others' mistakes."

"And what have you learned?"

"That women come out on the short end every time.
And once they become mothers, they're toast."

"How so?"

"Kids are leverage." That's as far as she was willing
to go.

"And you think that only goes one way?"

"Probably not," she admitted. "But most times it's
the mother who has to toe the line. That's if the father
even takes responsibility at all. Either way, Mom ends
up holding the bag."

The waiter appeared with their plates. Sole, pan-fried
in lemon butter. The aroma had Maddie salivating.

He brought a plate of risotto too, setting it between them to share, alongside a lightly dressed salad and a loaf of fresh bread. Adam had ordered it all brought at once because he knew she liked it that way.

She forked some risotto, savoring it. "I haven't had a bad meal since we met."

"So I'm good for something."

"You hit a ten on every sensual scale. Food, wine, and sex." She gave him a grin, determined to keep it light. "And cars," she added, lifting her glass. "Definitely cars."

He plinked his glass to hers. "Relationships have been built on less."

"The Roman Empire too," she said, making the point with her fork. "And look what happened to that."

"So you'll never marry and have a family?"

"Nope." She broke bread, handed him half. "You're looking at a crazy cat lady in the making."

"And if you fall in love?"

"I won't."

"You might."

"I'm immune. I was inoculated at sixteen."

"What happened at sixteen?"

She kicked herself, literally, a sharp toe to the ankle. Why did she have to win every argument, no matter the cost?

"None of your beeswax," she said, still keeping it light.

"Your father abused you, didn't he?"

It was a sucker punch, hitting her where she hurt most. She shot to her feet like he'd jabbed her with a cattle prod. "You sick fucking bastard." With both hands, she tipped the table into his lap.

He shoved his chair back so most of the meal missed him, but she didn't stick around to watch. She was halfway to the door when he caught her arm.

"Maddie—"

She shook him loose so hard she staggered when he let go. "Stay away from me. Stay away from my sister." She was a tiger, ready to claw out his eyes.

He held up both hands. "Forgive me, please. I didn't mean to offend you."

"Liar. That's all you ever wanted to do. That's what all this is about." Enraged, she flung an arm wildly, taking in the clubhouse, the track. "That was always the plan, wasn't it? Sucker me in, then humiliate me." She sneered. "Sorry I didn't cooperate by falling in love. What a blow to your ego that must be."

"Darling—"

She slapped him. "Don't *darling* me, you piece of shit."

She yanked open the door and got out of there.

OUT IN THE parking lot, Maddie eyed the Ferrari. She'd steal it in a minute if only she could drive.

She walked instead. The sky was cloudless, the breeze light and steady. It fluttered her skirt, navy silk with white polka dots, and tickled her arms, left bare by her white sleeveless top. On such a lovely day, she could walk five miles without breaking a sweat.

If not for her shoes.

Wedges, they were designed for slinking a few yards between cars and restaurants and yachts and villas, but decidedly not for hoofing miles of asphalt. She'd be hobbled before she reached the road, bleeding before she found friendlies who'd call her a cab.

Looking over her shoulder, she watched the Ferrari back around, then start her way. Surrender was a bitter pill she wasn't sure she could swallow.

Adam pulled up alongside, slowing to her speed. "Madeline. Get in the car." His voice was all business, the Adam LeCroix who'd forced her from her office at gunpoint. And why not? The jig was up. No reason to fake it any longer.

To her disgust, that hurt more than her feet.

She kept walking anyway.

"Don't be ridiculous," he said. "Let me take you home. You and Lucy can leave as soon as you'd like. Take my plane if you want to, or I'll book a commercial flight if you'd rather."

She stopped walking and he stopped the car. She got in without looking at him and they drove out of the racetrack in silence.

Staring out the side window, she tried to put her feelings in order.

Most were familiar to her—anger and humiliation and the blackhearted desire for revenge—but there was pain too, and she didn't know what to make of it. Centered in her chest, it throbbed along with her heartbeat, jagged and insistent, refusing to be ignored.

It sharpened when she thought about waking that morning, her rump backed up against Adam, his arms wrapped around her. She'd felt warm and snug and . . . safe.

Now she felt sick to her stomach. Hollowed out. Panicky.

It killed her to admit it, but Adam had gotten to her on a personal level. Made her *care about him*.

Anger rose up to the rescue. Damn it, she'd gotten *involved*. Fallen for his bullshit—

"Maddie."

She swiveled to face him. "Don't. Talk."

"You can't stop me."

She dug in her purse, came out with a nail file and held it to his throat. "Yeah, I can."

"You won't do it. It's a crime."

"No jury will convict me."

He gave a rueful smile. "Your conscience would eat you alive."

"You don't know me as well as you think," she ground out, hating that he was right.

"I know you'd blacken my eye given the chance, but you won't stab my jugular."

She threw the nail file over her shoulder. It landed on the road, never to be seen again.

She resumed her vigil out the window, glad to see in the side mirror that her cheeks wore red flags. Fury was better than heartbreak.

Oh Jesus. *Heartbreak.*

That's what it was. And it was everything she'd imagined, all that she'd shunned. A migraine, the flu, a bad fall down a steep flight of stairs. A hand around the throat, six broken ribs, the worst menstrual cramps in the history of the world.

Adam pulled into a turnout overlooking a breathtaking view. He killed the engine and angled toward her in his seat.

Her throat had narrowed to a slender straw. "You said you'd take me home."

"I will. But I need to talk to you first."

"No talking. Drive." She stared blindly off the overlook.

"Maddie. Darling."

That brought her head around. "I told you not to *darling* me!" And he had the stripes across his cheek to prove it.

"I'd like to oblige," he said, "but you *are* darling to me." He pushed a hand through his hair. "I wish it wasn't so. You're the last woman I'd imagined feeling this way about."

The pain in her chest didn't know whether it was

coming or going. She managed a snort. "Quit bullshit-
ting and drive."

"No, I won't drive. And don't bother pretending
you'll walk in those shoes. We're miles from home,
and you're not foolish enough to take a ride with a
stranger."

Grrr.

"Fine. Spit it out. Unburden yourself. Lie. Cheat.
Steal. I don't care, just get it over with."

For a long moment he watched her, his eyes a deeper
blue than the sky above him. He hadn't shaved, and
stubble shadowed his jaw. The wind riffled his hair
across his brow. She wanted to brush it back with her
fingers.

She sat on her hand instead.

He brushed it back himself, frustration in the movement. "This is all new to me," he said, "and I keep
screwing up. I'm not used to screwing up."

She could take a shot there, but she held her tongue.
And her breath. Because she was hanging on his
words.

"I'm not inexperienced with women," he went on,
the understatement of the century. "But I can't put
a foot right with you. You're a minefield, and I keep
stepping on them. Hurting you—hurting both of us—
without meaning to."

He laid an arm along her seat, slid his hand into her
hair, and shaped it to her scalp. "I'm trying to find out
why. Why you're so sensitive—"

"I'm not sensitive," she belted out, proving his point.
"Okay, I'm sensitive about some things. So why can't
you step off?"

"Because I want to understand you."

"I'm not that interesting."

"You're the most fascinating woman I've ever met."

He was getting to her. She was starting to eat it up.

She did a mental cheek slap. "I'm sure you say that to the legions."

"I've never said it to a soul." His fingertips stroked. Her nerve endings quivered.

She bucked up. "You brought me into this insurance thing to humiliate me."

"I brought you into it to put the arm on Hawthorne. But you're right, at first I took some delight in making you squirm."

"And you're still getting off on it. So to speak."

He smiled. "You see? Until last week, I never knew you had a sense of humor. I never saw it five years ago."

"You never saw my panties then either."

"No. But I did see your bra."

She glared. "Did not."

"Did too. In that dreary conference room with the buzzing fluorescents. You leaned across the table to shove some particularly damning bit of evidence under my nose, and your blouse gapped. I got an eyeful."

"I don't believe you." She crossed her arms. "Describe."

"Peach satin, scalloped edge, tiny white bow in the center."

Her arms uncrossed. "You're unbelievable. You should've been worrying about prison, and you were checking out my bra."

"I was checking out your tits. Your bra was in the way."

She laughed because, damn it, he was funny. Funny and so, so hot with the devil's own grin on his lips, and his eyes, so blue and so into her, crushing her willpower to dust.

He traced a finger down her throat, hooked it in her neckline, and peeked in. "Ah, virginal white today."

His lips quirked, and his fingertip dipped under the edge, slipping the strap off her shoulder a centimeter at a time.

"Maddie." His voice, exotic and bedroomy, trailed over her skin like his fingers. "I can't keep my hands off you."

"Then don't." Sex she understood. Sex she could handle. All the other emotional crap was just temporary insanity.

"I won't have you think I'm using you. That this is a trick, or a lie, or anything but desire. I want you. I want all of you."

"So shut up and take me." She grabbed a fistful of shirt and dragged him closer.

He covered her hand with his. "Do you believe that I care about you? That you're not like other women to me?"

"Yeah, sure." She wrestled him closer, but the console was a problem.

"Let's go home."

"Home, shmome." They'd work around the damn console.

She released his shirt, reached for his zipper, but he stilled her fingers. "Darling. It's important to me."

"Why? We don't need a bed. We can get it done right here."

"Not that. It's important that you understand."

"What's important is that I get laid in the next five minutes."

Exasperation made him short. "For Christ's sake, why must you make it so hard?"

Her instinct was to make the obvious joke, but the look in his eyes, the bubbling stew of frustration and lust and affection and more, shut her up.

It frightened her too. Because for once, for the first

time ever, seeing hunger and desire stir in a man's eyes made her feel . . .

. . . the opposite of heartbreak.

For a long, strange moment, she stared into those eyes. Then—*oh shit!*—it hit her. She was into him . . . *emotionally!*

She lost it, went off the deep end, freaked the fuck out.

Rearing back against the door, she threw her hands up, palms out. "Don't touch me. Don't."

"Maddie—"

"Drive. Drive the fucking car *now* or I'll walk on bloody stumps."

ADAM DROVE, EYES on the road, hands on the wheel, but with his mind ten miles behind him, back in the dining room, rewriting their lunch conversation.

In the revised version, he enjoyed her high spirits and the gleam in her eye, and kept his nosy questions to himself.

He was too fucking impatient, that was the problem. He couldn't wait for Maddie to open up on her own, so he'd pried and bullied, and now everything was fucked up beyond all recognition—FUBAR, as his SEAL trainer would say.

The miles rolled on in silence. Endless minutes ticked by.

He stole a glance at Maddie, saw she'd unwound enough to unglue her shoulder from the door and sit back against her seat. She stared blankly out the window, no welcome in her expression, not a scintilla of warmth. But at least she no longer looked homicidal, or terrified, or like she might leap out of the speeding car just to get away from him.

Against all odds, he took heart. Maybe, just maybe, things weren't FUBAR after all.

The kernel of a plan formed in his mind.

Examining it from all sides, he heard Henry's voice in his head. *Don't do it, Adam. Remember who she is. Remember what she tried to do to you.*

Henry was right. It was foolhardy, risky, a long leap of faith. But Adam was a gambler with one card left to play. Win or lose, he'd take his chances. Because the truth was, after five long years and five short days, he was quite sure he was falling in love with Maddie.

His forty-acre compound was fenced, the access road gated. He waited in silence while Gerard ran an expert eye over the Ferrari, then opened the gate and waved them through.

Bypassing his own villa, Adam continued around a sweeping curve, past a dense swath of trees, to another locked gate. Heart in his throat, he keyed in the code and drove through, braking at the door of a smaller, but no less luxurious, villa.

"Lucy told me about this place." Those were Maddie's first words in an hour, uttered listlessly, like she was too tired to care.

She'd perk up when she got inside, for better or worse.

He came around to open her door. She got out reluctantly. "I'm supposed to be on my way to the airport."

"Bear with me." His palm on her back urged her up the steps. "I'm about to share my deepest secret."

A petite maid opened the door. "Mr. LeCroix, how nice to see you." Her British accent sounded stiff, but her smile was friendly.

"Hello, Giselle. Would you please tell Maribelle I'm here?"

"If you'll wait in the living room," she said, and disappeared up the stairs as Adam led Maddie across the wide foyer and into a room as large as her apartment.

She looked interested now. Seeing her take a good long look around, he did the same for the first time in years, taking in the intricately tiled floor, the spare but comfortable furnishings in the latest Norwegian design. The fireplace was fronted with marble from his quarry. And the windows overlooking the spacious terrace had a Mediterranean view that rivaled his own.

Henry was right about one thing. Maribelle knew how to spend his money. But then, silence cost a great deal. More every year. Yet for all that she hated him and would gladly bankrupt him if she could, she guarded his secret well.

In a patented power play, she left them cooling their heels for twenty minutes while Maddie waited more patiently than he expected. When Maribelle finally appeared, slinking through the door like a Siamese cat, Maddie narrowed her eyes and assessed her.

Knowing as he did her vertical sensitivity, Adam could only imagine what she thought of Maribelle. All of six feet and slender as a snake, she owned any room she entered. He remembered the first time he saw her. He'd almost swallowed his tongue.

That was ten years ago. She was still as blond, as slim, as sensually beautiful as she'd been at that Hollywood party. But now she was a constant reminder that beauty was only skin deep.

She crossed the room at a measured pace, held up each cheek for his perfunctory kiss. Glancing dismissively at Maddie, she said, "I told you, Adam, Giselle's working out fine. I don't need another maid."

Nothing thrilled Maribelle like drawing blood. Like a vampire, once she broke the skin, she kept sucking.

He bit back a retort. "Maribelle, this is a friend of mine. Madeline St. Clair."

Maribelle hadn't lost her acting chops. She did Oscar-worthy wide-eyed surprise. "So sorry, Ms. St. Clair," she said, stooping just a bit as she extended her hand, as if shaking with a child.

"No problem." Maddie said, giving Maribelle's knuckles a solid squeeze. "And call me . . ." She seemed to reconsider. "You know what? Ms. St. Clair is good."

She showed her teeth in a smile.

God help him, he was in love with the Pitbull.

His feelings must have shown on his face, because Maribelle's plastic smile hardened to ice. Moving to the slider that opened onto the terrace, she took a half step outside.

"Dominick," she called with sick delight, "your father's here."

CHAPTER NINETEEN

Vicky: My heart is an open book.
I won't keep secrets from you.

Maddie: Except about that drunken
weekend in Barbados. That's in the vault.

WITH ADAM'S GLOSSY black hair and startling blue eyes, Dominick was the spitting image of his father. Streaking across the terrace, face alight with excitement, he pulled up sharply inside the door, and stared.

Maddie hinged her jaw, schooled her lips into a friendly smile. But it wasn't she who'd brought him up short.

She cut a look at Adam's grim face. Clearly, he wouldn't be swinging his son up onto his shoulder or wrestling him into a bear hug. The joy died out of the boy's eyes.

"Dominick," Adam intoned, "come and pay your respects to Ms. St. Clair."

The boy inched forward and extended one small hand, gravely. "It's a pleasure to meet you, Ms. St. Clair." His accent was Italian, but his English was perfect.

With equal gravity, Maddie shook his hand. "Likewise, Dominick. You can call me Maddie."

He flicked a glance at his father, who nodded once.

"Are you the new maid?" the boy asked politely.

Maribelle snorted a laugh.

"I'm a lawyer," Maddie said with a kind smile. "I've been doing some work for your dad."

"You're American," he said, blinking lavishly lashed eyes.

"That's right. From New York City. Have you been there?"

He shook his head. "There are bad men there. It's better if I stay here where it's safe."

That stumped her. She looked a question at Adam.

He ignored it, turning to Maribelle. "Is there anything I should know?"

She rolled a shoulder in a silky shrug. "Roland's upstairs."

"Dom's tutor," Adam said tersely to Maddie. "Excuse me a moment." He left Maddie with the boy and his mother.

Gee, thanks.

Maribelle didn't offer her a seat or a drink. Instead, she poured herself a glass of wine from the wet bar, sipped it as she looked Maddie up and down.

Dom's manners were better. "Would you like to sit down, Maddie?" Careful to keep his shoes off the white upholstery, he plopped on the sofa and patted the seat beside him.

She couldn't resist. He was charming and sweet and the spitting image of his father. Slipping off her sandals, she spread her skirt so she could curl her feet under her butt without flashing him.

"So, Dom, what grade are you in?"

"I don't have a grade. I have Mr. Roland."

"Okay. How about friends? Who's your best friend?"

"Henry," he said promptly.

"Adam's Henry?"

"Yes. He taught me to swim."

"You have a pool?"

"I can use Papa's when he's away."

"Only when he's away?"

Maribelle made a sound of disgust. "Quit interrogating him, Counselor." She sauntered into Maddie's view, folded her skyscraper legs, and draped herself across a chair, like a silk scarf floating down to the cushion from six feet in the air. "If you want to know what a shining example of fatherhood Adam is, ask *him*. Ask him when he last spent an hour with his son."

Maddie shifted her gaze back to Dominick. He blinked at her, his expression solemn.

She *had* been interrogating him. The truth was, she was taken aback. She'd half expected that Adam was bringing her here to show her the *Lady in Red*. To rub her nose in it.

Instead, he'd shown her the son the world had no idea he'd fathered. Dom was the best-kept secret in the Western Hemisphere. How had Adam managed it? And why?

Curiosity was an itch demanding to be scratched, but Maribelle was right. The person to grill was Adam.

She smiled at Dom. "Have you met John Doe yet?"

He shook his head. "Does he work for Papa too?"

"The other way around. Your Papa waits on John hand and foot."

Dom giggled like she was being silly, the first child-like sound to issue from the boy. "Papa doesn't work for anybody. Right, Mama? Papa's the boss of everyone."

He was repeating her words, no doubt. But she didn't look embarrassed.

"Right you are, sweetie. And you can bet your bottom dollar he's upstairs reminding Roland of that right now, giving him the dickens for letting you run around outside on this pretty day instead of holding your nose to the grindstone."

Dom looked down at the knobby knees sticking out of his shorts. A fresh scrape leaked a dot of blood. He flattened it with his fingertip.

"I didn't mean to get Mr. Roland in trouble." Dom's voice was small.

"Don't worry," said his mother, "I'll smooth his feathers after your father leaves."

Her eyes shifted to Maddie. "So. Who's John Doe?" Her smirk said she figured the name for an alias, like Adam could be harboring a spy. Or a hit man.

"John's a dog," Maddie said. "Adam rescued him after he was left for dead."

Maribelle sipped her wine, unimpressed. But Dom was all ears.

"Papa has a dog? Is he okay? Is he here?"

"Yes, he's okay," Maddie said, smiling at the boy, "and yes, he's here. Want to meet him?"

He jumped up. "Is he outside in the car? Can we go get him?"

"He's at your father's house."

"Oh." The boy sat down again. "I'm not allowed over there when Papa's home."

Maddie flicked a glance at Maribelle, whose shrug said, *I told you so.*

Maddie kept a straight face, but she thought, *What the fuck?* The boy was a treasure, yet Adam apparently lavished more love on a stray dog than his own son.

She ruffled Dom's hair. "I'll bring John over in a little while, okay?"

He brightened again. "Does he fetch?"

"He tries, but he hasn't gotten the hang of it. Maybe you can teach him."

He popped up again. "I have tennis balls. I'll go find them." He started for the door, then put on the brakes. "Is he big? His mouth, I mean."

"Big enough to catch a tennis ball."

He grinned, then ran out.

Maddie met Maribelle's eyes. The other woman looked bored, but Maddie wasn't buying it.

"Sorry," Maddie said. "I should've asked about bringing John over. Is it okay? He's had his shots. And he doesn't have fleas."

Maribelle shrugged. "Just keep him off the furniture." She faked a yawn. "Where did Adam find him?"

"In Brooklyn."

"So Adam's slumming now?"

Maddie's teeth set. "John was outside my apartment."

The perfectly shaped brows arched fractionally. "But you told Dom you live in New York City."

"Which Brooklyn is part of."

"Hmm. Well. What kind of lawyer are you?" The tiny crease between her bluebell eyes gave the lie to her phony nonchalance.

Maddie put it together. "Not family law, if that's what you're wondering."

Her relief was palpable, but curiosity kept the crease in her brow. "Then why are you here?"

Feeling a reluctant kinship with the woman, Maddie said, "I'm here because Adam's the boss of everyone."

Maribelle's eyes widened, her surprise genuine this time. But before she could reply, they heard his footsteps. Both of them turned. He stopped just inside the door.

"Maddie." He said it like she was supposed to dash to his side.

She stretched her arm along the back of the sofa.

He looked annoyed, but came further into the room. "Where's Dominick?"

Maribelle swirled her wine. "Looking for tennis balls to throw to your dog."

He cut a sharp glance at Maddie.

She smiled sweetly. "I'm bringing John over to play." She stated it as fact. She wasn't asking his permission.

He focused on Maribelle, who was giving Maddie another long study. "Roland said you gave Dom the day off."

"That's right." She tore her gaze away from Maddie. "It's too nice outside for him to have his nose in a book." She tipped her head toward the door. "He's building a fort."

"For what purpose?"

"For fun, Adam. Remember fun?" Maribelle's feet hit the floor. "Isn't it enough that he's stuck here on Gilligan's Island without any friends to play with? Can't he at least amuse himself?"

Adam's jaw ticked. This was obviously an ongoing battle.

Maddie couldn't help butting into it.

"Is his schoolwork suffering?" she asked.

Maribelle answered her, but glared at Adam. "Dom's a genius. Certifiable. He's college level in reading, math, and science. He doesn't need more studying. He needs more *fun*. And more time with—"

"Enough." Adam cut her off with one word. "Maddie, we're leaving." He headed for the door.

She decided not to argue. "I'll be back soon with John," she said to Maribelle, who lifted a careless hand.

Outside, Adam was holding the car door. "I'm not John," she snapped, brushing past him. "I don't come when you whistle."

"No," he bit out, "you come when I fuck you."

She stopped with her butt halfway to the seat, hanging in midair. "You did not just say that."

He nudged her shoulder, just enough so she landed in the seat. Then he shut the door.

She glared as he circled the hood.

He got in and started the car. But he didn't drive. Instead, he put his hands on the wheel and stared out the windshield, jaw rigid, shoulders knotted.

She gave him ten seconds, then "What the fuck, Adam?" She meant it any number of ways. There were half a dozen to choose from.

He turned his head, blasted her with blue flame. Then just as quickly, the fire died out of his eyes. He let his shoulders go slack. "Forgive me. It's just that you looked . . . chummy with Maribelle. It upset me. You don't know her like I do."

"Obviously. I don't have a *child* with her." Maddie's emotional chaos took a backseat to Dom. "Jesus, Adam. You've got a kid. *What the fuck?*"

He dropped his eyes. "It's a long story."

"At least nine years and nine months. And whatever it is, I don't care. The bottom line is you're keeping him and Maribelle prisoner."

He looked up, his expression incredulous. "You're joking."

"A gilded cage is still a cage." And abuse was abuse. Her heart beat like a hammer. "He's a hostage. You're using him to control his mother."

"Quite the contrary, Maddie. *She's* using him to control *me*. She always has."

Angry again, he threw the car into gear and pealed out of the drive. "She deliberately got pregnant when she knew I didn't want a child. Christ, I was twenty-six!"

The gate was still open. He hit the road going too fast, taking the turn like they were back on the race-track.

Maddie gripped the seat with both hands. "Are you married to her?"

"Good God, no. I was helpless about the child, but I wouldn't let her con me to the altar. And I made damn sure he was mine before I gave him my name."

"So you hide him here, your mistake. And his mother has to play along or you'll take him away from her."

He barked a laugh. "Wrong again, Maddie." The tires squealed as he braked in front of his villa. He shut off the engine and turned to face her again. "Maribelle calls the plays in this little game. Dominick turned nine this year, so the price of her silence is nine million. It goes up on his birthday each year."

"Then why pay it? Why are you hiding him?"

His hands gripped the wheel hard. "The pat answer, and it's true as far as it goes, is for his own protection. As my son, he's a kidnapping target. I don't know if I could live with that kind of worry."

His knuckles were white. "Here, I can keep him safe. Even if someone suspects he exists, this compound is impenetrable except from the air." He slid his eyes to hers. "For that, Gerard has ground-to-air rockets."

She tried to condemn him—"That's terrorist weaponry"—but how could she condemn a man who'd stop at nothing to protect his family? Again, he'd turned right and wrong on its head, and upended her principles in the process.

He must have sensed her halfheartedness, because he didn't engage. Instead, he said, "I told you that was only part of the answer. The other part is that he's an embarrassment."

Her back went up. She didn't equivocate about this.

"Dom's an amazing kid. You should be proud, not embarrassed."

"You don't understand. I'm not embarrassed by Dominick, per se. I'm embarrassed that he exists. That I let Maribelle dupe me." He raked a hand through his hair, self-aware enough to look sheepish. "It sounds foolish when I say it out loud, but there it is."

She grappled with it for a moment, then nutshelled it. "She tried to trick you into marrying her by getting pregnant. You got pissed and wouldn't give her the satisfaction. So you're torturing each other with the kid because you both took a shot to the ego."

She opened her door, but didn't get out. "Now it's a standoff. You've got the money, she's got the kid. If she meets your terms, meaning she keeps her mouth shut and hides the kid, you keep paying. If you stop paying, she blabs it to *People* for ten mil and takes the kid back to Hollywood."

She shook her head, disgusted. "No wonder you hate each other."

HANDS IN HIS pockets, Adam watched from the window of his study as Maddie disappeared down the path toward Maribelle's villa, John dashing ahead joyfully.

They were abandoning him. They didn't care that he was the mighty Adam LeCroix. He wasn't important to them. They were on to other things, other people.

He sucked a breath that carved through his chest like a blade. Not since childhood had he felt so lonely, so . . . unnecessary. Even John had turned his back.

Adam dug his hands deeper into his pockets. He didn't want a dog anyway. Better if John stayed with Dominick. He was an encumbrance. A nuisance. Always underfoot.

John, that is. He couldn't say the same about Dom, because the boy was barred from the main house when Adam was at home. Not that he hadn't snuck in on occasion, pestering Henry and Fredo, playing pranks to get Adam's attention.

Adam had no tolerance for it. He'd send the boy packing, then blister Maribelle's ear, sounding off, making empty threats. She'd fire right back at him, claws out, and it would escalate into a fight that neither of them bothered to spare Dom.

Before Maddie had waltzed off with his dog, she'd bluntly described them as a pair of self-absorbed, pigheaded idiots who had by some miracle created a great kid that neither of them deserved.

The woman didn't mince words. And she was right.

But there was nothing to be done about it, was there? Nothing except his duty, to see the boy cared for and educated, give him a leg up in the world. And if something about that didn't set quite right, well, he'd do what he always did where Dom was concerned—push him out of his mind.

Turning away from the window, he sat down at his desk to do just that, but damn it, Gio had taken his computer away to be analyzed.

And wasn't that another unsettling problem? So far the testing led to just one conclusion: The system had been disarmed from that unit, and Adam was the only person who could have done it.

Rising again, he paced the spacious room. Afternoon sun glanced off the polished floors, the mahogany desk. He paused at the bar, poured two fingers of Scotch, took a swallow, then set it down and forgot it.

He found himself back at the window, staring blindly at the path. The only good news was that Maddie hadn't sent for her sister. That meant he had one more night with her. He'd have to make it count.

For sure, he wouldn't be mentioning her father again. Her reaction left no doubt in his mind; she'd been abused, sexually, and dear old dad was the abuser.

That key unlocked so many of her mysteries. Like why she'd left home for good at eighteen, then sacrificed so much to care for her sister. Why she'd sworn off marriage and children of her own. Why she didn't trust the facade of a *nice* middle-class home.

What it didn't explain was why her mother hadn't protected her. His experience with his own mother notwithstanding, he knew that was what mothers were supposed to do.

Even Maribelle had that much of it right. Despite her threats, in his heart he knew she'd never put Dominick at risk. Just as she knew he'd never cut off the money. The fact that neither of them would admit it made their standoff that much stupider.

He paced some more, his troubled thoughts circling between Maddie's parents and his own, then inevitably winding around to himself and Maribelle.

For certain, Maddie'd had the worst of the lot. His own narcissistic parents looked good in comparison. For one, they'd never actively injured him. And even though he'd believed all his life that they hadn't wanted him, they'd never explicitly said so. For the most part, they simply ignored him.

As a father, he realized uncomfortably, he fell somewhere on the spectrum between his parents and Maddie's. He'd never physically abused Dom, as Maddie's father had abused her. But where his parents' greatest sin was neglect, he'd gone further and actively barred Dom from his home, repeatedly and openly rejecting his own son without a thought for how it might damage him.

And damage him it would. Look how his parents and Maddie's, with their separate brands of dysfunction, had warped their children's lives.

He sank his hands deeper in his pockets.

How had he, who took such pride in his unflinching self-awareness, not acknowledged before now what his callousness would do to Dom? He hadn't set out to wound the boy. But a knife wielded recklessly sliced just as deep.

He stepped back from the window and found the Scotch he'd abandoned, took a slug, and tried to salve his conscience. He'd make amends to the boy. Pay some attention to him. Ask him about his studies. He couldn't be the kind of father his son obviously wanted. There was too much history there, too much water under the bridge.

But even if he couldn't love the boy, he could at least quit being such a bloody bastard to him.

MADDIE HAD BEEN smitten with Lucy from the moment her parents brought her home from the hospital, swaddled in a pretty pink blanket. She'd changed Lucy's diapers, warmed her bottle, and sung her to sleep in her crib. When Lucy cried, Maddie distracted her father. When she started to toddle and knock things over, Maddie took the blame.

Then, when Lucy was four, Maddie went off to college and left her sister to their mother's dubious care. And she'd never gone back again.

In truth, Maddie had run away.

But through college, through law school, through the first hectic years as a prosecutor, Lucy was never far from Maddie's mind. And when Lucy entered her teens, Maddie hired a private detective to get a package into her hands without their parents' knowledge.

It held five hundred dollars, a cell phone and charger, and a note explaining what to do with them.

For three years, she didn't hear a word from Lucy. For all she knew, her sister had ditched the phone and spent the money on weed. But on Lucy's sixteenth birthday she stayed home all day and night. Just in case.

The call came at nine-thirty. The cab showed up at midnight. And just like that, Maddie had a little sister again. She quit the U.S. Attorney's Office the next day and took the job with the firm. And she hadn't regretted it for a minute.

But she'd never stopped regretting that she hadn't freed Lucy from that house sooner, before she'd had to learn things the hard way. Maddie would always wish that she'd shielded her from that disillusionment and pain.

Now here was Dom, with his intelligent eyes so much like Adam's, and the rolling laugh that had surprised her the first time she heard it, but that now seemed like the most essential part of him. He could still have a healthy and happy life, if his parents would only put him ahead of their own bruised egos.

Dom's laugh was constant and contagious as he galloped around the yard in pursuit of John, whose only game was keep-away.

Maribelle drifted off the terrace to stand beside Maddie where she was taking a breather in the shade. "Boys and dogs," she said, summing it up.

"Yep. How come he doesn't have one?"

Maribelle did the shrug, but it didn't seem studied now. "He never asked, and I never thought of it. I wish I had. I've never seen him so happy."

John pivoted on his back legs, swished past Dom just an inch out of reach. Dom spun to chase him, tripped over his own feet, and landed on his face.

Maddie tensed, expecting tears, while John circled back, tail tucked in apology. He dropped the ball to nose the boy, and Dom, laughing wildly, rolled over and grabbed it, then clambered to his feet and took off, John bounding merrily behind him.

"Tough kid," Maddie said.

"He gets that from his father." Maribelle gave her a crooked smile. "I cry if I break a nail. But Adam's built for pain. Taking it and dishing it out."

She seemed to mean the physical kind, so Maddie said, "Does he box?"

"No. He fights. I guess you haven't seen him after a brawl. Black eyes and bandages, arm strapped around his ribs until they knit."

This was news. "Wouldn't that make the papers? Adam LeCroix in a brawl?"

Maribelle slid her a sideways look. "You haven't figured out yet that Adam knows how to keep secrets?"

Secrets like having a kid. Stealing a Renoir.

"Remember that movie *Fight Club*?" said Maribelle. "A bunch of guys beating on each other, testosterone on the hoof. *The only rule is . . .* blah blah."

"Yeah, I remember it. Brad Pitt, totally ripped."

Maribelle grinned. "He's even hotter in person."

"That's impossible."

"But true. Anyway, that's Adam's deal. He's got a fight club."

"Why?" And why was she dishing about Adam with Maribelle?

Because the woman knew things, that's why.

"He grew up on the streets," said Maribelle. "But you probably know that. You prosecuted him over the *Lady in Red*."

So Maribelle had Googled her. "I *tried* to prosecute him," Maddie said. "My boss wouldn't let me. But I don't know much about his childhood except that his parents were big-time artists and he parlayed their paintings into zillions."

"Everybody knows that, how he turned sixty paintings into sixty million in five years, yada yada. But growing up, he was a vagabond. His parents were basically squatters, moving from one rich person's guesthouse to another's, wearing out their welcome, screwing around on each other, fighting like cats and dogs. And ignoring Adam.

"It's a real-life Dickensian tale," she said dryly, but not entirely without sympathy. "He was on his own, an easy target, despised by rich and poor alike. He got beat up *a lot*. And I have this from Henry, who knows everything there is to know about Adam. Henry keeps most of it to himself, but he's told me some stories over the years."

And she seemed more than willing to share them with Maddie, which only made sense, since she couldn't talk to another soul about them.

"So Adam got good at taking care of himself," she went on. "Fighting and thieving and guarding his turf. Which is why loyalty's everything to him. You mess with Adam once and forget it, you're on the outside forever."

And didn't that explain a lot about the man? Like his loyalty to his friends. The street skills he kept sharp by training . . . and stealing. And why he knew nothing at all about being a father.

Maddie looked up at Maribelle, six feet of supernatural beauty, and the look on the woman's face said she was living proof. She'd messed up, and now she was as far out of Adam's life as he could get her.

CHAPTER TWENTY

"LET'S GO SWIMMING," Maddie said to Dom. They were panting almost as hard as John, who'd flopped in the grass, his sides pumping like bellows.

Dom looked regretful. "Papa's in residence."

"I'll take care of *Papa*." Imagine barring his son from the pool. What a dick.

She sent Dom off for his swimsuit while she told Maribelle about it. "Want to come along?" she asked, grateful when Maribelle declined. Side by side in swimsuits, Maddie's legs would look even stumpier. And she could stand under the woman's bust like an awning.

"Don't be surprised when he throws Dom out," said Maribelle.

"If he does, I'll be sleeping over here tonight."

"I'll have Giselle get your room ready."

Maddie laughed. So did Maribelle. Unexpected camaraderie that neither knew quite what to make of.

On the path to Adam's villa, Dom walked soberly at Maddie's side while John herded them along like a Border collie. Now that he'd found Dom, he wouldn't let the boy out of his sight.

"Go ahead and take John to the pool," Maddie said, "while I get changed." *And while I show your father he's not the boss of everyone.*

Adam met her coming in. He must have seen them from the window, because his face was a thunder-cloud. She marched straight into the storm.

"You got the plane gassed up? Pilots on standby?"

That set him back on his heels. "No. I was hoping—"

"Good. Because I'm thinking I'll stick around a few days. If you can keep from pissing me off, that is."

"Okay." He raked his hair. "That's good. I want to talk to you—"

"Fine. Let's talk in the pool." She brushed past him, heading for her suite. "Dom's out there with John. We worked up a big sweat tearing around the yard."

"Maddie, I—"

"Get your suit on. I'll be right out." And she closed her door in his face.

Stripping off her sweaty T-shirt, she wondered if it was a mistake to stick her nose in. Too bad if it was. The kid deserved better.

Adam did too. He was stuck in a groove he'd dug ten years ago, back when he was still scratching and scrap-ing his way to the top of the shit pile, working hard and playing harder. Proving himself to the world and to every dickhead who'd ever doubted him.

It made all kinds of sense now, his need to constantly prove himself. Ignored by shitty parents, beaten up by bullies, tormented and picked on by pea-brained kids who were happy just to find somebody weaker to de-spise. He was still giving all of them the finger.

Even Maribelle. And once upon a time, she deserved it. But ten years of water had flowed under the bridge since she'd tried to trap him, and if Maddie was any judge of people, the woman had changed as much as he had. For sure, she regretted her treachery; it cost her a Hollywood career and forced her to live a lie. But just as surely, she didn't regret her son.

Maddie ripped the tags off another bikini, wriggled into the barely-there bottoms.

She wasn't wasting any sympathy on Maribelle. She was an adult, she'd have to fend for herself. But Dom was just a kid. He needed all the help he could get.

Slipping barefoot into the hallway, Maddie put an ear to Adam's door, but heard only silence. He could be in there changing into trunks, or outside sending Dom packing.

She sprinted for the pool, found Dom sitting on the side, feet dangling in the shallow end. John was doggie-paddling in circles, trying to lure him in.

No sign of Adam.

"How's the water?"

"Always the same. Eighty-six degrees."

The kid was too serious. She walked around behind him and shoved him in.

He sank like a stone.

"Shit!" She jumped in. The water was only four feet, but it was over his head. She hauled him up by his armpits, adrenaline pumping, mentally rehearsing her CPR.

He broke the surface laughing. She let go and he treaded water easily.

"You little shit. You scared me!"

"That's what you get for horsing around in the pool."

"Who's the adult here?" she grumbled. John paddled through the narrow space between them, and she feigned annoyance with him too. "Jesus, John, we've got Lake Michigan here. Spread out, will ya?"

Dom giggled. Then his face went slack.

Maddie glanced over her shoulder. Adam. Adam in board shorts.

Jesus. That body. Like Brad Pitt in *Fight Club.*

John paddled in his direction.

Tearing her eyes away to check Dom, she realized he was scared stiff. "Want to race?" she said. He blinked uncertainly. She looked over her shoulder again. "Hey Adam, want to race?"

It was the right thing to say. The man couldn't resist a competition.

He dove over John Doe, surfaced a few feet away from them, slicking back his jet hair. His eyes were bluer than the pool. "I suppose you'll want a head start," he said.

"Of course." She set the rules. "Two laps. When Dom gets to the far end, I'll start. When I get halfway, you can start. No calling interference on John, he'll be everyone's problem. Loser gets the drinks."

She lost. "It's John's fault," she griped, heaving herself up to sit on the side.

Adam swam over, grinning, and cupped her calf in his palm. "Drinks are in the cabana. Dom, what'll you have?"

The boy swam over, tentatively, keeping Maddie between them. "Coke, please."

"Gin and tonic for me." Adam slid his hand up behind her knee. It felt amazingly sexy. She dawdled, hating to break contact.

Then John paddled into the middle of things. He'd found a ball somewhere. Adam let go of her to hurl it the length of the pool, and with a collective whoop, all three males raced after it.

And that, thought Maddie as she clunked ice into glasses, made playing barmaid worthwhile.

OF COURSE, WITH Adam, things were never that simple.

"I want dinner alone with you," he said, managing to complain and command in the same breath.

"I already told Henry I'm eating with Dom." Maddie peeled off her suit, then opened the bathroom door enough to stick her head out. Adam sat pouting on the edge of her bed. "You're welcome to join us if you want."

"You and I have things to discuss."

"Whenever we discuss things, you piss me off. Let's take a break and enjoy a meal for a change."

He looked ready to argue, so she pulled her head in and turned on the shower, calling over her shoulder. "Maribelle can come too."

"No." All command, no equivocation. She smiled to herself. How to make Dom less objectionable to Adam? Make him the alternative to Maribelle.

"Okay, no Maribelle. Now get your wet ass off my bed and take a shower."

"All right, let me in." He stood outside the glass door.

"Beat it."

"Gladly, if I can watch you soap up while I do it."

"Har har."

He flattened a palm on the glass. "Why are you being so difficult?"

"Because I don't like you very much today. I'm still wondering if this whole trip is a setup to humiliate me. And even if it isn't, men who neglect their children are my least favorite kind."

He stepped back from the glass. "You don't understand. It's not black and white."

"Explain it to me."

"Let me in and I will."

She remembered his hand on her calf, the silky stroke up her leg.

She opened the door.

He stepped under the spray, locked eyes on her

soapy breasts. She let him look, while water streamed from his shoulders, sluiced down his arms.

Then he fisted his hands. His forearms flexed, his biceps jumped. And she couldn't resist; she reached out and touched them.

That was all it took, a skim of her fingertips. He pushed her against the wall. Pinned her with his chest, groping her, kneading her, thumbing her breasts. His mouth crushed her lips. He took her tongue like he owned it.

She let him handle her while she handled him back, feeding him her tongue, palming his taut ass, rubbing her slick belly along the rigid length of his cock.

Steam swirled around them, rose from their skin. His lips slid along her jaw, down her throat. And he moaned, deep and low, a mating call that vibrated through skin and bones, to her veins. Unconsciously, she answered with a hum that rose from her belly, galvanizing him, galvanizing them both.

He caught her arms and wrapped them round his neck. Boosted her thighs and hooked them over his hipbones. Then he brought her down on him as he thrust up.

He gave her a heartbeat, just one to adjust, and then went at her like a stallion mounting a mare. His teeth clamped her shoulder, his fingers bruised her ass, and she held on for dear life, riding the heat as he pumped.

Water coursed into her eyes and she closed them, heightening sensation. The stubble scraping her jaw. The slip and slide of wet skin. His cock stretching her, filling her.

It was hard and fast, too frantic for finesse. He worked her sweet spots, driving her higher. She fisted his hair, dragging him closer. Her back slapped the wall as he pounded her. He muttered her name like a mantra. And still it wasn't enough. She wanted him under her skin, running in her blood.

He lifted his face, eyes wild and blue. "Come," he panted, "come with me, all over me."

"Yes," she gasped out, "yes yes yes." Clasping his cheeks, she pulled his face down to hers and took his lips, kissing him as she'd never kissed a man before, taking the passion he poured into her, absorbing it, loving it, and trading her own, until they exploded, the violence driving their lips apart even as their bodies fused into one.

ROLLING OFF THE pillows they'd stacked in the middle of her bed, Maddie mumbled, "Whatever you're taking, you should buy the company."

He raised his head, eyed her. "Name your price."

She snuffled a snort, peeled back one lid. "Nobody gets it up again in ten minutes."

"You have that effect on me." He flopped back. "And you're increasingly addictive."

She rolled her eye toward the clock. "I'm getting Dom in half an hour. Is that enough time?"

"I should be good for one more."

"Funny. I mean is it enough time to explain."

He knew very well what she meant. But he wasn't in a hurry to change the mood. During sex, she focused on him completely, responsive and willing and up for anything. Trusting, as she was at no other time.

But when the subject shifted to Dom, he knew she'd cut him no slack. And he didn't want her to. What he wanted was to make her understand.

"Maribelle tricked me. I cared for her, more than I'd ever cared for a woman, but it wasn't enough for her. She got pregnant simply to tie me down, even though I had no imminent plans to leave her."

"But she knew it was coming, right? I mean, with your history, even up to that point, a woman would have to be brain dead to think you'd settle down willingly."

"Does that excuse bringing an unwanted child into the world?" He stuffed a pillow under his head. "She made a person, Maddie, and then demanded that I care about him."

"Do you?"

"You see the lengths I've gone to. He's safer than Fort Knox."

"So was your Monet."

"Don't remind me." He would have sat up, but she put a hand on his chest. Light as a feather, it nailed him to the bed.

He laid his own hand over it, hoping she wouldn't withdraw it. He'd keep talking if he must, just to keep it there.

"It's not enough," she said. "A good parent protects a child from more than gunmen. What about the bogeyman under the bed? Fear of the dark, the future, all the unknowns?"

"He's not alone. Maribelle, for all her faults, is a surprisingly good mother. Or rather, she's become one. In the early years, she didn't let Dom slow her down. She left him for weeks at a time. Monaco, St. Tropez. Back to Hollywood. Spending the money I gave her. She had affairs, slept around, trying to wound me, no doubt."

He folded an arm behind his head, remembering that he'd kept loose tabs on her, but that was all. And he'd left Dom to the nanny, feeling as little guilt as Maribelle had.

"She's grown out of that now," he said, realizing it was true. "She's seldom away for more than a few days. She spends most of her time with Dom."

"Stuck in that villa."

He shrugged. "She redecorates it twice a year, top to bottom. When I'm away, she and Dom have the run of the grounds. And I'm frequently away."

"Ever asked yourself how that makes Dom feel? Knowing that you despise him?"

"I don't despise him." He just didn't want to see him, didn't want to be reminded of the things Dom reminded him of.

"Have you ever hugged him, or ruffled his hair, or swung him up on your shoulder?"

"No. But my father never did those things to me either. He barely noticed I was alive."

"So it's a cycle of abuse. Emotional abuse. You're doing to him what your parents did to you."

It was one thing to admit it to himself, another to hear it from her lips. He wasn't quite ready for that. Sitting up, he glowered down at her where she lay curled like a kitten against the pillows.

"It's not the same," he said. "No one will ever drag him into an alley and kick him till he pukes, or hold him down while their friends beat his face to a pulp. No one will *ever* break that boy's nose, or his spirit. Not as long as I have a nickel to my name."

Her eyes had gone green against the rumpled sage sheets. Calm and deep, watching him with compassion, unusual for her.

He realized he was rasping, fighting for air. Sweat beaded his chest.

"I protect him," he said, his voice rough with emotion. "No one can hurt him here."

"No one," she said, "except you."

"PIZZA!" DOM SHOUTED, utterly at ease with Maddie. "Can John have some too?"

Two stories above them, Adam couldn't hear her response, but it brought on a gale of giggles as the boy wiggled his butt into the chair.

Henry had lit torches around the terrace perimeter. They glowed brighter as the sun inched below the horizon.

Now he cut the pie and slid slices onto plates, filled glasses with wine and soda. And unobtrusively removed the third place setting.

Adam watched them, his son and the woman he loved, sitting at a small round table on his terrace while the only dog he'd ever owned circled round them.

Behind him, the door opened and Henry barged in. "You're an ass," he said bluntly.

Adam glanced over his shoulder, then back down at the terrace. He couldn't argue the point with a straight face.

"Go down there," Henry urged. "Eat pizza with your son. Drink wine with your woman."

Adam shook his head. "I'd only raise false hopes all around. Mine as much as theirs."

"Why false? Why not claim this boy of yours? He couldn't be more like you."

"Is that supposed to recommend him?"

"To anyone else in the world, yes." He joined Adam at the window. "And Maddie. For the love of God, look at her. Thumbing her nose at the mighty Adam Le-Croix. Defying you just by eating pizza."

He turned to Adam, uncharacteristically impatient. "You're fucking it up, Adam."

He was right, and yet Adam stayed glued to the floor.

"Forget the Matisse," Henry hissed. "The Monet. The fucking *Lady in Red*. Your treasure's down there." He jabbed a finger at the terrace. "Go and get it."

Through the window, Adam heard Dom's giggling

again. Maddie wagged a finger at John Doe, who slinked away with a crust in his mouth.

It was a silly, homey sight, and he wanted to laugh at Henry, to scoff at the fancy of Adam LeCroix as a family man.

But he couldn't force a sound past the lump in his throat.

For ten years, since Maribelle betrayed him, he'd walled up foolish notions like hearth and home. Then Maddie, hard-nosed, smart-mouthed, pocket-sized Maddie, swanned right through the wall like it was tissue paper.

She was right, he thought, the whole business was a setup, but not to humiliate her. Just the opposite. The plot had been conceived, organized, and perpetrated by his back brain because his front brain was too stubborn to know what was good for him.

Half a decade ago, Maddie had intrigued him, attracted him, and nearly nailed him to the wall. Because that last part had pissed him off, he'd dismissed the rest of it and put her out of his mind.

He was—and he was just learning this—expert at burying inconvenient emotions.

But when the Hawthorne thing came up, his tricky subconscious put it all together and, voilà, once he was in the same room with Maddie again it was just a matter of time—say, five minutes—before even his thick-skulled front brain knew he had to have her.

It took a bit longer to understand that he wanted more than sex. After Maribelle, relationships involving organs located above his waist were off-limits. But with Maddie, he wanted it all.

Dom, though, was more than he'd bargained for. He'd deliberately—and cruelly—withheld affection from the boy since conception. Now, in one afternoon, he'd stopped seeing Dom as a gun held to his head or even as evidence of his foolishness.

Instead, he saw his son.

The change in perspective staggered him.

Henry crossed his arms. "There's no going back, you know. You can't pretend anymore that he doesn't exist, your own flesh and blood. I saw you in the pool. You were happy."

Happy.

Adam gazed down at the terrace, at the woman he cared for, the son she'd brought to his doorstep. Even the dog he'd craved as a child.

It was everything he wanted, though he hadn't known it until now.

The question was what to do about it.

HANDS IN HIS pockets, heart in his throat, Adam strolled onto the terrace. John loped across the flag-stones to greet him.

Rubbing the dog's floppy ears, he forced his lips up at the corners. "Sorry I'm late, I had some things to take care of."

Maddie's eyes gleamed in the torchlight. "No problem." She pushed out a chair with her foot. "Henry's bringing out another pizza."

He sat down. Dom hadn't said a word. Adam didn't know what to think. For years, the boy had begged for his attention, but these last few months he'd made himself scarce. Had he given up on his father?

He made himself meet his son's steady gaze, made himself hold those deep blue eyes, so like the eyes that looked back from the mirror each morning. And he made himself smile. Not the chilly slant of tight lips the boy was familiar with, but a warm smile that came from the heart. The same smile that had come so naturally while cavorting in the pool, but that now seemed like the biggest risk he'd ever taken.

And his son smiled back. Adam's heart beat again. He lifted his gaze to Maddie's. She was smiling too.

Finally, it seemed, he'd done something right.

CHAPTER TWENTY-ONE

Tiptoeing back to bed, Maddie took a minute to rake a greedy eye over the bod she was about to pounce on.

Adam had rolled onto his back, one long arm outflung, the other cocked behind his head, both corded with lean muscle. His chest and those one, two, three, yes, four rows of washboard abs looked extra tanned against the white sheets.

And a dark triangle of hair pointed south like a road sign, as if she might otherwise miss the three-hundred-thread-count tent that housed his most excellent equipment.

She'd have to be blind.

His eyes were closed, half hidden under a jumble of black satin hair. But his full lips curved into a smile. "I can feel you staring."

"Really? How does it feel?"

He opened his eyes, licked them down her naked body. Steam rose from her skin.

His smile deepened. His fingers did a come-to-me curl she didn't try to resist. Settling her cheek into the notch of his shoulder, she looped her thigh over his, a perfect fit.

A warm, fuzzy feeling fizzed under her ribs. She tried not to think about it, but it was hard to ignore. It had been humming along since last night, since they played Ping-Pong with Dom, Adam left-handed to give them a chance.

He'd routed them anyway, even with John on his team costing him a point for every stolen ball. And she—usually the sorest of losers—couldn't summon a pout, because they'd had so much fun, laughing and trash talking like a nice, happy family might do, if such a thing existed.

Which it didn't, as all three of them—four, counting John—could attest.

Yet for one night they'd forgotten that, and now, even with the morning sunlight slanting through the window, the warm fuzzies persisted.

She resigned herself to enjoy them.

For now.

Stroking her palm over the planes of Adam's pecs, she felt the rise and fall of his deep, steady breath. With a fingertip she traced a line lower, strummed the washboard.

"I don't get it," she murmured. "How can you have four rows with Leonardo cooking for you?"

"I work out like a demon."

"Pfft. You haven't lifted anything heavier than a wine bottle."

"I lifted you, darling, more than once."

True. And getting flipped and rolled and tossed around was The Hottest Thing Ever.

She snaked lower, fingertips dipping under the edge of the sheet. "So you benched me a few times. How else do you burn calories?"

"I climb. Run. Lift weights." He rolled his hips, urging her south.

She paused to play in the springy hair.

"Fight?" She couldn't help being curious.

He didn't reply. She inched away from the tent pole.

"Yes," he hissed out. "Fight, if you must know."

"Why?" She spread her palm on the flat ground between his hipbones.

"It feels good."

"Getting hit feels good?"

"Not at the time. But surviving feels good. Winning feels good."

"You're an unusual guy, Adam." She used her nails lightly.

"At the moment, I'm like any other man with a hard-on. Now for God's sake, Maddie." His hand came down over hers and shoved it under the tent.

"IT's BUSINESS," ADAM said, straight-faced.

Maddie pursed her lips. "Sounds like more fun and games to me."

"Hardly. The vineyard's a recent acquisition, overdue for a visit from the new owner."

Armed with facts and figures about the Piedmont region and the quantity and quality of the Barolo produced by his newly acquired winery, he braced for the grilling.

But after a long study through narrowed eyes, she simply said, "We're taking the Ferrari?"

"No, the Ducati."

Her eyes widened satisfyingly. "That explains the leather pants in my closet."

And didn't she look like a badass, strutting out of the villa in them? With the matching jacket, they fit like a second skin. She'd slicked on lipstick too, dead-sexy red.

He settled the helmet over her head. "I want your hands on my waist at all times."

"Afraid I'll fall off?"

"No. I'm afraid you'll get into mischief. I need my mind on the road, not on my cock."

He started off slow—like sex—to give her time to adjust. Then opened the throttle and they blasted off like a missile, the winding road vanishing in their slipstream.

He bypassed Genoa, weaving through the hills, past silvery olive groves, and grapevines laid out in lines straight and true, baking under blue skies and summer sun.

This was freedom. Behind the visor he was anonymous, just a man on a bike leaning into the wind, with his woman at his back and the world by the balls.

When his own vineyard came into view, he considered blowing past it, streaking north into the Alps, out of Italy, through Switzerland. Just driving, driving with her arms around him.

But he missed her face. That was the downside of the bike. They couldn't talk. He couldn't see her smile.

So he slowed, took the turn, and when they stood on solid ground again, helmets off, her eyes sparkling like diamonds, he lifted her in a testosterone-fueled hug that squeezed a squeal from her.

"That was *amazing*!" She couldn't stop laughing.

His arms around her tiny waist held her at eye level. "You're a speed junkie. So am I."

"Did my hair turn white? Because you took ten years off my life."

"Not white, but you do have helmet head."

"So do you." She poked her fingers through his hair.

"Unavoidable. But please don't stop."

"That's my line." Her wicked grin went straight to his balls.

Twisting her fingers in his hair, she leaned in, bit

his lip. Turned it into a kiss. His arms tightened. She angled her head, deepened the kiss. And he heard it, the humming in her throat. It vibrated through him, sapping his sanity.

When she pulled back, glassy-eyed, puffy-lipped, his breath shuddered. "Christ Jesus, Maddie, I can't get enough of you."

She managed a laugh. "So we're sex fiends and speed junkies. What does that say about us?"

"There's more between us than that." He wanted her to admit it.

"Yeah, two pricey layers of cowhide." She slapped his shoulders. "Put me down, King Kong."

He wanted her to speak the truth he saw in her eyes when he was inside her. But she wasn't ready yet, and making an issue would only harden her asinine resolve.

He let her slide down his chest. Released her reluctantly.

She peeled off her jacket, down to a silk tank. "This rig's too hot when we're not moving at light speed."

He tossed her jacket on the seat with his own. "I'm afraid we outpaced Fredo. He should be here shortly with a change of clothes."

"You're kidding."

"You said it yourself. Leather's too hot for a summer luncheon. Besides"—he did the knuckle kiss that predictably put stars in her eyes—"by the time we've sampled the wines of which I'm now the proud vintner, we'll be too drunk for the Ducati. Fredo will drive us home."

SHE COULD GET used to this. Not the obsequious buttkissing by every member of the staff, but the awesomeness of hanging out with Richie Rich, tooling around on his Ducati Streetfighter, wining and dining in the hot Italian sun.

Not to mention screwing their brains out in the back of a stretch limo with a mellow Barolo buzz.

No question, the man knew all the secrets of a woman's body. And he had The Best Toys money could buy.

And damn it, he made her laugh. At him, at herself. That shit was addictive.

So maybe it wasn't surprising that with all their screwing and laughing and having fun, he was getting The Wrong Idea about them. She'd have to set him straight.

She tapped his chest. He opened sleepy eyes, looked up at her from a sea of blue, and shifted his head slightly where it lay cradled on her lap.

"You sticking with your story that this was a *business* trip? Getting drunk in the sun and laid in the limo?"

He smiled, lazily, curled a warm palm around her wrist where it rested on his chest. "The latter part was the highlight, but I'd call it a successful day all around. We toured the facility, met the staff, sampled the wares, and enjoyed a pleasant luncheon with the key players, establishing a relationship and impressing upon them that I'm not a mere hobbyist, but a knowledgeable businessman with my eye on the bottom line."

He dug in his pocket, came out with a flash drive. "On here are the latest financials and, of particular interest to you, the most recent contracts with suppliers, insurers, and distributors." He tucked it into her cleavage. "Let me know what needs changing."

He was slick. She liked that about him.

In fact, she liked too damn many things about him. Like the annoying softness of his hair between her fingers. The stupid sexy bristles stippling his jaw. And the warm, melty look in his eyes.

It all brought on a bad case of the warm fuzzies.

She shook off his hand and crabbed at him. "Sit up, will you? You're as bad as John, always begging to be petted."

He grinned his mind-reading grin, the one that kicked up a little higher on the left side and made a roguish dimple on his suavely handsome face.

She got sort of light-headed gazing down at that grin.

Or maybe she was carsick.

Then he said, "I thought we'd have dinner with Dom tonight."

That really warmed up her fuzzies.

But it was sure to give him The Wrong Idea, so she shook her head. "You should have father-and-son time without me in the mix."

His eyes went soulful. "I need you in the mix. Dom and I both need you. Things are still awkward between us. I take full responsibility for that, but for now, it helps having you there." He linked his fingers through hers. "It's important to me, Maddie. Please."

The warm fuzzies snuggled around her heart. "Well, jeez, when you put it like that."

So maybe he'd get The Wrong Idea about it. She'd disabuse him of it later.

For now, she went for his zipper.

CHAPTER TWENTY-TWO

Vicky: I promise to walk with you through
the light and the dark,
the good times and the bad.

Maddie: Unless there are zombies,
then you're on your own.

LEANING BACK AGAINST the headboard, Maddie crossed her arms over her naked breasts. "All this sex is fucking things up."

Adam stroked a hand up her leg from ankle to apex. "An eloquent observation. Almost Shakespearean in its depth and complexity." He kissed the side of her knee. How could a knee be so appealing?

"Don't sweet-talk me. You know what I mean. Before we started screwing, everything was black and white. You magnate, me minion. I liked that."

"Darling, you *hated* that."

"I hated *you*. There's a difference."

He propped himself on an elbow, studied her troubled pout in the light of a new day. "And how do you feel now?" He knew how *he* felt. Like a lovesick puppy.

Her forehead furrowed. She didn't look lovesick. She looked annoyed.

"I feel like I should be earning the dough you're forking over to Cruella instead of fucking the boss blind."

"I see." He traced a random pattern on her thigh. "Would you feel better about fucking me if I fired you?"

She stuck out her lip. "If you fire me, I'll have to go home."

"And you'd rather stay here with me?" He wanted her to say it.

She shrugged. "This has been okay, but I have to get back to work sometime."

Stubborn woman. Why wouldn't she admit they were neck-deep in a red-hot affair that neither was nearly finished with?

He rolled out of bed, did the best Adam the Magnate he could manage with his junk hanging out.

"If it's work you want, Madeline, get your lazy ass out of bed. I'll keep your shoulder to the wheel all morning. But prepare to suffer a trip to the beach this afternoon. I promised Dom, so there'll be no wiggling out of it."

That got her attention. "You're taking him out in public?"

"It's my private beach. Gerard will secure it before we go." He lifted a hand before she could follow up. "I have to consider his security before going public. Gerard's working on it."

The subject made him edgy. He pushed a hand through his hair. "We'll bring Dom to New York with us next week, but we'll need more bodyguards. I've made do with Fredo because I can take care of myself. But Dom will need protection. So will you when our relationship gets out."

"Whoa." Maddie had her mule face on. "I don't need a bodyguard, because we *don't* have a relationship."

He stared at her, hard. Then, deliberately, he moved his gaze over the rumpled sheets, the scattered pillows. And back to her.

"It's just sex," she said, lamely. "Anyway. Is Maribelle okay with you taking Dom to New York?"

A neat change of subject. "She'll come along with us, to be at the press conference. Dyan's arranging it for a week from today."

"That's fast work, Adam. Two days ago you barely acknowledged the kid, and next week he'll be on TV? Are you sure you're not rushing it?"

"It's years overdue, as you so delicately pointed out." He pinched her toe. "As for you and me, you can't deny there's something between us. I knew it five years ago. Under different circumstances, we'd have gotten together then."

"Yeah, different circumstances. Like you not being a crook."

He let some smugness seep into his smile. "If I was a crook five years ago, then I'm still a crook. It doesn't seem to bother you now."

"That's because it's just sex." She gave him a bland smile. "Thanks for proving my point."

There was no winning an argument with Maddie.

THEY BROKE FOR lunch at noon, served by Henry at a poolside table shaded by an oversized umbrella.

Maddie spread a napkin on the lap of her turquoise sundress. Not exactly business attire, but as Adam loved to point out, this *was* the Riviera.

"I have to admit, you're okay at this magnate thing." The man held more information in his head than she could fit on a flash drive, and he accessed it as quickly as a computer. He never forgot a name, a date, or a detail, and when he said jump, people reached for the sky.

Adam put his tongue in cheek. "Don't gush, darling, it embarrasses me."

He poured a Barolo they'd brought back from the vineyard. She sipped. Delicious.

"Okay," she let on, softened up by the wine, "you're *good* at this. Not that you need me to tell you. You can look at your balance sheet." She stabbed lettuce with her fork and asked something she'd wondered five years ago. "When is enough enough?"

His brows inched up. His eyes couldn't be bluer. "Enough what?"

"Enough everything." She motioned with her fork. "You own all this. Hell, you own half the free world. But you're still buying stuff up. When will you have enough?"

He leaned back in his chair, looked around as if seeing it all anew, the villa, the lawn, Portofino below.

"I don't know," he said. "I never thought about it."

"Seriously? No goal, like richest son of a bitch in the universe?"

He shook his head. "It's not about money. Not anymore, though that was the root of it." He shrugged. "I suppose it's the power now. Knowing I can change the world for better or worse. Mostly better, I hope."

"Yeah," she admitted, "your foundation changes lives." Thousands of them daily. It was vast, effective and amply funded, like everything in Adam's world.

"I've plans to do more," he said, "and could use the help of a smart lawyer, if you know one who's interested."

"Not my area."

"You're a quick study. You proved it this morning. And I trust you. I don't trust many people."

For a moment, she was tempted. Working with Adam when he was in high gear was an adrenaline-charged roller-coaster ride. But, "Things are messy enough now. We don't need more complications."

"Ah, yes. All that sex fucking things up."

She raised her glass in salute. "Kidding aside, all magnates should be as generous."

"Yes, they should. But don't change your dour opinion of me just yet." He dropped his eyes to his glass, twirled the stem. "The unvarnished truth is that I grew up homeless and there were plenty who rubbed my nose in it. I had something to prove to them, and to myself as well."

He gave a short laugh. "You could say I've spent my life nursing my wounded ego. Not quite so heroic, is it?"

Oddly moved by his honesty, she touched his hand. "There's nothing wrong with proving you're not a victim anymore. But haven't you proved it by now?"

He met her eyes, and his were too knowing, too perceptive. "I'd ask you the same, Maddie darling."

She pulled back. "Listen, I don't . . . I'm not . . ."

He laid a hand on her thigh. Its warmth soaked through the thin linen, into her skin. "No one can hurt you anymore." His voice was a balm. "You're a grown woman, smart and savvy. You're nobody's victim, Maddie."

Of course she wasn't. She'd figured out long ago how to protect herself, and she didn't need a pat on the head from her friendly neighborhood felon.

She opened her mouth to snap him back, but the words didn't come. The anger that flashed so hot and bright had cooled under the stroke of his hand.

She searched his face for inspiration, a reason to rant. All she saw was kindness.

Kindness and love.

In her breast, emotions of another type surged up in response, a blast of feelings she didn't understand and couldn't control. The blue of his eyes pressed on her chest, the curve of his lips closed her throat.

Suddenly, desperately, she yearned to share her secret with him. Share the burden. She reached out, grasped his sleeve. Tried to force the words out.

But shame tied her tongue. Tears welled up, spilled over. Frustration and anguish.

"Oh, darling, forgive me." His voice cracked. Going down on one knee, he gathered her in his arms. John horned in too, pushing his head onto her lap. Kindness and love surrounded her. John slobbered it on her hands; Adam folded it around her.

Unable to resist it, she let her head rest on his broad shoulder, let her tears soak his shirt. When they petered out and she'd quieted, he brushed a kiss over her hair.

"We're two of a kind, Maddie St. Clair, though I'm sure it pains you to hear it."

She sponged her nose with her napkin. "Kick me while I'm down, why don't you."

He let out a laugh. "Darling, I adore you."

FLOPPING ON HIS towel, Adam closed his eyes against the brilliant sun. Even in triathlon condition, he was no match for a nine-year-old. If he'd lifted and tossed the boy once, he'd done it a hundred times.

Over the sound of the waves, he tuned in to Dom's hooting laughter as he boogie-boarded with Maddie. His son was a strong swimmer, a natural athlete. Why hadn't he known that before now? Why had he been so determined to shut Dom out?

For all the obvious reasons, of course, the ones he'd

relied on since the boy was conceived. But now he had to admit to at least one more.

Parenthood terrified him. He was certain he'd fuck it up, and he'd proved himself right by ignoring Dom for nine years. He'd be ignoring him still if Maddie hadn't come along and opened his eyes.

And how had he thanked her? By making her cry. Oh, he hadn't intended to hurt her. But that's when he did his best work, when he was too busy making his point to consider how sharp that point might be, and how it might hurt the person he jabbed with it.

"Papa!" Dom's panicky voice snapped him out of his brooding. "Papa, John's drowning! He's drowning!"

Adam was off the sand in an instant, tearing into the surf, cursing himself. He should have kept an eye on John. The dog had worn himself out romping in the waves, chasing Dom, chasing all of them.

Now the undertow had sucked him out. He was paddling, but no match for the current.

Maddie was already in the water, swimming hard, slowed by towing Dom's board. Adam dove through a wave, surfaced. But John had disappeared.

"Over there!" Dom bounced on his toes, pointing. Adam went into a crawl. His training was paying off now.

John bobbed up, briefly, and Adam swam harder, adrenaline powering his muscles past anything he'd asked of them before.

He passed Maddie, dove where John had gone down, breaststroked in a circle, squinting through the murk.

Spotting John's motionless body, drifting, sinking, he dove deeper, came up under the dog. Shouldered him and kicked hard for daylight, surfacing as Maddie reached them with the board.

"Get him on," she said. They wrestled the slack body,

dead weight, then Adam stroked hard for the shore, towing the board, the limp dog's feet trailing.

Dom met them at the water's edge. "Papa, can we give him CPR? I learned how to do it on a person. Is it the same on a dog?"

"I don't know." He laid John on his side in the sand.

Maddie ran out of the surf, breathing hard. "Check his mouth, make sure nothing's blocking his throat. Now straighten his neck. Hold his mouth closed and blow into his nose."

Adam did it all without question as she knelt beside John, started chest compressions on his rib cage.

Circling them, Dom called John's name, fighting tears.

A minute passed, a lifetime while Adam huffed air up John's nostrils and Maddie pumped his lungs. No response.

Adam streamed sweat. *Fuck me, if he dies . . .*

Then John heaved. Adam released his mouth and the dog coughed out a gush of water, shuddered, then coughed another trickle.

"John!" Dom flung himself on the dog, crying now, the great heaving sobs of a little boy who'd almost lost his best friend.

Maddie pulled him back gently, onto her lap. "John needs to catch his breath, sweetie." The boy clutched her instead, burying his face in her neck.

John quivered, exhausted but breathing, his trusting brown eyes resting on Adam. Adam stroked his head. "I'm sorry, boy," he murmured, shaken to the marrow.

"Papa," Dom snuffled, "is he okay?"

"He's fine. Gave us a scare, didn't he?" And a reminder that life hung by a thread, that losing a loved one was the work of a moment.

Looking at his son, his knobby spine, his slender

arms, Adam started to tremble. The boy was so small, so vulnerable. What if Dom had been drowning? What if Adam wasn't there to save him?

His gaze lifted to Maddie, delicate Maddie. Fragile as a twig. What if someone hurt her? What if Adam wasn't there to protect her?

They needed him. Dom and Maddie and John. They *needed* him.

Maybe Maddie saw the raw emotion on his face, or maybe she simply wanted a hug. For whatever reason, she opened an arm to him. He crawled to her, saw a sheen in her eyes.

"No more tears," he said, holding back his own. "We're all right. All of us. We'll be all right." And he wrapped them in his arms.

CHAPTER TWENTY-THREE

FINALLY, ADAM'S LIFE made sense.

Stepping into tan slacks, he laid out his plans to Henry, who leaned against the closet doorjamb, arms folded, attentive.

"We'll dine with Lucy and Crash tonight," Adam said. "Dom won't be joining us. I'm keeping him under wraps until next week."

"I'll set you up on the terrace?"

"Yes, good. And tomorrow, I'll need you to see Lucy and Crash to the jet. I'm taking Maddie to the lake."

"She's all right with that?"

"Well, she doesn't know about the lake yet, that's a surprise. But she's agreed to stay the weekend to help out with Dom. I'll stretch it into next week. We'll head to New York once the press conference is set."

"You're a cocky bastard, assuming she'll jump to your tune."

"Maddie knows I need her here. Dom needs her." Adam's head popped out through the neck of a silk T-shirt. "And she's in love with me."

Henry guffawed. "Does *she* know that?"

"She hasn't admitted it yet, but she will." Adam grinned at his old friend. "We're getting married."

Henry dropped his arms, caught flatfooted. "You're *engaged*?"

"We will be."

"You honestly think she'll marry you?"

Adam felt the first inkling of annoyance. "I'm not an ogre."

"No, you're a fucking thief!" Henry shoved his hands through his thinning hair. "So you're calling it off? The Matisse?"

"Of course not." Adam threw him a look. "Everything's in place?"

Henry nodded, reluctantly. "Fredo's been over the route a hundred times, and over the alternates too. As for the timing, my man inside assures me nothing's changed."

"Go over it again." Adam would walk all of them through it a dozen more times in the next forty-eight hours.

Henry folded his arms, recited by heart. "At precisely 9:15, you'll exit through the west gate. At 9:16, Fredo will pick you up in the black Maserati."

He laid out each step, minute by minute, all the way to the Matisse. "When you reach the southeast gallery, it's the third painting on the right, in the narrow gilt frame."

"Your man's sure of the location? There'll be no time for groping in the dark."

"He's sure." Henry followed Adam out of the closet and into the bedroom. "The security's a decade out of date. It's the easiest job you've ever done, a walk in the park compared to the *Lady in Red*. But Adam, are you sure you want to go through with it? If Maddie finds out—"

"I plan to tell her about it. After the fact."

"Are you mad?"

Adam slapped him on the back. "I won't keep secrets from my wife."

"You're taking a hell of a chance."

Annoyance prickled again. "Maddie and I aren't as different as you think. We share the same goals. We simply achieve them in different ways." He smiled, confident. "Once I explain that Rosales traffics in children, she'll understand."

Turning his back on Henry, he strode into the bathroom and unzipped, called through the door, "Now walk me through the getaway."

"MADDIIIIIEEEE!" LUCY SKIPPED across the terrazzo floor and caught Maddie in a hug. "We had the most epic cruise! You can't *believe* all the gazillionaires around here!"

"Yeah, the Riviera's known for gazillionaires." Maddie peeked around her. "Where's Crash? Did you dump him for a sheik?"

"Not a chance. He went upstairs to change, but I wanted to find you. Where's Adam? What did you guys do while we were cruising?"

"You know. Worked. And stuff." Maddie felt funny not mentioning Dom, but while she trusted Lucy to keep silent, she wasn't sure about Crash.

"By *stuff* you mean hot monkey sex, right?"

Maddie winced. "I was going to say we're kind of involved. Adam and me. Temporarily."

"And having hot monkey sex?"

"Sheesh. Yes. I don't want to talk about it."

"Prude." Lucy pinched her cheek, the only human to dare it. Tugging Maddie along, she headed for the terrace. "God, I love it here. I wish we didn't have to leave tomorrow."

"Um, listen, I'm sticking through the weekend. You could hang here with me."

"Crash has a Saturday-night gig. But I'm glad you're staying." She squeezed Maddie's hand. "I'm glad you're giving Adam a shot."

"Don't make too much out of it. He's a little diversion, that's all."

Lucy glanced up, over Maddie's shoulder. "Here comes the little diversion now. All six-foot-two of him."

Maddie couldn't help herself, she turned to watch him come, all six-foot-two of him. Gorgeous as sin, and his smile, wow. His lips said, "Hello, Lucy," but the smile was all hers.

Curling an arm around her shoulders, he snuggled her to his side. The presumptuous bastard. She reached for indignation, couldn't find any. Instead, she found her own arm curling around his waist.

Crash appeared, blond streaks lighter than ever. He hooked Lucy's shoulders. "Adam, man, your yacht's awesome. Thanks for the cruise." He shifted his infectious grin to Maddie. "Hey Mads. Nice tan. Been beachin' it?"

Maddie smiled, genuinely. The kid was a goof, but for now at least, he was head over heels for Lucy.

"We beached it today," she said. "John almost drowned."

"Oh, John!" Lucy wrapped her arms around the grinning dog.

"Adam fished him out of the water," Maddie heard herself brag.

"Which wouldn't have mattered if Maddie didn't know CPR." Adam bragged too.

"Aw." Lucy teared up. "You guys are so great together." She threw an arm around each of them.

Crash gave John a rub. "John, my man, you got great parents."

Parents?

Maddie wriggled out of the hug. "Listen, we're *not*—"

Adam cut her off with a kiss. Not a chaste in-front-of-your-sister peck, but a shut-up-and-kiss-me kiss. She put a hand on his chest to shove him back, but somehow her fingers curled into the silk of his shirt instead. He angled his head a little more, sank deeper.

And she hummed.

When they came up for air, Lucy and Crash had disappeared.

"Look what you did." Maddie rubbed her lips with her wrist like he'd forced her. "You embarrassed everybody. We probably won't see them till tomorrow."

He stroked a knuckle down her jaw. "Our Crash won't miss a meal. We'll find him working his way through the appetizers with your lovely sister. And I doubt either of them is embarrassed."

"Well, I am. I've never kissed anybody in front of Lucy. It's weird." And yet, walking out to the terrace she found herself going along with the arms-around-each-other.

Damn it, everything had changed. Every. Thing.

It all started with the sex, just as she predicted. Their bodies rubbed together and the sheets went up in flames.

But sex was just the bait he'd used to hook her. He reeled her in with his brains, his humor. And weirdly, his heart. She hadn't suspected he had one of those. And so much bigger than even he knew. He rationed his love—she could relate to that—but when he unleashed it on his friends, his son, his dog, it was a mighty force. It moved mountains.

Hell, it even moved her. In that moment on the beach when John coughed his first breath, she'd handed Adam her own heart and knew she'd never get it back.

Not that she needed it. Things hadn't changed *that* much. Not as far as relationships went—as in, she still wasn't having one, ever.

But—and this only made sense—since she was sticking around for the weekend, she might as well make the most of the endorphins fizzing through her bloodstream. They really amped up the sex.

And the lovey-dovey, couple-y stuff was kind of nice too. So why not play along for a few days? What harm could it do?

It wasn't like they were getting married.

CHAPTER TWENTY-FOUR

Vicky: I promise to help you get through
the hard things and the scary things
and to shine a light in the darkness.

Maddie: But if I see a zombie . . .

THE MORNING SUN glinted off the Ferrari's hood. Adam unhooked his aviators from the neck of his shirt and slid them on. "Relax, darling. It's a gorgeous day here, and promises to be the same in New York."

Maddie wrung her hands. "I should've ridden to the airport with them. What if the plane goes down?"

"It won't." He put absolute confidence into his tone. "And waving from the tarmac would make no difference in any case."

"At least I'd know I didn't abandon my sister to go catting off to the Alps to get laid."

Adam grinned. Leave it to Maddie to make a romantic getaway to his luxury villa on Lake Como sound like a hit-and-run at a sleazy motel in old Vegas.

Still, he couldn't bear to see her distressed. He

took her hand, squeezed it lightly. "Why don't I turn around? We can still make it to the airport."

"No." She let out a sigh, seemed to relax. "You're right, being there won't make any difference. But thanks for offering." She squeezed back, and he felt it in his chest, around his heart.

Slowly, it was sinking through his hard skull that the littlest things moved Maddie, the small acts of kindness. He'd given her a designer wardrobe and she couldn't care less. Handed her a five-million-dollar job and she'd turned up her nose. But the offer to turn around, which cost nothing at all, had won him his first heart-melting smile of the day and lifted the clouds from her eyes.

Why had it taken so long—all his life—to understand that money was no substitute for love? Not for others, like Dom and Maddie. And not for himself.

It did have its advantages though, like a place on Lake Como. Maddie's first glimpse of the spectacular mountains dropping sharply into the sapphire water, the castlelike villas clinging to promontories or carved into rock, the terraced gardens flowering abundantly, rendered her gratifyingly speechless.

Turning onto a narrow road, he skimmed past stone walls set with wide, sturdy gates leading to large waterfront estates, then hit the remote on his visor and drove through a narrow wrought-iron gate into a relatively modest compound, braking at the steps of a tidy stone villa.

Maddie looked it over, the flowering urns lining the front steps, the masses of rhododendrons drenching the air with cinnamon, the gray stone stairs curving down to the waterfront, then turned to him, concern on her face.

"Kinda puny, isn't it? People will wonder if LeCroix Enterprises is circling the drain."

He chuckled. "Don't worry, no one knows it's mine. The property's in Henry's name. No live-in help, just a gardener and his wife. She cleans and stocks the kitchen as necessary."

"It looks like it's been here forever," she said as they stepped inside. "Like it grew up out of the ground."

"Not quite, but some parts are older than others." Like the two-hundred-year-old tile on the floor, and the marble columns supporting the terrace roof.

"I've opened up the floor plan, made updates." He pointed them out as they walked through the house. Kitchen fixtures, Jacuzzi tub, and in the bedroom, a king-sized water bed.

Maddie smirked at the bed. "Is this where you film the porn?"

"Only if you're into it, darling." He tossed her into the center, causing a tidal wave.

She let out a giddy laugh. "I've never done it on a water bed."

"You'll love it." He climbed on, the surface rolling gently now. Propping up on one elbow, he gazed down at her as she gazed up at him. In her shining silver eyes, he saw his future, the woman to share his life, his work and his play, to mother his children.

Inside him, everything settled. "Maddie." He whispered her name, his mantra. "My beautiful Maddie."

A line formed between her eyes, and he braced for the pushback. But it didn't come. The line dissolved. Her smile deepened.

She lifted a hand to his cheek, traced her fingertips along his jaw. "Adam," she whispered. Her heart shone in her eyes.

His own heart swelled, expanding his rib cage, an almost painful sensation. The need to tell her all he felt overwhelmed him.

But she was a fawn, tiptoeing closer. One sudden move and she'd bolt.

He hadn't brought her here to chase her as she fled him. He'd brought her here, far from her sister and his son and the troubled pasts they evoked, to savor the present and, hopefully, take a step toward the future.

Not trusting himself to keep still, he pulled her palm to his lips. Her pulse tripped under his thumb. Closing his eyes, he let his pulse sync with hers so their hearts beat in time.

She was making a romantic of him, and he liked it.

She touched his chest lightly, fingers working buttons, sliding under the fabric. She touched his skin, just her knuckles, soft as feathers. Goosebumps rippled up his side.

Then she pushed him onto his back—gently, not her usual tooth-and-nail style. The mattress rolled as she straddled him.

"Ever get seasick on this thing?" she asked, tugging the shirttails from his jeans.

"Not yet," he murmured, "but let's make a tsunami and see what happens."

Her fingers worked his belt, his button-fly. Digging inside, she came out with his hard-on in her hot little hands.

Watching through hooded eyes, he palmed her thighs, bare under her scrap of a sundress. It was peach cotton, strapless, held up by a wish and a prayer. Later, he'd peel it down off her perfect handfuls.

Later, when she wasn't handling his cock.

For now, he hooked his thumbs in the sides of her shoestring panties, and snapped them. She sucked a little breath like a sip through a straw, and his raging heart beat harder.

More than his next breath, he wanted to put her on

her back, bury himself in her heat. But for once, she was taking it slow, pouring something more than animal lust into her touch. It was what he'd wanted, to take their time, explore each other.

And it was killing him by inches.

She looked down at his forearms, knotted with the effort not to manhandle her. "I love your arms," she said, the first time she'd used the L-word in connection with any part of him. "Flex them."

He laughed.

"I mean it," she said. "Take off your shirt and flex them like Popeye. Please."

The hunger in her eyes made him do it, made him spread his arms wide, then curl his fists toward his shoulders. When her pupils dilated to black, he forgot to be self-conscious and gave an extra squeeze, popping his biceps.

"Shit," she murmured, "I love your body. You're so hard. Everywhere."

"And getting harder." He brought his hands down to cover hers, stroking along with her.

"Good idea," she said, "you take care of that so I can do this." Sliding her hands out from under his, she flattened her palms on his chest, slid them up to his shoulders, slowly, then down the length of his arms. Up again, over his shoulders, her taut body stretching over him, her breasts a few tempting inches from his mouth.

He couldn't take it, the buildup. The heat.

Out the window went pretty ideas of lovemaking. Releasing his cock, he yanked her dress down to her waist, took the taste he craved, sucking one nipple, palming the other, while his spare hand went up under her skirt.

And found her soaking.

Christ Jesus.

Flipping her in one motion, he hooked his arms under her knees and unchained the animal, taking her with one plunge, claiming her with each stroke. Her breasts bounced as he pumped her. He dropped his head, lapped the sweat that beaded between them. Her nails, diamond sharp, raked his straining arms. She bowed beneath him, lean muscles flexing, sinews straining. Why had he ever thought her fragile? She was strong and tensile as a sword.

Her hips pistoned with his, a frantic rhythm. "Adam, I . . ." A gasping plea she couldn't finish. She clasped his face in her hands, locked her eyes with his. Accepting him. Accepting them.

"Come with me," he forced through clenched teeth.

And let the animal have his way.

ALL AFTERNOON THEY floated on Adam's huge lake of a bed, drinking wine and making love until hunger drove them to forage. Then they took cold chicken and green salads out to the terrace, feasting as the sun set behind the mountains, drawing the curtain on a perfect summer day.

Lights appeared in the windows of the villas strung out along the far shore. At the largest, the double-tiered terrace was hung with colored lanterns. It began filling with partiers as pleasure craft arrived, mooring in a loose half circle around the dock.

A little drunk, a lot mellow, Maddie sighed, deep and long. "How glad are you that we're over here instead of over there?"

"Infinitely." Adam topped off their glasses, then tilted back in his chair and stacked his bare ankles on the low stonewall.

"I miss John, though," she added.

"We'll bring a larger car next time."

She sipped her wine. Waited for the chill to race up her spine, or the blood to boil in her brain, or some other visceral reaction to his presumption that their *relationship* might drag on past the weekend.

It didn't happen. Instead, the warm fuzzies did a snuggly lap dance.

Adam's phone bleeped a text. "The pilot," he told her. "They've landed. Lucy and Crash are en route to the penthouse."

"Thanks for letting them stay there. I'm over the worst of it, I guess, but the thought of them banging in my bed . . ." She shivered.

"That much I understand." He reached across the small table, stroked a warm hand along her arm. "Lucy's a credit to you. Whatever she was dealing with before—and I'm not asking what it was—in your care she's blossomed into an extraordinary woman."

"I'd like to take credit, but Lucy's been special from the day she was born. And her talent staggers me. You might've noticed the paintings in my apartment. They're hers."

"I recognized them. I bought several at her Providence showing last year."

Her jaw dropped. "You're the anonymous collector?"

"I am. She's wonderfully talented. Her light infuses her work."

"Doesn't it?" Maddie beamed. Then, "Wait a minute. How did you know about the show? It wasn't advertised."

His hand slid up her arm, and down again. "I kept track of you over the years."

She stiffened. "Why?"

"Because you interest me. Haven't I made that plain this past week?"

"Nothing's plain about this past week." The warm

fuzzies took a vacation. "You appeared out of the blue and tied my life in a knot, then did a one-eighty and lured me into the sack. Now you're telling me you *kept track* of me for five years. What the fuck?"

He smiled, annoyingly. "It all makes sense if you think of it from my point of view. I had a crush on you."

"For five years?"

"If I'd met you ten years ago, it would've been ten." He ran his fingertips up the back of her arm, a delicious feeling she was too agitated to appreciate.

"That's nuts."

"I couldn't agree with you more. Which is no doubt why I rationalized my continuing attention as keeping tabs on an old enemy. I have a few on my watch list."

He must have seen her dismay, because his smile faded. "I promise you, Maddie, it was the lowest level of scrutiny. When you left the U.S. Attorney's Office, I knew about it. I knew your sister joined you at that time. I knew you moved to the firm, that she was accepted to RISD."

He shrugged a shoulder. "Since you were spending a fortune to send her there, I was curious about her work. I have an interest in young artists, as you know. I sponsor several, and when I saw the depth of her work, I considered sponsoring her as well. As you said, her talent is staggering."

Her skin felt cold. "Why didn't you?"

"Because I knew my involvement would offend you. So I bought some of her work instead, generated some interest in her by doing so, and left it at that."

He set his feet on the ground, turned his body to face her. "I can see it troubles you to think I was spying on you. Let me put your mind at ease. Gio tracks more than a hundred individuals on my behalf. People who interest me in some way. Because they used to work for me. Because I'd like them to work for me. Because they're competitors."

He smiled again, a slight tilt of the lips. "You're the only one who tried to put me in prison."

She relaxed a little. He wasn't a stalker, just a honcho with minions to do things like keep tabs on the prosecutor who almost put his neck in a noose.

"In retrospect," he added, "I should've bumped you off the list. At the firm, you no longer posed a threat."

"Again, why didn't you?"

"Because somewhere, in some complex and mysterious part of my psyche, I knew you were my woman."

"Bullshit."

"Word." His gaze never wavered, cerulean in the light of the squat candle between them.

She narrowed her eyes. "I'm not getting involved with you."

"Darling, we've been involved since you flashed me across the conference table. I've had a hard-on for peach lingerie ever since."

"Pfft. Lots of felons fantasize about doing their prosecutors. We could make a pin-up calendar and get rich selling it to inmates."

"I'll take one for every room."

She bit her lip. He was right, damn it. She was involved with him. In some ways, important ways, he knew more about her than anyone else. Not the things Gio dug up, but how she ticked. He got her. He knew how her brain worked. What turned her on.

Yeah, he was good at turning her on.

"Maddie."

She watched his lips move, let that voice wash over her, deep and exotic, the faint flavor of the continent making it uniquely his own.

He dipped a hand in his back pocket, pulled out a

swatch of crimson velvet, and set it on the table between them.

With a fingertip, he slid it toward her, a kind of envelope, two inches square.

She leaned back. "I'm not comfortable taking gifts from you."

"It's not the key to the Bugatti, if that's worrying you." He nudged it closer. "What's inside that pouch has no monetary value."

Mysterious. And tempting. Yet she couldn't bring herself to reach for it.

When she didn't move, he turned her hand over, emptied the contents into her palm.

A scrap of paper. She unfolded it.

D-O-M-I-N-I-C-K

She looked up at him, baffled.

"It's the code to the penthouse elevator. When we get back to New York, I'd like you to stay there. With me."

She dropped it like it was on fire. "Nuh-uh. Nope. Not happening."

He kept his eyes on her. "A compromise, then. Keep your apartment. Come to the penthouse when you like, stay as long as you like."

He was serious.

So was she.

"Listen, Adam. Don't take it personally. It's me, not you. And I actually mean that this time."

She took a breath, leveled out. "This"—she flicked a hand back and forth between them—"is the longest affair I've ever had. And frankly, it's about run its course. I've never been anybody's girlfriend and I'm not starting now."

She waited for "This can be different," "We're so good together," "Just give it a chance," or any of the myriad arguments she'd heard in the past.

When they didn't come, when his eyes dropped to the candle that guttered in the breeze, disappointment crept in.

Would it kill him to fight for her?

But that was ego talking. Who wouldn't want to be wanted by Adam LeCroix? In reality, his acquiescence was good, much better than groveling. She hated groveling.

In fact, maybe, since he was cooperating, since he got where she was coming from, maybe they *could* see each other once in a while. Just the occasional booty call. For sex, as long as there were no strings attached—

He lifted the scrap with two fingers and held it to the flame.

Whoa. "Why'd you do that?"

"I'm not one of your flings," he said, softly but firmly. "I'm not a convenient piece of ass."

"I never said—"

"It's written on your face. You can't bring yourself to cut me off, so you'll propose a friends-with-benefits arrangement. A steamy weekend now and then when loneliness gets the best of you."

Mind reader.

She sniffed. "I don't get lonely."

"Liar. You're lonely all the time. You've walled yourself up and you're afraid to come out."

That was bullshit. "I'm not afraid of anything."

"You're terrified of love."

"Baloney. I love Lucy. Vicky. John." Okay, it was a short list, and one of them wasn't a person. But still, she knew how to love.

"And how are you at accepting love? Even with Lucy, you're more comfortable giving than receiving it."

He had a point, but so what? "I don't need love," she said staunchly. "They do. I'm Lucy's whole family. And

Vicky, her father's dead, and you've met her mother. She's worse than no mother at all."

"So they're alone in the world, or nearly so."

"Exactly. And they don't deserve to be." It was so simple. Why couldn't he see it? "They deserve to be loved."

"Ah," he said, nodding his head as if the light had dawned. "They deserve to be loved. And you don't."

"I didn't say that."

"So you *do* deserve it?"

"I don't *not* deserve it. But I'm prickly. Some people say bitchy." She shrugged. "I'm just not lovable. Not the way they are."

"I see." His tone said he didn't, not at all.

"They're warm and friendly," she went on, making her case. "Full of light. They're good people."

"You're good too, Maddie."

He was unbelievably dense. "No, I mean they're *good*. They're"—she searched for the word—"*wholesome*."

"And you're what? *Un*wholesome?"

She threw up her hands. "What's your problem?"

"I'm trying to follow your train of thought. If I'm not mistaken, you're saying you can't accept love because you don't deserve it, and you don't deserve it because you're not *wholesome*."

"I didn't say that."

"Yes, you did, in a winding and irrational way. And my question is, where do you get such nonsense? For an intelligent woman, you have the most asinine notions about yourself."

He was starting to get under her skin. "Listen, Adam, you think you know me—"

"I do."

"You don't! We've spent a week together, doing nothing but fighting and fucking."

"I can't think of two better ways to get to know each other."

"Really? Is that how you get acquainted with all your friends? Piss them off and then screw them?"

"Don't make this about me. We're talking about you."

"No we're not. We're done talking. Let's go back to bed."

She stood up, but he caught her hand. "Maddie, you deserve to be loved."

"Shut up about it, will you?" Sweat started to roll. "I had a life before last Wednesday, you know. Before Adam LeCroix sashayed in and started bossing me around. Sic Gio on me all you want. Call in Homeland Security and the CIA. Snooping and spying won't tell you who I am. "

"Then you tell me."

She snatched up her glass, drank off the last of her wine. Inside, she trembled, but she held her hand steady and leveled a no-bullshit stare. "I'm your fuck-buddy. Let's go fuck."

He sat back in his chair. His stare stripped her bare. She fought the urge to shift her feet, made do with fisting a hand on her hip, all aggressive annoyance.

"I know you, Maddie," he said calmly. "I know you slap at me when your emotions run deep. You make what's between us sound ugly when your feelings frighten you. And now I know why. Because you don't feel worthy of this."

She mustered a sneer, but her palms went clammy. Her head spun a dizzy loop.

Damn it, she had to get away from him before she fainted. But not without firing a parting zinger, a ballbuster that would leave him clutching his junk for a week.

She opened her mouth to let it rip, and out came, "My father tried to rape me when I was sixteen."

Adam caught her as she crumpled.

CHAPTER TWENTY-FIVE

MADDIE CAME AROUND slowly, rocking on a gently rolling sea.

"There you are." Adam's voice soothed like a lullaby. He sat on the bedside, suffused in candlelight, holding both of her icy hands in one of his warm ones. With the other, he pressed a cool cloth to her temple.

"Adam." She released his name on a breath, adrift on their water bed, peaceful and—

Oh God!

She tried to sit up, to take it all back. "I didn't mean it. I wanted to shock you. So you'd quit pestering me."

He touched her shoulder, pressed her down.

"No, really—"

He laid a finger on her lips. Did her very voice disgust him? Was he too revolted to hear it?

Filled with dread, she searched his face, stunned to see only compassion. It flooded his eyes, swamping her.

"Darling, it wasn't your fault. You weren't to blame."

For almost twenty years she'd been telling herself that. But, "Maybe I tempted him. Flaunted myself."

"Is that what he said?"

She nodded.

"Tell me what happened."

She'd never said it out loud, not even to Lucy. Why now, in this strange place, with this unlikely man, did she finally feel safe enough to tell?

"My father," she began, "he's . . . well, for one thing, he's alive." She considered. "But you knew that, didn't you?"

He nodded. She couldn't drum up indignation. A tap had opened and her badass had run out.

"I'm not in contact with him," she said. "And now that Lucy's safe and sound, I never think of him. Not really."

She was tiptoeing in. Adam's patient gaze steadied her.

"Anyway. He was a son of a bitch. Always. To all of us. Lucy can spout a buttload of psychobabble about his multiple disorders. He's emotionally abusive, narcissistic, blah blah. In plain English, he's a monster. A predator. And with a houseful of females to prey on, he was happy as a pig in shit."

She pulled her hands out of Adam's, pushed herself up and stuffed a pillow behind her. She couldn't do this lying down.

"When I was a kid, he picked on me about everything. Every. Thing. Especially how small I was. Not just *small*, but underdeveloped, puny, stunted, scrawny, feeble. As I got older, he added ugly, stupid, useless, worthless. You get the drift."

"He devalued you. Relentlessly."

"That's Lucy's word for it, sure. But see, I wasn't as dumb as he told me I was." She tapped her temple. "I heard the names he called my mother. They were bullshit. I figured he was lying to me too, so I let most of his insults roll off."

"And others you internalized."

She shrugged. "I get defensive about my size. But that's all that stuck."

His jaw ticked, but he kept still.

"Anyway, it was awful when he got going, so we pretty much walked on eggshells, trying to stay off his radar. Then Lucy came along and changed the game. She'd cry, like babies do, and he'd lean over her crib, screaming at her to shut up. I couldn't stand it, so I'd distract him, make him focus on me."

"Your mother?"

"Mom was an empty dress by then. A domestic robot." She laughed without humor. "Vicky doesn't get why Mom didn't rise up and overthrow my father. But that's because her mother's the exact opposite of mine."

"Cowards like your father don't choose women like Adrianna Marchand."

"No. They want women with no skills, no family to run to. No self-confidence. My father had her completely terrorized. His best weapon was me. If she showed any spine, he'd threaten to take me away where she'd never see me again. And just like that"—she snapped her fingers—"she'd shut up, shut down, and bring him his slippers."

"I imagine he made the same threat about Lucy, and used it to control you."

"Yeah. And I can tell you, it works like a charm."

"What happened when you were sixteen?"

"I told you." She went hoarse, cleared her throat. "He tried to rape me." Easier to say it this time. Sweat prickled her armpits, but the room didn't spin.

"Did you report him?"

"No." She dropped her eyes. "Like I said, it worked like a charm."

"Counseling?"

"Too embarrassing." The stink clung to her still.

"Tell me." He said it calmly, matter-of-factly, like the world wouldn't end if she did.

For whatever reason, she believed him.

"Birthdays were a nightmare in my house. No cards or cakes, just another chance for him to harp on how disappointing we were. How my mother looked like a dishrag, old and faded. How I was still a runt."

She rubbed clammy palms on her thighs. "On my sixteenth birthday I went to bed at ten. Lay there in the dark, listening for him to lock my door from the outside like he did every night. But he didn't come, and I must've drifted off, because all of a sudden he was in my room. Leaning over my bed."

Her chest tightened. Her throat too.

"He'd never hit me before, which is weird, right? But I figured it was coming now. I'd mouthed off at the supper table. Lucy knocked over her milk and he screamed at her. Clumsy, gawky, spastic. So I called him a shit stain. It was the farthest I'd ever gone, and I figured he'd come to make me pay, so I covered my face with my arms.

"But it wasn't that. He grabbed my arms and pinned them to the pillow with one hand. Yanked off the blankets, right onto the floor. He said . . ." She wet her dry lips with her tongue. "He said I was asking for it. Flaunting myself with short skirts and high heels. He said that was how Mom used to be. Slutty. But he brought her into line, and he'd do the same with me."

Her hand covered her throat. She forced down a swallow. "He's big, did I say that before? Huge. Three times my size, easy.

"He pulled my T-shirt up over my face, and he . . . he pinched my breast. He said how my tits were mosquito bites, how I was a scarecrow." Her breath hitched. "I didn't like it. He kept saying I did, but I hated it. It hurt and I wanted to throw up. But I just lay there. I just lay there like a board.

"He dragged my panties down and shoved his fingers in. Hard." She covered her crotch with both hands. "No one had ever . . . and his fingers were so big. His nails were sharp.

"I started to cry, so h-he took his fingers out and pulled the T-shirt off my face. And he said . . . he said to get used to it, because I was sixteen now, old enough, and better than the dishrag downstairs. And then he stuffed the T-shirt in my mouth.

"I hadn't even thought about screaming, I don't know why. But when he did that, I sucked in a big breath, and I sucked the shirt down my throat. It stuck there and I couldn't breathe. And God, oh God, there's nothing worse."

She clutched her chest. "I lost my mind, completely. He wasn't expecting it. He was pulling down his pants and I just whipsawed my whole body, like a convulsion, because I was panicking, suffocating, and I caught him in the stomach with my knee. He let go of my arms and I pulled the shirt out of my mouth and I was just so glad to breathe."

She sucked wind as if was happening again.

"And then he came back at me, and, Jesus, I saw his hard-on sticking out." She covered her eyes but couldn't un-see it. "He was between me and the door, so I went for the window above my bed. It was August, it was open. He was trying to grab me. I dove through the screen headfirst."

She cradled her arm. "I fell two stories, snapped the bone clean in half. The last thing I remember before the pain put me under is him leaning over me, telling me if I said one word, I'd never see Lucy again."

There. It was over. Surely now Adam would see that she was all kinds of unworthy. Her bloodline was polluted, and she was obviously toxic herself to have made her own father lust for her.

Then, "Maddie," he said, his voice raw with emotion, "I'm sorry beyond words that you had to endure that. And I'm so very glad your father's not dead, because I'm going to kill him."

Her head came up. "You are not."

"I am, an inch at a time, while I explain to him why I'm breaking his arms, crushing his larynx—"

"No." She clutched his hands, balled into fists. "No, you can't."

"But I can. I will. Look how he hurt you. He warped your whole life."

She shook her head, kept shaking it.

"Don't deny it," he bit out. "You blame yourself for what he did that night. It's in every choice you've made ever since."

"Of course it is. There's a kernel of truth there. I *did* wear short skirts. And high heels to look taller—"

"Goddamn it!" He caught her shoulders. "I won't listen to you blame a sixteen-year-old child for that animal's perversion. I'll put him down like a rabid dog, and you'll dance on his grave in the highest heels I can buy you."

He was serious.

The nerve.

She bucked up. "Listen, Lancelot, I don't need you riding to my rescue. I've got issues. Who doesn't?"

"Yours run deeper than most, and for good reason. But you weren't responsible for his atrocities, Maddie. It's time to accept that and move on with your life."

"I'm fine with my life. You're just mad because I'm not going along with your plans for it."

His jaw went hard. He started to say more, to raise his voice. But he bit it back, took a deep breath and let it hiss out through his teeth.

"I'm sorry," he said quietly. "I'm venting my temper on you, when it's your bloody father I want to rage at." He took her hands, brought first one wrist to his lips, then the other. "Darling, you're the bravest woman I know."

She goggled at him. "How do you get *brave* out of that story? I told you, I crept around like a mouse for years. And that night I just *lay* there. If he hadn't suffocated me, I would've kept lying there while he raped me. What's brave about that?"

"You were a child, Maddie. You'd belittle yourself for doing what you had to do to survive? And it's not true anyway. You drew his fire away from your sister. And my God, you dove out a window headfirst!"

"That was fear, not bravery. When I got home from the hospital, I bought a wedge for my door and hid in my room for two years. And the minute I graduated high school, I ran away and never went back." She hugged her stomach. "Don't you get it, Adam? I left my baby sister there with that monster. *I left Lucy.*"

With those words, two decades of guilt steamrolled her. "I left her." It trickled out, a thin wail. "I left Lucy behind."

Adam took her shoulders again. "Stop it! You won't punish yourself for this, not while I'm breathing." He shook her. "What were you supposed to do? Tell me that."

"Take her with me!" Guilt ate a hole in her stomach. She covered it with her hands like a wound to keep her guts from leaking out.

"A four-year-old? He'd have taken her back. And then what? He told you he'd disappear with her, didn't he?"

She nodded. Tears rolled like rain.

"Then stop this." He released her shoulders, drove his fingers through his hair. "My God, Maddie, I don't know which is worse, blaming yourself for his perversion or torturing yourself for doing the only thing you could do."

He stood up, paced the floor. Turned to stare at her. "You contacted her, didn't you? Warned her, and gave her the means to get away if it came to that."

She nodded again. She'd done more than that. She'd hotlined him, anonymously. But her father was a pillar of the community, her mother a useless mess. And Lucy had nothing to tell social services when they asked, because he hadn't touched her yet.

He didn't, until her sixteenth birthday. Then Lucy didn't waste time with the system. She ran straight to Maddie. And since Maddie was a federal prosecutor by then, their father hadn't dared to come after her.

"You took her in," Adam said, "changed your life to give her all you could. You're doing it still, slaving for that she-wolf. Letting me use you like a pawn."

His own words sank in. Agony contorted his face. "I'm no better than he is, bullying you for my own amusement."

"No!" She leaped up, wrapped her arms around him. "You're nothing like him, Adam. I hate him. And I love you."

He went rigid. So did she.

Oh God!

She shifted into damage control. "I meant . . . I meant . . ." She drew a blank.

And then it was too late, because he kissed her.

Oh, how he kissed her, framing her face with warm hands, angling his head, taking her lips, her tongue, gentle but not soft, sweet but not easy.

There was possession in that kiss, and reverence, and passion. And love.

Yes, love.

His and hers. Unexpected, unfathomable. No warning, no net. Just a long, weightless tumble into uncharted space.

Falling. They were falling in love.

CHAPTER TWENTY-SIX

Vicky: I promise not to go to bed
mad or walk away from an argument
without listening to your side.

Maddie: But either way I'm getting
the last word.

"THANKS FOR COMING." Maribelle's smile seemed genuine. "Dom's thrilled."

"Thanks for the invite." Maddie glanced around the living room. It should feel weirder to hang out with Adam's ex now that they were—gulp—in love. "Adam's got some boring dinner thing. I guess being a honcho's not all fun and games."

Feet thundered on the stairs. Dom streaked into the room. "Maddie!" Throwing his arms around her waist, he stole her breath with his reckless affection. At her feet, John did his welcome dance. Her heart rolled over. Emotion clogged her throat.

Just a week and so much had changed. She'd found John and Dom and even Maribelle. And last night she'd laid down a burden she'd carried alone for almost twenty years. Just laid it down at Adam's feet, and they'd joined hands and walked away from it.

And today, well, today was the first day of the rest of her life.

Cor-ny! But she'd never felt happier.

Dom tugged her hand. "Come see what's for supper."

He led her out on the terrace, where Gisele was slicing a piping hot pizza with everything. Maddie let out an appreciative whistle.

Dom beamed. "I knew you'd like it, so I asked Gisele to make it."

Her heart, so long underused, did another happy roll. "Thanks, kiddo. You did good."

Dinner was fun, cheerful. Dom chattered his way through the pizza with blow-by-blows of John's hopeless attempts to catch a ball, a Frisbee, or even a biscuit.

But as the meal wound down and dessert came and went, he fell increasingly quiet.

When the last plate was cleared, he addressed his mother solemnly. "May I show Maddie my room?"

Maribelle seemed surprised. "Sure, if it's okay with her."

"You bet." Maddie ruffled his hair. Who didn't like frogs and goldfish, baseballs and dog bones?

But Dom's mood grew more somber as they climbed the stairs. At the end of the hallway, he stopped outside a door, shuffled his feet.

"What's the problem, Dom? You got a dead body in there?"

He shook his head, glumly, and opened the door to a perfectly normal room. Single bed with a toy box at the foot. Kid-sized desk. Books and stuffed animals and Disney crap everywhere. Messy but not a disaster.

She followed him in, shut the door behind her.

"Okay, buddy, it's just you, me, and John. What's on your mind?"

"Papa came over today. He said I can go to New York and stay with him in his penthouse."

"That's good, right? You want to hang with him, don't you?"

He nodded, but his eyes stayed downcast. "Papa never bothered with me before. Now he does. Is it because of you? Did you make him?"

The kid wasn't dumb. "I pointed out what he was missing. But no, I didn't make him. Nobody makes your dad do anything he doesn't want to do."

That got a faint smile. "Papa's the boss of everyone."

She snorted a laugh. "Not everyone. But he's the boss of himself, for sure." She plopped on the bed, but Dom stayed where he was, hand resting on the toy box.

His troubled eyes broke her heart.

"Look, Dom. Your dad's just a guy. He's a big, important guy, and he's super smart and real powerful out in the business world. But he's still a guy, like you, and he has feelings. In fact, he's a big softie, even though he acts like a hard-ass."

She blew out a breath. Child psych wasn't her field.

"What I'm trying to say is, a long time ago he got his feelings hurt by your mom. And he stayed mad at her for a long time, and that spilled over on you, even though you had *absolutely nothing to do with it*. You know how that works, right? You get mad at one person and then you take it out on everybody who happens to be in the neighborhood."

He looked uncertain, and she wondered if maybe that was just her.

"Anyway, he's over it now. He's not mad at your mom, and he's sorry he wasted time he could've been spending with you."

"That's almost exactly what he said." He hung his head.

"I gotta say, Dom, I thought you'd be happier about it."

"I would be. Except when he finds out what I did, he'll be mad at me forever." A fat tear hit the floor. "I ruined everything."

Maddie hopped off the bed, knelt in front of the boy. His tears could have been drops of her blood. "Dom, sweetie, you didn't ruin anything. Adam loves you."

"He won't. Not anymore."

She tilted his chin. Despair ravaged his little-boy's face.

"Tell me what you did and I'll help you fix it. I promise."

He searched her face, desperate to believe. She firmed her jaw, did her best competent-attorney-who-can-make-your-problems-go-away.

It must have convinced him, because he wiped his eyes with his sleeve, straightened his small spine. Then he opened the toy box, dug around, and came out with a roll of old canvas.

"I stole Papa's painting."

"ADAM, YOU'RE A fool. Let the Matisse go."

Adam flashed Henry a grin. "You said yourself it's a cakewalk."

"Oh, you'll pull it off right and tight. I've no worries there." He tossed Adam a shirt, dull black Lycra like the trousers he'd already skinned into.

"If it's Maddie you're fretting about, don't. She thinks I have a meeting—which I do, of a sort. She's having dinner at Dom's."

Just thinking of her had warmth flooding his chest. Last night at the lake, she'd quit fighting and accepted him. Accepted them. She hadn't signed on to happily-ever-after just yet, but she'd admitted she loved him.

Driving back to the villa this morning there wasn't a cross word between them. Not that her tongue had lost its edge. But her jibes were good-natured, and she'd held his hand on her lap, stroking his palm, tugging his fingers, love flowing between them like a current.

He was indeed besotted. And enjoying every minute of it.

"Maribelle's in on it then?" Henry shook his head in dismay.

"It's not ideal," Adam admitted. "But she knows her part."

He clipped his tool belt around his hips, snuggled it into place, then strode into the bathroom to smear blacking on his cheeks. "I've given Maddie the code to the penthouse elevator. And after some gentle persuasion"—holding her orgasm hostage—"she's agreed to use it."

Henry's brows inched higher. "She's moving in?"

"It's a process." Adam wiped his hands. "Maddie doesn't leap before looking. But she won't hold out for long. Why would she?"

Henry ran a speaking eye from Adam's black watch cap to his black leather boots.

Adam laughed, brimming with confidence and high spirits. "Have faith, my friend"—he clapped Henry's shoulder—"in the awesome power of love."

IF EVER MADDIE needed a cool head, it was now.

She waited a beat, then pasted on a smile. "Sweetie, your Dad's not going to kill you. He'll be happy to know what happened to his painting, and really glad to have it back."

Dom seemed to think she wasn't grasping the gravity, because he laid it out for her. "I snuck into his office and hacked his computer. I turned off the alarms and then I took his favorite painting out of the frame and stole it."

"Yes, honey, and that was quite an accomplishment. Your dad's going to ask exactly how you got around his hotshot security system, because he'll want to make sure nobody else can." She rubbed the boy's arms. They were stippled with goose bumps. "He's also gonna want to know why you took it. So do I."

"So he'd come home." He snuffled. "Sometimes when he's home I hide under the bar in his office. I can see him a little, and hear his voice."

The poor kid was starved for his father's affection. Now that he had it, he was terrified he'd lose it again.

Yet, even knowing the risk, he'd come forward instead of burning the canvas in the fireplace with no one the wiser.

"You're very brave to tell the truth, Dom. Your father's going to realize that and admire you for it." *Or he will when I get through with him.*

"I've got an idea," she said. "Why don't I bring the painting to him and explain the situation?" She checked her watch. Eight-thirty. Europeans ate late; he might not have left for his dinner meeting yet. "If I run, maybe I can catch him."

Hope bloomed in Dom's eyes.

Tucking the roll under her arm, she dropped a kiss on his head. "I'll be back in a flash, kiddo. Everything'll be fine. You'll see."

She took off at a run, down the stairs, through the living room, blowing past Maribelle on the sofa with her laptop. "Be right back," she called over her shoulder, sprinting out the slider.

Maribelle bounced to her feet, shot out behind her. "Wait! Maddie, no!"

But she was halfway home by then, eager to end Dom's misery, determined to persuade Adam to visit the boy before his meeting.

She streaked across the terrace, raced through the villa, zoomed up the stairs. His bedroom door was open. She heard his voice.

"Adam," she panted, bursting into the room, "I'm glad you're still—"

She stopped. Running, talking, breathing.

She stopped.

Adam was tricked out like a ninja in head-to-toe black, the only spots of color his startled blue eyes.

"My God. You're stealing something. *Tonight.*"

He took a step toward her. "Maddie, listen to me."

Her head swam, but fury drove blood to her brain. "You lying piece of shit fucking thieving bastard asshole."

He tried a smile. "I think that covers it, darling, no need to go on."

"I'm not your *darling*, you fucking felon." Ice trickled through her veins, the only movement in her body except for her lips. "You better lock me up now, because if you go out in that rig I'll drop a dime on your ass and bring the *polizia* down on this place in a motherfucking heartbeat."

His smile died. "You don't understand." He turned to Henry, standing stoically behind him. "Give us a moment."

When the door closed, he took another step toward Maddie. "There's a Matisse," he said, and she recognized his soothing, trust-me tone. "Some say it's his best. A man named Rosales bought it last month. He paid for it with blood money."

"And you're the superhero who's going to save the world one painting at a time." She had to work to put the sneer in her voice, because inside she'd curled up in a ball.

"He traffics in people, Maddie. He sells children to brothels. Boys and girls Dom's age, even younger." Fury edged his tone now, directed at Rosales but spilling over onto her.

"Got it. He's a villain. Which makes you Bruce Wayne. Fredo drives the Batmobile, right? And Henry plays Robin."

His jaw hardened. "I do justice my way, Maddie. The law's your crutch, not mine."

"So you write your own rules."

"While you blindly follow others'." He pointed a finger. "Your law sets too high a bar. Too many slide under it. Men like Rosales. Men like your father."

Inside, she shook, but she held herself straight as steel. "Speaking of fathers, you've done a great job with your son."

With a snap of her wrists, she unfurled the Monet.

He stared at it, stricken. "Not Dom."

"Yes, Dom. He wanted your attention." She laughed, and it was an ugly sound. "You must be so proud. Apples don't fall far from the tree." She let the canvas slide to the floor. "He loves you right down to his DNA. Try not to fuck him up any more than you already have."

Turning her back, she walked to the door. "Don't come after me, Adam. I never want to see you again."

THE SHAKING WORSENED as Maddie strode down the hall. On autopilot, she entered her suite, threw personal items into her purse—passport, toothbrush, phone—and strode out again. One foot in front of the other.

She held herself together as she crossed the lawn

onto Maribelle's terrace and stepped inside. She didn't knock or announce herself. Why bother, when Maribelle stared at her, white-faced, from inside the glass.

Maddie passed by her wordlessly, on a march to the stairs. She found Dom curled on the bed with John, weeping into the dog's patchy fur.

Calling up reserves from God knew where, she made herself breathe normally as she sat down beside him. The boy's swollen eyes peered up at her, waiting for the axe to fall.

"He's not mad," she said, praying it was true. "He's glad you came clean, and he loves you."

"H-he loves me?" Awe erased anguish from his eyes.

"Mmm-hmm." She'd like to tell the boy Adam's love meant something, but how could she, when he'd just proven otherwise?

She stroked Dom's hair, thick and black and soft as his father's. "Sweetie, something came up. I've got to get back to New York right away."

Dom sat up straight. "Is Papa going too? Can I come?"

"I'm flying solo on this one. I'm sure your dad will take you next week, like he said he would." Fingers crossed.

"What about John?"

She flicked a glance at Maribelle, leaning against the doorjamb, then looked hard at Dom, used her serious voice. "John's your dog now. That's a big responsibility. Are you up for it?"

He nodded gravely. "I'll take good care of him. And I'll keep teaching him to catch. We'll show you next week, okay?"

Her throat closed. God help her, she'd fallen in love with both of them. All three, counting John.

Maribelle stepped into the room. "Honey, Maddie has to go. You and John go to sleep now, okay?"

Maddie rose, leaving half her heart on the bed, dripping lifeblood as she walked away.

Downstairs, Maribelle said, "Adam called. He told me what happened."

"But you knew most of it already, didn't you?" Even Maribelle's betrayal stung.

"Not about the Monet. Jesus. Dom's a computer prodigy, but it never crossed my mind." She rubbed her forehead, then pushed it aside and focused on Maddie. "What're you going to do?"

"Call a cab for the airport and get the fuck out of here."

Maribelle picked up her purse. "I'll drive you. It's the least I can do."

The black Mercedes looked liked a Saudi sheik's car. "Armored," Maribelle said. "Sucks gas like a jet."

Maddie sank into the cushy seat, in no mood for small talk. As they wound down the mountain, she stared out the windshield at the neighboring villas, warm light spilling from their windows. Nice happy homes.

Ha.

She'd forgotten for a moment that there was no such thing. That was her first mistake.

The next—the biggest—was entrusting her darkest secret to Adam. Not because he'd breach her confidence—he wouldn't—but because he'd pried open her heart. She'd let him inside, let herself feel protected, cared for.

And like a rookie, she'd fallen in love.

Then in less than a day, he'd shown his true colors, the ones she'd known were underneath all along. He'd spit on what mattered to her. Asked her to abandon her principles. To understand, even applaud him.

The arrogant ass.

"Maddie?"

"What?" Couldn't she at least brood in peace?

"Adam's thing about art. It's complicated, but the quick and dirty is that his parents put art ahead of him, their own son." She spoke quickly, as if expecting to be cut off. "So he has no choice but to believe it's more important than anything. Otherwise, he'd have to accept that he had no value to his parents."

Maddie faked awe. "Gee, Maribelle, you understand him so well. I'm surprised you two aren't a happy couple."

"I understand him *now*. I banged my head against the wall for years before I got help."

"So this is secondhand therapy? No thanks."

"You're as stubborn as he is."

"Flattery will get you nowhere."

Maribelle snorted a laugh. "What a bitch. Why don't I hate you? You hooked the man I wanted, and you didn't even have to try. You captured Dom's heart in five minutes flat. Dumped a dog in my pristine home."

"Go ahead, hate me. See if I care."

"I can't." Maribelle shrugged one slender shoulder. "You accomplished a miracle. You opened Adam's eyes to his incredible son."

"Pfft. I shoved him down Adam's throat until he had to swallow."

"It worked, didn't it? Until you came along and shook him up, Adam was repeating the pattern that started with his parents, playing it out again with his own son." She reached out and grasped Maddie's hand. "I don't want you to leave. You're just what our dysfunctional family needs."

Maddie's heart beat painfully. She'd been ready to jump into that family with both feet.

She extracted her hand. "Thanks, but I've already got one of my own."

They turned onto the main road, began winding along the coast.

"By the way, where're we going?"

"Milan. It's a ride. You can sleep if you want to."

Fat chance. But she could pretend, which would at least shut Maribelle down. Who knew she'd be an Adam-apologist?

But first she dug out her phone, scrolled until she found Brandt's number. "Madeline St. Clair," she said briskly to his voice mail. "The Monet's been recovered. We're withdrawing the claim. As of now, I no longer represent Mr. LeCroix. Any further communication should be through his in-house counsel at LeCroix Enterprises."

Tossing her phone back into her purse, she muttered, "Have a nice day," and closed her eyes to "sleep."

CHAPTER TWENTY-SEVEN

ADAM GOT GERARD on the phone and grilled him like a steak. "What car did they take? What airport are they heading for? Do you have them on GPS?"

"They're in the Mercedes. GPS shows them heading for Milan. They should arrive in time for Alitalia's midnight flight."

"Listen to me, Gerard." Adam paced as he spoke. "Maddie's not a good flier. I want someone on the flight with her, to monitor her. Make it a woman. No contact unless necessary, you understand?" He scrubbed his face with one hand. "And see that she's upgraded to first class. Come up with a ruse. She can't know I'm behind it."

"I understand."

"I want to know the minute she checks in. I want her flight number, all the details."

"You'll have them."

Adam hit end and drilled the phone like a fastball at the sofa. "Fuck me." He kicked the desk hard, creasing the wood with his steel-toed boot.

"Assaulting the furniture won't bring her back," Henry said from well outside punching range.

"I don't have to bring her back. She'll come back on her own." But he wasn't sure of that, not at all. The hurt in her eyes . . . he couldn't accept that he'd done that to her, that his arrogance had jeopardized everything.

He fell back on belligerence. "She was startled, that's all. She'll come to her senses."

Henry's laugh was incredulous. "Are we talking about the same woman? Because the Maddie I know will see you in hell before she walks through that door." He shook his head in disgust. "You fucked it up, Adam, you arrogant ass."

Fear clutched his chest. He strode to the couch for his phone, dialed Gio, filled him in. "I want someone outside her apartment. I want to know when she arrives, when she leaves, where she goes. Round the clock, every move."

"Phone tap?" Gio asked. "Photographs?"

"No, no. Don't invade her privacy, for God's sake. I'm not spying on her." His fingers raked his hair. "I just need to know she's all right."

"I'm on it," said Gio, and disconnected.

"It's a fine line," said Henry, "between keeping an eye on her and spying. She's not likely to discern the difference."

"She won't find out."

"Like she didn't find out about tonight?"

"That was a mistake. One Maribelle will answer for."

"She couldn't have foreseen this, Adam. She didn't know Dom had the Monet, or that Maddie, bless her heart, would race over here with it."

Adam threw himself down on the sofa. "Why couldn't she leave it till morning?" His anger was unjustified, but there was so much of it, he had to put it somewhere.

"That's simple enough. She did it so your son

wouldn't carry it on his heart another night. So she could go back and tell him his father forgives him and loves him above all things."

He was right, of course. It earned him a glare.

Henry crossed his arms. "I'll stake my next paycheck that's what she did. Put aside her own broken heart to mend his, while you sit here feeling sorry for yourself."

He was right about that too.

Rising, Adam heaved a steadying breath. "I'll go talk to him."

"Remember," Henry added, "it's not the boy's fault Maddie left you."

"Maddie hasn't *left me*. She's upset, that's all. As for Dom, I can't allow him to think stealing's an acceptable way to make his point."

Henry simply raised his brows.

Adam dropped his eyes, and his shoulders. "Don't worry, I know who's to blame. For the Monet. And for Maddie."

ADAM'S PHONE JARRED him from a thousand-yard stare. Slumped at his desk, he'd been awake all night.

"Talk to me, Gio."

"She hasn't shown up at her apartment."

He sat bolt upright. "She should've been there two hours ago. Where is she?"

"We're looking into it. She could've hopped another flight. A train, a bus, a cab. She could be at a hotel. We're just getting started."

"Lucy's staying at the penthouse. What did she say?"

"We haven't spoken to her yet."

"Goddamn it, Gio! Do your fucking job!"

"Mr. LeCroix, sir. It's six in the morning in New York. I didn't want to alarm Ms. St. Clair's sister. I told my man on the ground not to disturb her until seven."

Adam took a breath. "Okay. All right." He paced to the window, stared down at the pool, sparkling under the noontime sun. "Track her credit card. Cash machines."

"We're on all those things."

"I'll talk to Maribelle. Maddie might've said something to her." He drove a hand through his hair. "Stay in touch, Gio. Close touch."

MARIBELLE GREETED HIM with a cocked brow and half smile. "Rough night?"

He stepped into her living room, a place he'd always hated, but that now seemed oddly comforting. Dom lived here. So did John, apparently.

And Maddie had been here only last night.

"She's missing," he said, facing Maribelle. "She never showed up at her apartment."

"I'm not surprised."

Or terribly concerned, by the looks of it. But why would she care? She'd hate Maddie in proportion to how much Adam loved her.

She lifted the phone. "Gisele, coffee please. For two." To Adam, "Let's take it out on the terrace."

"This isn't a social call."

"Dom's upstairs with Roland. He doesn't need to hear this, does he?"

How irritating that everyone else was so sensible while he was coming apart at the seams.

He followed her outside, paced while she sat at a café table under a purple awning. Gisele brought the coffee. Maribelle poured two cups.

"Thanks for coming to see Dom last night."

He snapped at her. "You needn't thank me for visiting my own son."

"All right then, I'm *glad* you came. He was happy this morning. The Monet must've weighed on him."

She was determined to be reasonable in the face of his bad temper. So be it. He could be civil too.

"I regret it came to that," he said, stiffly. "He shouldn't have had to commit a felony to get my attention."

"No, he shouldn't. But in a weird way, it worked. So let's just appreciate the irony and move on."

She smiled, damn her black heart.

He couldn't hold out against it. He was that desperate for comfort. Pulling out the other chair, he folded himself onto its lady-sized frame. "You've done well by him, Maribelle. With precious little help from me."

"He's a great kid, in spite of us both." She lifted her coffee, an air toast. "Now, about Maddie. You really fucked that up, Adam."

"She overreacted, that's all." He picked up his coffee, set it down without tasting it. "She'll see that, in time."

Maribelle shook her head. "No. You fucked it up. And before you think I'm crowing, I'll tell you that I tried to talk her into staying."

He let his doubt show.

"She's good for you, Adam." She spread her palms. "You're sitting here, right? Would either of us have imagined this last week?"

"I thought you might be jealous of her." He felt foolish admitting it, but her openness disarmed him.

"I *am* jealous of her, but not how you mean." She laughed, sounding almost carefree. "She can have your ornery ass, I'm not interested anymore. What I'm jealous of is how she stands up to you." She pointed a finger at him. "You're not the boss of her."

He looked down at his cup, sitting in a puddle on the saucer. He'd sloshed coffee over the rim, uncharacteristically clumsy of him. But then he was a mess, wasn't he? He'd been telling himself Maddie would get over it, but even he wasn't buying it.

Maribelle was right; he'd fucked up royally.

"What should I do?" he heard himself say.

"Let her go."

He looked up. "But I love her."

"Then quit trying to control her. And"—she pointed her finger again—"respect what matters to her. She made herself swallow the fact that you used to steal. But when you committed to a relationship, you as good as promised that you wouldn't do it again. That you wouldn't do anything that crossed one of her big, bright lines."

She leaned back in her chair. "What did you say to her when she found you?"

He made himself speak the truth. "That she used the law as a crutch. Mindlessly followed rules." And he'd dragged her father into it, hadn't he? He dropped his head in his hands.

Silence met his confession, a long, pregnant pause that left his mind free to turn on itself, guns blazing. He'd crossed Maddie's lines, all right, and then he'd belittled them. Belittled *her* because she'd caught him, embarrassed him, disagreed with him. And what was that but an attempt to control her through disparagement?

Well, she'd had plenty of experience with that in her youth. She'd had no trouble recognizing a bully when she saw one.

Maribelle let him stew while she sipped her coffee. Then she said, plainly, "People fuck up. They say—and do—stupid things when they're in love. Colossally stupid, self-centered, thoughtless things. Some they do in the name of love, some in spite of it."

She was right, of course. Apparently, she'd spent the

last ten years becoming more enlightened, while he'd become more entrenched in his arrogance.

He managed to meet her eyes. "I'm sorry, Maribelle. I should've forgiven you long ago."

She shrugged. "I did a horrible thing. It took me years to forgive myself. Don't wait that long, Adam. Forgive yourself now and go make things right with Maddie."

Humility was an uncomfortable new suit. "I don't know how."

"Make what's important to her important to you. Put her first. If you love her, that should be easy."

The easiest thing in the world, now that his head was on straight.

But first, he had to find her.

"SHE TOOK FIVE thousand from her bank account," Gio said, "Times Square branch, at nine o'clock this morning. Then she disappeared. Her sister hasn't heard from her. Neither has her employer. I tracked down her best friend, Victoria Westin. She denied contact, as did the veterinarian."

"Credit card?" Adam asked, though he knew she was too smart for that. "Cell phone?"

"She hasn't used either. I don't expect she will, until she's ready to be found." Gio paused. "Maribelle had nothing to add?"

"She says she doesn't know where Maddie is. I believe her."

Maribelle also said he should stop trying to control her. He rubbed his burning eyes. Who'd have thought he'd be taking relationship advice from Maribelle? Life's ironies were coming at him fast and furious.

"Let it go, Gio."

"Sir?"

"Call off the search. Drop it completely."

Adam ended the call. Gazed out the window at Portofino, the setting sun winking off windows, sparkling on the water like twinkle lights. In the harbor, boats bobbed at anchor. A yacht slid soundlessly over the sea, heading for open water.

Twenty-four hours ago, he'd been on top of the world, his life as he wanted it just beginning. He was in love, and it was glorious.

Now, he was still in love, and it sucked.

Holding out little hope, he dialed Lucy's number. She answered on the first ring. "Hello?"

"It's Adam."

"Oh Adam, how could you?"

His heart leaped. "You talked to her? Is she all right?"

She powered on. "Do you know how long Maddie's waited to fall in love? I begged her to give you a chance and you *totally fucked it up*! You *broke her heart*!"

"Please, Lucy." He clutched the window frame. "What did she say?"

"That you're a lying bastard asshole, and a lot more of the same. What the hell did you do?"

"Something stupid. Thoughtless. Arrogant. Idiotic."

"Did you cheat on her?"

"No! I love her. I need to tell her that. And apologize." He swallowed. "Lucy, where she is?"

"I don't know. When she called, it sounded like Port Authority."

Oh God. She could be on a bus to anywhere. Alone. Vulnerable.

"Fuck me!" He slapped the window frame, barely held himself back from punching through the glass.

But his temper fizzled as quickly as it flared, crowded out by other emotions. He rested his overheated forehead against the cool window. "I don't deserve her anyway."

"You're probably right," said Lucy. "She has the truest heart."

"And I crushed it." He thumped his head against the glass.

Silence followed, while he replayed the bedroom scene, the betrayal on her face.

He'd all but forgotten Lucy when she let out a long sigh.

"Listen, Adam. I don't know where Maddie is *right now*. But I know where she'll be a week from today."

CHAPTER TWENTY-EIGHT

VICTORIA WESTIN STACKED her heels on the porch rail. "So, what do you think?"

Maddie eyed Vicky's newly minted cowboy boots. "I think you'll rupture a tendon in those things."

"Oh, these?" Vicky rotated her ankle to show them off, black with pink stitching. "Apparently, ranchers don't wear ballet flats when they're mucking stalls. Who knew?" She wiggled the Chardonnay out of the pail of melting ice tucked between their rockers. "But I meant the ranch," she said, topping off their glasses. "What do you think of it?"

"It's . . ." Maddie wrestled down her knee-jerk snark, took a long look around at the barns, the paddock, the horses nibbling hay, and answered honestly. "It's different than I expected. It looks lived-in. Loved." She glanced at her best and truest friend, who was one day away from being mistress of the place. "It looks like home, Vic. It looks like you're home."

Vicky's smile was tinged with surprise. "I love it here. And the wildlife sanctuary, well, it's amazing." Ty was using the seven-figure award from his first wife's wrongful death case to create the Lissa Brown Memorial Refuge adjacent to the ranch. "We just rescued two elephants from a circus that went under."

"Cool. Can I see them before I leave?"

"Sure." Vicky paused. "You're such a city girl, I was afraid you'd hate Texas."

"It's an oven. But the wine's cold, so I'm good." Maddie tipped an icy trickle down her throat. Used her toes to rock her rocker.

"Um, you seem really relaxed," said Vicky, wincing like she'd lobbed a stink bomb.

Maddie knew what response she expected. *What do you mean, relaxed? How can I relax with giant smelly animals trying to stomp on me like I'm a cockroach?*

"I *am* relaxed," she said instead. "I've been on the road for a week, incommunicado. No phone, no texts, no e-mails, no Internet. And I realized, who needs them? They're a time suck."

Vicky nodded warily. "So, what did you do with all your newfound time?"

"I thought."

"I see."

"People don't think enough nowadays. We're always inputting data into the system, you know? And not taking time to process."

Vicky's heels hit the floor. "Okay, my turn to ask. Who are you and what did you do with my best friend?"

Maddie grinned. "I sound like Oprah, right? Don't worry, it's only temporary, until I finish sorting shit out."

"Good to know. But still. Not the Maddie I'm used to."

"Yeah, well, I got my heart broken." She held up a hand. "I know, I know. I said I'd never fall in love. It was a mistake. I'm over it."

And she was. Adam LeCroix was just a smudge on an otherwise perfect record.

"But to give the devil his due," she went on before Vicky could grill her, "he rattled some things loose. I was, you know, stuck. In some areas. And I had some breakthroughs."

It was hard to talk about, even with Vicky. But putting her thoughts into words was the ultimate truth test, so she soldiered on.

"First of all, Lucy's an adult."

Vicky nodded along, obviously waiting for the rest.

"That's it," Maddie said. "The big reveal. She's an adult and she's smart and kind and pure of heart. And she'll be fine. I'll always be here for her, but she's an adult now." She nodded. It sounded right and true.

"Okay. Good." Vicky smiled supportively.

"And my father." This part was harder. "I went to see the fucker."

"Oh, honey." Vicky touched her arm.

"I didn't talk to him or anything." She wasn't that brave. "I just spied on him in the diner where he bullshits with his cronies."

"He didn't spot you? Nobody spotted you?"

Here she could grin. "I dressed up like a boy. Hockey shirt, backwards baseball cap, roll of quarters in my front pocket."

Her smile faded. "The funny thing is, Vic, he's old. Old and gray and *not scary*." And hadn't that been a kick in the ass? "Biggest surprise? He can't be more than five-ten, one-seventy. I'd have staked my life on six-five, two-ninety."

"He was still twice your size. You had every reason to be scared of him."

"I know, I'm not beating myself up. It's a lesson, though. When something scares you, you exaggerate it in your mind." She lifted her shoulders, part shrug, part shrugging it off. "Anyway, it was an eye-opener. But don't worry, I'm not cured of all my neuroses yet."

"Phew. Baby steps, okay? I need time to adjust to mentally healthy Maddie."

"Har har. Anyway, the headline is, it was him, not me. I didn't deserve what he dished out. Neither did Mom. And neither did Lucy."

That's what ultimately convinced her. Her father had treated Lucy, who deserved nothing but love, the same way he treated Maddie. Which meant, in nonpsycho-babble, legal terms she could relate to, that he was the perp, and they were the victims.

It wasn't exactly a news flash. The logical part of her brain had always known it was true. But she'd never internalized it, not on an emotional level. How could she, when guilt and shame twisted her guts at the very thought of her father? Easier not to think about it. To bury her feelings under a mountain of hard work and a big pile of bullshit.

Then Adam came along and dredged it all up, dragged the details out of her, made her speak them out loud.

She'd like to hate him for it, to add another offense to his rap sheet. But in fairness, she couldn't. He'd broken her heart, for sure. But he'd also forced her take a long, hard look at the past—and the present. And she was better off for it.

If anyone could understand parental-induced trauma, it was Vicky. She clinked Maddie's glass. "Here's to surviving our fucked-up parents." They drank. Vicky topped them off again, then turned the dead soldier neck-down in the ice.

Comfortably buzzed and with the worst behind her, Maddie sucked it up and went the last mile. "I'm okay with the wedding too. You and Ty will probably be happy. So I'm good with it."

Vicky snorted a laugh. "I can hear your wedding toast now. Here's to Ty and Vicky, they'll *probably* be happy."

"Wait, I have to make a toast?"

"Yep." Vicky stacked her heels on the railing again. "Now quit stalling and tell me who he is. Or should I say who he *was*? Did you leave him alive?"

"He's not dead, just dead to me." She fanned at a fly like it was more important than Adam. "Your mother stuck me with a shitty assignment and I ended up at his place in Italy. He's rich and hot, and I was punchy from the wine and pasta." She dismissed it all with a shrug.

Vicky nodded sagely. Then she touched her fingertips together to make a bridge, preparing to drill down past half truths and facile lies.

Maddie cringed. Adam was the one area—the huge area—she hadn't finished processing. A thousand Greyhound miles, and she was still stuck on him. Still hurting. And *not* ready to talk about him.

Casting around for a distraction, she spotted a rooster tail of dust trailing a fast-approaching vehicle. "Looks like Ty's back." He'd driven to the airport to collect Vicky's mother, the she-wolf Adrianna.

Vicky shielded her eyes from the sun. "Nope, not Ty's truck. It's a car." She squinted. "A blue car. Who could it be?"

The mystery car disappeared from view, blocked by the barns. When it appeared again, it was much closer. And clearly visible.

Maddie shot to her feet. "The bastard!" Ignoring a startled Vicky, she charged down the steps and along the path to the circular driveway, planting her fists on her hips as the Bugatti rolled up.

The engine died and ticked. The dust cloud settled.

The door opened and Adam unlimbered his lean frame from the car. For a long moment he stood perfectly still, aviators aimed at her over the roof. Then he tossed them on the seat and shut the door with an ominous click.

Around the car he came, all six-foot-sexy of him, hair windblown, cheeks gaunter than she recalled, eyes as blue as the sky above.

From the porch, she heard Vicky say, "Whoa. Who's *that*?"

Trouble, that's who. Out loud, Maddie said, "You can turn your"—*excellent*—"ass around, LeCroix. You're not welcome here."

He kept walking. Pulled up a scant foot in front of her. At close range, his maleness was overwhelming. His eyes were hot and unyielding.

Holding her ground meant looking up at him, which pissed her off even more. She flattened her lips, tried to wilt him with her glare. "I said I didn't want to see you again."

"So you did. But we have things to say to each other."

His voice was a draft of cool water after a parched week in the desert. She lapped it up. And hated her thirst.

"How did you find me?"

"Your sister."

"She'll get an earful."

"No doubt. But you don't scare her, Maddie. And you don't scare me."

His gaze was locked on to her like a heat-seeking missile, so intense she fell back a step. She covered with a sneer. "Say your piece, tough guy, before I get a crick in my neck."

He advanced another step. "You ran out on me. Disappeared without a trace."

"What, your bloodhound couldn't track me?"

"No, he couldn't, as I'm sure you intended. So I worried myself sick, not knowing if you were alive or dead."

That explained the gaunt cheeks.

She refused to feel bad. "You made a fool out of me. You said you loved me, then you packed me off to Dom's so you could sneak out and steal."

"I planned to tell you the next day. I needed time to explain."

"How long does it take to say 'I'm a lying, sneaking thief'?"

"I don't see it that way."

"Exactly. *You* think you're the Caped Crusader. *I* think you're a felon."

THAT PISSED HIM off, oh yes it did.

After an interminable week of biding his time, Adam was living on the edge. He'd barely slept, couldn't eat. Only Dom and John had kept him sane. Foolishly optimistic, he'd left them in Austin with a promise to bring Maddie home, then driven agonizing hours through dry country with his heart bleeding on his sleeve, prepared to fall on his knees if she'd only hear him out.

Instead, she'd defaulted to sneers and name calling.

Irrationally disappointed, he fired back. "Still like to see me in prison, wouldn't you? Even with all that's passed between us, you're just as judgmental, uncompromising, and hard-assed as five years ago."

"All that *passed between us*, buster, were bodily fluids."

"If you believed that you wouldn't have fled at the first bump in the road."

"In my world, grand theft isn't a *bump in the road*. It's ten years in the big house."

Ah. Here was that big, bright line of hers. The last time they'd glared across it, he'd scoffed at it and at her, a mistake he'd had an endless week to regret.

"Maddie." He breathed in, then breathed out. "I'm sorry."

Her eyes narrowed to a gunslinger's squint. But her tongue, for once, stayed in her head.

Another deep breath. "I hurt you," he said, "and—"

The blonde from the porch popped up behind Maddie. "Hi. I'm Vicky." She stuck out a hand, then did a double take. "You're Adam LeCroix. Wow. I mean, welcome."

Adam clasped her hand. This was Maddie's dearest friend. His first instinct was to charm her, to recruit her in his war to win Maddie. But that would be more of the same, wouldn't it? Crowding Maddie into a corner, bending her to his will. He wanted her to choose him freely.

"I'm not here to crash your wedding," he said, politely. "I needed to see Maddie. She's been difficult to reach."

"So *you're* the client." Vicky raised a brow in Maddie's direction. "I'm sure you'd like privacy for this, er, discussion. But I'm afraid we're about to have company. Including my mother." She nodded toward the silver pickup turning into the driveway.

"Shit!" Maddie hissed like a cobra. "Go! Now! Quick!" She shoved his chest with both hands.

He didn't budge. "I'd like to see Adrianna," he said, poking the snake. "I have things to say to her."

"You want to tell her I took a week off? Too late, I already texted her." She tried to turn him around, but he crossed his arms, immovable. In bed, she got off on his strength. Well, she couldn't have it both ways.

The truck pulled up behind the Bugatti, Adrianna's sourpuss visible through the windshield. Shoving open the heavy door, she ignored Vicky's helping hand and slithered awkwardly down from the four-foot-high passenger seat, her pencil skirt riding up her nicely toned thighs.

A dust cloud rose when her feet hit the ground, filming her suede pumps. She didn't notice. She had bigger fish to fry.

"Tyrell," she announced, "drives like a maniac."

Busy unloading two suitcases the size of Smart cars from the truck bed, Ty called out in a long-suffering tone. "I told you, the speed limit's seventy."

"That doesn't mean it's safe." She sniffed. "Honestly, Victoria. Texas."

Her disapproving gaze tracked over the ranch house, the barns, the horses, and finally around to the people standing beside the dust-covered lump barely recognizable as the Bugatti. Her eyes bulged, then locked on Maddie like lasers.

Adam stepped smoothly into the line of fire. "Adrianna, how nice to see you." He smiled, charmingly.

"Adam. How unexpected. And delightful, of course." Her gaze slid to Maddie, and frosted over. "But if you've come all this way to complain about Madeline, you needn't have. She'll do her explaining to me."

Maddie pushed past him, simmering. "There's nothing to explain. We recovered the Monet, I notified Hawthorne, and then I took some vacation, of which I have plenty coming."

"If it was that simple"—Adrianna dripped venom—

"why did he call the office looking for you? Why did you turn off your phone? Obviously, you made a mess and skipped out on the consequences."

Adam cut in again, before Maddie could self-destruct. "On the contrary," he said, "Maddie uncovered the Monet and saved me a costly court battle that might have gone either way." He smiled, ruefully. "I even offered her a job, but she turned me down. It seems that if I want her services, I'll have to go through your firm."

That pacified the she-wolf. But Maddie went ballistic. "I'm not working for you!"

Adrianna flared up again. "You don't choose your clients, Madeline. I do. And if Adam wants you, he'll have you."

"He will not *have* me!" Maddie turned on him and did a two-handed chest shove, mad enough to knock him back a step this time.

"Madeline!" Adrianna started for her. Adam tried to get between them but Maddie kicked his shin. Then she spun on Adrianna, curling her fist. He caught her arm; Adrianna grabbed the other.

And Tyrell bravely stepped into the fray. "Whatever you folks think of Texas," he drawled, "we don't pull women apart like wishbones, even ornery women with smart mouths and bad attitudes."

Shaking off her captors, Maddie zapped him with a death stare. He ignored it in favor of neutral ground. "Nice car," he said, walking a circle around the Bugatti. "Never seen one like it."

Maddie's eye-roll as good as called him a bumpkin. "Of course not, it's a Bugatti Veyron. It goes for two million."

Three pair of eyes bugged.

Ty found his voice first. "What's the top end?"

"Just over two-fifty." She eyed the car longingly. "Zero to sixty in two point five seconds."

Adrianna said tartly, "And you know this how?"

"None of your beeswax," Maddie shot back.

It was the opening Adrianna wanted. She leaped through, jaws snapping. "You'll watch your mouth, Madeline, or—"

Vicky cut in. "Mother, please."

"Don't 'Mother' me. She goes too far. Skipping out on a client. Pushing him around. If she values her job—"

"Adrianna." Adam's magnate tone shut her up. "You won't fire Maddie on my account. She performed admirably as my counsel." He took a breath, skipped ahead to the part of the plan he'd been saving for last. "So well, in fact, that I'm giving her a bonus."

Taking Maddie's hand, he dropped the key in her palm.

Silence fell like a brick. Adam's heart stumbled through three endless beats while Maddie stared down at her hand. Then she lifted stunned eyes to meet his.

"What the hell, Adam?"

"You said you'd learn to drive if I gave you the Bugatti." He shrugged as if his fate didn't hang in the balance. "So here it is. No strings attached."

Her stormy eyes searched his face, slowly, as if details mattered, and he searched hers in return. She'd suffered too. Her hollowed cheeks scraped at his heart. The smudges under her eyes rubbed him raw.

He'd planned to save the car until after they'd reconciled, so she'd understand it was a gift, not a bribe. But the wheels he'd set in motion with his first phone call to Adrianna had brought them to a moment he'd never foreseen, where Maddie's livelihood was on the line because of him.

So, wisely or not, he'd jumped the gun, certain Adrianna wouldn't fire her in the face of his regard.

Of Maddie's reaction, he wasn't so sure. He waited for it now, breath locked in his lungs, hands balled in his pockets.

Her eyes dropped to her palm. She stroked the key with her thumb.

Then she walked to Tyrell. "Two million," she said, "will feed a lot of elephants." And tucking the key in his shirt pocket, she kept walking, up onto the porch and into the house.

The screen door slapped behind her.

Three pairs of eyes turned to Adam. He was hardly aware of them. Every muscle in his body itched to go after her. To make her listen, believe.

But a stronger instinct nailed him to the ground, made him wait and breathe and deal with the wreckage.

Ty dug the key from his pocket, held it out.

Adam shook his head. "It's hers to do with as she wishes."

Adrianna started to speak, but he held up a hand. "Not another word. And God help you if Maddie suffers from her connection to me."

That went down hard, but Adrianna buttoned her lip. With a stiff jerk of the head that passed for a nod, she turned her back and minced toward the house.

Watching her go, Ty let out a low whistle. "Hell's freezin' over, and I'm here to see it." He tipped his head toward the truck. "Hop in. I'll drive you to Austin."

"Thanks, but I'll call for my driver."

"Then you'll be waiting a while. Come on inside, have a cold one."

Adam had a better idea. "I'll wait on your porch, if you don't mind."

"Up to you." Ty plucked his hat off the truck's hood, slapped it on his thigh. "Change your mind, beer's in the fridge."

On the porch, an empty wine bottle bobbed in a bucket of warm water. Settling into one of the rockers, Adam texted Fredo just in case, then sat back to wait for Maddie.

It wouldn't be long. His presence on the porch would drive her insane. She'd pace, and she'd stew, and she'd curse under her breath. And eventually, long before Fredo reached Hill Country, she'd erupt like a volcano, exploding out the door to let him have it.

Then he'd lay his heart at her feet, put his fate in her hands. And win her, or lose everything—including his freedom—on one last desperate roll of the dice.

CHAPTER TWENTY-NINE

"Look at him," Maddie fumed from her station at the kitchen window, "sitting out there like he owns the place, idly rocking while his minions dance to his tune."

"Mmm," Vicky hummed absently. Chopping carrots at the counter, she'd apparently tuned out Maddie's long-running rant.

Ty stepped into the doorway wearing a hopeful smile. In the window's reflection, Maddie saw Vicky shake her head. He pivoted and tiptoed away.

Great. LeCroix's got me bringing down the bride and groom. "That's it. He's gotta go."

She found Ty killing time with his iPad. She stuck out her hand. "Gimme."

He feigned surprise. "What about the elephants?"

She wiggled her fingers. He dug out the key. She snatched it and stormed out the door.

Adam glanced up as she advanced, no surprise in his eyes. Annoyingly, he looked right at home on the weather-beaten porch, with his Levi's faded at knees and crotch—the major stress points—and T-shirt packed with pecs, a line of sweat showing between them. Add the finger-combed hair, the stubbly jaw, and he could have been an extremely sexy cowboy relaxing after a hard day busting broncs.

She stuck the key under his nose. "Giddy-up, cowboy. Saddle up and ride."

He looked at the key, looked at her. And stacked his heels on the rail.

She whacked his thigh with a backhand. "Vamoose. Skedaddle. Hit the trail."

"I'll wait. Fredo's en route."

"You can meet him halfway."

"Dom's with him. And John. I'm sure they'd like to see you."

Her mouth opened and closed like a guppy. Tears, stupid and treacherous, gathered behind her eyes. She blinked them back, but let herself ask, "How are they?"

He took out his phone, scrolled to a video. She leaned in.

A healthier, heavier John loped across the villa's green lawn. Off camera, Dom hollered his name as a tennis ball sailed into the frame. John did a one-eighty, leaped . . . and snagged it like a pro.

The camera panned to Dom's victory dance, then freeze-framed. Maddie realized she was grinning, a renegade tear trickling down one cheek.

Brushing it away, she stepped back. "Good." She nodded. "They're good. I'm glad. Now go."

He pushed the phone in his pocket. "The Bugatti's already registered in your name."

The video had blunted her hard edge, but not her resolve. "I can't accept it."

"Then sign it over to Tyrell. But before he drives it away, there's something in the passenger seat you'll want to see."

What now? The princess's emeralds?

She faked disinterest. "Unless it's the leather pants, I don't want it."

His lips curved slightly, a hint of her favorite half smile. "See for yourself. Then you can decide what to do with it."

She fought a pitched battle with curiosity, and lost. "Fine. Whatever." She marched to the car, pulled open the door.

Across the passenger seat lay a tubular package, large enough for a rolled-up canvas.

She peeked over her shoulder. Adam rocked slowly, blue eyes unreadable.

Tube under her arm, she strode back to the porch, dropped it across his lap. "Dom would've gotten up the guts to give it to you himself. You don't owe me anything."

He looked up at her, a strange expression on his face. "Maddie, it's not the Monet."

"Then what— Oh!" *Sweet Jesus.* The blood drained from her head. She staggered back a step.

He was up in an instant, scooping her up, setting her in the chair. "Head between your knees," he said, gently pushing it down. "You're all right. I've got you."

Why did that make her feel safe, when he was the reason she was fainting in the first place?

"Is it the *Lady in Red*?" she mumbled into her lap.

He rubbed circles on her back. "Mmm, yes it is."

"Why?"

"Because, darling, I love you."

"So?"

He chuckled, ruefully. "Romantic as ever."

Romantic? What was romantic about a stolen Renoir?

She sat up slowly. Adam was kneeling beside her at eye level, an unfair advantage for him. She had no choice but to gaze into those dark, dangerous depths.

"Maddie." His hand on her thigh was also unfair. "Whatever else you think of me, know this. I never meant to hurt you or betray you. The plans for the Matisse had long been laid, and I would've explained everything to you the next day. But it was too little, too late, and I'm sorry."

She wanted to look away, but his gaze mesmerized her.

"What I would've told you, if I'd had the chance, is that I have a thing about art."

She let out a short laugh. "No. You have a *thing* about sports cars. You have an *obsession* with art."

"Call it what you will. Henry has his theories about it. Maribelle too. They may well be right. But the why of it is beside the point."

His gaze bore into her. "For whatever reason, I care intensely about art. It sickens me when men climb out of the slime, wiping their feet on it to hide their bloody tracks, while the law, Maddie darling, does nothing."

He sounded so reasonable, so passionate. A thief with a cause.

"Feeling as I do," he went on, "I have no qualms about stealing art from criminals. And if I get off on the risk, as you astutely observed, I'll simply point out that the world is full of treasures to steal. If I did it only for the thrill, I'd have expanded my scope."

"But you haven't?"

A quick smile flashed. "If I had, you'd have discovered it five years ago. You were frighteningly thorough."

His smile faded. He took both her hands in his. "I stole the *Lady in Red* to keep it out of Akulov's hands. Now I'm putting it—and myself—in yours."

She didn't know what to say, what to do. She had

him cold; she should be fist-pumping. Instead she wanted to cry.

Why, oh why, had he waited until she wasn't his attorney to confess?

"I can see your mind working," he said. "Before you phone the FBI, let me finish."

"No, don't say any more." She shook her head, kept shaking it. "Not another word, Adam, until you have counsel."

"It's nothing incriminating, at least not legally. But I have to say what I came here to say."

He balanced her hands in his palms. His heart shone like diamonds in his eyes. "I can't change my beliefs for you, Maddie. My moral code. But I can accept that you don't share them. And I can"—his lips curved—"hang up my cape. I can do that for you. I want to."

"Why now? Why not a week ago, when it would've made all the difference?"

"Because, as you've frequently pointed out, I'm an arrogant ass. I assumed you—like everyone else—would recognize the error of your ways and fall into line with the world according to Adam LeCroix." He huffed out a laugh. "Believe me, it sounded less condescending and egotistical in my head."

He held her gaze, though it must have been difficult. "In any case, I was wrong. I crossed a line. I can only apologize and promise not to cross it again. I may cross others, and I've no doubt you'll snap me back. But this one, never again."

She pulled her hands away, scrubbed them over her face. "Jeez, Adam. It's not as simple as *sorry*. You just confessed to a crime."

"Which you've known for years I committed."

"But you said it out loud. I can't stick my head in the sand." She jabbed a finger at the tube that had rolled to the floor. "There's a zillion-dollar painting in there. I can't hang it in my apartment. I can't pretend it isn't stolen."

She forced her fingers through her hair. "Why do this to me? Why put me in this position?"

"To prove what you mean to me. What I'll risk for you. After your haunting description, I'd rather not go to jail. And I assure you, I'll spare no expense to avoid it. But I understand you can turn me in. I understand the risk I'm taking."

He cupped her face, stroked her cheeks with his thumbs. "I'm not the boss of you, Maddie. But I pushed you around, manipulated you, put your back to the wall." He pressed a kiss to her forehead. "Now, darling, I put *my* life in *your* hands."

And wasn't that a bitch.

THE AGONY WRITTEN on Maddie's face almost made Adam regret what he'd done. No matter his intentions, he always seemed to hurt her.

She gave him a hard stare from stormy eyes. "I'm between a rock and a hard place. If I let you walk away with the *Lady*, I'm an accessory after the fact. If I turn you in, you're going to jail." She poked his chest. "Why couldn't you stay in Italy and leave the *Lady* out of this?"

He smiled, more confident than he had any right to be. "Because I love you. It's as simple and as complicated as that. And I trust you. With my life, apparently."

"Not the smartest thing you've ever done."

Not smart, perhaps, but a leap of faith. He wanted her for his wife, the mother of his children, a partner in all he owned. If she felt half as much for him, she wouldn't turn him in. She'd accept who he was, believe in his promise. And they'd find a way to deal with the *Lady in Red*.

Backing away, she took her phone from her pocket, scrolled through her directory, and hit a number.

He tried to hold on to his smile. At least she hadn't dialed 911.

Then, "Madeline St. Clair for Senator Warren."

His heart sank like a stone.

"Michael, hi." A pause. "Yeah yeah, air hug. Listen, you've still got connections at the U.S. Attorney's Office, right?"

Adam stared at the floor. He'd broken her heart, and now she wouldn't have him.

Crisp and clear she went on, in full lawyer mode. "Good, because I've got the *Lady in Red*. I want to pass her off to you."

A pause. "No, I don't know where she's been. She just turned up on my doorstep."

Adam lifted his gaze, locked it on hers. The thunderclouds no longer swirled in her eyes. They were steady as steel.

"Don't think with your dick, Michael. If you implicate LeCroix, the government still has to prove it. And the headlines will be all about how *you* let him walk the first time." She listened, smiled a satisfied smile. "That's right, keep it on the down low. Milk it for favors."

Adam smiled as she rolled her eyes, made a yakkety-yak motion with her hand as Warren blabbed in her ear.

After a minute, she cut in. "Sure, sure, however you want to handle it. I'll meet you Monday, at your place." A pause. "No, not for dinner. I'll be in touch."

She ended the call. They gazed at each other.

"Very slick," he said at last.

"That's why I get the big bucks."

He stepped closer. Desire crackled across the narrow space between them. "You made me sweat it out."

"You deserved it."

"What if the good senator hadn't played along?"

"Pfft. You know how much mileage he'll get from this?"

"And what will you get?"

"Out from between a rock and a hard place." She eye-walked down his chest, got to the hard place. Her tongue flicked her lips.

The hard place got harder.

She took his hand in her small one, opened his palm, and placed the key in it.

"Maddie, it's yours."

"Damn right, and you're gonna teach me to drive it. But first, let's go parking."

His confusion must have shown, because she let out a laugh.

"*Parking*," she informed him, "is American for sex in a car."

TEXAS HILL COUNTRY was ribboned with roads that would serve their purpose. They got no farther than the dirt track behind Ty's stable, next to a rusted-out baler.

Adam shut off the engine, and she pounced, pawing his T-shirt up over his head so his chest gleamed in the sun. She slicked her hands over it greedily while he dug down into her bra, lifting her tits out like apples, biting and sucking.

It wasn't enough, not by a mile. He'd surrendered his pride and his heart; now she wanted his body. Around her, inside her. She unbuckled his belt, took him hot and heavy in her hands, in her mouth, as she sprawled across the console.

He had to abandon her breasts, so he went up her skirt instead, palms rough on her ass, fingers delving into panties. The car was a sauna, sweat poured off them like bathwater. She slithered over the console, into his lap, desperate to mount him. But he was too big, everywhere, and the steering wheel was unforgiving. He opened the door and they spilled out half dressed.

Into the stable they ran, ignoring the horses, the hay bales. A row of six saddles rode a waist-high beam. He bent her over the largest. She waggled her butt, a red flag at a bull, and he tossed up her skirt, yanked down her panties, and drove her up on her toes with one thrust.

She took all of him, gladly, his hands on her hips controlling the action, holding her where he wanted her, giving and taking with each scorching stroke. Foreplay was history; it was all about speed. Faster and harder. Skin slipping and sliding.

She tried to arch up, take back some control, but he was in charge now, one hand on her back, the other reaching around her. Driving her crazy, driving her higher.

She was desperate to touch him, his hard, sweaty chest, his straining arms, but she couldn't reach him. She twisted her head, but couldn't see him.

She could only feel him, above her, inside her. So she closed her eyes, met him stroke for stroke, their bodies all that existed, all that mattered. Everything else faded to black, insignificant, irrelevant, as tension built, and muscles clenched . . .

Until the universe, all of it, contracted to eight slippery inches . . . and exploded with a bang.

CHAPTER THIRTY

MADDIE HAD TO admit it. The wedding was actually kind of nice.

It took place during the golden hour, in a meadow dotted with wildflowers. The bride rode to the altar—a century-old pecan tree—on Ty's favorite horse, Brescia, the setting sun making spun gold of her hair, her simple white gown fluttering in the breeze. The wonder and devotion on Ty's face as he watched her approach stole Maddie's breath and erased her last doubts.

He lifted her from the saddle, then passed the reins to a beaming Dom. Maddie stepped forward with Vicky's bouquet, going up on her toes to kiss her friend's cheek. Then she stepped back to stand with Adam, part of the small circle of family and friends that closed around the bride and groom.

Most of them, Maddie already knew. Ty's brother, Cody, stood up as best man, his brand new wife, Julie, beside him. Vicky's brother, Matt, was there too, with his wife, Isabelle. And Ty's best friend, Jack McCabe, looked on benignly, while his wife, Lil, bounced their baby on her shoulder.

The preacher, a huge man named Buster who doubled as a bartender, handled the preliminaries. Then, as promised, Vicky and Ty spoke their own vows.

And as promised, the hankies came out.

It was a fairy-tale moment, one Maddie couldn't have predicted, where the love in Vicky's eyes and the catch in her voice turned those hokey vows into poetry.

The cynic in her wanted to sneer that they'd be broken again and again. But the magic in the air must have rubbed off on her, because a light bulb went on and she understood, finally, that perfection wasn't required, just a wholehearted effort.

A wholehearted effort, and love.

BY THE TIME it was over, the sun had gone down. Stars glittered like sequins in the twilit sky.

Dom led Brescia to the stable, Adam and Maddie strolling beside him.

Nudging her, Adam tipped his head at the saddle, raised an inquiring brow. She shook her head. "Ours had a bigger saddle horn. So to speak."

They snickered.

Over on the porch, the guests were nibbling appetizers. Buster poured drinks. Good-natured chatter floated across the grass.

"Happy couples," Adam said.

"Mmm. I guess it can happen."

He took heart from that, and from their lovely day, horseback riding with Dom and John, visiting the elephants. But in the morning, they'd leave for New York, back to the real world. What would happen then?

In the stable, he stripped Brescia's saddle, showed Dom how to curry her, then turned the brush over to him and stepped back with Maddie to keep an eye from a distance.

"About tomorrow," he said. "We can drive if you'd rather not fly."

"I'd always rather not fly. But I told Michael I'd be there Monday. I don't want to give him time for second thoughts."

"How about you? Second thoughts?"

"About the *Lady*? None."

"About us?"

She rubbed her arms like she was chilled, though it had to be eighty degrees. Not a good sign.

"I'm not ready to move in with you," she said at last. "But."

Happiness hung on a "but."

"Those vows," she went on, "the ones Vicky said. If we work on those for a while and it goes okay, then yeah, I'll move in." She lifted one shoulder, gave him a little smile. "Then, if we can keep it up when we're in each other's hair every day . . . I might, you know."

"Marry me?"

"Yeah. That."

He nodded gravely, biting down on the grin that wanted to burst out. "Fair enough. We'll take it slow."

"Good." Her smile widened. "That's good." Wrapping her arms around his waist, she rested her cheek on his chest.

Savoring her warmth, her scent, he cradled her close. Counted his blessings. Vowed he wouldn't rush her.

Then out came his mental calendar. He flipped through the pages.

"I can feel you planning," she said.

"Who, me?"

She lifted her head, gave him the beady eye. "You're working on a wedding date, aren't you?"

"Well, you won't let me plan another heist."

"Funny." She poked his ribs. "Remember, you're not the boss of me."

"If I forget, you'll remind me."

"You bet your ass." She settled her head on his chest again.

He went back to his calendar.

October was a nice month. Lovely weather in Portofino.

Read on for a sneak peek at Cara Connelly's
Save the Date series!

THE WEDDING DATE

A delicious holiday novella,
now available in print and
e-book from Avon Impulse!

THE WEDDING FAVOR

Cara's first full-length novel,
now available in print and
e-book from Avon Romance!

And don't miss the next book,

THE WEDDING BAND,

available in print and e-book in 2015!

An Excerpt from

THE WEDDING DATE

"BLIND DATES ARE for losers." Julie Marone pinched the phone with her shoulder and used both hands to scrape the papers on her desk into a tidy pile. "You really think I'm a loser?"

"Not a *loser*, exactly." Amelia's inflection kept her options open.

Julie snorted a laugh. "Gee, thanks, sis. Tell me how you *really* feel."

"You know what I mean. You've been out of circulation for three years. You have to start *somewhere*."

"Sure, but did it have to be at the bottom of the barrel?"

"Peter's a nice guy!" Amelia protested.

"Absolutely," Julie said agreeably. "So devoted to dear old Mom that he *still lives in her basement.*"

Amelia let out a here-we-go-again groan. "He's an optometrist, for crying out loud. I assumed he'd have his own place."

Julie started on the old saying about what happens when you *assume*, but Amelia cut her off. "Yeah, yeah. Ass. You. Me. Got it. Anyway, Leo"—tonight's date—"is a definite step up. I checked with his sister"—Amelia's hairstylist—"and she said he's got a house in Natick. His practice is thriving."

"So why's he going on a blind date?"

"His divorce just came through."

Recently divorced men fell into two categories. "Shopping for a replacement or still simmering with resentment?"

"Come on, Jules, give him a chance."

Julie sighed. Slid the stack of papers into a folder marked "Westin/Anderson" and added it to her briefcase for tomorrow's closing. "Just tell me where to meet him."

"On Hanover Street at seven. He made reservations at a place on Prince."

"Well, in that case." Dinner in Boston's North End almost made it worthwhile. Julie was always up for good Italian. "How will I recognize him? Tall, dark, and handsome?" A girl could hope.

"Dark . . . but . . . not tall. Wearing a red scarf."

"Handsome?"

Amelia cleared her throat. "I caught one of his commercials the other night. He's got a nice smile."

"Whoa, wait. Commercials? What kind of lawyer is he?"

"Personal injury." Amelia dropped it like a turd. Then said, "Oh, look, Ray's here. Gotta go," and hung up.

Putting two and two together, Julie groaned. Leo could only be the ubiquitous Leo "I Feel Your" Payne, whose commercials saturated late-night television, promising Boston's sleepless that he *would not quit* until they got every penny they deserved—minus his third, of course.

"How did I get into this?" she murmured.

For three years, since David died, she'd tried explaining to her sister that her career, her rigorous training schedule—she really *would* do the marathon this year—and their sprawling Italian-American family kept her too busy for a man. And Amelia, even though she didn't buy it, had respected Julie's wishes.

Until now.

The catalyst, Julie knew, was Amelia's own upcoming Christmas Eve wedding. She wanted Julie—her maid of honor—to bring a date. A real date, not her gay friend Dan. Amelia loved Dan like a brother, but he was single too, always up for hanging out, and he made it too easy for Julie to duck the dating game.

So Amelia had lined up three eligible men and informed Julie that if she didn't give them a chance, then their mother—a confirmed cougar with not-great taste in men—would bring a wedding date for her.

Recognizing a train wreck when she saw one coming, Julie had given in and agreed to date all three. So far they were shaping up even worse than expected.

Jan appeared in the doorway. "J-Julie?" Her usually pale cheeks were pink. Her tiny bosom heaved. "Oh Julie. You'll never believe . . . the most . . . I mean . . ."

"Take a breath, Jan." Julie did that thing where she

pointed two fingers at Jan's eyes, then back at her own. "Focus."

Jan sucked air through her nose, let it out with a wheeze. "Okay, we just had a walk-in. From Austin." She wheezed again. "He's *gorgeous*. And that drawl . . ." Wheeze.

Julie nodded encouragingly. It never helped to rush Jan.

"He said . . ." Jan fanned herself, for real. She was actually perspiring. "He said someone in the ER told him about you."

That sounded ominous.

Julie glanced at her watch. Five forty-five, too late to deal with mysterious strangers. If she left now, she'd just have time to get home and change into something more casual for her date.

"Ask him to come back tomorrow," she said. "I don't have time—"

"He just wants a minute." Jan wiped her palms on her gray pleated skirt. At twenty-five, she dressed like Julie's gram, but inside she was stuck at sixteen, helpless in the face of a handsome man. "I-I'm sorry. I couldn't say no."

Julie blew out a sigh, wondered—again—why she'd hired her silly cousin in the first place. Because family was family, that's why.

"Fine. Send him in."

Ten seconds later, six foot two of Texan filled her door. Tawny hair, caramel eyes, tanned cheekbones.

Whoa.

Her own sixteen-year-old heart went pitty-pat.

He crossed the room, swallowed up her hand in his big palm, and said in a ridiculous drawl, "Cody Brown. I appreciate you seeing me, Miz Marone."

"Call me Julie," she managed to reply. Her hand felt

naked when he released it, like she'd pulled off a warm glove on a cold winter day.

No wonder Jan had gone to pieces. He was tall, the way an oak tree's tall. Lean, the way a cougar's lean.

She gestured and he took a seat, his beat-up leather jacket falling open over an indigo shirt with pearl snaps and a belt buckle the size of Texas. When he crossed one cowboy-booted ankle over the other snug-jeaned knee, spurs jangled in her head.

Her mouth went dry.

She picked up her pen, clicked it off and on, off and on. "So, you're new to Boston?"

Cody Brown unfurled a slow, eye-crinkling smile. "What gave me away?"

She huffed out a laugh. "Okay, that was dumb."

God, she was as bad as Jan.

He waved a hand. "Not at all," he drawled, "you were just being polite." The December wind had stirred up his hair. The fingers he raked through it did nothing to tame it. "You're right, I'm brand new to Boston. Just got here last week, and been working every day since I touched down."

"I see," she said, staring at his stubble, the way it shadowed his jaw. She made herself look down at the yellow pad on her desk. "Are you looking for a house? A condo?"

"I'm thinking condo."

She made a note. "Your wife agrees?"

"I'm not married."

She glanced up. "Engaged?"

He shook his head. "No girlfriend either. Or boy-friend, for that matter." He broke into that smile again.

She set her pen on the desk. "Who referred you to me?"

"Marianne Wells. Said you found her dream house."

Julie remembered her, a nurse at Mass General. "Yes, I found a house for her. For her and her *husband*." She put an apology in her smile. "That's what I do. I match couples with houses."

Cody tilted his head. "Just couples? How come?"

"It's my specialty."

He nodded agreeably. "Okay. But how come?"

She shifted impatiently. "Because it is." *And that's all the explanation you're getting.* "Now, Mr. Brown—"

"It's Cody to my friends." He smiled. "Most of my enemies too."

She wished he'd holster that smile. It lit up the room, exposing how drab her office was. Tasteful, of course— ecru walls, framed prints, gold upholstery. But bland. She hadn't noticed just how bland until he'd walked in and started smiling all over it.

She clicked her pen.

His smile widened and a dimple appeared, for God's sake.

Then he spread his hands. His big, warm hands. "Julie," he said in that slow, Texas drawl. "Can't you make an exception for me?"

She tried to say no, to resist his pull. But he held her gaze, tugging her irresistibly toward blue skies and sunshine.

Her breath gave a hitch, her stomach a dip.

And her heart, her frozen heart, thumped *at last*.

CODY'D THOUGHT HE was too damn tired for sex, but from his first glimpse of Julie Marone—moss-green eyes, chestnut hair, slim runner's body—he'd been picturing her out of that business suit and spread across his bed, wearing a lacy pushup bra and not another damn thing.

Then her breath caught, a sexy little hiccup, and he was halfway hard before he knew what hit him.

Damn it. He didn't need to get laid half as much as he needed a place to live. After seven straight overnights in the Mass General ER—and an eighth that would begin in just a few hours—he was finally due to get some time off. Four days, to be exact, which gave him exactly that long to find a condo, sign the papers, and write the damn check.

But Julie wasn't cooperating. Not only did she have his cock in an uproar, she wasn't inclined to hunt up a condo for him. She kept feeding him a line about *couples*, like she was some kind of karmic matchmaker or something.

Seriously, what kind of realtor gave a shit who she sold to? A house was a house; a condo was a condo. Money was money. Right?

Whatever. She was hot for him too, and even if he wasn't in a position to do anything about it right at the moment, he wasn't above using it to get what he wanted.

Deliberately, in a move that had yet to fail him, he put his palm to his chest, rubbed it back and forth slowly.

Her eyes dropped to follow the movement.

He let her think about it.

She swallowed.

Then, shamelessly, he worked his drawl. "I'd sure be grateful if you'd help me out. I been staying next door at the Plaza—and don't get me wrong, it's swanky, for sure—but I need my own place so I can bring Betsy on east with me."

Her eyes snapped up. "I thought you didn't have a girlfriend."

"Betsy's my dog. Part coon hound, part Chihuahua." He did the smile again. "She'll like you. You both got that feisty thing going on."

Her brow knitted, and he bit his cheek to hold back a laugh. She probably wasn't sure how to feel about being compared to his dog. He could tell her it was a compliment—Betsy was the only woman who'd never disappointed him—but he didn't want her to get cocky.

What he wanted was for her to forget her cockamamie rule about couples and find him a condo in the next four days. That meant keeping her interested in him. So he played his strongest card, the one that worked with all the ladies. Worked too well in fact. But he wasn't going to argue with that now.

"The problem's my schedule," he went on, spreading his palms. "Me being a doctor and all."

He waited for her to rip her clothes off.

She didn't.

For five long seconds, she stared straight into his eyes. Then she opened a drawer and took out a business card, set it on the desk in front of him.

He dropped his eyes. *Brian Murphy—Century 21.*

What the fuck?

"Murph's a friend of mine," she said, her voice cool and flat. "I'm sure he can help you." She snapped her briefcase shut.

Cody couldn't believe it. The doctor thing *always* made women go crazy. So crazy that they stopped seeing Cody Brown the man and saw only Cody Brown, MD, their ticket to a McMansion in the burbs and vacations in Cabo.

But this chick was the opposite of attracted. She'd gone downright frosty.

He was in uncharted territory.

Desperate, he went into full seduction mode, hit her with the eye-lock sexy-smile combo, playing it out in super slow-mo.

First he caught her eyes. Held them. Let a long, silent moment slide by like a river of molasses.

Then slowly, leisurely, as if he had all night to get it done, he curved his lips. First one side. Then the other.

She paused.

He deepened his drawl. "I want *you*, Julie."

She clicked her pen.

"Give me one day," he crooned. "Just tomorrow, that's all."

Click click. "Are you sure you wouldn't rather rent first? Check out the neighborhoods?"

He shook his head. "I'm not picky. Someplace close to Mass General will do me fine, where I can take Betsy for a run."

She hesitated, obviously wrestling with some inner demon.

He put his money on the horny realtor.

"Beacon Hill could work," she said at last.

Not a smidgen of smugness seeped into his voice. "That where the Old North Church is? One if by land, two if by sea?"

She smiled, finally, a pretty sight. "No, that's in the North End. You could look there too, especially if you're a fan of Italian food. The restaurants are amazing."

He stood up. So did she. She was taller than he expected, which meant she had long legs.

He liked long legs.

"Let's go try one out," he said like it was only natural. "I'm sick of room service."

She looked startled. "Oh. Um. Thanks, but I have a date." She gave a nervous laugh. "A blind date, actually. And a closing in the morning."

"Seriously?" he blurted.

Her eyebrows shot up.

He did damage control. "A closing in the morning?

I shouldn't be surprised. You must have lots of those."
He nodded, sagely. Wondered why in the hell a looker
like her had a *blind date*.

One of her brows came down, but she arched the
other like she was assessing his intellect, wondering if
he was actually smart enough to be a doctor. Then she
lifted her briefcase and came around the desk, herding
him through the door. "I can give you tomorrow afternoon. I'll line up a few places, and we'll get started
around one."

"Sure. Let me give you my number." Maybe she'd get
lonely, give him a booty call.

"Give it to Jan," she said, sticking a fork in his fan-
tasy.

In the outer office, Jan looked like a Munchkin behind
her oversized desk. "Take Dr. Brown's number," said
Julie, on a march to the door. "Then go home. I'll check
in after the closing." And she was gone.

"Well hell," Cody muttered. She'd blown him off.
What about the eye-lock sexy-smile combo? He was
sure that'd put her in heat.

Huh.

He turned to Jan. A new sparkle lit her eyes.

"You're a *doctor*?" she said.

He let out a sigh.

An Excerpt from

THE WEDDING FAVOR

"THAT WOMAN"—TYRELL aimed his finger like a gun at the blonde across the hall—"is a bitch on wheels."

Angela set a calming hand on his arm. "That's why she's here, Ty. That's why they sent her."

He paced away from Angela, then back again, eyes locked on the object of his fury. She was talking on a cell phone, angled away from him so all he could see was her smooth French twist and the simple gold hoop in her right earlobe.

"She's got ice water in her veins," he muttered. "Or arsenic. Or whatever the hell they embalm people with."

"She's just doing her job. And in this case, it's a thankless one. They can't win."

Ty turned his roiling eyes on Angela. He would have started in—again—about hired-gun lawyers from New York City coming down to Texas thinking all they had to do was bullshit a bunch of good ole boys who'd never made it past eighth grade, but just then the clerk stepped out of the judge's chambers.

"Ms. Sanchez," she said to Angela. "Ms. Westin," to the blonde. "We have a verdict."

Across the hall, the blonde snapped her phone shut and dropped it into her purse, snatched her briefcase off the tile floor, and without looking at Angela or Ty, or anyone else for that matter, walked briskly through the massive oak doors and into the courtroom. Ty followed several paces behind, staring bullets in the back of her tailored navy suit.

Twenty minutes later they walked out again. A reporter from *Houston Tonight* stuck a microphone in Ty's face.

"The jury obviously believed you, Mr. Brown. Do you feel vindicated?"

I feel homicidal, he wanted to snarl. But the camera was rolling. "I'm just glad it's over," he said. "Jason Taylor dragged this out for seven years, trying to wear me down. He didn't."

He continued striding down the broad hallway, the reporter jogging alongside.

"Mr. Brown, the jury came back with every penny of the damages you asked for. What do you think that means?"

"It means they understood that all the money in the world won't raise the dead. But it can cause the living some serious pain."

"Taylor's due to be released next week. How do you feel knowing he'll be walking around a free man?"

Ty stopped abruptly. "While my wife's cold in the ground? How do you think I feel?" The man shrank back from Ty's hard stare, decided not to follow as Ty strode out through the courthouse doors.

Outside, Houston's rush hour was a glimpse inside the doors of hell. Scorching pavement, blaring horns. Eternal gridlock.

Ty didn't notice any of it. Angela caught up to him on the sidewalk, tugged his arm to slow him down. "Ty, I can't keep up in these heels."

"Sorry." He slowed to half speed. Even as pissed off as he was, Texas courtesy was ingrained.

Taking her bulging briefcase from her hand, he smiled down at her in a good imitation of his usual laid-back style. "Angie, honey," he drawled, "you could separate your shoulder lugging this thing around. And believe me, a separated shoulder's no joke."

"I'm sure you'd know about that." She slanted a look up from under thick black lashes, swept it over his own solid shoulders. Angling her slender body toward his, she tossed her wavy black hair and tightened her grip on his arm.

Ty got the message. The old breast-crushed-against-the-arm was just about the easiest signal to read.

And it came as no surprise. During their long days together preparing for trial, the cozy take-out dinners in her office as they went over his testimony, Angela had dropped plenty of hints. Given their circumstances, he hadn't encouraged her. But she was a beauty, and to be honest, he hadn't discouraged her either.

Now, high on adrenaline from a whopping verdict that would likely boost her to partner, she had "available" written all over her. At that very moment they were passing by the Alden Hotel. One nudge in that direction and she'd race him to the door. Five minutes later he'd be balls deep, blotting out the memories he'd relived on the witness stand that morning. Memories of Lissa torn and broken, pleading with him to let her go, let her die. Let her leave him behind to somehow keep living without her.

Angela's steps slowed. He was tempted, sorely tempted.

But he couldn't do it. For six months Angela had been his rock. It would be shameful and ugly to use her this afternoon, then drop her tonight.

Because drop her, he would. She'd seen too deep inside, and like the legions preceding her, she'd found the hurt there and was all geared up to fix it. He couldn't be fixed. He didn't want to be fixed. He just wanted to fuck and forget. And she wasn't the girl for that.

Fortunately, he had the perfect excuse to ditch her.

"Angie, honey." His drawl was deep and rich even when he wasn't using it to soften a blow. Now it flowed like molasses. "I can't ever thank you enough for all you did for me. You're the best lawyer in Houston and I'm gonna take out a full-page ad in the paper to say so."

She leaned into him. "We make a good team, Ty." Sultry-eyed, she tipped her head toward the Marriott. "Let's go inside. You can . . . buy me a drink."

His voice dripped with regret, not all of it feigned. "I wish I could, sugar. But I've got a plane to catch."

She stopped on a dime. "A *plane*? Where're you going?"

"Paris. I've got a wedding."

"But Paris is just a puddle-jump from here! Can't you go tomorrow?"

"France, honey. Paris, France." He flicked a glance at the revolving clock on the corner, then looked down into her eyes. "My flight's at eight, so I gotta get. Let me find you a cab."

Dropping his arm, she tossed her hair again, defiant this time. "Don't bother. My car's back at the courthouse." Snatching her briefcase from him, she checked her watch. "Gotta run, I have a date." She turned to go.

And then her bravado failed her. Looking over her shoulder, she smiled uncertainly. "Maybe we can celebrate when you get back?"

Ty smiled too, because it was easier. "I'll call you."

Guilt pricked him for leaving the wrong impression, but Jesus, he was itching to get away from her, from everyone, and lick his wounds. And he really did have a plane to catch.

Figuring it would be faster than finding a rush-hour cab, he walked the six blocks to his building, working up the kind of sweat a man only gets wearing a suit. He ignored the elevator, loped up the five flights of stairs—why not, he was soaked anyway—unlocked his apartment, and thanked God out loud when he hit the air-conditioning.

The apartment wasn't home—that would be his ranch—just a sublet, a place to crash during the run-up to the trial. Sparsely furnished and painted a dreary off-white, it had suited his bleak and brooding mood.

And it had one appliance he was looking forward to using right away. Striding straight to the kitchen, he peeled off the suit parts he was still wearing—shirt, pants, socks—and balled them up with the jacket and tie. Then he stuffed the whole wad in the trash compactor and switched it on, the first satisfaction he'd had all day.

The clock on the stove said he was running late, but

he couldn't face fourteen hours on a plane without a shower, so he took one anyway. And of course he hadn't packed yet.

He hated to rush, it went against his nature, but he moved faster than he usually did. Even so, what with the traffic, by the time he parked his truck and went through all the rigmarole to get to his terminal, the plane had already boarded and they were preparing to detach the Jetway.

Though he was in no frame of mind for it, he forced himself to dazzle and cajole the pretty girl at the gate into letting him pass, then settled back into his black mood as he walked down the Jetway. Well, at least he wouldn't be squished into coach with his knees up his nose all the way to Paris. He'd sprung for first class and he intended to make the most of it. Starting with a double shot of Jack Daniel's.

"Tyrell Brown, can't you move any faster than that? I got a planeful of people waiting on you."

Despite his misery, he broke out in a grin at the silver-haired woman glaring at him from the airplane door. "Loretta, honey, you working this flight? How'd I get so lucky?"

She rolled her eyes. "Spare me the sweet talk and move your ass." She waved away the ticket he held out. "I don't need that. There's only one seat left on the whole dang airplane. Why it has to be in my section, I'll be asking the good Lord next Sunday."

He dropped a kiss on her cheek. She swatted his arm. "Don't make me tell your mama on you." She gave him a little shove down the aisle. "I talked to her just last week and she said you haven't called her in a month. What kind of ungrateful boy are you, anyway? After she gave you the best years of her life."

Loretta was his mama's best friend, and she was like

family. She'd been needling him since he was a toddler, and was one of the few people immune to his charm. She pointed at the only empty seat. "Sit your butt down and buckle up so we can get this bird in the air."

Ty had reserved the window seat, but it was already taken, leaving him the aisle. He might have objected if the occupant hadn't been a woman. But again, Texas courtesy required him to suck it up, so he did, keeping one eye on her as he stuffed his bag in the overhead.

She was leaning forward, rummaging in the carry-on between her feet, and hadn't seen him yet, which gave him a chance to check her out.

Dressed for travel in a sleek black tank top and yoga pants, she was slender, about five-foot-six, a hundred and twenty pounds, if he was any judge. Her arms and shoulders were tanned and toned as an athlete's, and her long blond hair was perfectly straight, falling forward like a curtain around a face that he was starting to hope lived up to the rest of her.

Things are looking up, he thought. *Maybe this won't be one of the worst days of my life after all.*

Then she looked up at him. The bitch on wheels.

He took it like a fist in the face, spun on his heel, and ran smack into Loretta.

"For God's sake, Ty, what's wrong with you!"

"I need a different seat."

"Why?"

"Who cares why. I just do." He slewed a look around the first-class cabin. "Switch me with somebody."

She set her fists on her hips, and in a low but deadly voice, said, "No, I will not switch you. These folks are all in pairs and they're settled in, looking forward to their dinner and a good night's sleep, which is why they're paying through the nose for first class. I'm not asking them to move. And neither are you."

It *would* be Loretta, the only person on earth he couldn't sweet-talk. "Then switch me with someone from coach."

Now she crossed her arms. "You don't want me to do that."

"Yes I do."

"No you don't and I'll tell you why. Because it's a weird request. And when a passenger makes a weird request, I'm obliged to report it to the captain. The captain's obliged to report it to the tower. The tower notifies the marshals, and next thing you know, you're bent over with a finger up your butt checking for C–4." She cocked her head to one side. "Now, do you really want that?"

He really didn't. "Sheeee-iiiiit," he squeezed out between his teeth. He looked over his shoulder at the bitch on wheels. She had her nose in a book, ignoring him.

Fourteen hours was a long time to sit next to someone you wanted to strangle. But it was that or get off the plane, and he couldn't miss the wedding.

He cast a last bitter look at Loretta. "I want a Jack Daniel's every fifteen minutes till I pass out. You keep 'em coming, you hear?"

An Excerpt from

THE WEDDING BAND

DAKOTA RAIN TOOK a good hard look in the bathroom mirror and inventoried the assets.

Piercing blue eyes? Check.

Sexy stubble? Check.

Sun-streaked blonde hair? Check.

Movie-star smile?

Uh-oh.

In the doorway, his assistant rolled her eyes and hit speed dial. "Emily Fazzone here," she said. "Mr. Rain needs to see Dr. Spade this morning. Another cap." She listened a moment, then snorted a laugh. "You're telling me. Might as well cap them all and be done with it."

In the mirror Dakota gave her his hit man squint. "No extra caps."

"Weenie," she said, pocketing her phone. "You don't have time today, anyway. Spade's squeezing you in, as usual. Then you're due at the studio at eleven for the voice-over. It'll be tight, so step on it."

Deliberately, Dakota turned to his reflection again. Tilted his head. Pulled at his cheeks like he was contemplating a shave.

Emily did another eye roll. Muttering something that might have been either "get to work" or "what a jerk," she disappeared into his closet, emerging a minute later with jeans, T-shirt, and boxer briefs. She stacked them on the granite vanity, then pulled out her phone again and scrolled through the calendar.

"You've got a twelve o'clock with Peter at his office about the Levi's endorsement, then a one-thirty fitting for your tux. Mercer's coming here at two thirty to talk about security for the wedding . . ."

Dakota tuned her out. His schedule didn't worry him. Emily would get him where he needed to be. If he ran a little late and a few people had to cool their heels, well, they were used to dealing with movie stars. Hell, they'd be disappointed if he behaved like regular folk.

Taking his sweet time, he shucked yesterday's briefs and meandered naked to the shower without thinking twice. He knew Emily wouldn't bat an eye. After ten years nursing him through injuries and illness, puking and pain, she'd seen all there was to see. Broad shoulders? Tight buns? She was immune.

And besides, she was gay.

Jacking the water temp to scalding, he stuck his head under the spray, wincing when it found the goose egg on the back of his skull. He measured it with his fingers, two inches around.

The same right hook that chipped his tooth had bounced his head off a concrete wall.

Emily rapped on the glass. He rubbed a clear spot in the steam and gave her the hard eye for pestering him in the shower.

She was immune to that too. "I asked you if we're looking at a lawsuit."

"Damn straight," he said, all indignation. "We're suing The Combat Zone. Tubby busted my tooth and gave me a concussion to boot."

She sighed. "I meant, are *we* getting sued? If Tubby popped you, you gave him a reason."

Dakota put a world of aggrievement into his western drawl. "Why do you always take everybody else's side? You weren't there. You don't know what happened."

"Sure I do. It's October, isn't it? The month you start howling at the moon and throwing punches at bystanders. It's an annual event. The lawyers are on standby. I just want to know if I need to call them."

He did the snarl that sent villains and virgins running for their mamas. Emily folded her arms.

He stuck his head out the door. "Feel that." He pointed at the lump.

She jabbed it.

"Ow! Damn it, Em, you're mean as a snake." He shut off the water, dripped his way across the bathroom, and twisted around in front of the mirror, trying to see the back of his head.

"Was Montana with you?"

"No." Little brother's clubbing days were over. Montana spent his evenings with his fiancé now.

"Witnesses?"

"Plenty."

"Paparazzi?"

"Are you kidding?" He was always tripping over

those leeches. October usually ended with one of them on the ground, Dakota punching the snot out of him while the rest of the bloodsuckers streamed it live.

Emily dragged her phone out again. "Hi, Peter. Yeah, Dakota got into it with Tubby last night. Just a broken tooth and a knot on his thick skull. But the press was there, so expect pictures. Okay, later."

Dakota gave up on the lump. His hair was too thick. And too damn long. An inch past his chin for the western he'd start filming next month. A lot of trouble for what amounted to another shoot-'em-up just like the last one, and the one before that. This time there'd be horses instead of hot rods and six guns instead of Uzis. But no real surprises, just lots of dead bodies.

Emily handed him a towel. "Car?"

He glanced out the window. No surprises there either. Another sunny day in L.A. "Porsche. The black one."

She walked out of the bathroom, tapping her phone. "Tony, bring the black Porsche around, will you? And drop the top."

GOOSING THE GAS, Dakota squirted between a glossy Lexus and a pimped-out Civic, then shot through a yellow light and squealed a hard right into the In-N-Out Burger, braking at the drive-thru.

"Gimme a three-by-three, fries, and a chocolate shake, will ya, darlin'?" He glanced at Emily. "The usual?"

She nodded, phone to her ear.

"Throw in a grilled cheese for the meat-hater. And an extra straw." He pulled forward behind a yellow Hummer.

Still talking, Emily opened her iPad, fiddled around, then held it up for him to see. Pictures of his go-round with Tubby.

He shrugged like it didn't bother him, but it did. Oh,

he didn't care if people knew he'd had his ass handed to him. That was inevitable; nobody beat Tubby.

What pissed him off were the damn paparazzi.

Everyone—Peter, Emily, even Montana—told him the media was a fact of celebrity life. A necessary evil. And maybe that was true.

But he'd never forgive them for Charlie. For driving a good man to suicide, then tearing at his remains like the flesh-eating vultures they were.

And it wasn't only the paparazzi who'd made money and careers off Charlie's life and death. "Legitimate" journalists waded in too, exploiting his best friend's disintegration, never letting humanity get in the way of a good story.

The day they spread Charlie's corpse across the front page, Dakota swore off "news" forever. No papers, no magazines, no CNN. Never again in this life.

Pulling up to the window, he set aside his resentment and laid a practiced smile on the redhead inside. "Hey, Sandy-girl. What's shakin'?"

"Hey, Kota." Her Jersey accent was thick as molasses. "I like the hair."

"You can have it when I cut it off." He tipped her fifty bucks and she blew him a kiss.

Peeling out of the lot, he handed off the bag to Emily. She was still uh-huhing into her phone, so he plucked it from her hand.

"Hey! That was Peter."

"We just saw him twenty minutes ago." He rattled the bag.

"Honest to God." She unwrapped his burger and spread a napkin on his lap. Then she stuck both straws in the shake, took a long pull and passed it over, half turning in her seat to eyeball him. "So what happened last night?"

He sucked down two inches of shake, tucked it between his thighs. "Some asshole was hassling this girl. Feeling her up." Manhandling the poor kid. Pinning her to the wall and rubbing all over her.

"Tell me you didn't hit him."

"I was about to." And wouldn't it have felt great to lay that pretty boy out? "I pulled him off her. Then Tubby waded in and spoiled my fun."

"And the October madness begins." Emily tipped back her head and stared up at blue sky. "Why, oh why, couldn't Montana get married in September? Or November?"

"Why does he have to get married at all?" It made no sense. Montana had the world by the balls. Women loved him. Hollywood loved him. The critics loved him. He was the indie darling, offered one challenging, nuanced role after another, while Dakota got stuck blowing up cities and machine-gunning armies single-handed.

Sure, Dakota made bigger box office. But Montana had the talent in the family.

"Sasha's a great girl," Emily pointed out.

"Yeah, she's a peach. But peaches grow on trees in California. Why settle for one when you can have the orchard?"

Em punched his shoulder. "That's for peaches everywhere, especially California."

Dakota grinned and passed her the shake. "Call Mercer, will you, and tell him we're running behind. I don't want him getting pissed at us."

"Pfft. You never worry about anybody else's feelings."

"Because they can't kill us just by looking at us."

"See? You're scared of him too." She crossed her arms. "I wish you hadn't hired him."

"So you've said about a million times. But Montana put me in charge of security, and Mercer's the best." His guys were ex-Rangers and Navy SEALs. "He says he'll keep the press out, and I believe him."

"Well good luck with that. They always manage to sneak somebody inside."

"Not this time."

A beach wedding might be a security nightmare—not to mention just plain pointless since everyone was zipped into tents and couldn't see the water anyway—but Mercer had it covered. Airtight perimeter, no-fly zone. Saturday's guests and employees would be bussed in from a remote parking lot and wanded before admittance. Anyone caught with a recording device would be summarily executed—er, ejected.

Dakota gave a grim smile. "Believe me, Em, Mercer's got it locked down. Not a single, slimy, sleazy reporter is getting into that wedding."

"YOU'RE GETTING INTO that wedding." Reed aimed a finger at Chris. "Don't bother arguing. It's that, or clean out your desk."

"This is bullshit, Reed! Archie admitted it was his screwup."

"And his desk is already empty. But your ass is still in a sling, Christine. Your name was on that story."

"I told him not to go to print until I verified it! If he'd waited till I gave him the go-ahead—"

"You're missing the point. Senator Buckley saw *your name*—Christine Case—on the front page. *You* accused her of mishandling campaign contributions. It's *your* blood she wants." Reed's chair scraped back. "You wanted to do hard news, now you've got to take the heat."

Chris rubbed her temple. "I earned my byline, Reed."

With two years of writing fluff for the Living section. It finally seemed to pay off when one of Buckley's PR flacks—a guy Chris knew from covering the senator's thousand-dollar-a-plate fundraisers—handed her the story of a lifetime. Her big break. Guaranteed to run front page above the fold.

Reed had no sympathy. "You should've held onto the story until you locked it up. You handed Archie a stick of dynamite."

Oh yes she had. And it blew up in her face.

Reed was right. She bore a big chunk of the blame. She was lucky he hadn't fired her outright.

"Listen, Chris." Reed came around the desk, propped himself on the edge. "Emma Case is a hero to a whole generation of reporters. Your mother's coverage of Vietnam changed history. That's why you're still sitting here, getting another chance. That, and the fact that your father's the entertainment at Montana Rain's wedding."

"So now we're competing with the *Enquirer*? Sneaking into celebrity weddings? For God's sake, we're the *Los Angeles Sentinel*. Is this what journalism has come to?"

Wrong question. Reed stiffened. "Don't preach to me, young lady. I grew up in this business, and I can tell you the world's changed. Newspapers all over the country are hanging by a thread."

"The scoop on this wedding won't make or break the *Sentinel*."

"Maybe not. But it'll make or break your future here. I went to the mat for you and now you'll return the favor. I promised Owen an exclusive. *Where the Stars Are* rolls out in two weeks, and Montana Rain's wedding *will* be the centerfold spread."

"Come on, Reed. It's no better than a tabloid—"

He cut her off ruthlessly. "Your opinion's irrelevant. Owen's the publisher, and it's his baby. He's expecting it to boost Sunday circulation, and if it goes down in flames, it won't be because this office didn't do its damnedest."

Chris tried to stare him down, but Reed was master of the stare down. She crossed her arms. He crossed his.

Sand trickled through the hourglass.

Chris dropped her eyes. Thought about her mother, how proud she'd been when Chris graduated from Columbia with her master's in journalism. How disappointed when she didn't use her degree, choosing a troubadour's life with her father instead.

Well, it was too late to redeem herself in her mother's eyes. Alzheimer's had dulled Emma Case's razor-sharp mind. The woman Chris had admired and resented and loved with all her heart was, in so many of the ways that matter, already lost to her.

No, Emma would never know that Chris was finally following in her footsteps, or that her old friend Reed, managing editor of the *Sentinel*, had given Chris that chance.

But Chris knew. With no references but her family name, Reed had taken it on faith that she'd bring the same commitment to the *Sentinel* that Emma had brought to her Pulitzer Prize-winning career.

But sneaking into celebrity weddings, dishing on who wore what and who canoodled with whom . . . well, nobody won awards for that.

Still, she owed Reed. And with the balance sheet so far out of whack, what choice did she have?

None.

She'd have to suck it up, sing with her father's band at Montana Rain's stupid wedding, and bring back some useless gossip to hype Owen's pet project. Then she'd ride out her time in the penalty box until she got another crack at hard news.

Next time, she'd use better judgment, double-check her sources.

Next time, she'd make her mother proud.

Refusing to meet Reed's eyes, Chris punched in her famous father's private number. He answered on the first ring.

"Hi, honey pie."

"Hi, Dad." She cut to the chase. "Listen, is the offer still open? Can I do the wedding this weekend?"

"Abso-fucking-lutely." Zach Gray didn't miss a beat. "I'll work up a new set list and shoot it to you. We hit at two. And honey, security's tighter than a gnat's asshole. No phones, no nothing. Expect to strip down to your skivvies."

And the hits just kept on coming.

At Avon Books, we know your passion for romance—once you finish one of our novels, you find yourself wanting more.

May we tempt you with . . .

- **Excerpts** from our upcoming releases.

- Entertaining **extras**, including authors' personal photo albums and book lists.

- Behind-the-scenes **scoop** on your favorite characters and series.

- **Sweepstakes** for the chance to win free books, romantic getaways, and other fun prizes.

- Writing **tips** from our authors and editors.

- **Blog** with our authors and find out why they love to write romance.

- **Exclusive content** that's not contained within the pages of our novels.

Join us at
www.avonbooks.com

An Imprint of HarperCollins*Publishers*
www.avonromance.com

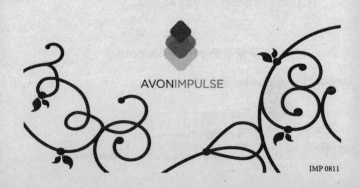